It approached Cen[...] perfectly level, nose [...] There had been a sto[...] washed air the great [...] gigantic fish in crystal-clear water. [...] the camera the lens picked out the white and green paint-work.

It was in line with the length of the Park. It seemed to make a slight correction to its course, but the loss of height remained remorseless. It was still higher than the buildings as it passed the camera, over the receiving reservoir. The cameraman used the zoom to get a close-up of the jet. Faces were at the windows. They were black faces, screaming.

It cleared the buildings on Central Park North by about three hundred feet, then the nose dipped, and as though on a slide the aircraft accelerated into Harlem. They saw it vanish, and then the explosion boiled up out of the city. A banner of flame leaped backwards along its path and brought the roar of impact with it. The pilot had been dumping fuel.

The thunderclap of noise grew and grew, as the buildings went down like dominoes. A vast cloud of smoke and dust and flame began to rise from Harlem. A dreadful and terrible sound was borne on the breeze, the noise of a battlefield, the noise of people dying.

Barnaby Williams began his career as a medical student, but left the profession to fly aircraft and race motorcycles, passions reflected in his first two novels, *The Comeback* and *The Racers*. He worked as a cropduster for many years and conceived the plot of *Soldiers of God* in the cockpit of an Ag Cat. The author of *Stealth Bomber* (also published by Sphere Books), he is now a full-time writer. He has an M.A. in the History of the British Empire and Commonwealth and lives in France with his wife and two daughters.

SOLDIERS OF GOD

Barnaby Williams

SPHERE BOOKS LIMITED

For Jeremy Lawson, with thanks.

A SPHERE book

First published in Great Britain in 1991 by
Sphere Books Ltd
A Division of Macdonald & Co (Publishers) Ltd
London & Sydney

ISBN 0 7474 0063 6

Printed and bound in Great Britain by
BPCC Hazell Books
Aylesbury, Bucks, England
Member of BPCC Ltd.

Sphere Books Ltd
A Division of
Macdonald & Co (Publishers) Ltd
165 Great Dover Street
London SE1 4YA

A member of Maxwell Macmillan Publishing Corporation

MASSACHUSETTS

The room was that of an academic. Books lined the walls, books from slight pamphlets to weighty tomes, covers of paper and bindings of leather, periodicals stacked together and periodicals bound in volumes. The tool of the modern academic was there too, in a corner by the window – the word-processor and computer. When Spencer came into the room from his kitchen he fitted the part; he favoured English trousers and polished brogues, and the word-processor had to be for storing and polishing his thesis, not for any exercises in cliometric history.

He moved slowly, because he was not long out of the hospital and had been immured many months while the bones set and the surgeons moved pieces of skin from his thighs, or bottom, or back, to the raw areas that needed them. He took a small portable television from a cupboard, placing it by a pile of volumes on the table. Limping back to the kitchen, he returned with a tall glass of iced tea. He switched on in time to hear how his wife could get even blood, grass stains and ground-in dirt from his son's football clothing, but the information was of little use to him, for both his wife and son were dead and Spencer washed his clothes with whatever box of powder came handy from the supermarket shelf. Then the advertisements stopped, the station identification music and world logo came up and coast-to-coast came the interview with former president Hugo Thomas, marking the occasion of the publication of his memoirs. Thomas had been a successful president, he had survived two terms and now his vice-president had been elected in his place. This was no mean feat in the America of the late twentieth century.

The presenter, the man who interviewed Thomas, was Edward K. Sims – an inquisitorial bully in Brooks Brothers suits. Spencer had found Sims's microphone under his nose when he came out of gaol, and had thought little of him. Sims had come a long way since then and it was unlikely he would try to bully Thomas, who had been no mean hand at the art himself. However, time was of the essence, and Sims wasted little of it in getting to the part everyone was interested in, if only because during 1,400 pages of solid chronicling of Thomas's rise through cub scout, college quarterback, attorney, Army Captain, Congressman, Senator, Leader of the House and President, Thomas had mentioned it only briefly, and in passing: what had happened, and what was happening, in the USSR.

'Mr President, you say little in your memoirs about the extraordinary events that began to rack the Soviet Union towards the end of your second term and which, as we speak, seem to be tearing her apart.'

'Well, Eddie, I wrote my memoirs, and I stuck to the things I was concerned with. I dare say if I had been General Secretary of the Communist party' – Thomas paused to allow himself and the viewers a slight belly laugh at the idea – 'then I'd have had a little more to say about it.'

'Is there any truth in the suggestion that we Americans had anything to do with fomenting dissent in the USSR?'

'There will always be people who interpret events in history in terms of conspiracy theories. Let me say that in my own modest experience of twentieth century history' – again, Thomas smiled avuncularly, he was not a modest man – 'I have found remarkably little evidence to support this way of looking at things. Make no mistake about it, what is happening in what is still for the moment called the USSR is one of the seismic shifts of history. Terrible the twentieth century may have been, but it has witnessed some events of great hope for the world, not least the unshackling of free peoples enchained by empire. The days of great empires are over, and the days of the last great ones are finishing too – the empire of the Tsars, acquired and renamed the USSR by the Bolsheviks. Free people in Lithuania, Kirghiz, Azerbaijan, the Ukraine, are all rising up against the yoke of their Russian masters, who will have as little success in containing them as did the British, French or Portuguese in resisting their colonial nations.'

'I'm sure you won't mind, Mr President, if I say that the suggestion has been made that we Americans did play a part in providing a spark, some tinder for what you rightly point out was some very combustible material in the Russian empire. More specifically, that it was your own administration that set about this.'

'You're talking about Mr Petrovsky's little book,' Thomas said amiably.

'Yes. Yossif Petrovsky alleges that you made use of the talents of Dr Victor Spencer, the covert warfare specialist.'

'It was my predecessor who employed Dr Spencer,' Thomas said mildly. 'I have never met him.'

Seated in his high-backed chair, Spencer smiled slightly and reached for his tea.

'What about the CIA connection? There's your man O'Neill, who Petrovsky claims was the one who advised Carmine Santucci to hire Dr Spencer. There's the Air America veteran – Air America was the CIA airline at the time of the Vietnam War – R.D. Marvin. Both of those men knew Spencer.'

'Can I refer you to some of your colleagues, Mr Sims? The investigative programme "60 Minutes" devoted a programme to Yossif Petrovsky and his wild little book. They interviewed Frank O'Neill and Mr Marvin. There's no evidence that Frank ever met Carmine Santucci, let alone advised him to hire Dr Spencer to investigate the Harlem atrocity. I should imagine that there are hundreds of former Air America employees who knew Dr Spencer. It was a very big outfit. Mr Marvin knew nothing of the events that Yossif Petrovsky claims happened. He's a small businessman in a little Georgia town. He has a flying business. He isn't in very good health, he could hardly have done the things Petrovsky writes about.'

Spencer's mouth twitched. Neither of them was in very good health. And sure, they were real grateful for what old R.D. Marvin had done for them, but it wouldn't have stopped them putting him in some unknown hole in Leavenworth and forgetting about him for ever, and R.D. knew it. Neither of them was about to spill a word.

'But Carmine Santucci's dead, and we can't ask him any questions. And what about the bomb? Doesn't it fit?'

'I don't want to speak ill of the dead, but I'd remind you that the Mayor was under investigation for having underworld contacts. I'd look in that direction to find who planted it, if I were you.'

'You don't believe in the Soldiers of God, then? What about the thousands who died in North Carolina? Weren't they victims in the gigantic covert battle between the USA and USSR that Yossif Petrovsky talks about? Victims just as much as those killed in the Nowruz Day Massacre? Or those who died in Red Square?'

'Mr Sims.' Thomas reached over to put his hand restrainingly on the interviewer's arm. He wore a long-suffering, slightly reproving air, like a wise schoolmaster talking to an erring pupil. His one-time fellow Senators would have recognized the expression. When Thomas had been responsible for getting the administration's business through the house, they said of him that he had two grips – the half-Thomas, when he put his arm around your shoulders and promised what he could do for you if you were cooperative, and if you were obstructive the full-Thomas, where he took both shoulders in his beefy hands put his great beefy face up close to yours and promised what he'd do to you if you weren't.

'Mr Sims. Let's stick to facts, not fiction. I'm happy to accept the findings of the independent inquiry into the disaster in North Carolina. It was a military accident. A terrible one, but one caused by human error, not by the machinations of some superhuman breed of fighting men. I think that sort of thing is best left to Hollywood and Arnold Schwarzenegger, don't you? As for the rest, there will always be those conspiracy theorists who see the hand of the CIA in any event, however far-fetched, and I assure you that to seek American involvement in the events that took place on Nowruz or in Red Square is stretching paranoia to its limits.'

'So there is no truth in Yossif Petrovsky's book at all?'

'Of course there's some truth. All good disinformation has some truth in it. But that there was this top-secret covert operation to destabilize the USSR, and that we did it? No, Mr Sims. I go along with the findings of the "60 Minutes" team, who found that it was most likely a KGB operation aimed at blaming the USA for what in fact the Soviets had themselves done. And I'll add my own little piece of intelligence. Do you know where Yossif Petrovsky is today?'

'No.'

'He's in Leningrad. As we speak. The USA took him in as a bona-fide refugee from political and religious persecution, as is the great and enduring tradition of our country, but Petrovsky was not the real thing. No, he was a KGB plant. For the last time, let me say that while like all civilized people I applaud the spontaneous struggle for freedom that is going on among the subject peoples of the Soviet empire, and call upon the Soviet leadership to speed the process before they are buried by History, let me place my hand on my heart and pledge to the American people that neither they, nor the man who was so proud to serve them as President for two terms, had any part in any crazy schemes to destabilize the USSR. Now, Eddie, shall we get on and talk about some of the things that actually happened instead of the ones that didn't?'

Spencer switched off the television and watched the light dwindle to a point before putting it away in the cupboard. He had the intellectual's contempt for television,

9

the people who worked for it and watched it. Thomas was not an intellectual, but in one vital respect the two men were the same. Neither was a good man. Both had understood that in the long struggle between the USA and USSR there could in the end be only one winner and one loser, and that in such a struggle good men were a liability. Good men could never save a great country, because they could not bring themselves to take the measures necessary. Thomas had used Spencer as his weapon, and he launched him the day Spencer went to see Carmine Santucci, Mayor of New York.

NEW YORK

Carmine Santucci saw Spencer at home, which was a full penthouse high over Central Park, and they ate steak with his family on the roof garden. As he said, the view was pleasant at that time of year. Before that they talked in the panelled study off the marbled hall, and Spencer thought that Santucci's grandfather would have rolled in his Sicilian grave with admiration if he could have seen how his son's son had taken the foolish foreigners and had them pay for the privilege.

Santucci poured Spencer a Jack Daniels, and himself a pale malt from Scotland. He was a handsome man, in his mid-fifties a little older than Spencer, and his immaculate silver hair was matched by the grey of his suit. In his tweedy clothes Spencer looked what he was, which was a college lecturer, but the set of his face said what he had been, which was a soldier. Santucci picked up two books from the rolltop desk.

'I've been reading your work. Tell me, how does a man who writes a thesis on Charles I and the English Civil War get to write this: *Instability and the State: Principles of destabilization and counter-measures?*'

'Same subject,' said Spencer. 'I've always been interested in the reasons and methods by and for which governments lose power and are replaced by those who have worked to unseat them – whether by election, civil war – which can include guerrilla warfare – or *coup d'état.*'

I'll say, thought Santucci. Didn't the son of a bitch control two Central American countries before Congress got to him?

'You don't mention terror.'

'Terrorism as a method of unseating a government does not tend to work. Any reasonably well-organized government can defeat terrorism, provided that it is willing to use sufficient violence and brutality.'

Spencer took a sip of his drink, and continued, 'This is not a view that those who regard terrorism as the inevitable consequence of legitimate grievance find able to accept. However, time and time again it has been shown that the terrorist reservoir is not unlimited, and that imprisoning or executing terrorists does not automatically bring forth new recruits. On the contrary, the more violence is applied, the more brutal and sweeping the anti-terrorist measures, the speedier and more absolute is the defeat of the terrorists. The blood of the martyrs may be the seed of the church, but it is not so for terrorism.'

He's a wordy bastard, thought Santucci. You'd never think he killed all those sons of bitches.

'The best examples of successful counter-terror of this kind are Iran under the Ayatollah Khomeini and the Argentine junta of the late 1970s. Terrorism does not exist in successful police states like the Soviet Union or those above because of their ability to deny the terrorists their life-blood – which is publicity – and to deploy devastating force against them. From this follows the corollary, which is that it is in open, democratic societies that terrorism is able to flourish best – leaving aside decaying, ineffective dictatorships and societies in a state of civil war, like Lebanon, which are special cases. In an open, democratic society the media are not controlled; knowingly or unknowingly they enter into a symbiotic relationship with terrorists who become active, in which the media provide the publicity vital to the terrorist cause and the terrorists provide the media with success in terms of ratings and circulation figures. Secondly, the government finds itself unable to apply the kind of repression necessary to eradicate the terrorists. The best it can do is to apply limited, half-hearted measures of repression, which it can be shown are far worse than none at all, in that they create the impression that the government is weak and that just one more determined push on the part of the terrorists will overthrow the system.'

'Are you saying that democracies can't defend themselves against terror?'

'Not at all. Democracies are perfectly able to defend themselves and retain civil liberties for almost all, *provided* they have the will to do so.'

'Uhuh.' Santucci grunted, getting out of his chair. He switched out the alabaster and silk lamp and, in the dark, he pointed out of the study window at the lights of the city.

'See down there, Victor? That's Harlem. The rebuilding's going on apace.'

He pressed a video remote-control switch, his television came to life, and he and Spencer watched the film they had seen many times before. If it had been daytime they could have looked out of the window and seen something very similar, except for the 747, because only one 747 had ever been that low over the city. It approached Central Park from the south, wings perfectly level, nose slightly down. It was losing height. There had been a storm the night before; in the newly-washed air the great aircraft glided downwards like a gigantic fish in crystal-clear water. As it came closer to the camera the lens picked out the white and green paintwork.

It was in line with the length of the Park. It seemed to make a slight correction to its course, but the loss of height remained remorseless. It was still higher than the buildings as it passed the camera, over the receiving reservoir. The cameraman used the zoom to get a close-up of the jet. Faces were at the windows. They were black faces, screaming.

It cleared the buildings on Central Park North by about three hundred feet, then the nose dipped, and as though on a slide the aircraft accelerated into Harlem. They saw it vanish, and then the explosion boiled up out of the city. A banner of flame leaped backwards along its

13

path and brought the roar of impact with it. The pilot had been dumping fuel.

The thunderclap of noise grew and grew, as the buildings went down like dominoes. A vast cloud of smoke and dust and flame began to rise from Harlem. A dreadful and terrible sound was borne on the breeze, the noise of a battlefield, the noise of people dying.

The smoke grew and grew, obscuring the north end of the Park. It rose high in the sky, whipping round the camera. Santucci cut the video and turned the lights back on.

'That was taken by Adam Ross and his cameraman, Charlie Harrel, who were shooting for a documentary in the area. You remember Ross, he was an action reporter for the television. Always in some nasty war zone or trouble area. The 747 going in finally flipped him, and a couple of days later he washed down half a bottle of barbiturates with whisky. By that time the fires were finally out and the White Supremacy League had made their famous, one and only, telephone call. You remember it, Victor? "We sent the niggahs into niggahtown, to do some slum clearance." They claimed responsibility, and that was the last anyone heard.'

Santucci paused to freshen his glass.

'We've been waiting to hold the trial, Victor. Waiting to see the guilty men brought here to the courthouse. We've been patient, just waiting to see justice done.'

The Mayor took a drink.

'Just last week I heard from the government. They cannot find whoever called themselves the White Supremacy League, or anyone else who might be responsible for the atrocity. They've been looking for eighteen months and they can't find who did it. They're keeping the file open, but they're taking the men off the job. There isn't going to be any trial, we've been waiting in vain. Does that surprise you?'

Spencer shook his head. 'No. Not really. The government isn't equipped to find them.'

Santucci's barbered eyebrows rose. 'Are you serious?

The government of the most powerful country in the world doesn't have the equipment?'

'No. The situation hasn't arisen where terrorism is perceived as a major threat to this country. All politicians from the president down *talk* a lot about it – just look at the column inches devoted to Gaddafy – but in reality, little is *done*. This is because, short of the situation where terrorism is perceived by government and governed to be a major threat, it is politically dangerous to keep in being the kind of forces capable of successfully combating it.'

'Is that what you meant about having the will to do so?'

'Right. As Colonel Grivas once said: to catch a mouse – or a rat – one uses a cat, not a tank or an aircraft carrier. Or, let me say, F-111 bombers. The mouse or rat represents the terrorist group, the cat the covert action capacity, or "active measures" as the Russians so delicately put it. The problem with having a cat is that it is often best in a liberal democracy for the people not to know that they possess one. The problem is what the cat does to the mouse or rat once it catches it. It is all very well if the intricate business of plot, bribery, corruption, double-cross and killing takes place out in the shrubbery, where the noise cannot be heard and the blood not seen; but once let the cat drag its victim on to the living-room carpet and there dismember it and all praise for the cat for freeing the occupants of the house from the disease brought in by the rat is forgotten, and the cry is for the horrible creature, red in tooth and claw, to be removed.'

There was a short silence.

'As I recall, one of the liberal papers wanted you to get life,' said Santucci.

'I was not charged with murder, Mr Mayor.'

'The president denied ever giving you authorization for what you did.'

'He did, and if that is what he said then I am sure that we must all believe him, and that I was mistaken for ever thinking otherwise.'

'You never said you thought otherwise at the trial.'

15

'No. But the president lived to fight another day.'

And you did only get five years, and serve half, thought Santucci, but kept it to himself.

'The other reason that the government has decided to shelve the investigation is undoubtedly that nothing has ever been heard since from the White Supremacy League. The one highly spectacular operation, the racist telephone call to the *New York Times*, and then nothing. I find this most curious. You see, the idea behind it was one of the most promising – I am speaking from the point of view of those who wish this country harm – in recent times. There are three good ways to damage this country, to decrease its will and ability to defend itself. There is first the obvious one, which is the one that naturally comes to mind – that of assassination, arson, hijack and destruction of airliners, destruction of property and so forth, with the intent of causing the breakdown of society, from the ruins of which will emerge some grand new order. It is the one always chosen by those who have not emerged from the terrorist kindergarten, so to speak. It appeals greatly to such intellectually confused young men and women as we have seen in recent years in groups like the German Red Army Faction, or our own Weathermen or Black Panthers. For these people terrorism was largely an attempted cure for their own personality problems, and even as flabby a government as that of West Germany was able to defeat the threat with relative ease.

'Far more promising, to my mind, is the encouragement of drug addiction within society. The long-term deleterious effects upon national morale and will cannot be underestimated. It has the added attraction of generating so much money that efforts to combat it can very largely be bought off. Witness the gulf between what the politicians *say* about drug abuse and what they *do*. The amount of money spent on organizations like the Drug Enforcement Agency and Coastguard is truly derisory.'

'Any group that seriously wished this country harm could inflict considerable damage by purchasing a few thousand acres of good farmland, cultivating it by using modern agricultural techniques and shipping the refined narcotic product to the major cities of the USA by means of fast aircraft and suitably trained and experienced pilots – Air America types. In terms of value for money, it would be a remarkably cost-effective way of waging warfare against us.'

Santucci finished his drink and freshened both their glasses. Spencer wondered if the Mayor's alcohol consumption had stepped up under the pressure of investigation. It wasn't necessarily so; his grandfather, and probably his father, had existed under the pressure of men trying to kill them on the streets of New York, not merely the threat of an investigative judge trying to remove them from office. He resumed.

'The third line of attack, and the reason I found the White Supremacy League so interesting – because it showed that someone was *thinking* – is the fostering of racial hatred between the different racial groups that make up our country. Terrorists have been very slow to realize that terror is almost always more popular against foreigners than against those of their own kind, or co-religionists. Sectarian appeal can be successful. With sufficient skill, dedication and effort, I could foresee the kind of racial war of which the White Supremacy League's launching was so clearly the spearhead as being most profitable – possibly sufficiently so to bring in the advocates of destruction in a successful role, allied with a greatly boosted pipeline of cheap drugs. The damage would be enormous. That's why I find it curious that the League should vanish from sight.'

'Hold on. You seem to be saying that someone outside this country was responsible.'

'Oh, certainly. The White Supremacy League was definitely a "false flag" operation. Who? Hard to say. Gaddafy? Syria through one of the Abus? You always have to put your money on the Soviet Union, if you could dig back far enough, *détente, glasnost*, disarmament talks or no. The operation itself illustrates that. The technical sophistication required to accurately crash a 747 into the part of New York you have selected quite definitely rules out a bunch of good ol' boys from Alabama or Georgia riding around in pick-up trucks wearing KKK nightshirts. That isn't to say that if you were investigating something like this you wouldn't look there. To get such a racial civil war rolling you need to mobilize the bigots, don't you? And from there move to the black ghettoes, and the poor Hispanic areas. Maybe throw in a bit of anti-semitism among the WASPs, and so forth. Oh, yes, you could get a good witches' cauldron boiling, if you really wanted to.'

'So why *did* the White Supremacy League vanish?'

'If they *have*, then maybe whoever started it had second thoughts. You see, doing something on that scale to a country like this is to write your own death warrant. Cats would suddenly be back in favour, and the cats would come and eat you one night.'

It was quiet in the luxurious apartment so high above the city, just the whisper of the air-conditioning and the creak of leather as Santucci moved in his chair.

'*You* were a cat,' Santucci said softly. 'Could you find who did it?'

'I might.'

'You'd be rehabilitated. Proved right. You could write your own ticket, I'd see to that. Sure wouldn't have to teach kids in college about politics any more.'

'I'd need favours, unaccountable money, political protection maybe. You might have to abuse your authority to get me what I wanted.'

Santucci's Roman face cracked into a smile. 'You can't have been reading the papers, Victor. Haven't you seen what they accuse me of? You get me the sons of bitches who did it and let me put them here in my courthouse, with my judge, and there'll be no questions from anyone.'

'I'll need to stay away. You know the best way to stop an investigation?'

Santucci spread his hands enquiringly.

'Kill the man doing it.'

18

Santucci smiled again. 'These terrorists have advantages over we Mayors, don't they?' he said dryly.

'I'll need to operate through a contact. I know one of your employees, he comes to evening classes at the college. Russian dissident refugee – Yossif Petrovsky. His father was a Jewish activist in Leningrad, he's studying for a Master's. Can you spare him?'

'Sure. Yossif'll do fine.'

'Very well then.'

The two men shook hands. Santucci looked at Spencer intently for a moment.

'What's it like inside, Victor?'

'Well, Carmine – may I call you Carmine? I once spent six months living in a hole in a hillside watching military movements, so I suppose I got used to cramped accommodation. Why do you ask?'

Santucci laughed shortly. 'Not because I plan to see one, I assure you. Opening a new one is as close as I intend to get. Okay, you hungry? My wife will give me hell if we stay here much longer.'

They went out on to the roof garden, with its plantings that made it seem as though the table had been set in a small woodland glade, and Spencer mentally added a couple of million to the value of the apartment.

Santucci turned up the gas under the coals.

'You think these people have quit, Victor, these terrorists? Do you think the 747 going was it?'

Spencer looked down from seventy-six floors at the cranes and the rising buildings where a great passenger jet had crashed at four hundred knots and killed thousands.

'No,' he said quietly. 'I think it was just the beginning.'

Santucci looked at him, then shut his mouth firmly.

'How do you like your steak?' he enquired.

'*Saignant*,' said Spencer.

'How's that?' asked Santucci, tossing herb mixture on to the coals. The air was suddenly filled with fragrance.

'Make it bloody,' Spencer told him.

19

WAYCROSS, GEORGIA

I got out of bed still half-asleep to answer the 'phone; I ached like a dog, the sweat on my body felt like glue as the night heat whipped the puny efforts of the old air-conditioner, but the cockroaches enjoyed the temperature and skittered out of my way as I stumbled down the corridor. Jimmy the telephone man sounded unhealthily fresh and cheerful.

'Mornin', R.D. Four-thirty a.m. Time to rise and be glad.'

'Uhuh. Thank you, Jimmy.'

'Okay now. Watch out for them wires, y'hear?'

'Yeah. They can ruin your whole day, them wires.'

I put water on to boil while I showered and shaved and got ready for the day's work. I gulped down some coffee and chewed on a cookie that turned to ash in my mouth. I had as much appetite as a bad hangover would leave you, but I hadn't had more than a can in weeks. Two jugs of Gatorade were waiting in the ice-box; I put them in a paper sack, I went back down the corridor and the roaches skittered about again like it was a formal dance or something. Going outside to the truck, the air wrapped itself around me like a warm, damp towel.

The truck fired up and rumbled through the hole in the muffler, the radio hissed because the station hadn't come on line. I crossed the tracks to get on to the wrong side of them, I came up to the store in the dark and he heard the truck coming; he grinned and I caught the reflection off his teeth. I stopped and he got in.

'Shore am glad it's dark,' he said as we pulled away. 'People cain't see me in here. Lookit that niggah, they say, riding in that sorry truck with them sorry white folks, ain't he got no pride?'

'Sheeyut,' I said.

'I got my position to consider. When you gone make some money, get us somethin' has some style to ride in, hey? I laked the Lincoln. That was my *kand* of vee-hicle,' he said, and looked at me and grinned.

'Sheeyut,' I said again. 'Don't you know pick-up trucks got class? Ain't you see them ads on the teevee, got some kind macho stud standing there with a chew in his mouth and a bulge in his pants and a cowboy hat, and all these good-lookin' women all over him?'

'This truck made in nineteen sixty-three, R.D. Ah believe some of the glamour has done worn off it by now.'

The radio came on – there was some show with two comedians called Hambone and Grits – and we drove out of town, and after a while they stopped shooting the shit and Tammy Wynette sang about cheating.

When we turned off the dirt road the eyes of the rabbits glowed and the lights caught the white of their tails as they bobbed away; a black snake slithered rapidly in front of us, by the beaver pond a big brown owl stared and circled briefly around the drowning trees before returning to his dying meal. On the radio Jerry Jeff Walker stopped singing about getting drunk and Hambone read the news. The disarmament talks had been suspended again for a month while everyone went home and counted their missiles. An Atlanta man had returned home unexpectedly to find his wife in bed with two neighbours and had reacted by blowing them away where they lay. One round got all three. Having barricaded himself in the apartment, he had a change of heart and started yelling that he wanted to join them. Emerging abruptly waving an assortment of firearms, the police obliged him by blowing *him* away, but took about thirty rounds to do the job. President Thomas wanted to double the budget spent on drug enforcement but was having trouble getting Congress to approve.

21

'Don't you know them drug people got themselves a Congressman in each pocket,' Billy Lee commented. 'Hell, the man's right, the President, 200 million ain't enough, them drug people can outspend him ten to one. Hell, my las' season, the quarterback was spending thirty thousand jus' to powder his nose.'

'That's a lot.'

'Hell, they gave him discount, on account he was so famous.'

We passed by the great girders of the Forestry tower and pulled up by the rig on the edge of the strip, white in the greying light; the big fat yellow bird was parked there in its tie-downs. We got out and Billy Lee started hauling the black and green five-gallon cans of chemical from the back of the truck and I put the Gatorade in the old cooler with the sack of ice.

'We'll hit Benroy's beans first,' I said. 'The armyworm's in them bad and he's screaming. Give me 350 gallons, two pints to the acre.'

''Kay.' He went over to the rig and began running the water into the mixing tank.

I went to the Thrush, opening the door, letting it hang down and checking that the switches were cold, the mixture lean, before I pulled the prop through. In the night the oil had a habit of creeping down past the rings into the lower cylinders; it wasn't very compressible, and if you fired it up without getting it out of there, there was just an expensive noise as the lower jugs parted company from the rest of the engine. With that done and the fuel drained I climbed up into the big old cockpit, made the switches hot and the mixture rich, primed it and called for a clear prop, then fired up. The smoke whipped past the cockpit in the sudden rush of air and the radial settled down to idle, and I climbed back down to organize work for the day.

Billy Lee was pouring the chemical in the rig, I was downwind as I caught the smell, that was just the smell of work – same as always for the past twenty years, off and on – and my knees buckled and my stomach heaved and I

22

parked my breakfast by the magnolia. I stayed down, waiting for the retching and shaking to stop, and Billy Lee hunkered down, supporting me.

'This is a dumb way to diet,' I said.

'That bush getting tired of having coffee for breakfast,' he said. 'It say, how about a *change*?'

'Yeah. Me too.'

'You want to stop?' he asked quietly. 'We can stop this shit, if you want. Go get you rested. Can come back next year, when you're better.'

'We can't. Hell, you know we can't, Billy. We need every dime . . . it ain't much more'n another six weeks, have it made in the shade by then . . .'

'Okay,' he said, and he helped me up. 'Hell, you prob'ly just getting too old for this shit.'

'Yeah, man,' I said. 'Give me that social security.'

He laughed over his shoulder, a huge black giant. 'You didn't keep up the payments.'

I took the country maps and work orders and went over to the bird in the grey light, untied the airplane and took its chocks away. I put on my helmet and mask and gloves, climbed into the cockpit and strapped it on, Billy Lee connected the Buckeye and pumped in the poison; when I had the load he cut me loose, and I gave it some throttle and waddled across the grass to the start of the strip.

My grandfather had worked this country, and his daddy before him. They had got up before dawn like me, gone out into the field, planted their corn, weeded by hand, shovelled shit to fertilize it; had gone to the chapel to beg the Lord to spare them from pestilence, from the looper and hornworm and armyworm, from rust and blight and mould; had worked eighteen hours a day and died old men before their time, just plain slap wore out, and I was doing the same, only with my big agricultural aircraft I did one thousand times the work. The technology had changed but the work hadn't, and it could still make you old before your time. If you got it wrong it could do it in a few seconds, one summer's morning.

23

I lined up, checked the mags and carb heat, saw the temperature and pressure in the green, set the fan brake and trim and gave it the fuel. The heavy bird accelerated sluggishly, I used plenty of rudder to keep it straight, then the tail rose, the control surfaces beginning to bite on the air; at eighty it lifted clear of the ground and I let it stay in ground effect as the airspeed built up, then eased back on the stick and let it climb out. Clear of the trees, I bent it around in a wide, shallow turn and headed for the field. The air was just like silk.

The soybeans were in three patches – a big 140-acre field, Benroy's pride, and two pieces of new ground. I'd sprayed them twice before that season, once with Benlate against fungus disease and once with Sevimol to kill cabbage loopers. Now the armyworm was in town and the little beasts were hungry; they could strip a field in a couple of days, less if they had all their relatives with them, and I had 350 gallons of 6.3, Toxaphene and Methyl Parathion, a quart to the acre in a two-gallon mix. I'd sprayed the area before and had my pattern ready, but I still flew around the three patches in the growing light, checking out the field furniture. I had had that lesson taught to me long before, learned it when I was working cotton in Arkansas one time, driving a Stearman; turned up at the field before dawn, got down in it as the light was coming up, laid in three swathes and there was this terrible *noise*, this godawful *bang*, and I horsed back out of there and there was a whole bunch of vibration and something flapping. I put it down in a pasture, and when I got out there was this festering great *pole* stuck in the fuselage about a foot below my balls, which promptly cringed up into their little sack when they saw what'd just nearly come to dinner. It had a red *flag* on it for Christ's sake, and I called the farmer and said what the hell, hey, and he said oh, yes, they was drilling this deep well so they could irrigate, and they had put the pole there, with a red flag on, so's they would know where it was.

The fields were clean. There was a light line across the

corner of one of the small patches and some snags you had to watch for where they had dozed the scrub trees. I swung it round and took the pump brake off and it added its rumble to the collection the big bird already had and came over the trees along the south edge, dropping it in over the crop and cutting on the spray; it was smooth as silk, no wind and the spray would be sitting there on the crop as pretty as you would want. The trees came up, the big tall pines, and I eased back on the stick and cut off the spray as I came up, just easing it on out of there, and when I was clear of them I put the nose back down and dropped it into the turn. You horse back on the stick to come out of the field with 340 gallons and 75 gallons of fuel, you will flat plain high speed stall it through those 100-foot pines at the other end, which will save your company the cost of your cremation, and when the preacher leans against the pulpit at your memorial service all he will say is that you didn't know how to fly worth a damn anyway, and everybody there will get up off the pews and yell *that's right*.

Outbound in the procedure turn I squinted back over my shoulder. The spray was sitting there like two coils of cotton wool settling into the crop and in minutes the worms would be hitting the dirt. While I was heavy I made a racetrack pattern in the main field and, as I lightened up, worked to include the smaller patches; it's like a dance, and you ain't never in a hurry, you're just always trying to save time.

When I was brushing out in the corners the sun was peering over the trees in a bloodshot fashion at its new day. I put on the brake with a few gallons of insurance left, and climbed out back to the strip. The land looked good in the sunlight. Mist hung like steam over the ponds and in among the trees in the branches and creeks, coming off the water. The pecan orchards were fat with nuts, we had sprayed six times earlier with Benlate and Malathion; the farmers would be checking the shakers and harvesters, doing a little maintenance, the corn was brown and the soybean fields beginning to yellow. The peanuts were still green. Here and there the white was showing in the cotton fields. King Cotton was making a comeback, looking strong against petrochemicals. All my own clothing was cotton except for the leather in my belt and boots. Cotton was cool and comfortable and, above all, when it burned it didn't melt.

I put it back down on the rough little strip and Billy Lee had the load waiting; the Briggs and Stratton motor put it in while he swabbed off the oil and bugs and chemical from the windshield, and we were turned round and ready to go again within two minutes.

I didn't *like* working out of the strip.

It was rough, of course, not necessarily a problem for an ag aircraft with its strong gear and flotation tyres; the trees were a problem in a crosswind take-off, the rotor turbulence got your attention, especially with a full load, but still that's what you were paid for. It was kind of short, which didn't worry the Forestry boys in their Maules, real STOL airplanes known for their ability to imitate helicopters; neither the trees nor the big window-maker powerline really worried them, but the latter did me. I wouldn't have used the damn strip at all. Previous years I'd worked the west territory off a farmer's strip; he kept an old Aeronca there and let me use it, but the previous winter they had put a by-pass slap through the middle of it and he had gone to Fernandino Beach on the proceeds – ain't no one seen him since, and the Forestry was all I could come up with, as the Thrush was too big a girl to work off roads – not that the Sheriff liked it anyway. I had to have a strip this far west, you can't make money when you ferry more'n twenty miles, even at two-gallon work, anyone knows that. So I worked it. But all in all, just another paragraph in a bad, bad year.

What got you whining in your sleep about using the little strip was climbing out after take-off; there was a period of about ten seconds when you had neither altitude nor – trying busily to get it on the step – did you have airspeed, and there was this period of time when if the big paddle at the front got tired of going round then

26

you had nowhere to go. You could – and of course *would* – dump your load, but you were still in poor shape until you cleared the powerline, and there were plenty of fields to choose. But on average I made say six loads a day out of the strip and sixty seconds out of a ten-or twelve-or fourteen-hour day did not seem excessive odds, not when you considered the basic nature of the job; or so I thought, but if it happened and you couldn't dump, or you were putting out something that wouldn't dump in a hurry – solids, like fertilizer – then every time they took off the Forestry boys could say, my, but ain't the trees and scrub looking good this year. Except for that big old burnt patch, there ain't *nuthin'* growing there.

I climbed out through the gap. If the engine had quit, or the governor had gone out, there would have been little to do except put it into the trees short of the powerline, because for sure you weren't about to fly into that, the damn thing was on a direct connection to the nuclear plant. But the old radial kept faithfully turning in front of me. As we came by the line I bent it around a little and looked down. Somebody had been doing some harvesting, there was a row of trees all cut down and lying on their sides, all the way up to a big old burnt patch. Wasn't *nuthin'* growing there. And in the middle, right where it should be, was a crushed and smashed and burned Thrush. Mine.

By midday the ground had heated up and the air was rough as a cob, the thermals were jarring my teeth and I was glad to have finished the morning's work over this part of the country. Billy Lee gave me 240 gallons to do Lee Roy Pierce's peanuts on the way back; he changed the barrel nozzles to 8s and himself set off for our home base, 25 miles away on the other side of town.

With the increase in gallonage per acre I dispersed the Bravo and liquid sulphur suspended in the water over Mr Pierce's 60-acre patch in no time at all and climbed to 1,500 feet as I crossed the town, letting down over the warehouses as the home strip came into view. Moe, my second pilot, was taxiing out in the second Thrush I'd leased. I made a couple of lazy S-turns on final as he opened the throttle, the tail came up and I sideslipped over the trees – the wings rocking a little in the wash as I flared – and taxied over to the rig. We had a concreted wash area with a sink pit, I dumped what little was left. Billy Lee had just driven up and had fifty gallons waiting in the rig; we put it in and blew it through; sulphur was bad for settling, you left it a few hours and came back to solid booms and nozzles.

I went through to the office and let the luxury of the air-conditioning wash over me like ice-water as I attended to the mail with Mrs Lyon, the middle-aged lady who ran the office for me in the spray season.

'Mr Williamson and Mr Roberson called wanting their beans sprayed,' she said. 'I told them that we could not do the work on credit, as you said. I don't think they'll be out.'

'No . . . they're strapped for cash. They owe from last year. They'll go to Sky Farmers.' I sighed. It was a dreadful year. I just flat could not afford to carry debts. The Thrush cost over a hundred bucks an hour to run even when I wasn't in it. Equally, I couldn't afford to lose my customers to the opposition. Sayings about rocks and hard places came to mind.

Sky Farmers was the opposition; they weren't strapped for cash, they could carry the stretched farmers awhile, maybe until their FHA loan came in, and once you had a customer he usually stayed. My own finance came from a more traditional source this year. The bank.

'A lawyer from Miami called while you were out working.' Mrs Lymon said. 'He asked for you to call back.'

'The hell with him,' I said. 'We probably owe one of his clients money. If he calls again, tell him I am out helping corner the soybean market.'

I called to Billy Lee and went and got cleaned up, put on a white shirt and Sunday-go-to-meeting pants and my shiny shoes. Billy Lee had clean jeans and plaid shirt on and we got into the truck and went downtown. The sign outside the Darlby Bank said 39 degrees, 2.56, 102 degrees, 39 degree, 2.56 . . . and we went in and the girl had us wait a few minutes to remind us who it was we were seeing. Then we went in and John G. Darlby III said how you doin', R.D., and enquired if it was hot enough for me; he didn't say anything at all to Billy Lee, although there would have been a time he'd have been pleased to be in his company, and boasted afterwards how he'd talked with the fast niggah who got the winning touchdown. Anyhow, we all sat down and if John G. was aware that being in the same room as him about made me want to throw up over his air-conditioned shag-pile carpet, then he gave no sign.

He leaned back in his leather and chrome chair, his manicured nails folded over his stomach. He didn't look like he had in days past out at the country club.

'You say you want to reschedule the loan, R.D. How's that?'

'Well, John, I'll be frank, we're just in a little bit of a tight – ah, you got the figures right there – it's just that right now we're owed a bunch of money from the customers, from the insurance on the Thrush, but I guess it's the old story; people got to sell the crop before they can settle, 'n insurance companies are slow, and right now we got bills to pay, what with having to buy gas ten thousand gallons at a time, 'n all. I think my accountant has it all laid out for you.'

'I do that, R.D., in effect I'm increasing the size of your loan. What security do I have?'

I looked at him and he looked at me, very bland, just like he didn't know that financially I was spread as thin as the last of the butter over two people's toast.

'I think you got all the deeds in your strong room,' I said quietly. 'But the ag business is in good shape. By next year we'll have all this turned around.'

'Your security ain't too good, R.D. I hear you sold your house, that right?'

'Yes. One of the engineers from the nuclear plant bought it.'

'But you had to spend the money . . . all those bills to pay . . . I hear you living out in niggahtown now, that right?'

'Sure is.'

'Like it there?'

'Should have moved years ago. I get all the barbecue I can eat.'

'Yeah . . . well, you know what they say, you can take the niggah out of Africa, but you can't take Africa out of the niggah.'

There was a silence while Billy Lee and I debated whether to solve our problems by tearing the president of the bank's head off and making him eat it. We waited a moment too long and Darlby leaned back again in his chair.

'You're a man of action, R.D. I recall you coming home from the war with all your medals, the Air Force Cross 'n all, and then you were gone again, and when you came back with the money to start your business didn't they say you got it working for the CIA some place? Maybe you should've stayed in that kind of work, R.D. Men of action don't always make good businessmen.'

'There's nothing wrong with my business ability. Some son of a bitch is trying to put me out of business, is what.'

He smiled, and it was all out in the open.

'Legally, R.D., you got until the first of the month.' His eyes looked very like a diamondback I shot in the woods one time. 'After that, the men with the legal papers will be there.' His voice was so low the hiss of the air-conditioning all but drowned it. 'After that, it belongs to me.'

We went out, and his voice followed us. 'Come back now, heah.'

We got into the baking truck and headed back for the strip.

'Sorry 'bout that, Billy Lee,' I said.

'Shit,' he said. 'He ain't careful, me and Jesse Jackson come by, burn a watermelon on his lawn.'

We grinned.

I got back in the Thrush and began working with Moe from the home strip. On climb-out I passed over land owned by John G. Darlby III. My land and his adjoined and were just about the right size for a shopping mall. Right location, right size. Of course, the town wasn't really big enough, but when the new brewery Busch was building was finished it would be about 10,000 people fatter. You went into town and the signs said you were entering the Progressive City. That's what they said. They built the mall and then, why I – R.D – would probably be a fucking millionaire same as John G. – unless he managed to steal my land first.

Around dusk we came in, me and Moe, washed down the planes and tied them down. It was that time of day a man turns off the lights, locks the door and goes home to his wife, has a drink, sits down at the table and gets outside that country-fried steak, creamed potatoes, collard greens, butterbeans and corn, mops up the sawmill gravy with the biscuits. Moe went off to his family and I went to mine.

There was a smell of cooking in the hall when I went in. My wife was waiting for me; she was sitting on the bed in a very fetching little outfit, had a little strap and lots of lace, her dark hair was glossy and tumbled down her shoulders. I bent and kissed her.

'After a day in the field, you a sight for sore eyes.'

'Better than all those soybeans?'

'No contest.'

She opened a can of Bud for me and took one herself.

'First of the day. When they going to make an ad about the sweaty cropduster coming in at the end of the day and getting his beer? You'd look good on TV.'

'That's Miller, ain't it?'

She sipped. 'It's all the same. I heard you go over this afternoon.'

'Uhuh. Did John MacArthur's beans south of 240.'

'I knew it! I could hear you giving it the gun coming out of the field, and brushing out. I timed you, I figured it was about one hundred and thirty acres.'

'Man, I don't know how we managing without you, girl. You better get off your butt, come back to work.'

She giggled. 'It was funny, I was listening to you working and I thought of when we were first together, you know that? Before we were married, you had that old 450 Stearman, working it off the roads, I was taking the orders in the little trailer we had and you used to land it on the pasture with Billy Lee hanging on the wing. That was when he was back from playing football, wasn't it?'

'Yeah. He ruined his knee.'

'And that was the first good season, wasn't it? Do you remember, we went off down to Miami after it was all through, had a room in the big hotel on the beach, with the balcony and all. Do you remember it had that smoked glass all around it and we was drunk one afternoon and you were standing out there, and I crept out and went down on you – and you having to keep a straight face with all them people wandering about out there.'

She laughed. 'Old silver-tongued Claire. Talk y' into anything.'

'No one better,' I agreed.

'We had fun, didn't we? Even if we were poor. I'm not saying I want to be poor again, but we have fun.' She looked at me a little anxiously, to see how I took this line of talk. 'Didn't we?'

'You know it,' I said. Someone put their head round the door, they looked at me and I nodded. I tipped back my can.

'How is everything at the house? I worry about you there all on your own.'

'No problem. Us professional pilots are real adaptable. I'm real comfortable.'

'You're still thin. Are you eating enough?'

'Man, this is my diet. I'm getting elegant and all. Gone look like Robert Redford in Waldo Pepper.'

'I could tell there was something familiar about you, the minute you came in the door.'

'Done bought me a silk scarf, leather helmet and all, already.'

'Fool.'

There was one more can of Bud on the table by the bed and I could hear footsteps out in the hall.

'They still allowing you just one can?'

'One a day. Isn't that *mean*?'

'Here, you give me your dead one and suck on that new one.'

'What about you?'

'They're forty-eight stores between here and home, I can stop off for one if I want it. Go on now.'

She did as I bid her to. 'Do you remember Bill Powers?' she asked, and I nodded for I was not likely to forget Bill Powers, ever.

'You did that for him. You were slipping him a sip when they weren't looking.'

'These places are bad enough even with a little help. He was thirsty. 'Sides, what difference would it have made?'

She looked at me and I realized what I had said; then the nurse came in and they wanted me to *go*, she tired easily, and I kissed her and went to the door.

'Stay clear of the wires,' she called.

'I will,' I promised.

I opened the door and her voice came after me.

'R.D.?'

'Sugah?'

'The big brown poles, too.'

'You know it, babe.' And I went out, and she worried about me losing weight when she was seventy-two pounds herself – it was a joke. I went down the corridor and someone scuttled out from a room to waylay me, and it was the man who sends out the bills – little fella in glasses and a pigeon chest.

'Mr Marvin, it's about your bill,' he said indignantly.

It usually was.

'We've sent you two reminders,' he said reproachfully.

'Sir, I am going to razz my secretary but good tomorrow,' I told him. 'She is supposed to keep up with this stuff. Ya'll just cain't get good help these days.'

'That is what you said last week.' He sniffed.

33

'Damn, but it must have slipped my mind. I been so busy and all, but listen heah, I'm going to have it in the mail first thing tomorrow morning.' I took my book from my back pocket with all the acres and fields and chemical notes and made an entry. 'First thing.'

He looked at me with the expression of a man who has seen the movie many, many times before, and I slipped out and went to the truck. Wasn't that one of the three great lies? 'The cheque's in the mail.' 'You'll have the car back by lunch.' 'I'm from Washington and I'm here to help you.'

I left the hospital and drove back to the shop, stopping off at the barbecue joint for a couple of sandwiches and a six-pack for me and Billy Lee. I drank one and he drank five. The aileron on Moe's Thrush was stiffening up, there was a frayed control cable there; we took it out and replaced it, and by the time it was swaged and all in place and moving freely it was midnight. In town the lights at Darlby Bank were still burning and I would have bet money that John G. Darlby III was still in there, figuring out ways to screw people. I drove past the fine house I used to live in with my wife, and Billy Lee said thuh nucluh man got hisself a deal there and I said uhuh, he sure had, but I was kinda getting a taste for living in mobile homes, and he said he had a real good shack his brother'd vacated if my taste matured any further. I took a left across the tracks and dropped him off, then re-crossed to the trailer the other side. Billy Lee was about right, I got any closer to niggertown they were going to make me an honorary member. When I got in the old trailer was like the inside of a baker's oven, and when I walked across the floor the cockroaches scuttled away and I was too tired and ill and old to do anything about it. I just took off my shirt and boots and pants and lay down on the bed under the rattling old air-conditioner and passed out, still thinking and wondering about the man or men who were trying and working so hard to ruin me, to put me out of business.

NEW YORK

Yossif Petrovsky went to meet Spencer in a Ramada Inn in Newark. As instructed, he left City Hall through the connecting tunnel under the Park to the Criminal Court, emerging from the civic centre to hail a cab to his destination. He found the procedure of concealment from those seeking him quite normal. He had grown up running the streets of Leningrad in this fashion – passing messages for his parents, taking notes, small parcels, arranging meetings of those who would learn Hebrew, learn Jewish history, absorb the culture of their people in a country become hostile to them – and the young boy had become adept in evading the militia, avoiding the attentions of the KGB. He accepted easily that there might be men anxious to kill his former college lecturer, Dr Victor Spencer, and that Spencer needed to conceal himself from their attentions.

The motel had been redecorated recently in Olde English. Yossif fought his way through a lobby that was the ground floor of a Duke's castle, manned by Beefeaters, across a lounge of greenwood where Brooklyn Maid Marions served drinks to the guests and an HIV-positive Merry Man was behind the bar. He got lost among the suits of armour, but was rescued by a page and arrived at a pressure-moulded ancient oak door where Spencer had his room. Spencer opened it and he went into a motel room thick with black plastic beams, a four-poster bed and a mural of the battle of Bannockburn.

'Afternoon, Victor,' he said. 'Some decor here, eh?'

'It is,' Spencer agreed. 'King Henry the Ninth meets the Grand Old Duke of York, I think. At least the coffee machine is twentieth-century American. Fancy a cup?'

'Please.'

Spencer had been sitting inside a small fort of files on a small refectory table made in Puerto Rico.

'Okay,' he said. 'I've been chewing through all this stuff. The first and most important point is that the aircraft was flown to the point of impact. We have the word of the Captain on that. "Some expletive deleted bastard is flying my expletive deleted airplane," was what he said. The 747 was taken from the control of its crew and guided all the way to Lenox and 125th, close by the underground station. A train was in at the time. The aviation authorities investigating the affair – the FAA and NTSB – have identified three alterations of course and two of pitch after control was seized. The aircraft was a Zambian Airways 747, which had flown in from Lusaka the previous evening and was now making the return journey, crewed by a former Lufthansa Captain, very experienced, aged fifty-two; a Zambian co-pilot, a relative of the President; and a former Lufthansa engineer, again most experienced – all on the flight deck – and a cabin staff of nine, all Zambians. The flight took off from JFK but shortly afterwards lost all power on one engine. From what we know, this was the first time that those responsible for the crash interfered with the aircraft. The Captain asked to return to JFK and was given permission to do so. The particular flight path used to bring him back brought him over New Jersey, where at eight thousand feet he had all control of the aircraft taken from him. The first he knew of it was that the aircraft made a standard rate turn to port of some eighty degrees, before rolling out on to its new heading, which was just about in line with Central Park. At this point the remaining three engines were shut down, and the aircraft trimmed into a nose-down attitude to glide at some three hundred and fifty knots. Two minor corrections of course were made, and one further of pitch, before it accurately struck the target.

'The aviation authorities surmise that the aircraft was

interfered with in its home base of Lusaka. Security is poor there, and it would have been possible for suitably trained personnel to have gained access to it. Modifications were made that enabled someone to take control of the aircraft, shutting out the pilots and engineer, through use of the automatic pilot. This was also the view of the Captain, who after he ran out of circuit breakers to pull was attacking the automatic pilot with a fire-axe as the aircraft went in. Of necessity much of this is surmise because after hitting a large building, a road and a subway station there was little recognizable, and what there was became less so after burning for a day.'

'Isn't the theory that it was modified to accept radio signals, say from someone on one of the tall buildings surrounding Central Park?'

'That's it. It's an attractive thesis, not least because it solves the problem of how the aircraft was guided. Someone on top of a skyscraper would easily be able to see the aircraft – it was a clear day – and with modern telemetry, would be able to fly it to its destination like a radio-controlled model. However, there is one small piece of evidence which suggests that it might have been done differently. In the mountains of wreckage, they found part of the arm of one of the aircraft's passenger seats. It had had a non-standard hole drilled into it, and although the arm is broken it is clear that the impact has torn something from that hole, the marks of which look very like a jack plug. Now this suggests something *much* more interesting, which is that the aircraft was flown in by someone on board, by one of the passengers, operating the automatic pilot by means of some piece of equipment – a disguised Walkman, maybe? – plugged into the jack in the arm of the seat.'

'Some kamikaze. A suicide bomber?'

'Yes. In recent years, in terrorist terms, a rare and fabulous beast. Not always so, of course.'

'But, hold on, Victor. How could he see where he was going? He'd be sitting in the back of the thing. To drive it he'd need to see.'

37

'Good point. But he wouldn't have done all this on his own, he couldn't have. He had an organization to insert technicians into Zambia to modify the aircraft, and they would have had someone – someone on that skyscraper, watching the flight – to tell him what to do, by radio. Through the Walkman's earphones. That's how they would have done it. We have a complete passenger and crew list for the flight. One hundred and ninety-two passengers were on board, plus the flight and cabin crews. Of the passengers, nine were Europeans and the rest native Zambians – members of the *Wabenzi* tribe, to be found all over Africa, the elite, those related to the President, the ones who drive Mercedes Benz automobiles. One of these people believed in something. To be a kamikaze, a suicide bomber, an assassin willing to die to take others with you, you have to believe in *something* very much. The certainty of entry to some wonderful place in the afterlife – paradise, Valhalla, heaven of some kind, will be there somewhere, so that the assassin is not dying but merely going somewhere better. But this is difficult. Members of the *Wabenzi* tribe are notorious for being so remarkably keen on the temporal pleasures of the flesh here on earth that they would be very reluctant to exchange them for more theoretical ones in the afterlife. Was it one of the Europeans? One of Gaddafy's terrorists? Or from the gang of Abu Nidal, or Abu Mohammed? Someone from the Japanese Red Army, or from a terrorist group we have never yet heard of?'

'The White Supremacy League claimed responsibility.'

'That's right. Never heard of before nor since. Why? Why did they do it at all? Given the sophistication of the operation, we can discount the image they were trying to present – good ol' boys in pick-up trucks from Alabama or Georgia getting ready to nail some niggah's dick to a tree-stump, give him a rusty razor and set fire to the stump – the old KKK apocrypha. What we can't discount is the effectiveness of the motive, which is the fomenting of racial hatred. I have always thought that for those interested in weakening this country, exploitation of

38

racial divisions in society is one of the most effective weapons available. We have what looks like a remarkably well-organized beginning to what could surely only be a remarkably effective campaign. Why did it stop?'

Spencer paused and looked at his watch.

'Past six,' he said. 'You fancy a drink, Yossif? There's a little refrigerator here somewhere.'

Spencer pulled at a section of Gothic panelling and some towels fell out. He moved along and got some coat-hangers. On the third go a small Westinghouse appeared, arrayed with bottles and fruit juice.

'Vodka?'

'A beer.'

'Remind you of home?'

'I don't need to be reminded of home. I am here in America now. A beer, a Schlitz or a Michelob or a Miller.'

Spencer opened two Michelobs and they drank from the neck.

'So where do we begin finding these men who performed one enormous act of terror, made one telephone call, and have vanished?'

'We follow our nose. Fortunately, we have something that stinks. We have something that stinks as bad as the cattle gut that the Ojo Caliente Apache were given to eat when they were defeated and had to live on the reservation.'

'Which is?'

Spencer rummaged in the fort on the table from Puerto Rico and emerged with a magazine, a copy of *People*. On the cover was a close-up of a drawn but handsome face, with burning buildings and vehicles in the background. Under the face, in black type, the words: 'When The Killing Became Too Much.'

'Our friend Adam Ross,' said Spencer. 'The man who was at the scene of the crime. He was *there*, with his ace cameraman Charlie Harrel, and they got the only newsreel footage of the whole thing. Two days later, Adam Ross went home and washed down half a bottle of sleeping pills with half a bottle of bourbon. He died about half an hour later. He left a note which can be summarized by the headline of the magazine. After so many years of reporting on death, degradation and disaster, the impact of witnessing the horror of the 747 going into Harlem unhinged his brain. Unable to take any more, he killed himself.'

Spencer tossed down the magazine. 'It made a lot of good copy for sob-journalists, but I do not believe it. I do not believe that two ace action reporters were present to record the action news event of the decade by chance. I do not believe that Adam Ross killed himself. I managed to track down a girl who knew him and she expressed her doubts. I quote: "Who do you know who kills the thing they love the best? When Adam looked in the mirror to shave in the morning he enjoyed the sight, he knew it was the best thing he'd see all day." End quote. That leaves Harrel. No one could find a whisker of evidence to suggest that he knew anything about the disaster before it happened, nor that he had anything to do with Ross's death. He couldn't have; he collapsed with shock after the crash and was still under sedation in hospital. He said that Ross had called him to take some film for a documentary he was thinking of making. Ross liked to do that when he wasn't out in the field.'

'So maybe they were just lucky. In the right place at the right time.'

'I don't believe it, and I'll tell you why. The media and the terrorists have a symbiotic relationship – especially television, which depends so heavily upon its ratings. They need each other. The terrorists want publicity for their "cause" and television wants something to get the people to watch their channel. They have been proven to need each other. Neither side has too many moral qualms about the relationship. I think that Ross was there because he'd been told there was something in it for him.'

'How can we find that out? He's dead.'

'Harrel must know something. I'll talk to him.'

'Will he talk to you?'

'Our Charlie has come up in the world. He's given up toting a camera for something more prestigious. He produces WashingtonWatch. Have you seen it? It's a weekly investigative reporting news programme, post-Watergate, Contragate, Irangate. Appeals to the vaguely paranoid liberal market. Of course Charlie will see me, I'm the sort of person he likes to make his programmes about.'

'Something bothers me about this thing with the 747. If the terrorists could modify it to accept outside commands, and if those who know say it would have been possible to make it obey someone – our man on the skyscraper – through radio signals, then why didn't they do so? What was the point of having a kamikaze do it? And if it was a kamikaze, where did they get him from?'

'That's the thing, isn't it?' Spencer agreed. 'The way it was set up, the crash was clearly meant to be the first in a series of large-scale terrorist incidents, perhaps all involving this mythical White Supremacy League. I don't know why they didn't materialize. Something must have gone wrong. But as for the reason they used a kamikaze, that's obvious.'

'Why?'

'To prove they could.'

Yossif Petrovsky pondered a vision of suicidally-piloted 747s raining in on cities across the USA.

'Have you got an hour to spare?' asked Spencer.

'I just have to do some reading, Victor. Final exams soon.'

'Like to see a real piece of history? A film from home?'

'Okay. What is it?'

Spencer got up and switched on the television above the VCR. On the news a small, bright green frog was explaining fiscal policy to the nation.

'You tell them, Kermit,' said Spencer.

'I want to see Miss Piggy explaining foreign policy.'

'She wouldn't be suitable. Miss Piggy has a very clear understanding of the realities of power politics. Dick and Jane would worry the people less.'

Spencer slipped a cassette into the machine and the financial expert vanished.

Spencer settled back in his chair with the remote-control and the motor of the VCR clicked and whirred. He pressed the command for play, and a figure familiar to both of them appeared on the screen.

'Palace of Congresses,' said Yossif.

The stocky figure in his well-cut suit was on the podium. Russian rolled from the speakers. Spencer saw Yossif's eyes prickle.

'I'm stupid,' muttered Yossif. 'To be homesick at seeing that man . . .'

'It's not him,' Spencer said understandingly. 'It's *rodina*.'

The President of the Soviet Union continued to bully, cajole, entice, lead.

'It's one of the ironies of history that the USA turned out to be the richest, most powerful nation in the world, you know,' Spencer said unexpectedly. 'It should have been the Russian Empire. Vast, rich in natural resources both human and material, it was poised to explode into growth early in this century. The First World War stopped that, and brought about the Revolution, as Lenin and his successors liked to call it. It wasn't a revolution, as a matter of fact, it was a *coup d'état*. And the irony of history was that the communists, who wanted to dominate the world, made sure that Russia could not, because their system of government was so bad, so stultifying, so inefficient. Yet without them, we would be living in a world in which *Russian* values mattered, not American ones.'

Spencer listened and watched for a few more moments.

'That's what *perestroika* and *glasnost* were all about, you know. That's what the whole changes in the system of government are for – the loosening up, the arms agreements to get investment away from the military and into productive sectors. They're to get it to work again. He could do it. He may do it.'

Spencer stared thoughtfully at the man on the screen.

'Everyone's writing off the Russians too early,' he said.

WAYCROSS, GEORGIA

It was Saturday. By late afternoon we had got caught up
and it meant we wouldn't have to annoy people by
working on the Sabbath – could maybe get up late, sit on
the front porch, barbecue ribs and sausage, crack a cold,
cold can, or in my case work on the airplanes. I'd been
out all afternoon with Billy Lee working the west territory and I got in about five, slipped it over the trees. Moe
had his Thrush tied down and beside it, looking like a lost
debutante who had unaccountably found herself in a
farmyard, was a pretty twin-engined Cessna 310. I shut
down and crawled out, sweaty and glad to get my helmet
off; the pilot was peering inside one nacelle the way
air-taxi drivers do, uncertain of the state of the
equipment.

'How'd you like the strip?' I asked.

'Bit short,' he said.

'Yeah, well, we don't see too many of you city slickers
out here. Us country boys find it fine. You done brung
someone, or you just out here seeing how honest folk
live?'

'I want to see horseshit I watch "Dallas" on TV,' he
said. He was a young kid, paying his dues doing part 135
work hoping to get a job with a commuter line. With a
mouth like his, he'd wind up right-hand seat of a 727
when he was 45.

'Brought two guys from JAX,' he said.

'Well, all right,' I said as I headed for the hangar.

'You cropdusters are mad,' he said, by way of a final
remark.

I went in and Mrs Lymon said that she had put them in

43

the office – they were from Miami, she said – so I went in, wondering who I owed money to down there.

'I'm sure sorry to have kept y'all waiting,' I said.

'We don't mind,' said a voice. 'We were sitting here enjoying all your cool air while you were sweating out there.'

I didn't know the first man, who was lounging back in the old stuffed chair in there; he had an alligator shirt on, and cut-offs and athletic sneakers, his legs were sinewy as if he ran. As I came in he smiled, showing even white teeth, but not as even and white as those of the second man, whom I did know. Only *he* was supposed to be dead.

'My airplane's air-conditioned,' I said. 'You stick your head out the window, you get all the air you want.'

'Business must be good, R.D.' said Ric. 'You're too busy to answer the 'phone.'

He got up; he'd been a good-looking man in his twenties, and now he was a handsome man. I shook his hand and it was real, solid flesh. Seeing him suddenly brought it all back, dust and blood, the smell of fuel pouring from torn lines, gunfire. All the scarred dents in my leg suddenly ached.

'A lawyer was calling me from Miami . . .'

Ric smiled. 'That's me.'

We all used to joke that it would be real useful for Ric to go on and study law after the war, so as he'd know how to defend himself.

'R.D., this is George Ryan. He's our farm manager.'

The second man got up smoothly and athletically, and I shook his hand too.

'You're in the farm business, Ric?' I asked, as I fixed some cold drinks from the refrigerator.

'I handle the business end. George and I work for Delloro tobacco, in Colombia. Delloro has about eighteen thousand acres of land some eighty miles east of Barranqilla, near Santa Marta. We're looking to hire some modern technology.'

'Have you worked tobacco, Mr Marvin?' Ryan asked.

'Why, sure. I started out on tobacco, as a matter of fact. I worked with Southern Dusters when I was a boy, as flagman and loader; when I was sixteen I flew a Cub for them, working some of the little patches the farmers cut out of the forest back then. This was big tobacco country then. Cotton, too.'

'We've had problems working our tobacco with ground equipment. Ground compaction is a problem, and a lot of the time the ground is too wet to get the equipment in to work it. Then you get the spraying problems, the number of Hi-boys you need, labour costs and all that. We're thinking of cutting it all out and using an ag airplane.'

'Makes all kinds of sense,' I agreed.

'If it works properly we'll buy our own aircraft and have our own aerial operation. We want someone in to do the first season, let us have the learning process. When I discussed it with Ric, he said he knew someone who was the best there was, back in the old days.'

I looked at Ric. 'You're very complimentary.'

He spread his hands and smiled. 'It's true. You're the best.'

'We'd like to offer you a full season's contract, to work our crop. You'd have to start in about six weeks. Would you be available?'

I didn't have to think, but I furrowed my brow a little and pondered.

'If we can agree rates, I guess I can do it, Mr Ryan, yes.'

He asked what I'd charge and I came up with four bucks an acre for five-gallon work, herbicide and fungicide, and three-fifty for two-gallon insecticide. Said we'd have to work on an hourly rate for fertilizer, but that it ought to come out around five cents a pound; would depend on the ferry.

'Our land is all around a central strip,' he commented, 'except for some on the coast. That's perhaps a little high, don't you think?'

'You could get some kid fresh out of ag school who'd

45

do it for half. Might do a million bucks' worth of damage to your drop. You pay me more, I'll make you more.'

We agreed on the prices and Ric borrowed the typewriter to fill in the spaces on the forms he had brought with him.

'There's one more thing. I hate to do it, but I have to have a CYA policy on this.'

Ric smiled. 'You feel you need to cover your ass, R.D.?'

'There's always a risk going that far,' I said. 'I can get all the way down there and maybe there's a change of government, maybe the bottom falls out of the tobacco market. Who knows? I need to cover myself.'

We settled on twenty-five thousand and I had feet on land that was still mine.

Ric passed me the forms and I sat down to read them. Some men rob you with guns, some with a fountain pen. But they were perfectly good, straightforward contracts. I signed, and Ryan did the same. Ric wrote out the cheque.

'I forget, R.D.,' he said, handing it to me. 'Have you worked that far south?'

'Not Colombia. Did a lot of work in Nicaragua and flew a DC-3 some, from Managua to Miami. That was before the revolution, of course.'

'Right. Colombia's very mountainous. Air transport makes a lot of sense. The company's bought a Convair to use as a workhorse. It's in Miami. Can you get it flown down for us?'

'It's a prop job?'

'Yes . . . a 240.'

'No problem. Leave it to me.'

'The other thing is, we need to start up a programme against malaria. We need to kill anopheles mosquitoes from the air. Have you ever done any mosquito spraying?'

'Sure. Had a couple of contracts to spray towns round here a while back. Easy work.'

'You use the aircraft you spray the crops with?'

46

'No, you can use just about anything you want because you don't put it out low, like you do on the crops. You put it out at about 500 feet, you use Malathion under pressure, ULV – that's Ultra Low Volume. Because you're at altitude you can use a single-nozzle set-up, and it gives you one hell of a swathe. You can spray a town in no time. The only thing you have to watch is wind. Too much wind, you could spray the whole county in a single pass!'

'We might be operating a long way from a strip. It'd be best to be able to carry a lot of chemical, to be able to spray a really big area before having to go back. Can you organize it for us? Give me a call and I'll send you the money once you'd found out about it.'

We went out into the sun and heat and they got into the Cessna. The kid fired it up and taxied out to the very end of the strip. He checked the mags and props, the engine note rising and falling, blowing a great plume of dust back to the trees. I saw Ric wave as the aircraft rolled. The pretty little twin climbed away towards Jacksonville and my fingers ran over the smooth paper of the cheque in my pocket. I figured I'd run down to the bank and put it straight in, just to spoil old Darlby's weekend.

I knew too much about Ric, about Ricardo Abdul Coluccio. I should have torn the cheque up and given Darlby the land instead. I should have known the interest on the money would be more than I could afford.

At 6,500 feet the air seemed cool, but it was an illusion, for the great thunderclouds were building. I threaded my way through the towers of cumulus in the Super Cub, heading 210 for Panama City. When I called the tower they warned me of a storm coming in over the bay – I could see it, the dark rain lashing the water – and they vectored me around behind an Air Florida 727. I landed long to avoid the wake turbulence and taxied off to the ramp, tying the little bird down firmly against the approaching wind.

The little old flying school had a couple of raggedy old buildings, an old 150, an aged 172 and a positively ancient straight-tail Skylane. I went in and said, 'Seen Hank Tyre?' and the child behind the desk stopped exercising her jaw muscles, said, 'Inna simulator room' and blew an obscene pink bubble. I went through a door with a worn notice saying 'Students Leaving Master Switch On Fined Fifteen Bucks', down the corridor, and he was sitting next to a rocking blue box, chewing an unlit cigar. I leaned in the doorway and he looked at me thoughtfully and spat a piece of leaf from his lip. The pen moving across the plastic table in front of him weaved and staggered like a spider that had wandered into a pool of spilt Mogen David.

'Forty-four Lima Pop, two mile outside the outer marker, cleared the ILS runway, 32 approach.'

The box lurched dangerously. 'Uh . . . Roger,' it mumbled.

'Polly wants a cracker,' said Tyre.

'Uh . . . Roger, forty-four Lima Papa is cleared the ILS runway 32 approach.'

Outside the storm rumbled and rain swept over the threshold of 14. A student in a hurry landed three times on 32 before sinking gratefully to the ground and scurrying off to its tie-downs.

'Tell him to expect turbulence on final,' I said helpfully, and Tyre grinned.

The box continued to gyrate. It looked like the bucking bull at Rod's Rodeo Ranch.

'Somebody taking a check ride?' I enquired.

The spider on the table weaved from side to side and Tyre peered through a slot in the side of the box, which was whimpering and muttering to itself. He winced and shook his head. The box reached full movement on its control arms back and forward, side to side. There was a muffled thud from inside and then just a long-drawn-out ooooh of disapproval from the gyros spooling down, and the box slowly sagged to its knees, looking dejected.

'Wassamatter? Wassgoinon? Huh? Huh? Wassissit?'

'Ah, Roger, forty-four Pop, understand that you have flown into an office block two and one half miles from the threshold. Do not execute missed approach at this time.'

'Huh? What?'

'You're *dead*, Lima Pop.'

'Sheeet.'

There was an amount of banging and cussing and then a door opened in the box and a young man fell out. His clean shirt was soaked to a dark blue and he appeared disoriented. Tyre grinned.

'What you all covered in sweat for, boy?'

'Shit,' said the youth. 'That mutha . . . that fucken machine.'

'Beats flying into an office block for real, though, don't it?'

The youth paid, Tyre signed his log book and told him to be back Tuesday for another try, and he staggered off for an appointment with a beer can.

'Simulator I, Students Zilch.'

'Damn if it ain't R.D. Marvin.' We shook hands. 'I read about you in the paper, son. Hear you been a bad boy, done sprayed all them trees with that naughty chemical.'

'Put-up job. Nothing wrong with 2,4,5-T.'

'Uhuh.' He looked at me closely and ate a fresh piece of his cigar. 'Well, it's good to see you, though matter of fact you looking kind of scroungy. You been ill or something, or is that just what everyone looks like, they get to be your age?'

'Age, hell. I just ain't been sitting behind a desk growing a belly; unlike some people I've been out in the field, working. Anyone that works for their living looks like this.'

'They do? I sure am glad I never tried it. What happen, you get in a wreck?'

'Yeah. Put a Thrush in, beginning of the season.'

'You did? You say you sure you done this kind of work before? What happened?'

49

'Was working out of the Forestry strip, had a hundred and eighty acres alfalfa to do, had loopers in there so bad they were flat mowing it in front of your eyes. I was going to let Moe, my pilot, do it, let him have some of the early work, but he came down in the night with a real bad toothache and had to go get it fixed, so I did it instead. I had my own Thrust in the shop doing the annual on it, and I took his. I was climbing out through the gap in the trees after take-off and the prop governor quit, rpms just wound back around the dial and the bird flat settled towards the trees.'

'You dump?'

'Hit the handle and the pin sheared, the thing flopped forward and I never lost a drop. Working out of that strip you had to clear this big, bad old widow-maker, one of the real big ones from the plant, and there was no way I was going to make it. The way it looked I was going to plug in direct to 580,000 volts, be a noise like someone playing "Duelling Banjos" with the volume turned up and nothing left but the *smell*, you know? Be people driving up for days saying "This the new barbecue joint? Gimme a bunch of ribs, pint of slaw and a Ripple to go." There's no room to go under the beast, and I put the nose down and put it into the trees.

'Done did some mowing of my own, collected a piece of a pine tree that came through the windshield and separated me from my senses, and when I came round – couldn't have been long – the bird was on fire. I was so damn dazed I didn't have any strength, the doors were still shut and the flames hadn't got to me, but the hopper'd burst and I'd got the chemical all over me.'

'What were you using?'

'Methyl and ethyl parathion, 6.3.'

Hank shuddered. 'That stuff used to scare me to death. Closest thing to nerve gas you can come across outside wartime. How'd you get out?'

'My load man, Billy Lee. He always watches when I take off, to see that I climb out safely. He saw the bird go down and piled into the truck, got to the end of the strip and came running through the scrub. Found me still in it, pawing at the door latch, weak as a kitten. He hauled me out, got cut up and burned some doing it.'

'Brave fella. You're lucky as hell to be here, you know?'

'Yeah. I was staggering out with Billy Lee and suddenly I got these little twinkles around my eyes, little bursts of light, and then I couldn't see. Went blind. Billy Lee got me to the loading area and hosed me down, then he got me to the hospital. I was in a couple of days, had me on atropine and 2-PAM: They wanted to keep me in some, but there was work to be done so I left.'

'It sure messed you up. You walked in here and I said, who's this damned Chinaman coming in here?'

'You're looking kind of fit yourself. I was expecting to see you all pale.'

'Was one of them open places. We grew vegetables and all.'

'So what are you doing here, teaching kids to shoot bad approaches?'

'When you're starting over, R.D., you got to start somewhere,' he said soberly.

I met Hank back when about a couple of hundred of us would go down to Nicaragua to spray for them. We did a season together, and when we'd finished a guy offered us money to fly a very old DC-3 for him; we made the run from Miami to Managua and then on down to Colon in Panama and back up to Miami twice a week, got so we could do it blindfold. Flew all winter, and then it was ag time again. Hank was smart, he saved all his money and bought an old Beech 19 and got out of the bug-killing business, and all the rest turned up and I left the DC-3 and its owner (who was busy going out of business) and went and got back in the Stearman. Everyone said see old Hank ain't here this year, guess it was too tough f'r 'im, haw haw, yes sir, he hauling grits from Bugtussle to Chitlin Switch, haw, haw. Because you weren't a *real* pilot if you didn't spend half your day in a 100-degree

51

bank at fifty feet pulling four gees, looking back over your shoulder at where you just been – anyone knew that – and we all continued working ten and fourteen hours a day in the air for four months and buying new Caddys when we got home and drinking a lot of Blue Ribbon and teaching kids how to fly, our way, and flying old eighty-fours for the Reserve. And then back we'd go, see old Jake ain't here this year, guess it was . . . and it could have gone on for *years* if it hadn't been for the war; and we all trooped off to teach kids in uniform to fly, or maybe wear uniforms ourselves, and the ones that did get shot at, a whole bunch didn't come back, and the ones that did weren't the same, and not too damned rich either. And old Hank, he still hauling grits from Bugtussle to Chitlin Switch and a whole bunch of other places too, and they about to deregulate things, folk thinking about the Commuter airline business. Hank was getting all set, ready to *go*, and give him a few years and it's all just downhill to the shiny Porsche car, and the house with the ponds and ducks and the secretary with the hair and the lungs and the mouth. Old Hank he got to work one morning real early, but not earlier than the Internal Revenue Service, who had a platoon of people there already when he arrived, all of them busy, and they had all his books including the real ones. It took them about six months, but when they were ready they took his ass outside and just naturally hung it from the highest piece of timber that they could find, and after twenty years' worth of hard graft he was again worth as much as when he first came into the world.

None of which would have concerned me, only that three months before he had unexpected visitors I had loaned him forty thousand dollars.

It had made a lot of sense at the time. I had had a very prosperous season. *Very.* I wanted to broaden my base, give myself some protection against the lean years. He was temporarily short of ready cash and needed liquid capital. We made a deal, my forty-grand loan for six months, after which it was to be repaid with reasonable interest. Or if he couldn't repay, I was to be allowed to have stock in his company.

Which was what I wanted. Hank was smart, always had been, much better at business than me; he knew that no one got rich working for someone else. I knew he was a sharp operator, but then no one gets rich without being dishonest somewhere down the line. I wanted in.

I sure could have used that forty grand, right then.

'So what you doing here, R.D., apart from old times?'

'You still remember how to fly?'

'Maybe.'

'Convair 240?'

'Didn't own but two.'

'Need one taken down to Columbia.'

'I seem to remember you know how to fly multi-engine airplanes.'

'I'm taking a Thrush down there. Got a contract to work tobacco.'

'Good. What does it pay, taking the old junker down there?'

'Three hundred and a ticket home.'

'You come to the wrong door, son. The Charity offices are down the street.'

We settled on five.

'How much do I get to keep?' he asked.

'It's yours. I don't want five hundred, I want forty thousand.'

'I owe it.'

'I know. I want you back on your feet. The sooner you're back in business, the sooner I can have my money.'

He looked at me quizzically. 'You have a lot of faith in my business skill. I'd remind you I'm worth about the price of a pizza'n a jug at Luigi's Pizza Parlor, right now.'

'You'll be rich again.'

'Be more careful of the IRS, that's for sure.'

The storm had passed through, the tarmac gleamed wet in the sun. I'd be in time to call by and see Claire. She'd had her treatment, she'd be tired and ill. No beer tonight.

'You doing a full season down there?' asked Hank.

'Yeah, six months.'

I went out to untie the Super Cub and drain the fuel, and it occurred to me that by the time I came back from Colombia Claire would be dead. One day she'd been healthy, the next in hospital. It was burning her up like a flame.

ALBANY, N.Y.

When Charlie Harrel had followed Adam Ross from one trouble spot to another war zone, he had rented an apartment in Staten Island where his wife led a lonely existence during the large part of the year that he was away. Now that fortune had smiled on him he had moved to Albany, where he had a handsome house. He took advantage of modern technology to work at least two days a week from home, and it was there that he agreed to meet Spencer.

Spencer drove out in his Ninety-Eight Oldsmobile, which he parked a block away before walking to his destination. It was a good neighbourhood, he noted, white, crime-free, with neatly trimmed front lawns elevated slightly from the road and children of prosperous parents in evidence. He went up the front path and rang on the door chime.

Harrel answered within a few seconds and the two men stared at each other on the doorstep. Harrel had trimmed his beard to outline his jaw, and a regular diet and lack of periodic dysentery had filled out his figure somewhat.

'The Cold War Warrior himself,' he commented. 'You'd better come in.'

He guided Spencer to a work room where there were shelves of books, a computer terminal, several televisions with VCRs and a large glass table. On the walls were various photographs in which Harrel smiled out at the world alongside unshaven men in turbans, head-cloths, *kaffiyehs* and fatigue caps. Sunshine glinted on teeth and oiled jowls and gun-barrels. Adam Ross gave an Action Man smile into the camera without anything burning in the background. A small shelf of awards proclaimed Harrel's ability. A bottle of Perrier water and a glass stood on the glass table, and Harrel and Spencer each sat on one side of it.

'So you're working for the Mayor,' said Harrel. 'You make a habit of associating with losing causes. Did you see the feature we did on Santucci? Judge Connel is going to fry his ass.'

'I don't watch television.'

'You think it's for stupid people, right?'

'That's it. And the political problems of the Mayor do not concern me. I have been asked to do some investigation into the terrorist 747 crash in Harlem, some eighteen months ago. Fifteen thousand dead, and their relatives would like to know who did it.'

'Spare me the bleeding heart, Spencer. It doesn't fit.'

'Something else doesn't fit, but we'll come to that in a minute. Let's start at the beginning, with you. You're the producer of a weekly television news programme. How'd you get the job?'

'Ability rewarded.'

'I didn't say you couldn't do the job, but promotion from camera-jockey to prime mover is not an easy one. You must have made a deal with someone. Try again.'

'I was offered the post and accepted.'

'After Ross died?'

'Yes.'

'Dead man's shoes, then.'

'I . . . inherited it, if you like.'

'It would have been his.'

'Yes.'

'Why?'

'Adam would have fronted the programme, with responsibility as producer. I would have been in charge of the shooting.'

'So Ross was a good television reporter. It's still a big jump.'

'Not really,' Harrel said frankly. 'It was a logical extension of the kind of reporting Adam did anyway. He'd discussed it with the executives before. Then he had a big piece of luck, he had film of the Jumbo disaster in Harlem. He took it to them and they were able to make a deal on the spot. It was a deal from everyone's point of view.'

'Except the people of Harlem and the people on board the jet,' Spencer said dryly. 'But it was *Adam* who did this, not you. And yet you were the one who shot the film. Why weren't you there?'

'I was . . . very upset. By witnessing the accident, I saw mass murder.'

'Yes . . . but you're no stranger to violence and disaster, are you? And yet you were upset. You were taken to hospital suffering from shock, weren't you?'

Harrel nodded.

'But why? Why did it shock you so?'

'It got to Adam too,' Harrel reminded him. 'No one who knew Adam would have ever thought he'd commit suicide, but he did.'

Spencer shook his head. 'No. No, I don't subscribe to that theory. Adam Ross had emotions of flint. He was an egomaniac of some proportions, and the suffering of others bothered him not at all. I believe that he was murdered by those who caused the crash of the 747. He was murdered because he had known *in advance* that the aircraft would crash, and the terrorists were tidying up loose ends. *You* didn't know why you were there on that rooftop, but afterwards when the disaster had taken place you realized that Ross must have known in advance. Maybe you had suspected that something might be going to happen. It wasn't shock that put you in hospital, but guilt. Because you and Ross, you'd done it before. Isn't that right?'

Harrel stood up, very white.

'Let's get this into perspective, Spencer. I'm not some poor Sandinista you can interrogate or torture. I'm the producer of a coast-to-coast news programme, and you're the sort of person I can put on it. In the equation of power, I'm up here and you're down there. You're not

57

even in the CIA any more. You're an ex-convict who's going to find himself on TV again next week.'

Spencer spread his hands in conciliatory fashion.

'Okay, okay. Let's not get heated about this. How about a drink to calm things down? You have any bourbon?'

'You drink this early in the day?' Harrel sneered.

'Some people drink any time. The time of day doesn't matter to them. What about a Scotch?'

'No.'

'Gin, tequila, rum, vodka. Anything'll do.'

Harrel gave no response and Spencer sighed. 'Then it's a good job I bought some with me.'

He took a flat bottle of 100-proof vodka from an inside pocket of his sports jacket and placed it on the table between them. He cracked the twist-cap and the oily fumes began to invade the air.

'You want a glass? Or do you just take it from the neck?'

'Put it away.'

'Don't you want any? No? You know what, Charlie, if I didn't know better I would have said that you were a reformed alcoholic. I say reformed, because once a lush, always a lush, eh? It's hard for them, staying on the straight and narrow. You always worry about booze being around, being a temptation. You know I knew a guy once, he was a lush, and he went for dinner with some people and they served a sweet – it had fruit and sponge, and in the sponge it had sherry. They didn't *know* he was a lush, you see. He ate the sweet and left early. Went on a bender that lasted a week. That was all it took to put him back to square one. So if I didn't know better I'd say that you were horrified by the sight and smell of this vodka here because it was so dangerous. It's the strong stuff, the sort the alks love. It gets them going fast, you see.'

Spencer leaned forward to put his hard, flat face close to Harrel's. 'But I *do* know better. It isn't you that's trying to stay off the sauce, is it? It's your wife.'

Harrel had gone completely white with rage. 'Keep my wife out of this.'

Spencer sighed. 'Everyone says that. As though when you have blood on your hands you can prevent some of it from getting on those you love. And you do love your wife. It's a nice quality in you, Charlie, it makes you much nicer than people like Adam Ross. Your wife's a good woman, but weak. She found it difficult to take your long trips away into dangerous places, became attached to comfort from a bottle. But she's better now. Dried out. You've got your new job, doing well. You're trying to have children, although it's still not easy. The booze doesn't help, does it?'

Spencer reached over and screwed the top on to the bottle.

'I was married once. I had a wife and a young son. Like you, I was away from home for long periods, doing a dangerous job. I came back one evening, after a couple of months in the field, very tired. I'd been up for seventy hours or more. I saw my wife and son, had some supper and went to bed. Passed out cold. In the night my son woke with a pain in his stomach and a fever. Maybe the excitement of me coming home. I was so unconscious that my wife decided to take him to the hospital herself rather than try to rouse me. She left a little note by the bed to tell me what she had done and went downstairs with our son. She decided to take my car, which was already outside. I was awakened to read her note by the blast of six kilos of F-14 plastic explosive going off.

'It had been meant for me. Because of my job I had blood on my hands, and some of it got on to my family. Because of it I now live in a pit of grief and guilt. It is a very horrible place to live, Charlie, and I hope that you never find yourself there.'

Spencer looked up, and stared into Harrel's eyes.

'I fear that you will, though. You have blood on your hands, Charlie, and it has a way of splashing on to those you love. It would be all too easy for your wife to return to the booze. Much, much too easy. And then you would find yourself living where I do, in that pit, because you will have been responsible.'

Harrel leaned forward and put his head in his hands. He could not but see Spencer as anything but the embodiment of evil. He was afraid of him, and believed him capable of anything.

'Tell me, Charlie,' Spencer said softly. 'Tell me what you know. Get the blood off.'

Harrel hesitated.

'It was Adam, wasn't it?' Spencer prompted softly. 'Adam set it up.'

'Yes.' Harrel let out his breath in a long gasp. 'Adam always set it up. When we were going somewhere new Adam would always go first, to make a reconnaissance. And then when we were there we'd always be in the right place at the right time . . . we always got the best stories, the best film.'

'You got the assassination of Setchin Singh, didn't you?'

Harrel nodded.

'And the Palestinians, when they got the school buses. Weren't you on board the Mil when they caught the Contra supply column? Didn't you get Cameraman of the Year for that one?'

'Yes,' said Harrel quietly.

'Why didn't you show them when they burned the villages afterwards and shot all the people?'

'It didn't fit. Adam knew what the people back home wanted to see.'

'Yes. There's a fine line between doing your job and being accessory to murder, isn't there?'

'You should know! How many have you murdered?'

'When I worked for the government it was always understood that killing the enemies of my country was a part of the job. You seem to have been in on the killing of other people's enemies. Anyone's enemy. For a good story.'

Harrel stayed silent.

'So you realized that Adam had known that an aircraft

60

was going to crash into Harlem. What made you sure?'

'He was listening to a radio. A Walkman-style radio, through headphones. I asked him what he was doing and he said catching the news, but Adam wasn't interested in the news unless he was on it. I realized that he must have been listening – maybe to the pilot and the control tower, so as to know where to look and when to get me ready to take film. Once the crash had happened I knew that Adam had known – that someone had been in touch with him and told him where to be, and when.'

There was a short silence and then Spencer launched the single, deadly word.

'Who?'

Harrel shook his head. 'Adam never ever told me who he dealt with. Not at the beginning in Cambodia, not at the end in Central Park. That's it, Spencer. That's all there is to know. Now get out. I don't want to talk to you any more.'

Spencer reached out and put the flat bottle of vodka away in his jacket pocket.

'It's filthy stuff,' he commented. He wrote two numbers on a piece of card and put it on the glass table-top in front of Harrel. 'That's the number of Yossif Petrovsky, who works for the Mayor. He can get in touch with me any time if you want to talk to me.'

'Why would I ever want to talk to you, Spencer? I know as much as I want to about brutality.'

'Perhaps not enough,' Spencer said quietly. 'I'm not the one you ought to be afraid of, Charlie. Do you think that Adam was afraid, right at the end, when they forced him to swallow the pills? When he gagged on the raw liquor? As he felt himself going under, dying as they held him down, and he realized that at long last he'd gambled and lost? You ought to be afraid of those people, Charlie; you ought to be afraid that they might come round and want to talk to you too.'

He got up and went to the door. 'You couldn't cope with them. I could.'

Harrel watched Spencer go out and down the path and

along the street, walking back to his car. Rage flared in his stomach and he picked up the phone, his fingers flicking through his book.

'Judge Connel, please. Charles Harrell, "Washington-Watch".'

He waited while the secretary transferred his call.

'Judge? Charles Harrel. I think we met last year . . . yeah, that's right. Aren't you conducting the enquiry? The Mayor, that's right. I just thought you might be interested. Santucci has hired Dr Victor Spencer. He says to investigate the terrorist crash of the 747 that went into Harlem. The White Supremacy League. Yeah, he is an expert on terrorism. Hell, he was one, wasn't he? The government of this country employed him for that very task, that's why he did his time. Yeah, I thought you might be interested. Okay. Me too.'

Harrel put the telephone down, lit with the pleasure of striking back. The glow burned within him as he sat at the table until, like a shot of raw liquor, the fire faded away, leaving only the dull ache of fear behind.

WAYCROSS, GEORGIA

The leaves on the beans began to yellow and the farmers had their combines checked and running. The ground peas had fattened up; John MacArthur came by with a mess of early ones and Moe's wife boiled them; we ate them after work for a couple of days – they were real good, salty and firm. I preferred them like that, not roasted. We put out defoliant on 500 acres cotton and that was the last work we did, the harvest was coming in. I settled up with Moe, who'd had a good season; he took his money and went on back to Columbia, South Carolina, with his family for a vacation before taking up his winter job of flight instruction. I added it all up and I was still just in business, thanks to the tobacco contract. I thought of Moe – maybe there were advantages to working for twenty-five per cent.

The two-holer, Mike Sierra, had less hours on it, and it was useful to be able to haul a loader or spares when you were working out in the sticks, so we pulled an annual on it and got it in jam-up shape and late on a Saturday I went down to Panama City to collect Hank. There was a Sigmet out for a squall line associated with a cold front from Tampa St Pete to Jacksonville. The Thrush was not remotely an IFR airplane, being built for the fields and not the clouds, and I tied it down and went out to eat oysters with Hank.

The oyster bar was doing good trade, with folk stopping off for a couple of beers and a dozen, and with some tourists. It was a little early for the snowbirds, but there were enough people to keep the shucker busy; we had a couple of dozen raw with hot sauce and a couple of dozen roasted, and plenty of crisp saltines and a pitcher, and when we were through Hank said there was a place down the road that had country music so we went along. It looked like it had been a warehouse at some stage, had a whole bunch of tables and chairs and booths and a big old long bar; it was packed with college folk, all boisterous and mostly drunk.

'How 'bout them *dawgs*?' hollered the leader of the band, and the crowd roared. We squeezed into a booth with our cans of Blue Ribbon.

'We gone be shit*faced* tonight,' he promised, and they stamped their feet and yelled.

'Gooooooo dawgs,' Hank called. 'Guess the Bulldogs kicked ass,' he said to me.

'You a football fan?' I asked.

'I had two seats in the stadium at Athens, before I had my little piece of trouble,' he said. 'I got a head start, back when I first had the 19.I set up a run on game days; used to pick up a whole bunch of rich rednecks from out in the sticks, pick them up from Tifton and Waycross and Alma and Vidalia and Dublin, haul them up for the game and haul them back on the Sunday. They used to stay at the Ramada. I did so damn well at it I got a DC-3 the next year, had a little stewardess and a bar. Those old boys loved it. I'm telling you, the Bulldogs got me started, and I am grateful. When I die, I hope to go to Vince Dooley's house.'

He drained his can and brought back two more. 'You kind of slow there, boy.'

The band finished its set and filed off for lubrication, and to line itself up some ass.

'We gone be raht back,' the man promised. 'So ya'll don't leave, now, heah?'

The jukebox came on with country music and Hank grinned at a table of young women, a couple of whom looked interested.

'We ought to check out them gals.'

I felt very tired. It was the end of the season. Five hundred and sixty hours of flying. For a moment I wished to God I wasn't going down to Colombia to do it all over again. I drank some cold beer in an effort to revive myself.

'How's instructing?' I asked.

'Aw, shit. You do much instructing, R.D.?'

'Plenty. They made me a mission I.P. after I recovered, that time.'

'You must have been good.'

I finished the beer and felt very little better. On the jukebox the Kendalls were singing about going to bed with someone else's husband.

'You mustn't ever think you're good. You can know you got the skill, you can know you got the experience, but you mustn't ever think you're *good*. The day you go out there and there ain't just a little bit of wariness in you, you in trouble. Day you say, I'm GOOD, that's the day you have agreed to have an accident, some day, some time in the future, probably near. Day you say, I'm GOOD, you start discarding all the little tricks and manoeuvres you devised to protect yourself and keep yours alive when you were inexperienced and afraid. The day some small brown men in black pyjamas filled my airplane full of holes, killed my passengers and co-pilot, almost separated me from my leg, I was firmly convinced that I was GOOD. The only mystery was why the Lord hadn't done the job properly and given me white feathery wings and a nightie to wear, I was so good. It was my opinion that I could not only fly any airplane anywhere in any conditions in any attitude I chose, but should someone have temporarily taken the airplane somewhere I could probably do the same in the box in which it had arrived.'

I got up and stumbled some. 'I was, you see, GOOD,' he repeated.

I staggered off to the men's room. Outside on the jukebox, Jeannie Kendall was having an orgasm. I felt weary, almost beaten, all the way into my bones. A large man with an expensive paunch relieved himself next to me as I propped myself up against the wall.

'Quickest buck in town,' he grunted.

When I got back to the table, Hank had lured a healthy-looking female to the booth and was busy being charming. The band was re-forming on the stage.

'Well, *all right*,' the man yelled and the people roared. I felt so weary I leaned my head back in the booth and closed my eyes for just a short while, just to rest, and never even heard the opening notes of 'Ain't Living Long Like This'.

It was the noise that woke me up. I came conscious with a mouth like owl shit and heard all this noise. I decided that either Hank was fucking someone or he was having an extraordinarily exciting dream. Though what he was doing having either in a beer joint I did not know. So I opened my eyes and found that I was lying on the floor of someone's apartment. I couldn't remember driving back at all.

My mouth tasted quite disgusting, so I got up and looked for the bathroom to go borrow a toothbrush and passed by the bedroom.

She surely was an athletic gal.

When I came back the action was over and the happy couple were lying on the bed smoking cigarettes.

'Way to go, R.D.,' said Hank, and they giggled. 'Way to stay sober.'

'Shit,' I said. There was a second bed over by the wall and I went over and lay down. 'If ya'll don't mind.'

I drifted on back to sleep.

'Marylu, honey,' said Hank. 'It ain't a bit of good in the world you doing that, I don't believe it is going to get hard again *ever*, the things you have been doing to it.'

He swung his legs off the bed and went out to the bathroom.

'Why don't you try R.D.?' he chuckled. 'He looks raring for action.' Sod off, I thought, and continued going to sleep. It was the gal hauling off my pants that woke me. They build them strong in the South. Built to last.

'R.D. Marvin,' I said. 'Pleased to meet you.'

When I woke early in the morning the gal was gone and Hank was fixing coffee.

'Morning,' he said cheerfully, and I grunted and took a mug.

'You look terrible,' he said heartily.

'I feel terrible.' I drank some coffee, debated whether to throw up for a moment, then decided it was all right and took some more.

'You must have something wrong with the water here,' I complained. 'You ought to get it checked.'

'Water, hell. You were sloppy ass drunk, is all. Though how you did it on half a pitcher and a couple little bitty cans I don't know.'

'I don't know either.'

'You want some Tylenol, something?'

'I don't take pills. I despise them things.'

I drank the coffee and went off to take a piss and shower. After I stopped pissing I realized that I was going to have to go see a doctor when I got to Miami. The joke said that a cropduster that went over a thousand feet got a nose-bleed. The water in the bowl was dark red. I was pissing blood.

Hank drove us to the airport. He was in high good humour. Clearly, he wasn't bleeding through his kidneys.

'Man,' he said happily. 'That old gal sure was a fine piece ass, wasn't she?'

'Uhuh.'

'I'm telling you,' he boasted joyfully, 'you lucky I took the edge off her before she got her hands on you. She about like to kill someone in your state of health.'

'Shit,' I said. 'She just wasn't *satisfied*. She needed a real man, was all.'

Hank laughed and stirred the gears.

'Lord,' I said wearily, 'the oysters here ain't up to much. I ate two dozen last night and only one worked.'

He drove along making noises on his teeth like a man working on a piece of steak, reliving his pleasant memories of the evening.

'You become some kind of enthusiast or something, Hank?'

'I'll tell you something, R.D., that's odd, but before I lost everything and went to the jail I *liked* ass, you know? But I liked steak too. I could afford both, no problem, and then I lost everything and I couldn't have either for eighteen months, shut away, and I came out and – I don't know – it's all changed. I eat a steak and I can taste the blood, I get with some good-looking gal and it's *vivid*, you know, and it's funny, I can't get enough of either, and it's so damned good, it really is.'

I had a load man one time, he was a nice fella, even if he had done five for manslaughter, but he had the same thing, only it was liquor. You couldn't rely on him, he hadn't had any all that time and when he came out he enjoyed it so much he was always going off and taking a hit, and I had to let him go.

The FSS confirmed that the front had gone through and was dissipating its rain on the Barbadians, there were ceilings of around 2,000 broken and five miles viz, so we got in the Thrush and grumbled along. We stopped at a little airfield down among the lakes and refuelled and had a coke, and arrived at Opa Locka in Miami around noon. The Convair was parked with some light twins and a couple of army helicopters on one of the disused runways near the customs house. Billy Lee was there, busy taking the wings off the Super Cub prior to putting it inside the Convair. I'd decided to take it along as a scout plane and general runabout. It burned six gallons an hour compared to the Thrush's forty-five.

'That the loader you were telling me about?'

'That's Billy Lee.'

'I believe his daddy was a black man. Big son of a bitch, isn't he?'

68

'He used to play ball for the Falcons, before he smashed his knee.'

I switched the son of a black man to rigging the ferry system on the Thrush that converted the hopper to a vast fuel tank, and set about looking for a doctor.

It wasn't easy. If I had one receptionist telling me oh, no, Dr Fatbucks only saw members of his own practice, none of whom were hicks from out of town anyway, I had a dozen. Two or three offered to fit me in in three weeks' time, a lot of good, I thought, but finally I got a Dr Mendez in Hialeah whose receptionist said he could manage it. We had a little difficulty communicating; her English wasn't good and I hadn't spoken Spanish since I had worked in Nicaragua years before, but we made it. I took the truck we'd brought the spares down in and drove off into the traffic.

It took a while to find him but eventually I got there. His surgery was in a little run-down street next to some large garbage containers stencilled with forbidding commands not to dump dead animals in them, nor to start fires, and promising large fines should they catch you incinerating your dog in one. The surgery was run down, as you might expect, although clean; it gave me the creeps, as always – hate them places, man, hate to sit next to all them diseased people, God knew what they had. Luckily I didn't have to wait long and the olive-coloured gal showed me in. I was the only white guy in there.

Mendez was a Cuban expatriate. He looked a bit like Ric, only younger, thinner and not as good-looking. He sat behind an old desk and had a worn but clean examining table. Beside the desk he had a three-tiered wire basket system that held brown files – of patients, I assumed; on the walls were shelves of second-hand medical books, and a handsomely framed diploma telling us all that Carlos D. Mendez was allowed to do it.

He had a fresh file and asked my name and address, and what I did.

'I'm a pilot.'

'So what is the problem, Captain? How can I help you?'

'Got up this morning and pissed and it wasn't the right colour. Kind of bloody.'

He scribbled and, without looking at me, said: 'And you have lost weight recently.'

'Yes. I had an accident last April. I work the crops, I'm an ag pilot. I got some chemical on me in the wreck that's kind of toxic.'

'It relates from then? And the yellow hue of your skin?'

'Yeah. 'Bout then.'

He asked a little about ag, and about Ethyl and Methyl, saying he wasn't familiar with them, and asked me to spell Parathion. His nurse took some samples and money from me and he asked me to come back in a few days. I went out to where a dog was defiling the front wheel of my truck and thought that I really could have saved my time. If I hadn't felt so damn ill, I wouldn't have bothered to go at all.

PATTERSON, ARKANSAS

It was a dry county, Yossif Petrovsky had been warned by a Texan who said he was something in 'all'; sitting next to him on the Eastern flight and hearing his destination, he said that there was nigh-on eighty mile that was dry as a bone heading that way; on reflex Petrovsky had ordered a beer with the meal that came on a plastic tray, although normally he drank nothing in the day. His Hertz rental Ford took him through autumnal colours by way of a series of small towns, and eighty-odd miles from the airport he came to the one he was looking for. Only downtown had more than one storey of building. He went past a respectable motel, a large filling station, car lot and tyre and silencer stockist, side by side, and made the turn by Winn-Dixie as he had been instructed. The people of the little town were not fond of alcohol, at least officially, but they went in proper fear of the Lord, for there was a large church standing in well-kept grounds which he passed before taking a right into a very quiet street of wood-and-brick porched houses with neatly trimmed, orderly front yards. He pulled up behind an elderly two-door Cutlass.

He thought that he must have come to the wrong house. Adam Ross had made the most of his chiselled good looks, and although fatigues and safari suits had formed his television wardrobe they had been tailored to best advantage. A portable hair-dryer and gel had ensured that his appearance was action-swept at all times. The woman who stood enquiringly in the doorway was almost deliberately plain. Although only in her early thirties she wore no make-up at all, with her hair drawn back into a bun. She was slim, and possibly possessed of a good figure, but wore a rather drab shirtwaister dress and flat shoes.

'Miss Ross?' he said hesitantly.

She smiled, showing even white teeth. 'You're Mr Petrovsky, aren't you? We don't have any accents like yours around here. Now come right in.'

They went straight in to an off-white painted living room, and he was shown to a leatherette sofa, where he sat down.

'You rest here while I get you some iced tea. I was just marking the children's exercise books while I was waiting for you.'

She went through to the kitchen and Yossif heard the chink of glass. The room was plainly furnished, and the only decoration was a wooden cross on one wall, and some embroidered religious tracts framed under glass. The sister of Adam Ross came back with a tall portion of iced tea. It was very cold and very sweet. She sat down opposite him, on a hard chair by a little table which held a pile of exercise books.

'So you've come about Adam,' she said, holding her hands folded on one knee.

'Yes, Miss Ross. As I told you, I'm with the Mayor in City Hall, and I've been working on the investigation into the terrorist disaster in New York, when the jumbo jet was crashed into Harlem.'

'It's been eighteen months now. I heard that unless anything new came up, the investigation was closed.'

'Well, that may be so for the government, but the Mayor isn't happy that fifteen thousand of his people died. He still wants to know who did it, and bring them to justice.'

'Is that the one having such problems of his own? It is good of him to still care after all this time.'

Petrovsky made a note not to treat this plain woman too lightly.

'As you know, Miss Ross, your brother Adam was nearby, with his cameraman, Charlie Harrel. They got

72

the only pictures of the jet going in. They were shown around the world.'

'Adam was on television often.'

'They say that the effects of seeing violence and death so much in his work had an accumulative effect on Adam.'

'People may say what they wish. Whether it is true is entirely a different matter,' his sister said, and her lips tightened.

'He died three days after the crash, from the effects of alcohol and phenobarbitone.'

'Adam could sleep at will. There was nothing on his conscience. He had no need of sleeping tablets.'

'The coroner returned a verdict of suicide, while the balance of his mind was disturbed.'

Helen Ross's eyes closed tight in pain for a brief second, and then opened angrily.

'The coroner was a fool. Why are you here, Mr Petrovsky? Are you here to taunt me with what gives me pain every day?'

'Suicide is not a crime, Miss Ross. Shouldn't one feel sympathy for – '

'In the law of men, Mr Petrovsky,' the woman said intensely, cutting through. She leaned forward. 'But not in the law of God. It is the Lord who gives us life, and the Lord who takes it away. It is not ours to dispose of. Those who do so face His Almighty displeasure.'

Petrovsky's Aunt Rachel had been a much older woman than Helen Ross, but he sensed the similarity – an elderly but fierce little lady in her one-roomed apartment on the Mojka canal, who would solve any dispute with finality, reaching out and saying: 'Let us see what the Book says.' For his Aunt Rachel the book had been the Talmud, and for Helen Ross the Bible, but both beliefs were the same.

'We don't think that your brother committed suicide.'

'Tell me,' she said, stone-faced.

'We think that he was murdered. We think that the reason he was there with Charlie Harrel, his cameraman, was because he knew something was going to happen, because he had been told. By the people who caused the aircraft to crash. Now tell me, does it ring true to you?'

She nodded, very slowly and with finality.

'Of course. They must be going to do it again, Mr Petrovsky, otherwise why kill Adam? Adam has been useful to evil men many times. But this time . . . this time they could not leave him, knowing what he did . . . '

'You don't seem surprised, Miss Ross.'

She shook her head, looking into the distance, into the past.

'Surprise? No . . . I knew my brother well, Mr Petrovsky, very well. Shall I tell you a story about him? It may help you understand who you were dealing with. Don't believe what you saw on the television. People watch television and take its lies for truth, but in this impure world only the word of the Lord is truth.

'Many years ago when Adam was still at school, in his final year, he needed top grades to make sure he went to college. He could have done it anyway, because he was clever, but he wanted to make sure. He wanted to do it anyway, because he could love evil . . . There was one of the teachers, a lonely, middle-aged man, with a weakness for the little girls. He would not have done anything, not left to himself, but Adam put temptation in his way. He arranged for one young girl – not yet fourteen, but fresh and pretty – to make up to the teacher, to go with him . . . '

'How could he do that?'

Helen Ross looked at Petrovsky with faint pity. 'Well, because he had already been with her himself and the young girl hero-worshipped him, that is why. And Adam was hiding, he took photos . . . Adam passed out top of the school, you see. Adam never looked back.'

'Blackmail.'

'When you burn to succeed, no weapon is turned away. When you burn to succeed in this world, you may burn in the next. You cannot have come all this way merely to tell me this, merely to give me relief in knowing that my brother did not at least break one of God's greatest commandments, if he broke others. How can I help you?'

'We believe that he may have made a tape of something over the radio. We think it may help us find the terrorists.'

She nodded. 'Yes. Which tape? What date?'

'There are tapes?'

'He kept many tapes in a safety deposit. Which do you want?'

'The date of the crash. The twenty-seventh of May.'

She got up and went out of the room. When she came back she had a 60-minute Sony cassette in its clear plastic cover. When he looked at it, on its card was written the date and the letters HS/AJ, in bold strokes.

'You may have it,' she said. He knew it was time to leave.

'Thank you,' he said. 'And thank you for the tea.'

'Thank you for your news. It will give me hope, when I pray for my brother's soul. Do you have any brothers or sisters, Mr Petrovsky?'

'No. I was an only child.'

'And your parents?'

'Are dead.'

She paused by the door. 'I am sorry.'

'They were murdered, in a Soviet psychiatric hospital,' he said suddenly. He wondered why he had told her. It was a thing he kept to himself. She reached out and held his hand with cool, strong fingers.

'There is so much evil in this world,' she said, somehow comfortingly. 'But not in the next. May I pray for them? And for the souls of those responsible?'

'You must pray for many people,' he replied.

'For many. For my brother Adam, and for poor Mr Ellis, always.'

'Mr Ellis?'

'The schoolteacher. He committed suicide, Mr Petrovsky. Just two years later. Did you see the big church on your way here?'

75

'Yes.' Yossif knew who the little, pretty girl who had hero-worshipped Adam Ross was, now.

'They would have buried him in the churchyard, but those who take their own life cannot rest in hallowed ground. Mr Ellis lies in common earth and his soul rests not in Heaven. Goodbye, Mr Petrovsky.'

He put the tape into his pocket and went out to his hire car. On the way out of town he stopped at the big church and went inside. Kneeling at the back, he covered his head with a handkerchief and said prayers for the souls of Mr Ellis, his lover Helen Ross, and her brother Adam.

MIAMI, FLORIDA

We fired up, talked to ground and waddled off to 27 Right, ran it up, called the tower. A student 152 came in, landed it four times and went around and we were cleared to go, departing on a left downwind. The Thrush lumbered into the air and I enjoyed the luxury of a shallow climb out over no trees. I took a heading of 240 degrees, avoiding the MIA International TCA, an upside-down wedding cake packed with the clipper ships of the twentieth century, jet airliners. The great city of Miami lay spread out to our left, sprawling over the flat land. Clear of the TCA, I climbed gradually aiming for 8,500 feet and we left the city behind, flying over the swamp and scrub of the Everglades, home of the alligator and mosquito.

The Thrush grumbled along at 1900 rpm and 20 inches. Back in Opa Locka Hank and Ric would be preparing for take-off. Although not that fast, the Convair was faster than us, because from A to B we were slow. A hundred and thirty across the *field* is fast. After Key West there was nothing, just ocean, eight and one half thousand feet below. I chewed some gum and Billy Lee chewed some tobacco, and spat from time to time into his big spit cup.

The air was smooth, which made it easier to hold course. With no heading indicator I was flying on the old whisky compass, not known for its gyros. Although there was no doubt that by flying in this direction I would hit the Mexican coast after a while, I was particularly anxious not to penetrate Cuban airspace. The Russians were out there, they had given the Cubans radar and MiG interceptors; they looked at you with one and if you were close enough they sent the others up to make you come down.

We had a coffee break and munched a sandwich, and in the clear air three hours out there was the dark smudge of Cuba intruding into the horizon on our left. We stayed out of their airspace and in another two hours we saw the coast of Mexico, the Yucatan peninsula, then we began our descent and landed on the island of Cozumel not long after. The Convair was already there. With its big ferry tank it could have flown direct, but the Thrush couldn't, so they stayed with us and carried out spares, staying in touch on 122.9. Ric had the customs all sorted out – it was all hassle-free, very unusual.

'Your buddy's an aviator,' Hank said laconically, while Ric was gone.

'How's that?'

'Wanted to know how everything worked. I had to let him fly it, too.'

'How'd he do?'

'Good. He's got a mind like a trap. You only have to tell him once.'

'Yeah. He's sharp, all right.'

Hank rubbed the corners of his eyes. It's always a strain, flying old airplanes. You keep waiting for something to stop going round. Or fall off.

Hank shot a glance at me. 'It's more than that, you know, R.D. There's something wrong with the mother.'

'What do you mean?'

'I mean he scares me. Behind that smile and good looks he is driven, R.D. For a while, before they found room for me among the other white-collar criminals, they kept me in the Dade County prison, and let me tell you, there are some very strange and bad people in places like that.' He looked me in the eye. 'Ain't but one of them would have called your buddy sir. I'm sure glad it's you working for him down there and not me.'

I shrugged. There wasn't much to do. Hank was right, of course. Ric was dangerous as hell. I put it out of my mind and got on with organizing for the ten-hour haul to Colombia early the next morning.

I kept a very cautious eye out while I was doing so, because this was Joe Powers country. There'd been a time back when big Stearman biplanes had been very popular among the South Americans for spraying; we had plenty in the USA and wanted to sell them our old technology to make way for getting our own new equipment, like Ag Cats and Thrushes. Old Joe, he heard about all this and decided on one of Grumman's big Cats, so gets his old Stearman out and heads south. He was in Mexico, making for Venezuela, when he lands at a little town to refuel; hardly gets on the ground before the local sheriff arrives, fat and greasy and swathed in bandoliers, arrests him on a charge of illegally overflying Puta City, slings him in jail.

They kept old Joe there about three months before releasing him, thirty pounds lighter and needing a week's worth of hospital treatment for various ailments, put him out by the crossroads to ride his thumb north. The Stearman they'd already sold.

So I kept a sharp eye out, but all ran on rails. Ric was responsible for that, all the paperwork was correct, all the correct palms greased. And Ric could talk to them; unlike old Joe who only spoke Arkansas at best, Ric spoke English, Spanish and Italian – that because of his father – and Arabic, on account of his mother. When I'd known him he'd had a good smattering of Thai, too.

The weather we had been given proved accurate for a change, and it was an uneventful if long flight, the only excitement threading our way through a line of thunderstorms near Honduras. We hit some moderate to severe turbulence and Billy Lee lost his spit cup.

We came out the other side and I saw the familiar sight of the Botaderos and Agalta mountains over to the west. When I'd been flying the DC-3 with Hank we'd come trucking in on Airway II, up at ten thousand with the mountains below like a great rug flung down on the floor, and Managua on the other side. It was a long time since I'd been there and I'd probably never go again, but I'd done the route so many times I could have found Managua in my sleep. My chances of having to do so were small, since the revolution that had ousted Somoza. Norteamericanos weren't popular, and the place was full of Russians and East Germans. They were also fighting the Hondurans across the border. Central America had always been a violent and volatile place and it didn't seem to be improving with age. To the west, Guatemala and San Salvador, both in a state of civil war. I hoped that Colombia proved more stable.

The Barranquilla TCA was 75 miles in radius. I made a guesstimate based on my ETA and the sensitivity of the elderly VOR receiver in the Thrush. I dialled in 113.7 and got a vague twitch out of it, and contacted approach control on 119.1, informing them confidently that I was eighty nautical out, just like I had DME to tell me so, inbound on the 310-degree radial. No, I was not IFR. They sounded vaguely disappointed and in effect told me to keep on trucking. About forty minutes later we landed on the splendid 9,800-foot runway and taxied off to the ramp. They put us by the customs, next to the Convair which had already landed, and we got out happy to ease our aching muscles and cricked backs.

Ric was dealing with the paperwork with his usual efficiency. As the Thrush wasn't carrying anything, most of the concern centred on the Convair and its load but one official took an interest in the spray plane, never having seen one. He spoke quite good English, and asked the usual questions about what were the booms and nozzles for, and why did it have the little propeller beneath. Billy Lee told him we taxied with it.

'What is the big door for?' he asked, pointing at the hopper hatch.

'That where the deadly poison go,' said Billy Lee. 'Here, lemme open it so you can take a look. You got a safety mask fo' the man, R.D.?'

'No, no,' the man said hurriedly. 'You are too kind . . . '

He scurried away and me and Billy Lee looked at each

80

other, both knowing perfectly well that all the hopper contained was about eighty gallons of 100 Low Lead. Apart from the two Colt .45 automatic pistols and ammunition, that is. There were still parts of Georgia in Toombs and Ware, places like that, where it didn't hurt to have a gun, and I doubted that some insurance wouldn't come in equally handy here.

The next morning we flew out over the cargo ships moored in the big port, hauling coffee and machinery and crude, over the swamp, following the road that picked along the thin peninsula edging the bay. On the other side of the bay the Sierra Nevada towered up, showing cold white peaks in the clear air. I flew by the map Ric had provided me with, skirted Simon Bolivar's airspace, saw the town of Santa Marta to my left, nudged into the coastline, flew another ten miles and picked up the road that crawled up into the valley. Ric's bread isn't done, I thought; you couldn't land anything short of a helicopter on *that*. But it climbed up to an elevation of about 3,000 feet and the valley flattened out. On the slopes there was a rich profusion of trees, evergreen and deciduous, and on the floor of the valley itself was the cultivated land – and Lord, won't you look at that, not a power line anywhere. And the sinuous little road widened out like a mountain river reaching the flatlands, but straight as a die for maybe ten thousand feet, and a hundred and fifty feet wide, it was as good as a runway. A third of the way from the end the road was cut by another at right angles, and it made a cross. On one arm of the cross was a ramp area, in front of a group of buildings, where the Convair stood. I landed and taxied in. Ric and Hank and Billy Lee were there, also George Ryan and a smallish, dark-haired woman. Billy Lee had organized some of Ryan's workers to get the Super Cub and the spares out of the Convair.

The buildings were arranged in an L-shape around the tarmac ramp area. There were two big tobacco barns, a kind of office area and a big long shop with rolling doors; inside I could see a lot of farm machinery, a top-of-the-line model John Deere harvester and a new 4000-series tractor with the twin wheels, chemicals tanks and harrow and drag rig held up at the back. Parked outside were several tobacco harvesters, ungainly as parade floats.

'How do you like it?' Ric asked.

'Fine strip. If you can't get off on that, you can't get off.'

The dark-haired woman was standing next to him.

'R.D., meet Miss Ellen Tyler,' said Ric. 'I'm not here all the time, but Ellen works for us – she's an interpreter, among other things – and as you're not from these parts she will smooth the way for you. We also have a favour to ask.'

'It's a pleasure to meet you,' I said to Miss Tyler.

'I live in Santa Marta,' she said. She had a curious accent, very precise, rather pleasant. 'I'll be on hand if you need any help.'

'We would like to learn to fly,' said Ric. 'Perhaps in the Super Cub . . . '

'It'll be a pleasure,' I told him. Ric pointed to the carcass of the Super Cub, emerging from the Convair.

'We put wings on it,' I assured the girl, and she smiled. 'Are you from up north somewhere?'

'Not quite. I come from England.'

Where I came from northerners were known as 'damyankees', and someone from England would be a '*real*damyankee', but I kept my musings to myself and got on with the arrangements.

Billy Lee spent most of the day getting the Super Cub into one piece and I worked with Ryan. He had a 500-gallon mixing rig which we converted with one of my Buckeyes so that it would mate to the Thrush's loading system. By the ag shop there was a locked metal building where the chemicals were kept, neatly stacked pile of drums, boxes, sacks, Bravo, Sulfur, Sevin, Lannate, 2,4-D, Pounce, 6.3., Ethyl and Methyl, Benlate, Cutwork bait, Furadan, MH-30, Ammonium Nitrate, Compound D, Ortho Paraquat, Nalcotrol and all the other tools of the modern farm industry.

Late in the afternoon Ric and the English lady returned, in a Mercedes.

'Are you happy with everything?' he asked.

'It all looks good so far. Good equipment, good organization.'

'I'm glad.'

Now we were here I wanted to see the land I was going to work. Billy Lee was sitting on the tyre of the Super Cub, now whole again, amusing himself by spitting Levi Garrett at passing bugs and killing them. Nicotine is a nerve poison. His accuracy was phenomenal.

'Hey, Billy Lee,' I called. 'You done test flown that thing yet?'

'Sheat, no. I just work on them. Ain't nuthin' in my contract says I got to go fly my work. Might fall apart,' he said, and grinned. When he was running for the Falcons they called him 'The Man With the Smile', because when he scored he grinned so wide. After he got crippled, of course, they didn't call him at all.

'I want to go take a look at the valley,' I said to Ric. 'You want to come up and fly a little?'

He looked at me quizzically.

'It's safe,' I said. 'He's just kidding. Ain'tcha?'

Billy Lee grinned.

We got in; Ric in the front with the instruments and me behind. I fired it up and we taxied out, rather erratically, since I had Ric do it. When I was first instructing on T-33s I used to give them the full nine yards of chat beforehand, during and after, until I discovered that people learned best by *doing*, and when they did it wrong you explained how to do it right.

'You start off by pushing it the way you want it to go,' I said, as we weaved along. 'It's a taildragger, and once you've got it started the tail wants to keep going and wind up in front of the prop, so then you push the *opposite* way.'

He caught on fast, and by the time we got down to the runway he was keeping it straight. He swung it around and I gave it the throttle for him, *little* movements, *little* movements, back on the stick, and we went spectacularly up into the air. Ric's first flying lesson had begun.

After a while I took it over and he pointed out the main features of the valley. The fields were well laid out, large, with strategically placed lines of trees to act as wind-breaks. The John Deere was harrowing what looked about a 250-acre patch down below, turning the fruitcake-dark earth. The valley was prime land. With good management, you'd get a top quality and yield crop from it. At several locations in the valley stood deep, glinting ponds, reservoirs of moisture should the rainfall be less than desirable. In the store, I had seen big irrigation guns undergoing maintenance to ensure their performance should they be needed once the season came around.

We stayed up for about forty minutes, about par for the first lesson, and came down. I talked Ric through the traffic pattern and took it on final, telling him to follow me through so that he could feel how it was done.

'That was very pleasant,' he said when we got out. 'A little different from when we flew together in the past, I think.'

'A bit.'

'I didn't know you flew together,' said Ellen Tyler.

'But yes,' said Ric. 'We worked for the same company, years ago.'

'What was that?'

'It was a sort of airline. Called Air America,' I told her. 'Would you like to fly too?'

The name appeared to mean nothing to her. Which was fine. It was all a long time ago.

'Oh yes, please.'

'Okay,' I said. 'Before we fly, we always pre-flight the aircraft. Check it to see that everything is in order. Like anything else to do with flying, we do it a certain way. I'll do it this time, and next time we'll have you do it.'

The familiar patter came out as smooth as a long-playing record. I must have made my little speech several hundreds of times, to folk of all ages and both sexes, their only common denominator their eagerness to be a bird.

We came around the little high-winged airplane and I showed her the importance of free movement of the controls, to check the brakes and tyres – that they should be in good condition, that there should be no leaking brake fluid.

'Always check the fuel. Use the little cup here and drain some out of the tank. Very important out here in the sticks, where contaminated fuel's common. You're checking for trash, and for water. Trash's easy to see, water's a little harder, but just as important. The engine prefers to run on gas. Water usually shows up as globules in the bottom of the little cup. Would you say that specimen was okay?'

She peered at it. 'Yes . . . it's all uniform, there's no globs in it.'

'But it *might* be all water. It's clear . . . a heavy rain, a leaking cap could give you an inch of water at the bottom of your tank.'

She nodded.

'So smell it. Make *sure* it's gas.' I held it out to her and she looked at me curiously, a little embarrassed.

'I'm afraid I don't have any sense of smell, Mr Marvin.'

'None?'

'None. I was born without it. It's a rare birth defect.'

'Well . . . I never heard of that. Well, tell you what, there's a couple of other ways, hold it up to the light and it's pale blue, isn't it? Then if you pour a little over your hand you can feel it evaporate, it's cold, water won't do that.'

She did so.

'Gas?'

She smiled. 'It's petrol.'

'Okay. No sense of smell at all?'

She shook her head. 'No. None at all.'

We fired it up and taxied out. She had a *lot* of trouble getting the feel of the pedals and I handled the take-off

85

and climb-out; I let her have it when it was trimmed straight and level and she enjoyed herself tacking about the valley at various altitudes. We stayed up about half an hour and then came in and tied it down in the tie-downs we had dug and filled in the ramp.

Ellen Tyler took us into Santa Marta, where we had rooms in a little hotel that seemed clean. She showed us the basic layout of the place and we all had supper. I was feeling beat, as usual, and afterwards I went on back to the hotel to go to bed. Billy Lee said he'd have a couple more beers, and Hank said he was on the 707 in the morning and it had been some years since he'd had any South American ass, so he thought he'd go look for some. I thought it unlikely, the place looked kind of conservative to me.

I went back, took a shower and went to bed. I woke around dawn, with a grey light creeping through the window. I'd have slept longer, but someone was beating on the door.

I had a headache, as usual. I got up, put on my shorts and went to the door. It was Ellen Tyler.

'The days start early here?'

'You better come,' she said grimly. 'Your friend's in jail!'

'Billy Lee?'

I pulled on clothes and boots. 'The other one,' she said. 'The white man.'

'Hank? Hank got drunk?'

We went down and there was a dark blue Fiat at the side of the road with a very big, thickset man of about forty at the wheel. Despite the hour he was dressed in a suit and was clean-shaven. It was raining, and the streets were empty.

'This is Captain Quesada of the Santa Marta Police force,' Ellen Tyler told me. 'He's . . . a friend of ours, and he got in touch when he heard.'

'I was on my way from duty,' said Quesada. I wondered if his lack of uniform meant he was a detective, or what.

'What's the bail going to be?' I asked. 'Or do you just pour them out of the tank in the morning and have the judge set the fines?'

Quesada slowed at a junction. At some time in the night two cars had collided and the drivers had simply abandoned them where they were, scrunched up the middle of the crossing, each still asserting their driver's absolute right of way over the other.

'There will be no bail,' Quesada grunted. 'He will stand trial in the high court.'

'For getting drunk?'

'He was drunk, it is true. But he is not charged with that.'

'What, then?'

'He raped a woman,' Ellen Tyler said quietly.

Hank never knew old Joe Powers, and he never would, and that was kind of a pity because Joe had become an involuntary expert on how to survive in a prison south of the border, and you a gringo. Old Joe knew about crabs, body lice, the food, corrupt guards and the other prisoners who'd kill you for the shoes on your feet, and it sure was a pity he couldn't have filled Hank in, because from the look of it he was going to need all the help he could get. Quesada got me in and they took Hank out of the holding pen and he looked bad.

'Damn, Hank,' I said, as he rested his head in his shaky hands. 'You must like these places. Just done got out of one, couldn't wait to get back.'

The left side of his face was all swole up where someone had put a boot on it, done had the tread marks in it.

'I feel awful bad,' he muttered.

'Did you do it? Were you drunked up, or what?'

'Damn, R.D., I don't remember much. Ric came by, I asked him if he knew anywhere to meet a few women, he said he'd drop me off somewhere and we went off in his car . . . I guess I must've drunk a bit, the next thing I knew I was on the floor in some room and there was some gal screaming and carrying on and some cops trying to cave my ribs in.'

'You know what they're charging you with?'

'Yeah . . . hell, I never raped anyone, R.D., never had to . . . You think they're going to put me inside?'

'I don't know, Hank,' I said, because he'd learn soon enough, I didn't need to tell him just yet. Quesada said a knife had been involved. He said it would be fifteen long years.

They put him back in the pen as I left and a tall Indian with muscled arms showing under a ragged shirt had stolen his thin mat; he showed his teeth in a smile, daring him to try and take it back, and Hank sat down on the filthy floor and rested his face in his arms.

Back when I was flying Skyraiders out of Nakhon Phanom for my uncle we had one pilot who was a great Jim Croce fan, had all his albums on 8 track. The singer was killed when his plane crashed within the airport boundary at night, which would have upset old Lee had he known about it. The world of aviation is small, all those thousands of miles away we sat in the cockpit with him, tired after his show, saw him fail to transfer his attention to his altitude indicator as he rotated, the horizon vanishing in the dark. He didn't catch the airspeed and heading and the twin rolled on to its back in the night and died. That must have been how it happened, we surmised, it was such a common accident. There wasn't any need to surmise what happened to Lee; ground fire hit him near Mouong Souang and for a moment all the gas and ordnance turned the night into day and Jim had someone to greet him at the gates. I know, I was there, I saw it.

In my mind I was sitting by the hooch watching the monstrous thunderheads building over the river, the flashes glowing in the dark, way high, far higher that the loaded Skyraider could climb, listening to Mr Jim singing on the tape.

'When I get out of this prison I will be forty-five, I'll

know I used to like to do it, but I won't remember why. Five short minutes of lovin' has brought me twenty long years in jail. It wasn't worth it . . . it wasn't worth it . . . '

No. It surely wasn't worth it.

NEW YORK

Yossif Petrovsky met Spencer in a theme hotel. The whole place was like a woodland glade; there were carpets of green grass, waterfalls burst out at the unwary from pastoral murals and it was staffed by pixies, elves and gnomes from Brooklyn and Queen's. Petrovsky found Spencer in an autumnal room where the lighting system left dappled sunlight on a counterpane of fallen leaves and a lakeside glittered through a *trompe-l'oeil* picture window.

'You sure you fit in here, Victor?'

'I'm the bad fairy, Yossif. The one who puts an evil spell on the beautiful princess. Would you believe this place costs three hundred bucks a night?'

'You have to have money to live in wonderland, Victor.'

'Now there's an idea for a theme hotel. Some place run by the Red Queen. Still, those who wish us evil will hardly think of searching here. Anyhow, they have attack-hobbits guarding the place. So what did you get?'

'A tape, just as you thought. But it's odd. It's just a cab controller giving instructions to one of the drivers. I played it driving the car back to the airport. The really odd thing about it is that the cab driver yells something right at the end and it stops suddenly.'

'How did you find Miss Ross?'

'Somewhat strange. She had religion. She could have been good-looking, but deliberately made herself frumpy. The fault of her illustrious brother. He was screwing her when she was a little teenage girl. He was a psycho, Victor.'

'You would be surprised at what you would find if you could lift the stone off the psyches of some of the really driven. The ones who really *have* to succeed. Like Adam. Let's listen to the tape.'

Petrovsky fed the cassette into the machine and started it turning.

'Here we go.'

A voice came out, over the radio.

'*Solo one one. Do you read me?*'

'Foreign accent.'

'Puerto Rican, Hispanic?'

'I don't think so.'

'*This is solo one one.*'

'Different accent.'

'African. This is it, Yossif.'

'Stand by, I have a customer for you.'

The tape hissed on, blank, for a minute or more, and then the controller came on again.

'*Solo one one, go to Stamford Street.*'

'*Roger.*'

In the next minute and a half the controller spoke three more times.

'*Take a left. Okay.*'

'*Take a right. Okay.*'

'*Step on it.*'

Ten seconds later the driver's voice was heard again for the last time. It came off the tape with shocking suddenness, a howl of triumph, a chant of vindication, cut off midway.

'That's it. That's the odd part.'

Spencer reached out switched the tape off. His near-black eyes glittered.

'Know what he was saying, Yossif? "*Inna li Allah, wa inna ilayhi raji'un. La illaha ila Allah, wa Muhammad rasul Allah.*" "To God we belong, and to Him we must return. There is no God but Allah, and Muhammad is His Prophet." It is the traditional Muslim prayer to the dead. He was saying it to the passengers of the 747, and to the people of Harlem below. If the jet had not struck

91

the ground he would have completed it. That tape is a recording of the instructions from someone on the ground to someone in the 747, and that person's acknowledgement. When we match up the timing we'll find that the instructions fit with the changes in heading and pitch of the aircraft. When he says "Go to Stamford Street" that's the order to put the aircraft into a standard rate turn to port. That's three degrees per second. The aircraft turned eighty degrees, and there's a pause of a little over twenty seconds before the controller says, "Okay now." That's the signal to roll the aircraft and cut the power. Then we have two minor course corrections and the final order, "Step on it." That's when they have the target made and they pitch the nose down to accelerate the aircraft into the city.'

'So who?'

'On the card of the cassette Ross has written HS/AJ. Let us assume that these are the two people we've heard. Where's the passenger list? Anyone with the initials HS?'

Yossif ran his fingers along the alphabetic list of passengers and crew.

'No.'

'Let's say he was the controller. What about AJ?'

'AJ . . . yes. Got one here, one Ade Jumbe.'

'Any information on him?'

Yossif looked among the pile of files that Spencer had with him, and fished out a box from which he extracted a slim folder. He shook a photograph out of it, which Spencer picked up. It showed a big, powerfully built and handsome man in combat clothing.

'He a soldier of some sort?'

'Let's see . . . it's a still from his book. He wrote an autobiography called *Bush Fighting Man*. He was some kind of guerrilla leader during the Rhodesian civil war. Okay. As a young boy, brought up in Nigeria, not Zambia, by relatives after his parents had been killed. Left during the Biafran war, went to university in Florida. Played ball for the Gators. Returned to Zambia, began making his way in politics in the Lozi tribe, of which he was one. Formed an alliance with Joshua Nkomo to fight the white Rhodesian regime over the border, and was instrumental in providing support and training-camp facilities for Nkomo's fighters.'

'That would make sense. The Lozi and the Ndebele – Nkomo's tribe – are quite similar. Big, strong, brave, good fighters. Each a minority tribe, the Lozi outnumbered by the Bemba in Zambia and the Ndebele by the Mashona in Rhodesia/Zimbabwe.'

'Okay . . . it seems he backed the wrong horse in the civil war and it was Mugabe and the Mashona who won, leaving Nkomo out in the cold, so Jumbe went back to Zambia and concentrated on his power base among the Lozi. He had considerable influence within his tribe, but did not hold any government position.'

'He couldn't. Again, wrong tribe. The Lozi enjoyed considerable autonomy under British rule, but in a wrong-side-of-the-coin way have been kept down by the Bemba ever since independence. They don't like it. What religion was Jumbe? Christian? Muslim? Did he follow the traditional beliefs?'

Yossif Petrovsky's Aunt Rachel believed that *schwartzers* from Africa wore bones in their noses and worshipped stone idols.

'I don't know, Victor. It doesn't say. You know, maybe we haven't got the right man. A power-broker, a big-league politician where he comes from, a guerrilla leader – don't men like that get other men to die for *them*? He just doesn't seem a likely kamikaze.'

'That's right. Maybe we can get a voice-print of him and match it to the tape.'

'What about the other voice, the controller?'

'That's the other thing. I know that accent, I spent some years in its owner's country. The man giving Ade Jumbe his instructions is from Iran – from the Islamic revolution of the Grand Ayatollah.'

93

SANTA MARTA

When we began, the tobacco was ready for its first application of fertilizer. They were using ammonium nitrate and some trace elements the ground was short of. The rain had made the fields impenetrable to ground equipment, so we were ready to use the Thrush. We had a big auger rigged up; I'd taxi under the sock, Billy Lee would open the hopper door and tug the handle and vroosh, in would go, 3,000lb granular and the bird would settle a little on its gear; he'd shut the hatch and out I'd waddle on to the big straight road, and off I'd go.

I'd got my calibration done the day before. They wanted 300lb an acre, had the gate set on 8½ by the time I had my time right; I was using an airfoil spreader that gave me sixty feet, and that's how we had the markers placed. Putting out fertilizer was more relaxing than spray in some ways; you only got to go across the field about once, and forty feet up, but it was still hard work in that your loads were so short you made maybe eight to fifteen loads an hour. Unlike spray we didn't have to worry about showers, in fact you want the moisture to wash the fertilizer in, but it still took us eight days' work and I was tired at the end of it.

There was just me and the farm workers in the pretty valley. A few animals – occasionally as one came in to a field I'd see a deer bounding away. And the military. Little groups of them moving about, patrolling. It was almost as though they were guarding the place.

I got down late in the afternoon on the eighth day to find Ric there with Ryan. It was the first time I'd seen him since Hank got into trouble.

'Any news of Hank?' I asked. They'd taken him to the jail in Barranquilla.

'The mills of God grind exceedingly slow here as in other places,' he said. 'It'll be six months before they get him to trial.'

By which time I would be back in Georgia.

'I want to check that last field for coverage,' Ryan said. 'Want to ride along?'

I'd been looking at the fields for eight days, but I said okay and we all piled into Ryan's Renegade jeep. Ryan was a very capable farmer, efficient, ambitious, humourless despite his ready smile, a fitness nut who went jogging around the fields every morning about dawn. We drove up the road and turned off down a dirt lane that led to the field, the four-wheel drive and the big off-road tyres carrying us over the soft ground. We passed between the cultivated fields, the Eagles leaving wide, heavily-patterned tracks.

'This is pretty good land,' Ryan commented. 'I've been working on it about three years, got the pH right, given fertilizer and trace elements. But it sure costs money. And that's before you even put the seed into the ground. You can see why poor countries can't do it. They're still getting eight bushels an acre when we can get fifty – for beans, say.'

We passed by the smooth harrowed fields with the even rows of small green plants rising from the soil.

'Nice fields,' I said. 'Got good weed control. What did you use?'

'Paraquat as a pre-plant herbicide. It's effective.'

'Yeah. It's okay here, where you got a big farm, but it's no fun to use on a small field, or anywhere you can hurt something with drift. Drifting paraquat'll burn the shit out of everything.'

'Paraquat's not the same as 2,4,5-T, is it?' Ric asked innocently.

'No, it ain't. Not at all,' I said slowly. 'Why'd you ask?'

'Didn't you have a little trouble with it earlier this year?' he said smoothly. 'I wondered what it was.'

95

'It's a herbicide. But selective. Paraquat will kill any plant, but 2,4,5-T goes for broad-leaf plants. What happened was, early in the year, I got a call from a man owned timber in the north part of the state, and it was coming up time for him to have his forest sprayed with herbicide to take out the weed growth. Standard procedure. The only glitch was that he'd got himself caught with fifteen grand's worth of chemical in store that he couldn't use: 2,4,5-T.'

'Why couldn't he use it?'

'It's illegal. It's banned, taken off the list of ag chemicals you can use. Anyway, him and me trade on it; I make him a price a bit higher than normal but not so high he's hurting, and he gets to use his chemical. It all goes fine, except on the last day I suddenly find myself up to my ears in chemical cans and also representatives of every regulatory body you can find. I was red-handed, pants down around my ankles. They fined the shit out of me.'

'You're obviously waiting for me to ask, so I will. Why is 2,4,5-T illegal?'

'Depends who you talk to. Some people say there's evidence that it's toxic to people and wildlife – a kind of Agent Orange. However, for those sufficiently cynically minded there is an alternative theory. It kills broad-leaved plants. Can you name me a broad-leaved plant that grows in a forest?'

'Tell me.'

'Marijuana. Currently the Number One cash crop in California. It's grown at home these days, you know, on a commercial scale. Saves all the hassle of importing it. They grow it out in the commercial forests and what the managers were doing, spraying with 2,4,5-T, was destroying a very valuable crop. So, the cynical people in the business believe, the drug growers put a lot of money into getting 2,4,5-T banned.'

'Which version do you believe?'

'I'm with the cynics, I'm afraid. Think of the money involved.'

Ryan turned in to the last field. The second flagman

was walking in from the far end, an Indian whose face contrasted with the international orange jacket he was wearing. It was a fine field, well-prepared, good soil, rectangular in shape, 220 acres all told, no wires. The little plants were about a foot high. I bent down at the edge of the field and the granules of ammonium nitrate were there, evenly spread over the soil.

Ric's voice came from behind me.

'We don't use 2,4,5-T here either, R.D.'

I got up from examining the young plants. They were healthy, green, uniform and vigorous. But not tobacco.

'I'm kind of slow,' I said, 'but I get there in the end. You're back in the same business.'

Ric smiled. 'I never left, R.D.'

I looked across the field: 220 acres best marijuana. To go with the other 2,240.

'We wouldn't ask you to work for the same rate. We'll pay a lot more. You'll leave a rich man. What do you say?'

He held out his hand and, after a little while, I shook it.

WASHINGTON

The black woman opened the door to Spencer's knock and stood back.

'Well, come on in before some newsman catches you on film,' she said.

Spencer went in, she shut the door and regarded him sardonically.

'I wouldn't want people thinking you were the kind of company I normally keep.'

Spencer smiled. 'It doesn't bother me. I've had to keep all kinds of strange company in my time.'

The ebony features cracked in the famous smile, and she gestured for him to go into the study beyond.

'Thank you, Senator.'

Senator Lloyd sat down in a leather swivel chair by a baize-inlaid desk and crossed the equally famous legs. Spencer sat in a large armchair. On the walls were photographs of her as a younger woman, with various well-known people. Similar photographs including her would be on their walls, too.

'You know, I'm sorry you retired from the business,' Spencer said. 'I saw all your films.'

'It wasn't big enough,' she said frankly. 'Once you're in, any damn fool can get to be a movie star. I wanted to move in a bigger game. Ronald Reagan made it respectable for people like me to do it, and I did.'

The famous legs re-crossed under the grey silk dress.

'Okay. I owe Carmine a couple of favours, which is why I agreed to see you. What is it you want?'

'I'm investigating the terrorist crash of the 747, the one that went into Harlem.'

'You're doing this for the Mayor?'

'That's it.'

'Carmine is going to Spiro Agnew, Dr Spencer, do you know that? Do you think it'll do any good for the pair of you to be associated? I'd have said having you on the payroll would add a year or two to his sentence.'

'If I find who was responsible for the crash and he is seen to have been the one to bring them to justice, it might get him off altogether.'

'There's something in that. Some fascist white group, wasn't it? The White Supremacy League?'

'False flag. The group doesn't exist. It is someone else who was responsible, and I'm trying to find out who that someone is.'

The perfect eyebrows rose in disbelief. 'By talking to me?'

'You were one of the very last people to talk to one of the men on board – Ade Jumbe?'

The full lips pressed into a line.

'Ade was *killed*. He went in with the jet. He could hardly have had anything to do with that crash.'

'Did you see him often?' Spencer asked blandly.

'Whenever he was over here.'

'You were friends? Do you mind me asking these questions?'

'No, I don't mind. Yes, we were friends. Very good friends. I miss Ade very, very much.'

'Why did the two of you get on so well?'

'I've done well. I succeeded as a movie actress and I have succeeded as a politician. I'm not all through yet, either. Do you know how difficult all of this has been, for someone from my background?'

'Yes, I do.'

Lloyd stared at Spencer for several seconds. 'Yes, you probably do. You were a prime mover yourself. Didn't you come from Nohope, Arizona, or somewhere like that?'

'Somewhere like that. Though people called it worse than that.'

'Okay. When you succeed like me, it does something to you. You may be able to eat wholefood yoghurt for lunch, but for your personal relationships you have to have real blood and meat. Most men you chew up and spit out. When you find the real thing, you hang on to it.'

'Ade Jumbe.'

'Ade. Ade was as strong and tough and ambitious and as capable as I was, and it was good for both of us.'

'What faith was he, do you know?'

'Faith?'

'Was he a Baptist or a Methodist, a Deist or a follower of Kali. Was he a Muslim or a Buddhist?'

'I don't think Ade believed in anything particularly, except himself. He believed he could do anything, if he wanted to.'

'Was he brought up in any particular faith, do you know?'

'He was brought up by relatives in Nigeria. His parents were killed when he was very young. I think they were Muslims.'

Suddenly, she had become wary.

'Why do you want to know about Ade? He's dead, God rest his soul.'

'It's about the air crash. We believe that the 747 was guided in to its point of impact by someone on board.'

She sat silent, waiting for him to finish.

'We think that man was Ade Jumbe.'

Senator Lloyd, from the wrong side of the tracks in Mobile, Alabama, sat silent for a long time. Then she looked up, piercingly.

'You going to get these people, Spencer? The ones who did this?'

'Yes.'

'Will they die?'

'Yes.'

She stared at the wall for a few seconds.

'God help me,' she said quietly. Then she turned back to Spencer.

'I'm going to tell you something, and if you ever make

100

it public I'll find some way of getting you back inside that jail. Worse, I'll get you into Leavenworth.'

'Everyone knows I'm a practised liar,' Spencer said mildly. 'They'd believe you, not me.'

She smiled crookedly. 'I thought only white man speak with forked tongue.'

Spencer grinned.

'Okay. Listen. I saw Ade the night before the plane crashed. I had been *supposed* to see him one month before. He was coming to see me and he never showed. I called up his people; I spoke to James Njoya, who they call "Iron Man". He was Ade's number two, and he told me that Ade had had to go to Paris suddenly. I thought it a little strange that he hadn't contacted me, but I was busy and didn't pursue it. Then he turned up, the day before the crash. He'd flown in, and said he was going back to Zambia the next day. Now, to most people he'd have seemed the same, but he wasn't. Spencer, there was some other man inhabiting his body. Okay, that sounds very dramatic, very film-actress. Let me give you three things that are concrete.

'One, he was on his own. Spencer, when you're a politician in Africa you don't move without your bodyguards. "Iron Man" Njoya should have been there, with two or three goons at least. He was alone. Two, Ade was a man who lived life to the full, he wanted power, money, food, liquor, women – had them all and enjoyed them to the full. Okay, we went out to eat and Ade ate, but drank no alcohol. He said he'd had jaundice and that the doctor had forbidden it. Now, he did look as though he'd been ill – he was thinner and his face was drawn – but I didn't buy the jaundice. When we went home he didn't make love to me. He said it was the jaundice, and jet-lag. Spencer, that man once flew to see me after having been shot! He bent me over a chest and pleasured us both with a .223 round still in his body, and we went out and got drunk afterwards!

'The strangest thing happened in the night. I woke up and he wasn't in the bed next to me. I looked at my watch and it was about an hour before dawn. I could hear his voice, very faint, in the reception room. I crept out, very quiet. He'd lit a candle, in the dark. He was praying. He had a little mat rolled out and he was prostrating himself . . . Spencer, I was afraid, I knew that something really bad had happened to my man. He never came back to bed. A little later I heard him let himself out. He caught the shuttle to Washington, and the Zambian 747 to his death. I had a full day on the housing bill, it wasn't until nearly evening that I heard what had happened.'

'You tell anyone about this?'

'No.'

'Why?'

'The tide's not running for women the way the libbers thought it would. Look what happened to Geraldine Ferraro. Can you imagine what they'd make of it if it came out my lover had been responsible for the biggest act of terror this country has ever endured? I'd be out, Spencer. I wouldn't even get a job as an extra in a remake of *Uncle Tom's Cabin*.

'Now. One final point about Ade. He was a wealthy man; he left half his money to charity.'

'Very commendable.'

'Spencer, the man *despised* charity. He said that it was through playing on the guilt of the white liberals to get aid – which he saw as charity – that Africa was the mess it is. You know much about Zambia?'

'It's pretty much like the rest, isn't it? One man one vote, the president being the man and his the vote. Downhill all the way since independence. Shattered economy, corruption rampant.'

'It's their only service industry. And yet it's potentially one of the richest nations on earth. Terrific natural resources, fabulous agricultural climate, enormous tourist potential. I don't know why I think it's important for you to know what kind of raw power Ade Jumbe had, but I do. He was a man in a million. Maybe more. Very rare. He was going to turn Zambia right around, make it great. He could have done it. Would have.'

'He was going to be president?'

'About one year ago there was an unsuccessful *coup* attempt – led by Ade's number two, James "Iron Man" Njoya. It failed, because "Iron Man" keeps his brains in his prick. It was Ade's *coup* – if he had been in charge of it, it would have succeeded. But he was got at, he was brainwashed, wasn't he? Find out who did it, Spencer.'

Spencer got up. 'I aim to.'

Lloyd sat, still looking at him.

'I was in Congress when you were investigated, you know. You were better than Ollie North. Someone once described him as "Rambo with a Ph.D." You actually did have a doctorate. Do you know what I felt when I watched you?'

'No.'

'Envy. You were a warlord, you had absolute power. You were responsible to no one, and you pursued your objectives to the end. You were great for this country.'

'Which is why you destroyed me.'

'That's how politics works in this country.'

'At the moment.'

'Now you're some kind of private eye. Do you manage?'

'I get by.'

Senator Lloyd stared at him, unblinking, with the famous dark eyes. 'For a man like you, it must be like living in hell.'

Spencer was on his way to the door when she called after him.

'Oh, something I forgot. When we were in the restaurant and I was trying to make conversation, wondering what the hell had happened to my man, I said, trying to be bright and cheerful, "So where have you been?" And he said, "I saw Najaf and Karbala." I think that's right. Najaf and Karbala. I don't know if they're people or places.'

'Places. Two cities in Mesopotamia.'

103

'It mean anything to you?'

'Yes.'

When he had gone, the Senator realized that Spencer had suddenly been pleased. Very pleased.

SANTA MARTA

The most valuable vegetables this side of Natchez could fatten up without me for a while; we'd be treating them with fungicide when they were a little bigger, scouting for hornworm which I'd treat with a Pounce/Methyl mix – had good results with it the previous season; a little later we'd put out MH-30 for sucker control. I spent a few days teaching my two students. Ric was in Santa Marta for a week, came out twice a day and soloed, much to Miss Tyler's chagrin. Ric had always been a natural athlete, his coordination between hand and eye was excellent. He departed to do business in Bogota and I was left with Miss Tyler.

She was like few students I'd ever taught. Even in tandem trainers students prefer to turn to the left, it's easier. Not so the intrepid Miss Tyler. *She* turned better to the right. Not well, admittedly, but better than her turns to the left. Her flare for landing began anywhere from twenty feet up to where she would have been, ten feet below runway elevation, had the runway not been in the way. Possibly due to generosity of character, she gave us not one landing per attempt but three, and sometimes four. Turns about a point were as thrilling, and followed much the same path as a ride on the roller-coaster.

I began to look forward to the sessions, to see what the gal was going to come up with next. I felt not unlike a zoologist with a new and unusual species to study.

'I'm fed up,' she announced after one particularly exciting flight. We were both covered in sweat and she was exhibiting most of the signs of extreme frustration including resentment of her instructor.

'You don't *know* how infuriating it is. The nasty little aeroplane won't do *anything* I want it to, but *you* take it and it eats out of your hand; you give it back to me and off it goes again. Anywhere it wants and nowhere *I* want.'

'I've been flying since I was fifteen, there'd be something wrong if I didn't have some idea how to do it. Just stay with it. It'll come.'

I signed her logbook and she drank some coke from the icebox.

'I don't understand it,' she said, trying to analyse her disability. 'I'm coordinated, I was in the gym team at school. And I can't fly a stupid little aeroplane.'

'Like I say, stay with it. It'll come.'

'You must think I'm stupid,' she said moodily. 'I'm not. I bet I'm much better at lots of things than you are.'

'Ain't hard,' I agreed.

'Are you good in bed, Marvin?'

I thought about it. 'I guess that would depend on who I was there with. Don't usually get many complaints. I ain't one of them short-time boys.'

'Sixty-minute man.'

She lived in a little white house in Santa Marta, near to her office. It was Saturday, early evening, and she had finished work for the week, it was cool and dark in the house; her serious little face told lies about her lovely body, and she made love far better than she flew.

'Did you like that?' she asked.

'I did.'

'Do you want to do it again?'

'In a moment.'

'I thought you said you were a sixty-minute man.'

'I am. You give me sixty minutes, I will be right back with you.'

She had the local beer in the icebox and I drank the first of two or maybe three for the evening. Insomnia was no problem to me then – you gave me two, three little bottles and I departed the scene. She didn't join me but put on a cool white cotton shirt and lay back on the bed.

'Why are you here in Colombia, Marvin?'

106

'Just working the crops, honey. And teaching you to fly.'

'No, you aren't,' she said. 'You just joined the narcotics trade. I didn't notice it caused you much anguish.'

'You know about that.'

'Of course. I told you, I know lots of things you don't.'

'I need the money,' I said after a while. 'I am in a deep, deep hole financially, not all of it my own fault. There are some people who have been trying to put me out of business. Ag is hard, ain't many pilots do it much more'n into their fifties, and I have seen some of them wind up old and tired and broke. It ain't gone happen to me.'

'Drugs are nasty things. *They* ruin people too.'

'Don't get moral with me. It's voluntary. Nobody makes a person become an addict, it's their own stupidity.'

'Rationalize it,' she said. 'Or are you an expert on drugs?'

'No. I know a bit about hauling them, though.'

There was silence in the little room. Outside, people were beginning to stir in the evening.

'I worked in Laos for Air America when I left the military. We flew out of Vientiane, all kinds of stuff, Caribous, Otters, C-46s, Gooney Birds. Aerial trucks is what they were; we used to haul rice and hard rice – that was ammo and guns – and all kinds of supplies, take them in and out of awful little rough strips hacked out of the jungle. Make maybe sixty missions a day. Short, short flights. Twelve-hour day. It was an awful place. Mountainous as hell, and the weather there had three seasons – foggy, windy and rainy. There was a war going on between the CIA, the Communists and the drug barons. The people on the ground who called us in were the customers. Ric was one of them. He was a young guy then, but sharp as a tack. He was with the drug barons – was in Long Pot with Vang Pao, and you knew that if you went there then more than likely you were hauling dope out. So that's what I mean when I say I know about doing it. I got shot up going into Long Pot in a Caribou. That was the last time I was there. The guys in the black pyjamas filled the airplane full of holes, killed my crew, put six bullets in my leg. I put it down, but the thing was on fire. Ric forced his way into the airplane and hauled me out. He's a tough guy, but he's brave as gangbusters and I owe him my life. They took me out in an Air America Huey, and I spent the next six months in hospital. While I was there, I heard that Ric had been killed. Turns out he wasn't. But I thought he was until I saw him sitting with Ryan and Hendricks at my strip.'

'You can't kill Ric,' she said. 'Not without silver bullets. Even then you need a stake, and crossroads.'

'He's tough,' I admitted. 'Anyhow, that's all I know about drugs. I never had anything to do with them after Long Pot.'

'Welcome back,' she said. 'Welcome back.'

She had some scented oil in a little bottle – her hand slid, her teeth and nails were suddenly sharp. I came alive as though she had turned on a switch and forgot that I had meant to ask what the hell she was doing on the fringes of the drug trade.

I had a couple more beers later and said hello to the sandman, and still forgot to ask. I went to sleep with a vague sense of unease, because things didn't add up. I could fly, I was good enough to make it all look easy to anyone else, unless they tried it. Ellen Tyler couldn't fly an airplane worth a damn, but she could fly the box the bed came in. I wondered where she got that kind of expertise. I wasn't under any illusions about myself. I'd liked ladies ever since Betsy Ann Carter helped me lose it on the back seat of a '53 Chevy while the Creature crawled out of the Black Lagoon up on the screen, and the ladies seemed to like me too, but I was no champion, whereas Ellen Tyler you could have entered in competition with good hopes of getting a prize.

And there was something else. It came to me as I was slipping away. Deep down, hidden from sight, for some reason, Ellen Tyler did not like me at all.

NEW YORK

Yossif Petrovsky met Spencer at the Plaza Athenee, where he waded across silver-grey carpet and by dining rooms of exquisite elegance where well-heeled folk paid two hundred dollars a head to eat tiny portions of food that were works of art, and be insulted by waiters wearing the uniforms of Louis XIV's footmen. He found Spencer in a room stuffed with very lovely antiques, reading Dostoevsky in Russian.

'Your taste is improving, Victor,' he said.

'I've finally realized the purpose of being in government employment,' Spencer told him. 'You try to spend as much of the taxpayer's money as you can. Beer?'

'Please.'

A small Sears refrigerator hidden in a *dix-huitième siècle* commode offered up *bière d'Alsace*, and the two refreshed themselves.

'Okay,' said Petrovsky. 'We've got Ade Jumbe, who unbeknown to anyone else was a religious fanatic ready to sacrifice his life for some cause, as yet unknown to us. Where do we go from here?'

'As much as anything else, I'd like to know how it was done. Religious fanatics ready and willing to commit murder in the full expectation of martyrdom aren't new; they crop up all through history. The *sicarii*, for example, operating in Palestine around the end of the first century AD, who murdered their enemies in broad daylight, in crowds, using a short sword, the *sica* – hence the name. They anticipated martyrdom with a frenzy of religious joy and believed quite irrationally that after the fall of Jerusalem the Romans would be defeated, and that God would reveal Himself to His people and deliver them. They weren't and He didn't, but it made little difference to the *sicarii*.

'You find similar features among the better-known Assassins. They also operated in secret and killed always with a dagger, because it was a sacramental act. You find that feature among the Thugs, followers of Kali. The act of killing – with a silk tie, for them – was also sacramental. I don't think we're going to be able to get any association there; I cannot see that death by 747 can be sacramental. I get the feeling that in purpose the 747 crash was quite definitely meant to achieve something, but that that something was for the people who made Ade Jumbe into this religious fanatic. For him, I would have thought that he sought martyrdom in the full expectation of assured entry into paradise. That has to be the ultimate motive. It was for the Kamikaze, those of the Divine Wind of Shinto. We know that Ade Jumbe had been converted to Shi'ia Islam, not Sunni. His words – that he had been to Najaf and Karbala – prove that. For a Shi'ia Muslim, a single pilgrimage to the holy cities of Najaf and Karbala is worth 70,000 pilgrimages to Mecca.

'It isn't that it happened – Jumbe being converted – it's the speed. I agree that you can turn round some silly, bored little rich girl like Patty Hearst, but even then it was the glamour of it, the posing with the urban revolutionary outfit that appealed. I don't know that you'd have got her to embrace *martyrdom*. How they turned someone as hard and tough-minded as Ade Jumbe in such a short space of time, I do not know.'

Yossif helped himself to another pale blonde beer.

'The Mayor's getting anxious for some news on this, you know, Victor.'

'The hounds are closing in on our Carmine.'

'Judge Connel is, anyway. You might want to remind him about the need to keep security. About you. I heard one of the girls telling old Mr Champe that the Mayor had an expert in terrorism investigating the crash. She didn't mention your name, of course.'

'What's that, now? Who is Mr Champe?'

'The father of two girls who died in the crash. He calls our office every week to check if any progress has been made.'

'Every week?'

Spencer suddenly seemed very interested, but Yossif could not see why.

'Yes. He calls every week on Wednesday. At ten o'clock on the dot.'

'He called yesterday?'

'Yes. That's when I heard Debbie telling him we had the expert investigating for us.'

'He calls from Zambia?'

'Yes.'

'Every week at ten?'

'Yes.'

'Yossif,' Spencer said gently. 'Have you ever heard of "black time"?'

'What do you mean?'

'You know how things work here in New York. Everything runs on a timetable. Businessmen try to fit in more work by having working breakfasts, working lunches. Lovers fit in time to go to bed by matching Filofaxes. Everyone tries to get twenty-five hours into a twenty-four-hour day.'

Yossif nodded. 'That's right.'

'Africans don't,' said Spencer.

'You mean they're idle?'

'It's not that. They simply do not have the same mind-set that people in New York have to excess. They would think people here mad. In Africa, most people do what feels right at the time. If any typical Zambian made an appointment to see you on Wednesday they would probably be there Wednesday, but it might be Thursday.'

'Some people in Russia are like that.'

'A lot of Africans are *very* like that. They would never, never call you every Wednesday at ten each week for eighteen months, even if the Zambian telephone system would let them, which it won't. You couldn't guarantee

111

to call Ndola from Kabwe at the same time every week, let alone another continent.'

'So Mr Champe isn't Mr Champe?'

'No.'

'So who has been calling us all this time?'

Spencer leaned forward in triumph.

'The terrorists.'

STATEN ISLAND

Charlie Harrel was on his way from a meeting held in Staten Island to the mid-town studios when the telephone rang in his Shogun.

'Harrel,' he said briefly. A hated and feared voice spoke in his ear.

'This is Spencer.'

'We have nothing to say to each other,' Harrel said, and put the phone back in its socket. Within a minute it had rung again.

'For the good of your health,' said Spencer, 'hear me out.'

Harrel stayed silent.

'You remember the people we talked about? The ones whose identity you claimed not to know?'

'I *don't*,' Harrel burst out. He braked very suddenly to avoid running up the rear of the car in front, and someone behind hooted aggrievedly.

'I have very good reason to believe that they have become interested in you. If they find you, I believe that they will use methods unwelcome to you to ascertain the extent of your knowledge. I know that by yourself you cannot deal with them. I, however, can.'

Harrel thrust the phone back down again. The Shogun drifted across the centre line and cars coming towards him swerved, hooting and flashing their lights. Abruptly, he made a U-turn, breaking his journey and heading for the toll tunnel to New Jersey. Once through he headed north on 17, to Sloatsburg. People waited for him in the studios, for a long time.

The garage to his home was open and he went straight

in, parking the Shogun. Inside the house, he called his wife by name.

'Molly?'

There was no reply and he went through the rooms, calling out. His wife was nowhere to be found. He checked the yard, to no avail. Inside the house, images began pounding through his mind, images seen through a camera lens all over the world. Desperate, distraught relatives waiting by the phone. The grisly parcels arriving in the mail, bearing parts removed from the living, loved one. The opened trunk of a car, containing the bloody, bound corpse.

A car drew up on the street and his wife got out. In the time it took for her to get out, pick up her small athletic bag and walk up the path, Harrel struggled to bring himself under control, to banish the horrors that had paraded through his mind and conceal the anxiety and relief that he had felt. He contained the knowledge of things she must not know, things she had to be protected from, for she was quite unable to cope with them. She was a beautiful, delicate plant, crushed and damaged once by reality. He saw the little soft bag containing her exercise clothes and remembered that this was one of the three days a week she went to yoga class. She was slim, and moved easily, with flesh on her bones and colour in her cheeks as she had learned to eat again. There was life in her eyes, that had been dull, as she had learned to live within a safe routine, with a husband who was there when she needed him. All this was threatened by monsters from Harrel's past. He forced himself to hide his fear and beam at her as she came through the door.

'Hi, honey.'

'You're home early,' she said, pleased. They embraced.

'The meeting finished sooner than we thought. I only had a couple of calls to make, so I thought I'd head back.'

He moved towards his work-room.

'How about some hot tea?' he said.

'I'll put a kettle on.'

He went into his room, shutting the door, and sitting at the glass table called the number Spencer had given him.

'Yossif Petrovsky.'

'This is Charles Harrel. Spencer called me a little while ago. I want him to call back. I am at home.'

'If you stay by the telephone I will have him call,' said the voice of Yossif Petrovsky.

Harrel had to wait only a short while before his telephone rang.

'Harrel.'

'This is Spencer.'

'How reliable is this information of yours?'

'Very. I believe that the 747 disaster was not an isolated incident but part of a well-thought-out campaign. For some reason the campaign has been delayed, but is now moving again. Adam Ross served his purpose and was eliminated. Sufficient time has passed for you to be removed as well, after having been squeezed first. The latest information I have leads me to think that they will come for you soon.'

'What can you do about that?'

'I can provide protection, somewhere you and your wife will be safe while the terrorists are identified and eliminated.'

'Very well then.'

There was silence on the other end of the line.

'I said it was okay,' Harrel repeated, becoming anxious.

'Protection of this kind is very expensive,' Spencer said patiently. 'I would need sufficiently valuable information from you to justify it.'

'Christ, Spencer, you've told me we may be killed! Aren't you going to protect us?'

'Not unless you tell me who these people are, the ones who will come for you.'

Harrel's heart was pounding.

'You do know, don't you?' said Spencer.

'Yes,' Harrel whispered. 'Adam told me. Right

afterwards. He was afraid . . . even Adam was afraid, he wanted to make me know, to share the responsibility . . . '

'So tell me.'

'No. You set up the place to go, you set it up, and then when we're there I'll tell you. When we're safe I'll tell you.'

'Come now then.'

'No. In the morning. The house is safe here, it's protected. The neighbourhood is patrolled, the house is burglar-proof. I'll need the evening to get my wife used to the idea of going away. She is fragile – it will have to seem like a sudden holiday.'

'All right. Tell her a client is letting you use a villa in the Virgin Islands.'

'Yes.'

'Be ready to leave in the morning. I'll call.'

Harrel went out of his work-room, and in the living room his wife had put two mugs of tea and a small plate of cookies. Once it would have been a single glass and a large bottle of cheap Chablis. Harrel made himself smile.

'Well, honey,' he said, 'we're going on holiday.'

Harrel went quietly around his house, ensuring that the doors and windows were locked. He checked that the alarms were armed. Before it was dark, the house was sealed up tight. Outside, children came in from playing and prepared for bed. Men and women came home from work and the police patrolled the streets.

Charlie and Molly Harrel both bathed, and ate a light supper watching a film on television. By ten o'clock they were in bed. Molly Harrel went to sleep quickly, her husband stayed awake. Once he was sure she was asleep he slipped out of bed and once more checked the house. The security lights were on front and back. He was drawn tight as a wire. Looking through a window he saw a black-and-white cruise slowly past and was reassured. He went back to bed, but it took for ever to go to sleep. He turned restlessly, waiting for the dawn, but finally his breathing relaxed and became like that of his wife beside him. The house was quiet.

There was a soft rustling in the bedroom as the door of the large fitted wardrobe pushed outwards, brushing against the pile carpet. It opened fully, and a man stepped from the darkness into the room.

SANTA MARTA

We were working down on the coast; they had a strip in the middle of all the tobacco, pointing straight out over the ocean. You got engine failure there, you just put it down on the sea and swam in. The wind got up around midday and we knocked off for a while to let it lay – sat in the shade and had something to eat.

Ellen Tyler drove up in her little car about then. She got out and came over.

'How's life in the drug trade?' she asked, smiling her English smile, the one that never reached the grey eyes the colour of cold, cold sea.

'Ain't so bad,' I said.

She looked around at the piles of chemical cans by the mixing rig.

'Is this stuff safe?' she enquired.

'Won't hurt you. Unless you're a fungus or a tobacco flea.'

'You're not using that other stuff that's banned?'

'That's 2,4,5-T. That ain't dangerous either. I saw one of those scientific fellas drink a glass of it one time. Said it didn't taste much like Boone's Farm Apple wine, but it wouldn't hurt him.'

'Is he still alive?'

'Hell, no. Died a week later.'

'Well . . .'

'Got hit by a Mack truck. Killed him stone dead.'

'You have such faith in the technology. You think it's the only way, don't you?'

'Sure. We'll go to the stars one day.'

'That's it. I don't *want* to go to the stars. The Shuttle

118

blows up, and people like you brush it aside and say "Build Another One," and when you do the tough, competent, hard-nosed people queue up to get in it, but half the rest of the world are like me – they don't know why the light goes on, or where the water comes from, and technology terrifies them. You put out the spray on the crops and yes, I believe you, you know when to stop so it doesn't drift, but people like me are terrified that if it does drift and gets on us we'll die. They are frightened that the nuclear plant down the road will blow up and irradiate their children; they're scared that the weapons stored by the military will have an accident, or get stolen by terrorists, or that there'll be a mistake and the nuclear rockets will fire.'

The wind blowing the palms seemed to be lessening, although you could hear the boom of the waves a quarter of a mile away at the other end of the strip, beating on the shore. Red and blue birds perched in the palms; close by a red-headed woodpecker jumped about the trunk, gripping with his powerful claws, fragments of bark falling from the tree, his head cocked to one side as he listened for the bark insects underneath. He paused, put his head in the operating position and drilled rapidly. Pulling out the insect in triumph, he gulped it down.

'It's all in the Bible, you know,' she said.

'It is?'

'I would have thought a good Southern boy would know the Bible. "Surely he shall deliver thee from the snare of the fowler, and from the noisome pestilence. Thou shalt not be afraid for the terror by night; nor for the arrow that flieth by day; nor for the pestilence that walketh in darkness; nor for the destruction that wasteth at noon-day. A thousand shall fall at the side, and ten thousand at thy right hand; but it shall not come nigh thee. Only with thine eyes shalt thou behold and see the reward of the wicked." How do you interpret that? All of those awful things won't happen if you believe in God and follow His will. Do you believe in God, Marvin?'

'Of course I do.'

119

'Of course. And will he deliver you from the snare of the fowler? You'd better hope He will, because to me you're good and trapped.'

'What you talking about?'

'You've been had, caught, trussed up. You're in the drug trade, Marvin, and once in, never out.'

'That ain't so,' I said uneasily. 'I need the money, is all. It's strictly a one-time thing.'

She gave a bitter crow of laughter.

'*Nothing* to do with drugs is a one-time thing. Once you're in, it's a lifetime thing. Don't you know anything about it? Don't you know that it starts in school, where they got people getting the kids on dope, on pills. For some of those kids of twelve and thirteen their lives have been ended before they even start. Don't you know that most of the crime in your country is because of drugs? Most of the violence. Haven't you seen what it does to people? They have no hope. Once you're in, you pay and pay. There's no pleasure, just pain and more pain, and more paying and more paying.'

'Nobody has to take drugs,' I said weakly. 'It's their own damn fault. Anyway, if you feel so strongly about it what're *you* doing here, with all these religious nuts, helping grow all this damn stuff?'

'Oh, you're right,' she agreed. 'I'm no better than you are. I'm just afraid of having to go back to jail. I've got an unfinished ten-year sentence waiting for me back home.'

She was small, neat and ladylike, sitting cross-legged under the wing. I could not conceive of why they would put her in jail, nor what she could have done to get there.

'I'm twenty-seven,' she said. She glanced across to see if Billy Lee was listening, but he was still stacking z's. With her dark hair and crisp features she was not unlike my wife Claire, who before her illness had caused her to lose sixty pounds and the radiation and chemicals had removed all her hair, had been as good-looking a woman as you would hope to rest your eyes on, a woman that

120

just about any man in the county would like to have —
and some had.

'I'm twenty-seven,' she repeated. 'My father works in
the city, my brother's a doctor, my sister's married to a
man in advertising. I'm the youngest. I met Ric in Rome,
where I had a job working as an interpreter. I met Ric
and he had done so many things, and been so many
places, he was so competent and clever, he seemed
wonderful to me and I fell head over heels for him. And
he gave me a little powder, introduced me to the stuff;
you just put a couple of lines on a mirror and snuffed it
up, and you felt so good, all your problems went away. It
wasn't dangerous, that's what he told me in the beginning. And afterwards, I didn't care anyway.

'It was free . . . if you felt down all you had to do was
slip off to the loo and take a little more and back you
were. And to come down you just popped a couple of
'ludes, and they let you down like a parachute.'

'What're they? They the same?'

'No. Nooo . . . no . . . no.' She giggled a little. 'Good
old straight R.D. *He* drinks a beer to get off. No, the
point is, if you stay on too long it's not nice, it hurts, and
after a while you'd like to unwind, 'cause you're like a
clock spring and one more click of the key's going to
make you snap. But coming down's awful too, unless you
pop a couple of 'ludes and then it's okay. I was doing
quite a lot of that. Heroin will do the same job,' she said
idly. 'I was skin-popping it, so I could tell myself I wasn't
an addict. I was, of course.'

She had a casual, macabre expertise. The VOR-A
approach for drug addicts.

'I was using a lot of the stuff, stuff I couldn't have
afforded if Ric hadn't given it to me, so I couldn't very
well say no, not when he wanted me to do favours for
him. He hired me out as a toy for a while, to people he
wanted things from. I had to be good; if I wasn't good
with them he cut me off . . . I've been with women, and
I'm not that way. Sometimes I had to steal documents
when they were asleep, or take photos. Finally he wanted

me to take things for him, to England. Get the stuff in. It was ingenious. I carried it on my tummy, I was disguised to look pregnant. He had a make-up man fit me out every time and it was very realistic. I made nine runs before I was caught.'

I had caught on by now. 'No sense of smell? Not a birth defect?'

'The only defect's in my brain. I have a plastic insert, up here in my nose, because the toot rotted the real one away. I can't tell the difference between ammonia and a rose. They got me, and they gave me ten years. After six months, they moved me from Holloway to a less secure place outside. And then Ric appeared, one day. You see, it was odd, I shouldn't have been caught, because Ric had a *man* – customs man, that he bribed. I called him all that day, before I went, and he wasn't there . . . Anyway, he came back for me, he persuaded me to come . . . with ten years ahead of me it wasn't hard, and he got me out of jail, and out of the country on a boat. That was nearly three years ago, and here I am rotting in Colombia.'

'You still use that stuff?'

She looked at me pityingly. 'Where would I get it? Why would Ric need to give it to me now? He's got me where he wants me.'

Billy Lee stirred, and I realized that he must have been listening to some of the conversation.

'Drugs is bad shit,' he said. 'I used a little coke back when I was playing ball. It don't do you no good. Lot of ball players get a drug problem, making good money, brothahs especially – get other blacks prey on them, maybe start out taking codeine for the pain, go from there . . . it ain't none of it good. You bettah off with beah.'

'What is playing ball?' Ellen asked.

'Billy Lee was a pro football player,' I told her. 'Had two years with the Falcons before he hurt his knee.'

'This must be a little different,' she said politely. She was always very polite with him, much more than she was with me. Probably didn't want to appear prejudiced. She

122

was trying not to say that Billy Lee had sure come down in the world.

'Billy Lee isn't an employee, you understand,' I explained. 'He's a partner in the business.'

'Oh.' Again, she was too polite to ask what the hell I had a buck nigger load man as a partner for, so I explained.

'Me and Billy Lee have worked together a whiles. I *need* him to be a partner, I need him to have an interest in the business. Sure now I could go out, hire me a blue-gum nigger – excuse me, Billy Lee – hire one for minimum wage and what would happen? Like as not, I'd be out of business at the end of the year. Be more'n likely. All he'd have to do would be mess up the chemical. My Lord, he could put paraquat in my load instead of Orthene the day I went out and sprayed 400 acres of tobacco, and that tobacco would flat ass *die*. The farmer would be some hundreds of thousands of bucks out of pocket and would rightly sue my incompetent ass right out of business. Your load man can make or break you.'

'This the hardest side of aviation there is, lady,' said Billy Lee. 'It make a man old in twenty years, or it makes him old just one sunny summer morning. You got to be a team, everyone got to work together if it to go right.'

'When I had my accident earlier this year I went in, the airplane caught fire. I had ethyl and methyl all over me and I was *gone*, 'cept that Billy Lee always watches when I take off – see I climb out okay – and he came running, got me out, got burned himself, got me to water to get the chemical off. And that is just one of the reasons why when we leave here with our money we gone sit down, work out the accounts, distribute the shares, same as we do each season. Billy Lee gone make some stash this time. Hell, he liable to go hog-wild, buy him a new Mercedes.'

'Yeah, man. Gone have one in burgundy, with the tinted glass and air-conditioning and the leather seats. People gone see me go by, they say look at that Jewboy go, Lawrhd, he *know* how to ride.'

The wind was dying down, from the rustle of the palms it was coming below 10 mph.

'Why you?' I asked. 'Why did Ric choose you? Or was it an accident?'

'Oh, no,' she said. 'No accident. He *found* me, I was what he wanted.'

She looked at me piercingly.

'He found me just the same way he found you, Marvin. He was waiting and planning to have you a long while before he came to see you in Georgia . . . ' She pointed a slim finger at herself. 'I know, I know Ric. Tell me, can that Thrush there take you back home? Could you fill it with fuel and fly away?'

'Yes.'

'*Do* it. You are in great danger.'

'From Ric?'

'Yes.'

'Hell, Ric's all right. We go back a long way.'

'Ric is *not* all right. Ric has *never* been all right, but he has become something very terrible. Ric is lord of this fief here. Do you know how?'

'No.'

'This drug operation belonged to the del Rey family. Ric defeated them. He took it from them, and to prove who was now boss to the men he needed, he did something. He took the whole family to the hangar, where you keep the aircraft. He hung them all from the centre beam, swathed in sacking, lined everyone up, so they could see, and his men soaked the sacking in kerosene. Then he set fire to them. You can still see the marks on the concrete floor. *No one* gets in Ric's way here.'

She got up and walked to her car.

'Don't look around, Marvin. Something dreadful is following you.'

'I've been in danger before,' I said. 'The Lord's looked after me so far.'

She got into her little car and started the engine.

'You haven't been listening to me,' she said. 'There is no God. It is the Devil who is in charge.'

124

She drove off down the strip, and Billy Lee stirred beside me.

'Poor little gal,' he said. 'You kin tell she's been on the needle. They ain't never right in their head after. You kin see it in their eyes.'

SANTA MARTA

I got back from work one day and there was someone waiting for me in my room.

'Have you escaped, or are you out on bail?' I enquired.

Hank had lost a few pounds – the diet's never so good in these places – and he smelled kind of antiseptic, so I guessed that Ric had done taken him to the hospital to get the lice and nits and crabs off of him. But all in all, he looked in fair shape. Of course, freedom has that effect on you. After you had been expecting fifteen to twenty, that is.

'Charges been dropped,' he said succinctly. He sucked on his bottle of beer.

Ric had to be behind it. He was sitting there in a chair, sipping his glass of ice-water, so I asked him.

'How'd you do it?'

'We have a little influence here. I managed to persuade the authorities that it was in everyone's interests for Hank to be free.'

'Well, damn, son, I'm glad for you. I guess you catching the next flight out, huh, afore they change their minds?'

There was a short silence, and Hank set about chugging the rest of the bottle.

'Well, almost,' Ric said. 'Hank is, ah, very grateful to us for securing his release, and he has volunteered to do a little job for us on the way. You see, R.D., we have to deliver those fine crops you have been spraying. Or rather, we have to deliver last year's. Get them to market. In the past we have delivered by sea, but we have had some unfortunate setbacks because of the increased

126

efficiency of the US Coast Guard and Drug Enforcement Agency. We lost two ships to them; we had a fast power-boat, but it was caught by a Cobra helicopter off the Keys. It's very uneconomic. We're going to get it in by air.'

'The Convair,' I said. I was a little slow, but I got there in the end.

'The Convair.'

'The road in the valley. It's a runway, isn't it? I always thought it was too damn big.'

'That's right, R.D. So Hank has volunteered to fly the Convair for us.'

I helped myself to one of Hank's bottles of beer, the first of three before bedtime.

Hank opened another and drank some of it. He had a real thirst on him.

'Well, here's to you, kid,' I said. 'Have at it.'

'There's just one thing, R.D.,' said Ric.

'What's that?'

'Hank doesn't want to fly it all by himself. He wants another pilot to go with him.'

They seemed to be looking at me.

'You want me to go with you, Hank?'

'You're the man. I'm a good transport pilot, but I don't know shit about low-level, nap-of-the-earth intruder missions. You do. You were the best, the Agency said so.'

'It was a long time ago. And I near got killed last time I did it.'

Ric smiled. 'This isn't a combat mission. For someone like you, it'll be easy. And we'll pay you up front, we'll give you forty thousand for the trip.'

Forty grand. Lord have Mercy, it would get Darlby off my back, right then. Not at the end of the season. But . . .

'Don't suppose I'm supporting more'n about seven or eight head, right now,' I said, after a while. 'Then there's all them folk at the bank. I don't suppose any of them been skipping meals lately, neither.'

There was silence for a while and then Ric coughed.

'It's been a while since I lived among shitkickers,' he

said. 'You're going to have to translate for me, R.D. Are you saying that you will, or that you won't?'

The right seat was old and worn and frayed from the countless backsides belonging to countless co-pilots wriggling about on it wondering if the goddam captain was going to let them get hold of the controls this trip. I didn't mind. Hank could fly it all he wanted to.

The thing was built like a truck, all big strong levers and great pedals like dinner-plates, which was good, and all of it about twenty years out of date, which wasn't.

'Damn, this thing's old.'

'They pretty good old airplanes,' Hank said.

'Except that it's old.'

'Shit, we all getting old. You so gloomy today.'

'I'm just tired of sitting behind twenty-year-old engines while I grumble along at five feet and a hundred and twenty, with the pines coming up, wondering if the paddle's going to stop going round.'

'Well, that's ag. Ag's for crazy folk. Hear, we got two engines, gonna take us high above that.'

'This bird's over gross. We lose an engine on take-off and I guarantee you that the other will transport us to the scene of the accident.'

'Ain't gonna *be* no accident. Now will you kindly shut the hell up and start reading the check list? We got to *move*. There's a front coming through over there.'

'Ain't got no weather radar either,' I moaned.

We fired up the big old Double Wasp radials and the smoke whipped away. We did all the checks from the worn, grubby manual and taxied out to the very end of the big road that was a runway. Air was flowing down the valley at about ten mph, and that meant that we would be making an undesirable downwind take-off, but for sure there was no way we were going to take off *up* the valley, the ground got altitude faster than we would. *Damn*, but it was heavy. When it had been the darling of someone's airline, hauling rich folks drinking little bottles of

128

bourbon and smoking on big cigars, the big round engines would have been putting out 2,500 horses a side, and at max gross the bird would have left the ground just short of 5,000 feet, sea level, standard day. It sure was going to be interesting to see what twenty years of deterioration and an extra 3,000 lb would do.

We completed the before take-off checks and I skipped the part that said what to do if an engine failed after V_1. There was no point in depressing ourselves unnecessarily. We both knew that the bird would fly with difficulty on both, and not at all on one.

'Let's roll.'

It took us nine thousand feet and one minute seven seconds to get airborne. I know. I timed it out of morbid curiosity. Luckily the valley went downhill from then on. I got the gear up and Hank put the nose down and coaxed the unwilling creature on to the step; the pines started getting smaller and we began climbing to 10,000 feet. It took us an hour to get there, we got it trimmed and set the props and leaned the mixture. Hank set the old autopilot and hooked it up.

'Electric niggah On,' he said.

We watched it beadily for a while to see if it was trustworthy. It seemed to have an idea that it knew what it was doing, and we relaxed a little and allowed it to carry us northwards.

'Well,' I said to Hank, 'it's one way to get your ass out of jail.'

'I believe there ain't many things a man wouldn't do to get himself out of one of those places,' he agreed.

'Bad?'

'Man, it was awful. About the worst part was they put me in this damn cell with three niggers. Sheeat. I ain't never been wild with enthusiasm for our coloured friends but having to *live* with the bastards . . . man, they is so fucking sorry . . . There's three things you cain't give a niggah, my daddy used to say; you cain't give him a black eye, a fat lip, and you cain't give him a job. And I reckon he was about right.'

'I remember, a few years back I was farming fifty-three acres sweet onions, which was a mistake, 'cause I was so damn busy with the spraying and, man, I was hurting for field help come harvest. The bearing went out on the pump on my Stearman and I went into town for another, passed by this *big* old healthy-looking coloured gal; man, she looked like she could about lift up you and me both, and I stick my head out of the pick-up and say, "Hey, gal, you want to earn some good money, come work in the field a couple of weeks?" And she looks at me and says, "I'se don't have to work, I'se gets a cheque! Man, that made me so mad, I was about ready to bite nails in two. There I was, working a seventeen-hour day covered in sweat all the time, paying taxes out the ass for her to sit on her fat behind on welfare.

'I got calmed down some and thought about it, and it wasn't the fact that she was black, 'cause there was plenty of sorry white folk about too – still are, folk that don't want to work, hold down a job – so who's at fault. Seemed to me that the fuckin' system's wrong. If that big gal had got up that morning'n there hadn't been anything to eat in the house 'cause she wasn't on welfare then, man, she'd have been more'n happy to come to work, 'n would've felt better about it, done have some pride in herself. You give money to able-bodied folk like they do on welfare, you automatically make them sorry. I don't care what colour they are. Take Billy Lee, now, he's more valuable to me than any white man I know. Works like hell, I couldn't run my business without him. Don't reckon skin's got anything to do with it.'

Hank shook his head. Niggers were sorry, and he knew it.

Our eyes ticked around the panel, checking the gauges. At ten thousand feet we were running in and out of cloud and each time we went in our eyes swung across to the flight instruments, checking that the automatic pilot was not about to play an unwanted joke on us.

'I remember back when I was eighteen,' Hank said. 'Folks had done died and I was living in an aunt's back

130

room in Jackson, Mississippi. I was going for my commercial ticket and I needed money bad to finish up – done got me a job working a postal round out in the country; ten hours' work paid for one hour flight time, one hamburger and a Bud at Joe's Café. There was this section out there they call the loop, on account of that was what it was – you went in one end and wound up back where you started. At the beginning of the loop there was J.B. Stone's farm. He was one mean man, and ugly, too, but he had these lovely daughters. There were two big gals, 'bout my own age, and damn if each time I went by one of the gals would come with me to ride around the loop. They always wanted a cigarette, because their daddy was strict and wouldn't let them smoke. And every time, we'd stop out in the woods and frig. Man, them gals loved to frig. This went on for near a couple of months, I was about getting ready to get my ticket, and then one day instead of one of the big gals their little sister Betty turns up, says *she* wants to ride.

'So I say hold on now, you too young, but she says oh, please, so I say okay, and she is the sweetest little thing, but I say only to ride now – I mean, goddam, she only thirteen, real young, but we get out there and damn, there she is, snuggling up to me, and I say hold *on* now. But after a while, I'm telling you, it ain't a bit of good in the world me saying no, honey, you too young, my peter was was hard as that bulkhead over there, wasn't a bit of good me telling it no, get down, she only kidding.'

'So you did, huh?'

'We did. And would you know, I was not the first fella inside her pants. No, sir. Not by a long way.'

'These country gals start early. They see all the cows 'n horses getting it on. What happened?'

'What do you think happened? Her daddy found out about it. Lord, but J.B. Stone was a mean man. There is no doubt in my mind, even today, that he would have liked to kill me if'n he could've got a hold of me.'

'You left town, right?'

'Left town? Man, I left the *state*. In fact, I left the

goddamn *country*. What do you think I was *doing* down there in Nicaragua with you guys? Man, I didn't know Jack Shit about dusting, I was scared shitless all the fuckin' time.'

'Yeah, your first few weeks were kind of interesting. When we had time off, me and the crew used to come watch you. It was cheaper than the movies and more entertaining.'

'Yeah, I swear I have been getting into trouble over pussy 'bout since I discovered your peter wasn't just for pissing through. But this time, this here is the first time I ever got the trouble without getting the pussy.'

'You didn't do it?'

'No. Drugged, framed and set up. The whole damn thing was faked.'

'By Ric.'

'By your good buddy. I'd like to kill him.'

'I believe people have done tried. You say that gal was thirteen?'

'Sure was.'

'That's like the joke, ain't it? Middle-aged fella's at a party, meets this sweet little gal and they trot off to the bedroom, and he's hauling down his pants and he thinks, hey, she does look a bit young and he says, "Say, how old you, honey?" And she says "Thirteen." "Ho Lee Shit," he hollers, 'n hauls them straight back up again. Little gal looks at him, puzzled, 'n says, "Wassamatter, you superstitious or sump'n?" '

The Convair was cranking along at a respectable 260 mph, but it was still a long way to 9,000 feet of wartime runway in Georgia. We spent the time chatting about the price of used trucks, liquor we'd drunk, women we'd known, and the politics of the President. We drank coffee and munched on the sandwiches we'd brought. And, compulsively, we checked the gauges.

The left engine was running hotter than the right. The right generator seemed weak. Little things. Little things I didn't like worth a shit.

Outside of radar range, with the Florida coast coming

132

up, I disconnected the autopilot and brought it on down. We were cruising at 10,000 feet and I lost 9,950. We came in over the ocean well outside the Marquesas Keys to stay away from Key West radar. The weather was starting to deteriorate, and I was concentrating hard; at that sort of speed we were covering a football pitch in under a second, and at that altitude a guy fishing for tuna is liable to hook something a bit bigger, gone spoil everyone's day.

The weather was poor, bad viz and we didn't see the Marquesas Keys, but soon afterwards we picked up the Ten Thousand Islands coast. I was squinting hard through the rain-streaked windshield and got it, the little uncontrolled airstrip of Marcos came up on the nose. I put it a half-mile off my starboard wing, the runway grey and slick in the poor light, and then I climbed, going for 4,500 feet. As far as anyone was concerned I had just taken off.

We passed Naples and stayed out to sea to keep clear of Tampa-St Pete's airspace, didn't want to talk to them fuckers, didn't want to talk to *anybody*. Once I had some altitude I tuned in the TWEB on Vero Beach's vortac, and the weather was going marginal VFR most of Florida on up into Georgia, Alabama, Louisiana. Sounded like it would be IFR down to precip fog within a few hours. I wasn't overly worried. I had been trained by my government to find, land *and* take off again from strips that looked like scars in the jungle – short, rough, dangerous – and I'd got so good at it they made me teach other people how to do it. I believed I could find 9,000 feet of concrete runway clearly marked on a sectional chart and not far from both an NDB and a VOR. I mean, I was good at this kind of shit.

The weather continued to deteriorate. Rain made the windshield opaque, from the side windows low scud was blowing across the dark ocean. We came over the north Florida coast in the late afternoon with Tallahassee somewhere ahead of us in the murky light; on the 288 radial of their VOR we picked up the Chattahoochee river and then we had it made. We let down, and on schedule the long wet strip of concrete appeared. We checked the gear, the gas, the pitch, the flaps, the speed and the safeties on our .45s. Hank painted it on and we taxied over to the waiting airplanes.

There was an old twin-engine Bonanza, a couple of Mooneys, a big fat Stationair, an Arrow and a Skylane, and a fuel truck. On the runways were painted the big yellow crosses that told you not to use it, and cut green grass and weeds that had grown in the cracks lying sliced and wet because we had.

The packages were sealed in plastic, all labelled. The men came to fill their airplanes and cold gas swelled the great black rubber of the ferry tank as we refuelled to go back. The metal of the gun in my jacket pocket was warm and slick with the sweat from my hand. It was all too much like the days gone by, when I'd been young and hadn't known any better. The fog was thickening rapidly. As the small airplanes left, we lost them as they rotated and they were just engines climbing out to the clear stuff above.

The twin Bonanza left the ground, we closed up the cargo door and fired up. Anxious to leave, we lined it up on the centreline and gave it the fuel. The visibility was closing fast and it was near to an ITO as we entered the clag and got clear at 800 feet, heading south.

Hank was flying and I was pouring coffee and looking at the engine instruments; the coffee was tired and the left engine was running hot. There was fog below us and the left oil pressure was sagging. The temperature suddenly started to move across the face of the dial and the pressure went the other way.

'That is fixing to quit on us,' I said, and we shut it down before it could; we cut the mixture, feathered the prop, shut the cowl flaps and wound in trim. I got out the check-list and called out the items, we tied it all up and put it to bed. The prop stopped and the blades swung with the sharp parts into the wind; we came in with take-off power on the right engine and wound in more trim and it had all gone to rat shit in the space of a minute. And in that time we'd come down 400 feet. That's what the vertical speed indicator said, it was firmly pegged there.

'Ain't gone stay up long.'

'I need an approach. Give me an approach.'

I got the Cairo NDB and put it in the ADF, the needle swung and Hank brought it around. I got him the approach plate out of the Jep binder, we came over the beacon at two thousand two and headed outbound. The fog was white below us and as we entered the procedure turn Hank said, 'This is a goddamn non-precision approach and it's gone be zero zero in that shit. I want the other engine back on line if I have to go around, do it again.'

With only one engine, if we didn't get the runway first time it was too bad, because we were coming down. With two on line we could climb out and try again – assuming the sick one hung together that long.

We were going to bust minimums, for sure. I wished to hell we were coming in at a bigger airport, one of the ones where they got HIRL and RAIL and REIL and MALSR and VASI and ILS to slide down. And when you hurting a bit you duck under a tad, and you see any of them pretty lights waving at you, you back on the power and it coming down, boy – all the way to that good hard runway, and thirty-eight Victor clear of the active, what's that, sir, well, yes, sure looked like half a mile viz to me, didn't it to you, Zeke, that's right, yeah, guess it must have cleared a tad as we came in, what's that you say, we the only plane landed here today, well you surprise me. Yes sir, we sure would appreciate you send someone out here in a jeep to guide us in, cain't see a damned thing out here.

I checked the chart and there was nothing shown on the approach that looked like a tower, just hoped that civic pride hadn't ordered up and paid for a new water tank. Hey, man, what all them twisted old girders. That the

135

water tower. Couple drug runners done flew into it one afternoon.

Hank went outbound in the procedure turn, the ADF needle pointing to the station behind our left wing, and I got out the check-list to fire up our weak engine. I made the mixture rich and gave it the fuel, brought the prop out of feather and it jerked reluctantly. It went about a third of a turn and stopped. We began to turn inbound to the station and the ADF needle faithfully showed us where it was, where the sweet, hard runway was waiting for us. I was going to get out and kiss it.

'Bump it.'

I bumped it with the starter, there was a frightening rate of discharge from the load meter, the prop ground again, the engine coughed, smoke gushed from the cowl and then it stopped, the ADF needle swung slackly away, the off flags came up and the radios went tits up, and we were flat plain S.O.L. Purely Sierra Oscar Lima for the day, just shit outa luck.

'Missed approach,' he said calmly, just like we were on a training flight and not going to die in about a minute and a half. The electrical system was dead. The batteries were dead. The generator on the working engine was dead. The avionics were dead. The good engine was delivering take-off power and we were coming down. When we hit the ground the fire would burn off the fog in the area and make it like a summer's day. Not that we would be there to see it.

We weren't running off the ferry tanks, we were on the mains. Hank feathered the prop and flew and I scrambled back into the cargo compartment and blessed my pessimism in bringing a tool-kit. Plumbing connected the fat ferry tank to the fuel system; I got out the pipe wrench and fitted it around the big locknut. The thing was stiff and the rubber tank didn't help by giving as I heaved. It slowly began to turn. Terrified of striking a spark as the fuel began to dribble out I wrapped a handkerchief around the cut, the fitting came loose and the fuel burst out into the hold in a flood. I scrambled back to open the cargo door and when I got it open we were in the fog.

I ran up the cargo hold, slithered and fell on the gushing fuel, and got to the cockpit.

'Give me a right turn.'

Hank didn't ask, just did as he was told. We were down to 500 feet blind. When I went back into the cargo bay, fuel was spewing from the door and the plane was filled with fog and fuel vapour. Just one spark. Hey, man, whatever happened to that guy, used to spray the crops? Hell, he got turned into fried chicken, five miles SE of Cairo, 450 feet, MSL. I jumped up and down on the tank.

The flow turned to a dribble, after what seemed like an age. I went back to the door and fog whipped by. In a little while, I was looking down at it. We were climbing out.

I shut the door and went back to the cockpit – out of breath, frightened and reeking of fuel. I sat down in the right seat and made myself go through the ritual of counting up to ten, real slow, get my tones measured, like I did when it was IFR and you deep in it, hurting bad to get out of the CB or out of the icing, or in the fighter and the Low Fuel light glaring at you and needing the straight in real bad.

'Well, all right,' I said. 'Guess we'd better go look for some VFR weather.'

'Let's transfer some fuel,' I said. 'You holding trim there. Shift some across from the left tanks.'

Hank didn't move. He was soaked in sweat, it ran down his face and stained his shirt and he brushed it away from his eyes. I thought that he hadn't heard me.

'C'mon, c'mon. Shift the fuckin' gas.'

Very slowly, he turned to look at me. Maybe he'd counted to ten too.

'The fuel pumps are electric,' he said.

We didn't have very long left to fly. Our good engine

137

was burning fuel from its tanks in the right wing, which was becoming lighter. We wanted to transfer fuel across from the left to keep our lateral centre of gravity within limits. If we couldn't, we'd correct with aileron and rudder right up until we ran out of control authority and the right wing swapped air with the left.

I looked at the chart.

'Steer 265,' I said. 'Go to Panama City.'

'What the fuck good will that do?'

'The towers. They should be sticking up out of the fog. They have those fucking great towers there, you know. Maybe we can work something out. Get some kind of a visual reference. Do it. *Do it.*'

Hank flew and I sat with the charts and tried to work out some way to descend through 300 feet of cotton wool, and hit hard runway and not Harry's Oyster Bar complete with car park and patrons. It was getting dark and I took the flashlights from the flight bag. When they teach you to fly they always train you to carry a flashlight when you fly at night, in case of failure of the instrument lighting, and like most old-timey captains I had arrived at the stage of carrying three, of different sizes and makes, just in case. I struck up the big 5 D-cell military model and it was bright, because I'd changed the battery cells before the flight and checked that they worked.

The time ticked away and on cue, like candles on a frosted cake, the tall towers and masts of the city appeared, red lights blinking against the fog. Hank gently swung around the area, favouring the good engine.

'The VOR Alpha approach here has circle-to-land minimums,' I said. 'It should be straight in, seeing as it's within thirty degrees. Reason it ain't, it's got this tower in the way, can't risk having some cat fly into it.'

I showed him what I had found on the map.

'Now, all we got to do is find the tower.'

'That's WYOC's tower – see, it's got the freak here. Yeah, look, it's that one over there. And the ones over that way are the telecommunications towers. WYOC. Got good country music.'

'Ah swear, we get down I will play their fuckin' station all night in the motel. Right, got it, got it. That's our tower over there. Way I see it, ain't hardly no wind, we'll fly the approach on the headings.'

Hank looked at me, his eyes white in the failing light, and he took his hand from the wheel.

'You worked it out, R.D.,' he said. 'I guess that gives you the honour.'

'I got it.'

'You got it.'

I took over and headed outbound, descending to 1,600 feet, and Hank shone the flashlight on the panel so I could see the gauges. The flight instruments were all fine, because they were driven off the suction pump on the good engine. I gave him the second flashlight in case the first quit.

Inbound, I dropped it down over the fog, we came in on a 236-degree heading with the tower above us and to the right, about three swathe widths, enough to clear the guy wires, started the time, I came back on the power and we came on down.

'I want lights.'

'I'll call.'

'What type.'

'Roger. Hey, R.D.?'

'Yeah.'

'Pointy end forward.'

'Right.'

'Dirty side down, too.'

'You know it, babe.'

The gear was down, we had flap, the grey outside was turning black, going down into the well, 200 feet coming up on the altimeter, time coming up; both of us forward on the seats, the big old transport carving a tunnel in the fog, a hundred feet, eighty, and way below minimums.

'I hope this ain't Fernandina Beach.'

139

The time was *up*, and we had to *be* there, unless I had done fucked up, in which case we about to join someone in their living room, and Hank yelled in alarm for the *lights* and we caught the hangars and planes and Ho Lee Shit the fuckin' control tower whipping out of the fog, and I came in with the power and cranked it across to the open side of the airfield in a nasty skidding turn because I was afraid of catching the wingtip on all the things I could see whizzing by. And we went under the tower and cleaned it up and climbed it out and came on out of the fog like a submarine. I wound in some more aileron trim and it wasn't too bad, at least there wasn't anyone shooting at us.

'You kill me now, R.D., and my creditors gone be mad at you.'

'We were about 300 feet off. To the left.'

'Yeah. Shame on you. Just done failed your check ride.'

'I'm running out of authority. About used up most the aileron. We fuck up a second time I'm going to take it out over the bay, try and ditch.'

'What's with the "we" shit? You the driver here. Anyway, I cain't swim.'

'May have to learn, son.'

'I like to eat oysters, I didn't say I wanted to go live with them.'

We came in one more time, and the time and the altitude and the heading all came up and Hank called for *lights, runway lights*. I came off the gauges and transferred outside and we were on the fucking *money*, the bright white glow pumping through the moisture, and I was back on it and the rubber chirped once, and twice; and I was on the brakes, because all we had was the white glow as the lights came into view and whipped past, guess it must have cleared as we were coming in, looked like half a mile to me, didn't it to you, Zeke, yes sir, we sure would appreciate you send a jeep out here to guide us in, cain't see a damned thing out here.

But that wasn't what we wanted at all. We were sitting

140

in a very hot piece of equipment indeed and the Man would want to have a long and serious talk with us, culminating in a long and serious holiday at his expense, and we would never ever fly again, so when I got it slowed up I kept it rolling. The red runway end lights came up and I rolled straight through them, went a thousand feet into the dark until the nosegear piled into the runway fence. I shut the faithful Wasp down, we grabbed our bags and opened the door and jumped down into the swirling fog.

In the car we went over the bridge across the bay with all the snowbirds going to eat oysters in the fog, and the smell of the paper mill and the smooth hard tar underneath our wheels.

'Whatchoo say them folk were called?'

'WYOC. Couple turns down the dial. Good country music.'

'They kin play fuckin' reggae for all I care. I'm gone listen till we get out of range.'

Merle Haggard was singing about catching trout and drinking bourbon, I popped the top of a cold can of Blue Ribbon, the beer was good and sharp in my throat, I had a second somewhere near the Georgia Florida border and left, or passed out while the beautiful vibrato voice of Emmylou Harris sang about Sin City.

THE CATSKILLS

Hassan Sadeq and Ali Bahonar had worked together, had cooperated, for many years. They had trained and graduated as officers together, had survived the revolution together, even survived through the years at the front line in the endless war together. There were few like them left, and the revolutionary government was glad to find them when they were needed.

Hassan Sadeq and Ali Bahonar worked together on Charlie Harrel, according to the instructions they had been given. He was strapped to a heavy wooden chair that was bolted to the floor of the cellar, and he was blindfolded. The heavy band of cloth was the only clothing he wore. His wife lay in the corner of the room, tied, and sobbed and shrieked. The noise penetrated not at all from the subterranean chamber. Hassan and Ali asked but very simple questions from the thing that jerked and squealed in the chair, as they had explained they would before they had started. They asked only – who it was that had been brought in to investigate the 747 disaster? Where could he be found? What did he know? What had Charlie Harrel told him?

The answers came urgently, the words stumbling one over the other in their eagerness to please his tormentors. When they had come forth Hassan and Ali did it again, because they well knew that a very strong man might hold up under torture and give the answers he wanted to give, not the ones the interrogators wanted to hear. But the answers came forth the same, Victor Spencer. Yossif Petrovsky. His telephone number. He didn't know. No, nothing . . .

142

They worked on Charlie Harrel five times, but got nothing else, and at the end he was incoherent, dying and insane, joining his wife who had lost her reason early on in the proceedings. Life slipped away from him gladly as Ali crushed his larynx with a garotte, the pain infinitesimal compared with the relief. They unstrapped the corpse and put it into a heavy rubber body-bag, then left it in the cellar with his wife, locking them in while they went upstairs.

They ascended into the sunlight of a bright winter morning, with the lake sparkling over the deck and birds singing in the trees. Their clothes were splashed with vomit and excrement, their hands smelled of burned pork. They put the clothes into the trash and showered. When they had changed, they had breakfast looking out over the Catskills. Their knowledge they would keep until they returned to New York and could use a payphone. The food and hot coffee revived them. It had been a very long night since they had hidden in the wardrobe while the woman was out at her meditation class.

Ali wiped his mouth and put his plate to one side.

'You going to rest?'

'Sure. We'll have to wait until it's dark, now.'

'You want to fuck the bitch?'

Hassan shook his head.

'I think I will,' said Ali.

'Sure. Why not?'

They went back down into the cellar and brought the woman out. Like their clothes had been, she was soaked in fear, vomit and urine, and gobs of blood that had flown across the room. After they had washed, the smell, sight and sound of her was foul. She keened continually.

'She's not very exciting, Ali,' Hassan said. 'Just kill her now.'

'I'll wash her down.'

Ali stripped all her clothes off and pushed her into a shower, where she remained for some minutes. When he took her out he rubbed her with a towel to dry her, enjoying the sensation.

'See,' he said, showing her off. 'She is not so bad to look at.'

Hassan regarded the woman dispassionately. 'She still making that awful noise.' He recognized the symptoms. They were the same as those shown by some men at the front whose reason had been destroyed by endless combat and endless shelling. They were given to the field police, who took them away and shot them.

'Give her a drink.'

There was a tray of liquor at the side of the room. Ali took a bottle of brandy and made her swallow, forcing the glass neck into her mouth. When he took it away she began sobbing, continually.

'Ai . . . ' Hassan said mockingly. 'Ai . . . see with what passion she awaits your tryst . . . she trembles with desire for you . . . '

Ali grinned and, taking the woman by the wrist, led her unresisting down the corridor. There there was a special bedroom, secure and windowless, for the containment of captives.

Hassan got up and went over to the liquor tray himself. They would rest soon. He poured himself a large bourbon and stood staring out over the lake. Years of involvement with extreme suffering had rendered him, like Ali, almost immune to its effects. He wanted only that he not endure it himself, nor a woman, and two small children, at home. Better that the man from the television suffer. And was there not poetic justice that this voyeur of disaster, this peddler of other people's agonies should finally taste that which he sold?

Sounds as from a farm came down the corridor and Hassan sipped his drink, feeling himself relax. It would be good to sleep soon. The sobbing died away, becoming muffled as Ali locked the door, and he appeared pulling on and belting up his robe. Like Hassan, he poured himself a drink.

'How was she?'

'Is it not true, as the Imam Ali says in the scriptures, "All women feel the same, when you mount them in the dark."?'

Hassan guffawed; Ali had been quick to learn amusing parts of the Qur'an during their re-education. Ali hitched the belt around his belly – he was running to fat away from the front, taking advantage of the good food in the land of Satan. But like Hassan he was still strong, trained and dangerous. Both men were in their early thirties, olive-skinned, with black hair in tight curls. Both were marked: Ali's face had been remodelled by the blast of an RPG-7, and Hassan's body was pecked with shell splinters.

Ali raised his glass. 'There is no God but Allah,' he said.

'There is no God,' Hassan replied. They drained their tumblers. It was their own private toast.

The two men were tired. They had been awake for over twenty-four hours and had succeeded in completing a critical mission. They went to bed, to sleep. It was the afternoon before they awoke, with the winter's sun fading fast. They ate lasagne from the freezer, heated in the microwave, and when it was dark began completing the job. Ali fetched a body-bag from the store and Hassan went to get the woman. He unlocked the door as Ali came up the stairs unpacking the bag, and peered in. He hesitated for a moment, then pulled the door back shut.

'Ai . . . Ali, she awaits her lord,' he said solemnly. 'She trembles at the power of your loins, she cannot wait to consummate your love again . . . ai . . . greatest of the world's lovers you are, you have but to lie with a woman once to make her forever yours . . . '

Ali looked at his comrade in exasperation. 'What's going on? Here, let me – '

He pushed past Hassan and opened the door. The ceiling light was on, casting a gruesome pink glow over the scene. Walls, ceiling and floor were spattered with gouts of sticky, drying blood. The naked, empty body

145

sagged across the bed. The woman had succeeded in prising loose a hard shard of plastic from the headboard of the bed, and had opened her carotid artery with it.

Hassan began to laugh, continuing his joke, comparing Ali with Rudolph Valentino – the greatest of all Latin lovers were but amateurs compared with Ali . . . the words gasped out between the laughter and Ali began joining in. They laughed so much the tears ran down their faces, and they staggered in the corridor, bouncing off the walls, putting their hands on their knees to support themselves. It was nearly twenty minutes before they were sufficiently composed to stuff the body in the rubber sack and begin swabbing away the blood with towels and buckets of water.

When they were finished they took both corpses in the weighted sacks down to the boathouse, together with the two suitcases they had forced them to pack – in the middle of the night in their home, when Hassan and Ali had emerged from the wardrobe – before taking them out on the drive into the Catskills to die. A Riva speedboat suitable for water-skiing was tied to the dock. They purred out over the smooth surface of the lake and when the lights of the house were small diamonds glittering in the wake they tipped the grisly cargo over the side.

They sent the Riva curling back across the lake. They had a report to make, another mission to undertake. They were undercover soldiers, fighting far behind enemy lines.

WAYCROSS, GEORGIA

'It's a shitheel town,' she said. 'And I'm beautiful.'

It was one of my wife's better days. They had taken her off the radiation treatment that kept you alive but made you feel as though, at some time while you slept, relays of people had come by to kick you in the crotch. I didn't know what they had her on, but it was obviously good. She was trying to explain something to me that was quite clear in her own mind, but which was taking a while to come out. But it was one of her better days and I hoped that she would enjoy it as she had but a small stock left.

'When you're beautiful, it's different.'

'I guess.'

'You shouldn't marry beautiful people and put them in little bitty sticks towns, R.D.'

'Guess that's what you get for marrying a cropduster, honey. We kind of always live in little bitty sticks towns. It's where the work is.'

'Piss on it,' she said resentfully. 'I wanted to live in a beautiful two-storey house with all old antique furniture and silver and maids and shit, you know?' She looked at me cunningly. 'I did, too, didn't I?'

'You did, Claire.'

There was silence for a while.

When we'd been young, just married, we used to talk things over, about what we had to do. I guess I'd come by out of old habit, but of course it was far too late for that. Had been, for a long time.

'I suppose I'm just trying to say I'm sorry I been such a lousy wife to you, R.D.'

'Yes. Me, too.'

'Fuck you,' she said quietly. 'I don't know why I said that, I'm not sorry at all. I just want to get better, so's I can go out and do it all over again.'

I got up to leave. 'I know.'

'I'm beautiful, you see. It's different for us.'

'Yeah. I know.'

I got up to leave and left my wife, weighing 62 pounds, bald in a wig and doped to the eyeballs – and they didn't have a mirror in her room, not one.

As I went out down the corridor, the little man in the coat beamed at me because the bill was paid.

'Oh, Mr Marvin,' he said. 'Have you a moment? Dr Jones would like a word.'

He showed me to a little room with the light on the wall where they look at the x-ray and tell you how long you got, and there was this young fella behind a desk reading notes. He was short-haired, with round glasses. He got up to shake my hand and he was wearing earth-coloured clothes and Jesus sandals.

'Mr Marvin,' he said, 'I'm so glad I've finally caught you.'

'What can I do for you, doc?'

'I just wanted to ask you a few questions, concerning your wife's illness.'

'Uhuh.'

'It really concerns her diet. What was she eating in the weeks before she came to hospital seeking medical help?'

'Hell, I don't know. Steak 'n' lobster, I should think.'

He looked rather shocked at my lack of concern.

'Mr Marvin, you must know. It's important, you see. There is no doubt in my mind that her carcinoma was caused by something she ate.'

'You can get cancer from eating things?'

'There is a lot of evidence that some of the preservatives and agents used in food preparation may have harmful side effects,' he said seriously.

'Yeah, man,' I said. 'All them folk going to MacDonald's and falling over dead in the street.'

He flushed. 'You're not taking me seriously.'

'I got the opposite problem, doc. I get withdrawals if I don't get my tartrazine. Give me those Es.'

He smiled in a wintry fashion. You could tell he ate brown rice and believed in biorhythms.

'Anyway. What did she eat?'

'Doc, I don't know. My wife was not living with me at the time, having left me for a wealthier man.'

He flushed again, bright pink. He was only young, and not a Southerner. He was a damyankee of some sort.

'Oh . . . ' He shuffled his papers. 'Uh, Mr Marvin, did this give you feelings of intense anger towards your wife?'

'Hell, no. I was kinda grateful. She's an expensive bitch to run.'

He was almost choking, poor boy.

'I mean, you wouldn't have considered . . . uh . . . '

I finally saw what he was driving at. 'You mean, would I have wiped her out. By giving her some nasty stuff?'

He nodded gratefully.

'Aw . . . I can see you don't know how things are here. You from the north?'

He nodded. 'Wisconsin.'

'My Lord . . . how you wind up heah. This is the deep South. Now, a man mess with another man's wife, you got a choice of action. You can let it go. You want to do something about it, you still got a choice. If she ovah at his house, 'n' you drink half a bottle of Jack Daniels 'n' go round with your Winchester pump twelve-gauge 'n' send them to Heaven, then you in deep shit. Ain't no one gone approve of you busting into another man's house and committing murder.

'Now, they grabbing ass in a motel, 'n' you stop off at the bar for a few before blowing them away, you get five years, out in three, 'n' everybody say she drove you to do it.

'Now, ifn' they stupid enough to get it on in *your* house, 'n' you scatter them over the wallpaper before

149

sitting down for a slug before the sheriff arrive, then when he come he gone grip you by the shoulder 'n' say, "Mah Lawrd, how could they do this to you, son?" Then you home free.'

Poor Dr Jones was looking at me with his eyes goggling behind his granny glasses.

'Now, me, I let it go,' I said. 'It wasn't the first time she gone off with someone else, even if it was the last.'

'Oh . . . I'm sorry, I didn't know.'

I got up to leave. 'Well, you the only one in town who didn't, son.'

I was by the door when he spoke again.

'But it's still so,' he said. 'She ate something that gave her cancer.'

'Probably went on a health-food diet,' I said. 'The three-bean-salad done done her in.'

I went out to the truck to go drive down to Jacksonville, and once again read the letter in the package that had been waiting for me with the rest of the mail in the box. There'd been a lot of it, it hadn't been emptied in a while.

Dear Mr Marvin,

I have called the number that you left me many times in an effort to talk to you, but without success, so I am writing to you in the hope that this letter will reach you.

The results from the tests we made after you came to see me indicate that the chemicals Ethyl and Methyl Parathion which you became contaminated with in your aircraft accident have inflicted quite serious damage on your body. Most specifically, they have damaged the soft tissues of your liver and kidneys.

In addition, the tests show that you have become sensitized to the whole group of organo-phosphorous compounds to which these chemicals belong. You are in the condition of someone who is allergic to – for instance – the sting of a wasp. To an ordinary person the wasp's sting is painful but not serious, whereas to the allergic person the sting may prove fatal.

A similar situation exists. Whereas I recall you have been in close association with these chemicals for many years without suffering any ill-effects, now in your changed condition even as much as the smell may be sufficient to induce nausea. Should you ever become contaminated again, it is likely that serious injury or death may result.

· Bluntly, I am telling you that it is *essential* that you retire from the field of dispensing agricultural chemicals. However, should you accidentally come into contact with them in the future, you should take action to counter the effects. I enclose a prescription for a kit that you should always have close to hand. It comes in a small box, containing a pre-loaded syringe, and is based on the military model issued to troops to counter the effects of nerve gas. The needle should be pushed into the upper thigh and the plunger depressed.

'DO NOT carry it and continue to work with the chemicals, considering it to be prophylactic. It is merely in the category of life insurance, as the man allergic to wasps carries antihistamines. The prescription may be repeated three times.

Yours sincerely,
Carlos Mendez. M.D.

The address was from between two garbage containers in Hialeah, Miami, one of which asked you not to start fires in it and the other ordered you to put dead animals elsewhere. Both promised fines if you disobeyed.

Back when I'd been in high school we did some work on the early days of the industrial revolution. They were pretty dangerous times for the workers. Match-makers got something horrid called phossy-jaw from the phosphorous; iron-puddlers were immensely strong men who died, always, before they were forty; hatters went

151

mad. At the end of the twentieth century, ag pilots who took a bath in the more ghastly of the chemicals got to be one step from dying.

There was only one problem. I couldn't stop. Not yet. I'd just have to be careful. Very, very careful.

NEW YORK

Yossif Petrovsky met Spencer in the General Grant Hotel
on the edge of Harlem. There were cockroach tracks on
the furniture and the room had a bed that claimed to give
a soothing electro-vibro-massage for a quarter.

'I wish we could meet somewhere else, Victor. I'm
getting some pretty odd looks in these places.'

'They think we're gay,' Spencer said. 'And AIDS has
altered the cultural viewpoint of heterosexual New York
towards men going with men. You get here okay?'

'I did. I've got a cab downstairs. I figured in a place
like this I might not get another. Pity the 747 didn't take
out this bit too.'

'Yeah. You're still using the tunnel? No one following
you?'

'No. I'm careful. Okay, about Charlie Harrel. I went
with the police when they went to his house. There's
nothing broken or disturbed, the house was locked up
and the burglar alarms armed. Inside there were no signs
of any struggle, the house was tidy and the refrigerator
was emptied of things that would rot. The trash had a bag
full. Upstairs the drawers and closets had gaps in, as
though clothes had been taken, and in a cupboard Harrel
had a line of various suitcases. From the marks on the
carpet two are missing. Things like cosmetics and tooth-
paste are missing from the bathroom. Mrs Harrel's auto-
mobile was in the garage, but his Shogun was missing.
The police found it this afternoon in one of the car parks
at JFK.'

'I called him back when you gave me the message that
he'd called. I told him that I was fairly certain that he

would be receiving a visit from the people who caused the 747 disaster. He asked me if I could provide protection for him and his wife, which I said I could, but only if he had some information for me. You see, I was sure that he knew who had done it.'

'Did he?'

'He claimed to, but said he would only tell me what he knew once he was safe. I was to get him out next morning. But when I called there was no reply.'

'Do you think he just got up and ran?'

'His television people, "WashingtonWatch", they don't know anything?'

'That's the bit I've been keeping, Victor. They got a short note from him. It just said: "I have to go away for a few days. Will be in touch." It was typed, and signed Charlie.'

'It was his signature?'

'Yes . . . but here's the thing. I took a photocopy. I know this girl, you see, Victor, I dated her a few times, she makes a living analysing people's handwriting. You know: "Send me a sample of your handwriting and ten bucks and I'll predict your fortune." She makes some good money out of the kooks.'

'And?'

'I showed Harrel's signature to her. I didn't say anything about it, I just asked her to comment. She only took one look. She said that he was in terror of his life when he wrote it.'

'Maybe the people who were after him are sufficiently terrifying.'

'She seemed to think it was greater than that. It was immediate.'

'Yeah. When you're frightened enough to take off and run, you don't clean out the refrigerator.'

'Where do you think he is?'

'Dead, at a guess,' Spencer said sombrely. 'Listen, I'm going to be out of town over the weekend. I'll see you on Monday. Do you remember the Ramada where we first met?'

'The King Henry the Ninth decor?'

'That's it. I'll meet you there at midday.'

'Okay, Victor.'

'What are you up to at the weekend?'

'Well, tomorrow afternoon I'm playing baseball. The Mayor's team's taking on Marks, McCann and Erikson. They're a big law firm.'

'I didn't know Russian folk played baseball.'

'I've learned.'

'Like a lot of things. Any speciality?'

'They bring me on as the new Russian immigrant and put me in as relief pitcher sometimes. I've got a good curve ball and it fools them.'

Spencer grinned. 'What's your secret? A foreign substance?'

'Certainly not. Everything I use is made right here in the USA. Hair gel makes it wobble really well.'

Spencer grinned. 'Anything planned after the game?'

'Oh, we'll have a few beers in the evening. Go for a pizza. I think I'll enjoy Saturday, because Sunday's tough.'

'Why?'

'Lunch with my Aunt Ruth. I mean, it's great to see her, but Mrs Abrams will be there.'

'You don't take to Mrs Abrams?'

'It's not that. It's *Miss* Abrams. Miss Rebecca Abrams. The ladies – Aunt Ruth and Mrs Abrams – would like us to see more of each other.'

'And Miss Abrams has a face like a boot, right?' Spencer said sympathetically.

'Oh, no, Victor. She's a pretty girl. But she's twenty-four.'

'Yes . . . Oh, I see. Young Jewish ladies only have a shelf-life of about twenty-five, isn't that right?'

'That's it. Twenty-five and she's *on* the shelf. I think that I'm being voted into the position of the US Cavalry.'

'Riding to the rescue in the last reel? Well, I suppose most of us get married in the end. It might not be so bad.'

155

'Aunt Ruth worked so hard to get me out of the Gulag . . . she had petitions, and people calling for my release . . . it would be hard to refuse her, but I don't think I would make Miss Abrams a good husband.'

Yossif looked up at Spencer suddenly. 'I don't fit, you know, Victor. I'm here in my new, foreign, country, and I don't know why people do things. I work with people and they're worrying about whether to have the BMW or the Porsche, and it *matters*. Or about which boutique to shop at. The lawyers at Marks, McCann and Erikson all have plenty, yet they're giving themselves heart attacks doing things that don't matter. When I was home, I knew what mattered – it was avoiding the KGB, and passing the messages to and from my parents. And in the Gulag, I knew what mattered. It was staying alive, and getting enough to eat so that you stayed healthy enough to do the work to get enough to eat. And avoiding the attention of the guards. Staying alive. But here . . . so many people, so concerned about so little . . . '

'Why are you telling me?'

'You I understand, Victor. You're like me. You know what matters.' He glanced again at Spencer. 'Don't listen to me. I'll go home and be a couch potato – eat a steak and baked potato and watch the big game. If I was in Moscow I'd be in a one-room apartment above a big family that ate cabbage soup every evening. I just don't know when I'm lucky.'

'You'll get used to it. It's the first forty years that are hard. Okay, we ought to go. The Ramada midday on Monday. You got enough for the cab? The meter'll have been running.'

'The Mayor can pay.'

Spencer smiled. 'Yeah, I believe he can afford it. How are things going for him?'

'He's still talking about being re-elected.'

'Think he will be?'

'I think he'll be lucky not to do time for corruption.'

'It's an old American tradition. You know what they say, we have the best politicians that money can buy.'

Yossif got up and went to the door. 'What do you think of this decor, Victor?'

'Oh, just standard late twentieth-century American sleaze. See you Monday.'

'Have a nice weekend.'

Yossif went downstairs, avoiding the eye of the clerk, and got into his taxi. They set off, making steady if slow progress through the traffic, heading for Brooklyn. He rented a bachelor apartment in the Brownstone belt. A black slum some years before, the wheel had turned and it was now a humming community of young, upwardly mobile people in which Yossif sought cover like a chameleon. He paid off the cab close by, obtaining a receipt, and walked to his apartment block.

The lift was waiting, an old-fashioned affair with trellis gates that one shut by hand. He got in, and took it to the third floor. There he went through the routine of un-locking his apartment, and let himself in. He turned into the miniscule kitchen, undecided whether to have a coffee or begin the weekend with a beer. The water was moaning in the pipes as his neighbours prepared themselves for the evening. They were party people, a couple who found it hard merely to be together and sought satisfaction in a crowd, so they would be getting ready for the evening. The noise of the shower intensified the feeling of Russian gloom that had been gathering about him. Such moods possessed him at regular intervals. When they built up to a peak he would spend the evening drinking a little too much before falling into bed, where he would dream – he would dream that he was a young boy again, running the clandestine messages for his parents through the streets and tenements of Moscow, and he would wake at the dead of night sobbing, with tears running down his cheeks. What was wrong was that he was crying because the dream was over.

He turned abruptly, deciding to shower, and change himself and go to Flanagan's, his favourite local bar, where there was cold Blue Ribbon on ice, home-made hamburgers and a waitress who thought that the young

Russian exile was cute. When he came out of the kitchen into the hall there was a man standing there. He was tall and well-built, with olive skin and dark, curly hair. Dressed in a blue coverall, he held a clipboard in one hand.

Hassan smiled, showing even white teeth. 'Good evening, Mr Petrovsky. We have your washing machine here.'

Yossif's mind wasted no time wondering about any mythical washing machine. He knew he was in danger and his lungs drew in breath to yell alarm; his body was turning away from Hassan to reach the door, but Ali was right behind him, stunning him expertly with a sap and felling him to the floor, where the two men quickly gagged him, slid a needle into his arm, folded him up like a chicken prepared for market and put him into a heavy cardboard box that had once contained a Sears washing machine. They had a workman's trolley with them, suitable for wheeling about heavy and bulky boxes, and they put the case on to this and took him out into the corridor.

'Good night, sir,' Hassan called into the empty apartment. 'Have a nice weekend.'

He closed the door and they went along the corridor to the elevator that was still waiting. Inside they shut the doors, pressed the old shiny brass button and slid out of sight. In the street they opened the loading door of a big Chevrolet pick-up with a camper attachment, and with practised ease lifted the box and trolley inside. They closed the door, and within twenty seconds were driving off down the street. They crossed the narrows of Richmond, picking up 278, and once in Elizabeth took the New Jersey Turnpike heading for the Catskills.

Yossif came conscious to the pain of his bruised head. He was lying on the floor of the pick-up bed and it was dark. A gag obstructed his mouth, tied between his jaws, and he was breathing through his nose. Through the tinted glass of small windows came the intermittent light of moving cars. He decided to try to sit up and gasped in pain as he found that he was tethered – neck, hands and feet – to ring-bolts set in the pick-up bed. He sagged back on to the hard metal, fighting down the panic that he could feel surging within him. He reminded himself that he had survived bad situations before, as he used to do in the camp. He would come through. He thought about trying to shout through the gag, but realized that the only people who might hear him were those whose attention he did not want to attract. He tried out the bonds as they went up the highway, but they were well tied and secure.

Gradually, the frequency of the car lights became less. After a period of some minutes of darkness the vehicle slowed and turned off the road, lurching and swaying as though on a rough track. Then it stopped, and the engine died. A man climbed into the back and untied him; the other was outside and together they dragged him out like a sack of vegetables. Blood rushed back into the starved tissues with agony. The air was fresh and cold, and there was a smell of pine trees. His feet would not obey his commands and they hauled him into the building with them dragging. Lights jarred his eyes as they pulled him down steps, their feet echoing. There was the thud of a heavy door being pushed back, a smell of something dead in the air, more pain as he was thrown into a hard and unyielding chair, pressure and discomfort as they pinned him with heavy strapping. One stood behind him, while the other went over to a wooden table by the wall where heavy, sharp, metallic objects chinked and clattered in his hands, and he was suddenly young again.

When you went to the dentist as a child, the surgery was cold with brown walls, the chair was large and hard with a big bright light above which they brought down to blast into your face, and the nurse stood behind the chair; her overall was greyish-white and when she bent over you to hold you down her breath smelled of stale vodka. Before she held you down the dentist sorted through his tools on the table by the wall and you peeped out of the

159

corner of your eye in terror to see the big syringe with its needle; then he came over and the big hands came down on your shoulders. They opened your mouth and the dentist would say 'This won't hurt' before he slid the sharp metal into your gum. But it always did, and would hurt more in a minute, because the dentist took the anaesthetic to use on patients who paid, and all he was injecting was water. The drill was black and driven by cord pulleys, and you could see them running; when the electricity wasn't at full strength, it ran even slower than usual. To make himself brave, the little boy who ran the streets with secret information for his parents would make believe that it was the KGB that was torturing him.

Now he was adult, and as Ali turned from the table and came towards him with wires trailing from one hand he knew that it had happened. Ali bent over one of his hands and he winced in anticipation as a heavy crocodile clip bit into his thumb. Ali straightened up and stood in front of him.

'Okay, *jahel*, tough guy. You are the man who makes contact with Victor Spencer. Victor Spencer, who is the man investigating the crash of the 747. Okay. We want to know one thing. Where is Spencer? Where can we find him. Now, we're going to encourage you. The machine there goes from level 0 to level 10. I'm going to start at 0 and work up to 5. Through your thumb. If when we stop you don't want to talk we'll start at 5 and work up to 10. Through your balls.'

He turned, and Yossif craned his neck to follow him.

'You don't have to. I can tell you now.'

'Not yet. Afterwards,' Ali said, and began to turn the dial.

Pain – terrible, pounding pain of a hammer smashing rhythmically into his thumb and up his arm – came crashing through the crocodile clip and he screamed in agony. Ali half-turned his head.

'It is only on two,' he said, and twisted the dial.

Blood was running down Yossif's head where he had banged it against the back of the chair, and from his lip that he had bitten through trying to compensate for the pain by the time Ali reached 5. Then it was gone, leaving only the pain of a thumb smashed by a hammer, not the actual blows themselves.

'Okay,' said Hassan from behind the chair. His voice was friendly. 'We don't want to hurt you if we don't have to. Where is Spencer?'

'I don't know,' Ivan gasped, blood spattering from his mouth in a fine spray. 'I'm meeting him on Monday.'

'But where is he *now*?' Ali asked patiently.

'I don't know. I'm meeting him in the Ramada on Jefferson in New Jersey. Midday on Monday.'

'But we want to know where he is now,' Ali repeated. 'You're not being co-operative.'

'I am. I *am*. I just don't know where he's gone,' Yossif said desperately.

'You need more persuasion,' Ali said finally. Yossif felt hard, competent fingers undo his trousers and he cringed as his private parts were exposed to the air. The crocodile clip crushed the soft skin of his scrotum and gripped a testicle. Ali turned the dial and chopping knives of agony rushed up his intestine. He jerked in the chair and was violently sick.

'Where's Spencer?' Hassan said softly.

'He's gone,' Yossif screamed.

'Gone where?' Hassan said again. There was a faint noise at the door, and he looked up. Ali turned round, bent over by the table, twisting in alarm.

'Gone here,' said Spencer.

SANTA MARTA

Miss Ellen Tyler soared over a powder-snow white hill and swooped with glee down into the valley. Mist whipped over the canopy for a second or two and then we burst back into the sunlight and she chuckled with pleasure.

'Stay out of the puffy white things,' I warned.

'You're such a spoilsport,' she complained. 'It's such fun.'

'Outside. Not inside.'

'What's the difference? The plane still flies.'

Miss Tyler was full of confidence. She liked to fly. In fact, like she'd said earlier, 'I can fly. I just have trouble with the take-offs and landings.' But now Ellen was a proud pilot. She had soloed. Done gone up all by herself, *and* come down. And now we were swooping like an eagle around the big cumulus cloud.

'Okay,' I said. 'Let's fly through the cloud from one side to the other. Just for fun.'

Her English reserve temporarily on holiday, Ellen cackled with pleasure and we hurtled into the marshmallow. It was white, and then it was grey. The turn coordinator that Ellen was not looking at hesitated first one way and then the other before deciding to lean up against the stop. The vertical speed indicator also took an interest in life and swung rapidly towards its own stop. Downwards. The altimeter started to unwind and the airspeed headed briskly through the yellow arc towards the red line. There was a noise out of a World War Two movie, rising in intensity.

We came out of the cloud near vertical in a spiral dive and Ellen, tramping frantically on the controls, managed

162

to get us out. We pulled five gees as she came back on the stick, snap rolled and went vertically upwards into the belly of the cloud where we stalled, and spun out of the bottom a few seconds later.

I helped her just a tad by coming back on the dual throttle and the Cub, being good-tempered by nature, fluttered its way out and Ellen got it back into level flight.

'You still got it,' I reminded her, not wanting her to lose all confidence. 'That's why you don't fly into the puffy white things.'

'But people *do*,' she protested, back on the ground. 'You do.'

'Sure,' I said. 'But you got to be trained. In the clouds you got no outside reference, so you have to scan your flight instruments to know what the airplane's doing. So now you've soloed, we're going to put you under a hood, make believe we're in a cloud.'

'I didn't know it was like that.'

'Flying into instrument conditions without an instrument rating kills private pilots all the time. They did a test one time, took some guys with forty hours' flight time but no hood or instrument training, flew them into real clouds with a safety pilot on board, and the best one lasted three minutes. 180 seconds. I like my students to have maybe ten hours' hood time before they go off for their ticket. It helps keep them alive afterwards.'

When we taxied in there was a van parked by the building, and Ric was supervising some men loading equipment into it. We parked the Super Cub by the tie-down, next to its new big brother.

We had a new airplane. No one was about to knock on the control tower door in Panama City and say 'Can we have our Convair back, please?' And the Convair hadn't been a good idea anyway, it was old and slow, and exactly the right sort of airplane to catch the Man's attention, as there was only one type of cargo valuable enough to bother running it.

I gave advice, and a bank account in Miami disgorged a little over one and one half million dollars and a couple

163

of one-way air tickets, and Hank and I flew up there to collect it. You didn't get a lot of aluminium for your money, but what you got was good. It was a Mitsubishi MU-2, very sleek, rounded high-wing turbine twin, designed in Japan and the basic airframe shipped to Texas where it was put together and outfitted. While you still retained propellers to do the hauling instead of a jet turbine to do the shoving, it was about the fastest around. A Lear Jet would go quite a lot faster, but a Lear didn't have the Starfighter-style gear that could land on a rough strip, and a Lear would go off the other end if you tried to put it into an 1,800-foot ag strip. The MU-2 could do it, and the AiResearch turbines were built; you could load it to the gills and get out of your 1,800-foot strip with the torque limiter off and the turbines delivering 110 per cent power. If that's what you wanted. It had 350,000 dollars' worth of radios that enabled you to navigate on or off airways . . . at fifty feet, if that was what you wanted. It had a navigation system that was smart enough to take you anywhere on earth that you wanted; you could use it to set up an approach to somewhere that didn't have a published approach. Like an 1,800-foot ag strip . . . if that was what you wanted.

When we got there there were two sitting side by side, identical in dark blue with a thin silver line painted down the side. The chief salesman joked that we could have any one we wanted, so long as it was dark blue. We took the one on the left. We flew it back to Colombia and it was a pleasure to use something so efficient, so new and reliable. The only area you had to work at was putting it on the ground. It wasn't sweet-natured, like the Super Cub, or even the Convair, which had been an amiable old thing when it was running properly. The MU-2 was something of a prima donna, as the salesman said, or a squirrelly bitch, as Hank did when on his first landing he didn't so much paint it on as *arrive*.

We got out of the Super Cub and Ric came over to me.

'We decided to store the mosquito-spraying equipment

164

in town. We won't use it for a while, we don't want it to deteriorate.'

'Sure,' I said. I had investigated in depth for Ric before we had flown out from Miami, and had bought a high-tech outfit you could fit to a sophisticated twin. You could spray at anything from 150 to 300 knots, and micro-chips monitored the rate of flow of the poison, which was ultra-low volume. It was in use to spray corridors in Africa against Tsetse fly. Used to spray great blocks of territory, with a fast twin you could cover vast tracts in a day. Hooked up to something like a modern navigation system, you could programme it and sit on your hands while it did the work for you. Ric had ordered ULV tanks of 1,200 gallons capacity; you could spray a swath from Colombia to Natchez with a load like that.

'You come to fly?' I asked.

'Yes,' he said.

Ric had taken to aviating, and once we had the MU-2 he insisted on being checked out in it, and had put in the time. He made quick progress, as always.

'I've got to put out cutworm bait,' I said. 'We can go up in the MU-2 after that, if you like.'

'I thought I'd come with you in the Thrush, if that's all right.'

I smiled. 'After my job, I can tell.'

Putting out cutworm bait was quite easy work. You did it about tree level, as it was granular, like fertilizer. At that altitude Ric in the rear cockpit was able to follow me through on the controls, see how you lined up for a swath, using the markers, kept your latitude, opened and shut the hopper gate to release and stop the flow of the chemical pellets. We made a number of trips, covering one hundred and ten of Ryan's acres, and towards the end I let Ric try his hand.

Cutworm does what its name suggests, it eats through the stems of seedlings like a tiny beaver, causing them to fall over and ruining your chances of bringing a smile to your bank manager's face that year. The only thing was, the marijuana was too big to be affected by it.

On the last pass, when I'd finished I came down low and ran my wheels through the light green of the little plants. I got back and parked it, and as I was tying it down with Billy Lee I went round to the gear that was stained green with the little plants stuck in and around the brake discs and pucks. I pulled some out and stood looking at them while Rick leaned against his van in the cool of the evening.

'It's just another crop, R.D.,' he said, and after a while I tossed the handful of crushed poppies away, and they lay on the ground among the dust left from the sacks of bait.

Ellen Tyler had been right – once you were in, you only got deeper. Ric knew I wouldn't protest, and once I'd tossed the poppies away he moved on to the next subject.

'Is the MU-2 ready to work?'

'Sure. You want to make another trip?'

'We will. But first I want you to go the other way. Take something out of America, not into it.'

'That's unusual. What's the cargo?'

'Just some people,' he said casually. 'A private charter.'

'Where from?'

'New Mexico.'

'Going to?'

'Nicaragua.'

THE CATSKILLS

There was an automatic pistol on the table and Ali had it in his hand as he turned. Spencer was in the dark outside, looking in, and as the gun came up he shot Ali twice in the head. The impact of the bullets blew him backwards, sliding across the table to fall with a crash on the floor where Charlie Harrel's wife had finally gone insane. Standing behind Yossif Hassan put his hands high in the air and Spencer came into the light.

'Stand over there and put your hands on the wall. Legs apart.'

Spencer searched him and removed a Ruger revolver. Spencer himself was carrying a nickel-plated .357 Smith & Wesson. His ears sang from the noise of the rounds going off in the enclosed space.

'On the floor in the corner. Kneel, put your forehead on the floor and your hands behind your back.'

Hassan obeyed and, watching him, Spencer released Yossif from the chair. Fumbling with his burned hand, he did up his trousers and watched as Spencer ordered Hassan into the chair in his place. He made him strap his legs and one hand down himself, then secured the second hand and checked the bindings. Hassan shuddered slightly, but otherwise his face remained impassive. Once it was done, Spencer turned to Yossif.

'Can you keep going for a while?'

Yossif nodded dumbly. In one corner of the room there was a sink and Spencer went over and filled a glass with water. In his state of shock, all Yossif could think of was that he looked out of place in his grey trousers, checked sports jacket, brogues and silver revolver, in a torture-chamber. Spencer came back with the glass; then, putting his revolver in a waist holster, he took out a strip of capsules in foil and, pressing them, gave two to Yossif, putting the debris back in his pocket.

'Take these. They'll stop the pain.'

'Thanks.' He swallowed and waited for some relief. 'Let's get the cops, Victor.'

'Soon,' Spencer said soothingly. 'Soon.'

He took a couple of kitchen chairs that were by the wall and put them near Hassan. 'Sit down a moment.'

'Victor, have you checked?' Yossif asked anxiously. 'Are there any more terrorists?'

Spencer sat down on one of the chairs and Yossif did the same.

'There are no more here,' Spencer said reassuringly. There was something strong in the capsules, Yossif could feel the pain and terror receding. He felt removed from the room, as though he could see the three of them from a great height – very small, through crystal-clear air.

'He's not a terrorist, though,' said Spencer. He seemed a long way off to Yossif, yet he could see every line in his face, could separate each black eyelash from its neighbour.

'He's a soldier. A soldier a long way from home, doing a terrifying job. He's fighting under cover. It's frightening. I know, I have done it too. You are always afraid of what will happen to you if you're caught. Undercover soldiers are always treated as spies, and any rules of warfare cease to exist for them. In primitive societies they are given to the women to be killed, ritualistically, over a period of time.'

Hassan sat in his own torture-chair, immobile, his face blank.

'Of course, this one is lucky, he's been caught in a democracy and we don't do that kind of thing. He can expect a fair trial, with a long sentence. He's been told that he won't have to serve his full time, that some deal will be made. All he has to do is to sit tight, eat three meals a day and watch television, and sooner or later the doors will open. He has to keep his mouth shut, of course. That's most important. It's a shame he got so unlucky.'

The room stank. The stench of fresh blood and excrement exuded from the corner where the corpse of Ali lay. Vomit splashed down Yossif's clothes, and his numbing flesh smelled of burning.

'I thought you said he was lucky,' he whispered.

'He can be either,' said Spencer. The flat black eyes stared at Hassan. 'He can be either, because he has been captured by me. I can do with him what I will. He's lucky because he can help me and, if he helps me, I can spirit him away. I can see to it that he lives the rest of his life in safety and comfort. He's unlucky because he may want to remain loyal to his masters. Perhaps he believes, like a real Shi'ia Muslim, that if he dies here in the land of Satan then one of the larger rooms in Paradise will be his.'

Something twitched deep in Hassan's eyes.

'The choice is his,' said Spencer. 'If he wants to go to Paradise I will arrange it as he sits in his chair, because he's never going to trial.'

The picture of the room was getting further and further away in the lens of Yossif's mind. Another figure came into view, a big man who came up behind his chair.

'Electrical burns, hand and scrotum,' said Spencer, many miles away, and the big man reached down gently and picked him up like his mother had done when he was a little boy. As he went up the stairs, he heard Hassan speak.

'Hallo, this is Mr Champe calling. I am asking you if you have any news to give me concerning the crash of the jumbo jet that killed my daughters.'

The accent was straight from Zambia. Yossif had heard the voice on the telephone. Then it changed and he spoke again.

'I am Hassan Sadeq, Dr Spencer. What do you want of me?'

*   *   *

169

When Spencer and Hassan came out of the house there was a van by the pick-up, and they had brought up Spencer's big old Ninety-Eight Oldsmobile. It was damp by the lake, and the breath of the three men waiting was frosting in the chill air. The tail-lights of the ambulance taking Yossif away flickered through the trees of the rough track that led to the house.

'Down in the cellar,' said Spencer. He turned to Hassan. 'Any more dead bodies we need to get rid of?'

'No. What will be done with Ali, that you shot?'

'We'll incinerate the body. That worry you?'

Hassan shrugged. 'The rest of us are mixed with Persian mud and Persian sand, so why should it bother me?'

They walked over to the Oldsmobile and the men went into the house.

'What about Charlie Harrel and his wife?'

'In the lake,' said Hassan. 'Well out. Will you leave them there?'

'Yes. Do you want to drive?'

'Do you trust me?'

'Of course. You and I are comrades now, aren't we? We need each other.'

'Of course.'

Hassan got into the driver's seat and they put on their lap-belts. 'I haven't seen a steering wheel this size since I came here to train,' he said.

'Was that with your friends? Those who are mixed with Persian mud and Persian sand?'

'We were the Immortals.' Hassan fired up the big V8 and shifted into gear. 'The Guards of the *Shahanshah*, the King of Kings.'

'Ah. I was there, you know, in the years of his downfall.'

'Yes, I know.'

'Who told you?'

'Hojat al-Islam al-Tasdeeq.'

'The Vicar of Islam, of the Divine Intention as revealed in the Qur'an. It's easier in Arabic, is it not? I knew the

170

Vicar when he was but an ambitious mullah. Is he your commander?'

'Yes, he is head of the Islamic Council of the Revolution. Are you familiar with it? It is somewhat confusing to know who wields power in Iran today, but you may say that the Council has some of the power of the old SAVAK inside the country, but also has agents and ambitions outside, both in *ja'er*, other – evil – countries of Islam, and in *Shaytan Bozorg*.'

'The Great Satan. Here, where you are. Turn right now, as if you were heading back to New York. So how is it that an officer, a member of the Shah's Imperial Guard, is now working as an undercover agent, a submarine in *Shaytan Bozorg*, for a man as dangerous as Hojat Tasdeeq?'

In the woods eyes shone as the animals stiffened, watching the lights of the car going down the road.

'After the Shah had left, and after the Grand Ayatollah had returned, there was a time of great confusion. Of the generals and senior officers, those who did not escape were shot. A time came when we were disarmed, and those of us who had been loyal to the Shah were imprisoned. Well might we all be there today but for the Iraqis. Fanatics fought to the last man at Khorramshahr, but the Iraqis took it anyway. You can clear a minefield by having child soldiers run through it, but to fight a real war you need real soldiers, and especially real officers. We, the officers of the Imperial Guard, were the ones who arrested the Iraqi advance. We who led our men and pushed them back into their own land.'

'The war is still going on,' said Spencer. 'Why are you not there, mixed with mud and sand like your fellow officers?'

'So many died . . . have you read about the First World War, in Europe?'

'Yes.'

'Sassoon, Graves, Sherriff . . . Our war has gone on longer than that, with like dead, but no one writes about it like that . . . I would be dead too, and Ali, but once

171

again we had something that was wanted. First they wanted us to fight their war, because we were professionals, and then later, Hojat Tasdeeq wanted us because we knew the United States, we had trained there, we could pass easily for two of the expatriate Iranians who fled with the coming of the Grand Ayatollah.'

'Why did he want you here?'

'To mind his plans, to do what we were told to do.'

'Why did he not think that once you had both escaped the war and come here, you might not merely vanish?'

'We have family. I a wife and two small children. Ali was from a large family. His parents, brothers and sisters are all living. It was explained to us very clearly what would happen to them if we did not remain totally loyal.'

They came out from the woods and began running along the edge of a lake. Pools of mist were forming in the inlets and they ran in and out of it, thin moisture showing up the shape of the lights.

'If you do what I want, I will extract your family from Iran. If you are successful you will never want for anything. You will live safe and with your family. It is also possible that you may die.'

'That is a professional risk for a soldier. If I die, you will look after my family?'

'Yes.'

'Will I return to Iran?'

'For a time. You will have help. Someone of power will aid you there.'

'Is Hojat Tasdeeq concerned in this?'

'In part. Why did Hojat Tasdeeq have Ade Jumbe crash the jumbo jet into Harlem?'

'I do not know. But the African Jumbe was special to Tasdeeq. He called him the Soldier of God.'

'What is the significance of that? Pull off up here, where these vehicles are.'

'I do not know. But you should understand, where Hojat Tasdeeq is concerned, you should know how much he hates the United States. There are those who vie for power who do not hate you so very much, who could co-exist, but he is not one. For him, *Shaytan Bozorg* is not simply a term of abuse, it is the very truth, this country is where *taghut* – the devil himself – resides. You are *mufsed fel-Ardh*, corrupters of the earth, *muharib an al-Allah*, evil ones who wage war on Allah. Hojat Tasdeeq is from an older age, the age of Mohammed himself. If it was possible to wipe the United States from the face of the earth he would do it without questioning.'

The Oldsmobile drew up behind the two cars parked in the pull-off by the lake, and Hassan dimmed the lights.

'I know,' Spencer said quietly. 'I know of Hojat Tasdeeq, he tried to kill me once.'

A man got out of the car in front of them and stood waiting.

'He didn't succeed.'

'You'll be going with the car there,' said Spencer. 'No, he didn't succeed. He killed my wife and son instead.'

There was quiet in the car, just a ticking as hot metal cooled in the chill air.

'You must tell me. Are there more of these Soldiers of God? More *Enteharis* like Ade Jumbe?'

'It was very urgent, once Tasdeeq knew that it was you who was investigating the Harlem disaster. We were told to kill you at all costs. Tasdeeq knows of your reputation as a hunter of men. I have to say that there must be more. Somewhere out there are others.'

173

NEW MEXICO

There were 400,000 dollars' worth of radios in the MU-2 and the computer in the Omega/VLF navigation system could fly an approach to a deserted, straight desert road marked only on a county map a thousand miles from its starting point in pitch darkness, provided only it was given both sets of co-ordinates and was allowed to update itself with a way-point or two on the journey. That night it did just that; we put it down on the blacktop in the middle of nowhere and when we rolled to a halt they were there, a little huddled group that ran forward and were quickly inside as Hank handled the door. I was forward on the power and we were on the ground for no more than a minute.

We headed south, and near the coast Ric came through the door.

'Mind if I sit in?' he asked Hank, and Hank said he didn't mind and went on back with the passengers.

'I'm going to let it overfly the Jamestown vortac,' I said, pointing at the Omega/VLF. 'Give it an absolute fix, it won't get any over the water.'

Ric sat in the ivory leather seat and watched as the VOR needles flicked left, right, and the lights of the coastline vanished behind the windshield to be replaced by black night. We went over the ocean at 200 feet and 280 knots. It was a calm night, otherwise we'd have been jarring our fillings.

'How does it work?' he asked.

'Runs on P.F.M.' I said.

'*What* is that?'

'Pure Fucking Magic. No, you've got two nav. systems

backing each other. The VLF uses the Navy communications stations, very low-frequency, high-power stations they can use to talk to the subs when they're under water. The Omega uses a different system; I saw a drawing of it once, it looks like a women's knitting pattern. Compares radio waves, basically.'

'And from here it can find a coastal strip on the Mosquito Coast in pitch darkness.'

'Same as it found the desert road back there.'

Ric was quiet for a while, just sitting and looking.

'I've got a proposition for you,' he said. 'You don't just fly, you know how to fix the machinery, make it do things the manufactuer didn't intend. I want to be able to take an aircraft like this, put a payload in it and leave it. At a certain, pre-programmed time, I want it to start up on its own, taxi to the runway, take off and fly – say to one of the strips we've used before, and when it gets there, land. On its own. Can you make it do that?'

'Nobody in it?'

'No.'

'Have to modify it some,' I said, deadpan. 'The FAA's going to ask us for a Supplementary Type Certificate.'

Ric stared at me and I saw a look of suppressed fury cross his face.

'Joke,' I said, and he relaxed.

'Oh, of course.'

I sighed inwardly. Ric had had a sense of humour once, before he got crazy.

'I could do that,' I told him. 'Your problem will be not getting it to take off and fly to the destination but having it land. It will *do* it, Cat III airliners do it regularly, but they do it at airports with the right equipment. We would need the landing site equipped.'

'Let's split it up,' he said. 'Two sections, the taking-off and flying there, and the landing. I'll pay you a hundred thousand for each section. Start with the first, taking-off and navigating.'

'Okay,' I said. 'Be useful, I guess,' I ventured. 'Then you could be somewhere else when the trip was made.'

175

'Yes.' Something flickered behind the intense eyes and I realized that Ric was trying to remember how to make a joke.

'*Vorsprung durch technik,*' he said.

'How's that?'

'That's what the Germans say: "Forward with technology".'

At the appointed time the coastline of Nicaragua came up on the radar.

'Here we go,' said Ric. He spoke a few words into the microphone as the MU-2 cranked itself around and lined up. We were descending into a cypress swamp at one hundred and forty knots with the gear out and the lights went on, outlining the strip. I uncoupled the autopilot and flew it the rest of the way by hand. It was the first time I had touched the controls since leaving the desert road.

It was a long dirt strip, perfectly adequate. As we rolled to a halt Ric was unbuckling. Our instructions were to turn around and go straight back out. Twenty years, and nothing had changed except the location. Then Laos, now Nicaragua.

I was looking out of the side of the windshield as they left and I saw the passengers properly for the first time. With Ric were three tough South American men, soldiers with pistols, and then – so very out of place – a thin, bespectacled man in a suit and two little children, a boy of about eight and a little girl about five. Father and children were frightened, and were hustled along by the soldiers. The little girl had braces on her teeth and was crying.

'Okay, buddy,' said Hank briskly, dropping himself into the right-hand seat vacated by Ric. 'Let's put the pedal to the metal.'

We left the strip as fast as we had come in and accelerated away over the ocean.

'Your buddy's smart,' Hank said, staring straight ahead. 'Makes sense for a man in his business to hide away there. Uncle Sam can look all he wants, in Nicaragua.'

'Did we just kidnap some people, Hank?' I asked slowly.

Hank turned to look at me, as though I was being very naive.

'He ain't making us rich men to haul grits, is he? And why did he come to you in the first place? Didn't he know you'd done worse, in your time?'

177

THE CATSKILLS

Dew was forming on the grey Ford, and mist pooling around the rocks on the edge of the lake. The lights of the car taking Hassan away flared briefly as it approached the road, and then it purred away and Spencer opened the passenger door of the Ford. As he got in the courtesy light illuminated the features of the man at the wheel. He was a white man, Spencer's age, and despite the hour was clean-shaven and dressed in a grey suit. When Spencer had been in Iran he had been a departmental head of intelligence with the CIA. Now he worked at the White House. Officially, his responsibility was security, but he had the right of direct access to the President.

'His name's Hassan Sadeq. One of the Shah's Guards officers. Recycled as one of Hojat Tasdeeq's submarines. He's going to do just fine.'

'You said there'd be one out there.' The driver's name was O'Neill, he spoke with a Chicago accent little blunted by his many sojourns in foreign parts.

'It was only a question of finding him. I'll spend some time with him during the next few weeks. We want to make sure he's ours before we send him out there. Okay. Tasdeeq was responsible for the 747 at Harlem. You said you had something on whatever happened to Ade Jumbe.'

'Right. Your Ade Jumbe had a Judas. One James "Iron Man" Njoya.'

'Didn't he lead that failed *coup* a few months afterwards?'

'That's him. Ade Jumbe's right-hand man. No fool, very ambitious, but not ultimately bright enough to

178

realize that he should have settled for the number two slot instead of bucking for boss. He didn't have all the reins firmly enough in his grasp and the *coup* came apart. The usual bloodshed and massacre of the lesser folk, while "Iron Man" himself had a Learjet waiting. He left in it, taking the Lozi's bankroll with him.'

'A *coup* isn't easy at the best of times. Something as slight as a ten-minute delay in the appearance of fighter-bombers, or the Minister of the Interior's car breaking down, can screw you up. Blending the ingredients takes a master-chef – try taking over half-way through and you'll wind up eating out of a tin. Is that what happened to "Iron Man"? I take it that had he succeeded he would now be "Great Father of His Peoples" or some improved epithet.'

'Sure. Well, "Iron Man's" plain Mr Njoya now. Lives in a fortified mansion in California. We were able to tap his balls a little. We pointed out that it would not be hard to have him shipped home in an airfreight crate, if we chose.'

'Yeah. And what would be waiting for him back home?'

'Depends who we gave him to. The Lozis would dispense with a trial. They'd assemble those of the tribe who were around that day and string him up by his feet over an ant-hill, smeared with honey. The State Department's already been approached by the Zambian government, demanding that "the traitor Njoya be returned to answer for his crimes".'

'Ouch.'

'Yeah. They'd give him a trial and stand him up against a post for firing practice on the next public holiday.'

'They use the Nigerian method there?'

'Starting at the feet and working up? Yeah. One shot a minute. Takes a while. Anyway, he's enjoying the good life in California. Steak, liquor, videos and white women.'

'Loose shoes, too.'

O'Neill grunted in amusement. 'Yeah. Anyway, he was ready to talk to us. He was approached to sell Ade Jumbe. The man was guarded, right.'

'By his buddy, "Iron Man".'

'That's it. Arrangements had to be made to detach him from his security and, furthermore, make it look as though nothing had happened. Only his right-hand man was in a position to ensure that.'

'He was paid?'

'Handsomely. And got a crack at absolute power himself. Now, the details of it all don't matter. It was done, those buying took delivery and those selling provided the goods and got paid. What's *interesting* is who bought.'

'Iranians?'

'Yes and no. We are sure that that's where Jumbe ended up, but the arrangements themselves were handled by an Arab who went by the name of Yusuf Ghesuda. Now, the point about all this is that when "Iron Man" was a young man, young ambitious Africans coloured by the experience of colonial rule took the trip to Patrice Lumumba to get educated Soviet-style.'

' "Iron Man" went to the Soviet Union?'

'Right. He was there for three years, getting a good grounding in subversion and Communism. It doesn't seem to have done him much good, or had any lasting effect, but one thing "Iron Man" is familiar with is Russians.'

'And?'

'He said that Yusuf Ghesuda looked like an Arab, talked like an Arab and behaved like one. But he, "Iron Man", says he was a Russian. Or rather, someone from the Soviet Union who'd been educated as a Russian. From Uzbek, or Turkmen maybe.'

A solitary car swished softly past in the night, and its lights glowed up the road.

'The Russians. How strange, that they should be involved . . . I'll be seeing Borodin soon, in Paris. I'll put it to him.'

'Okay. Is there anything you're going to need?'

'Only the money, for Hassan. In Geneva.'

'I'll do it.'

There was to be nothing in writing, ever. No tapes, no documents, no shredding machines. No Watergate, no Contragate, no parade of witnesses through Congress. President Thomas met Spencer only once, in secrecy so total that O'Neill was the only other man living who knew of it. He turned to Spencer.

'Does Hassan think that there are more of these Soldiers of God out there?'

'He does.'

'So do we,' O'Neill said sombrely. 'Last Wednesday a man called Davidson and his two small children went missing. He was divorced from his wife, who had custody of the children, and she used to take it out on him by being difficult about visiting rights. She moved from Ohio to New Mexico after the divorce, and had a habit of taking the children elsewhere when he was supposed to be allowed to see them. Anyhow, the children and Mr Davidson have vanished and Mrs Davidson that was is in the morgue with her throat slashed. The police are looking for her husband with a murder warrant.'

'But you're not?'

'Davidson was a scientist working at Fort Detrick. He was a leading light in the Brimstone gas project.'

'What's Brimstone?'

'Son of VX. Nerve gas. It's really nasty stuff. Designed to be put out through ultra-low-volume equipment as microscopic droplets. One drop inhaled or on the skin is enough to cause death.'

A car went by and illuminated their faces for a second.

'We hope Davidson did come unwrapped and take out his former wife. We hope he is on the run somewhere. We just hope to hell he isn't the captive of one of these Soldiers of God. Find them, Victor. We may be short on time.'

SANTA MARTA

There was dew on the MU-2 as I untied it in the new light. The long, drooping wings rocked and little rivulets ran down the windshield and along the fuselage, collecting water as they went and exposing the shiny polished surfaces underneath. A Mercedes came driving up the runway from the town and parked by the hangar. Ric got out and walked over, his shoes making crisp noises in the still air.

'You ready?' I asked, and we got in, shutting the door behind us. The seats were cold and shiny, the chill penetrated my shirt. I sat and watched the dials, all at rest except for the clock which ticked steadily.

At 07:00 there was a small, solid thud as a relay closed, and a red light glowed as the Master switch denoted that it was on. A fuel pump whined and the cockpit trembled very slightly as the starboard propeller began to move. The turbine spun up and there was a muffled bang as the igniter lit the fuel. The throttle advanced, and the turbine spun up to 95 per cent power and then back. The process was repeated for the port engine. The brakes came off and the MU-2 rolled off the ramp and on to the runway as we sat on our hands and watched. At the end of the runway the Omega/VLF instructed the autopilot to turn around. We waited while the autopilot cycled the props to put hot oil through them, then the throttles moved in front of us and we accelerated down the runway.

'It's looking at a small radio transmitter at the far end, on the centreline,' I said. 'Once we're over it, it will unhook and enter its programmed flight-path.'

The MU-2 rotated rather abruptly, but we were off the

ground. The gear came up and we flew dead straight down the runway, climbing at 1,500 feet per minute. As we came over the numbers the Omega/VLF unhooked and the MU-2 entered a climbing turn on to course. At 10,000 feet it levelled off, and the throttles and props moved themselves to cruise settings.

'It'll go to Miami if you want.'

'It'll do,' said Ric. He motioned with his hand. 'Let's go back.'

I unhooked the autopilot, and sent the twin turning back for the base. It was the first time either of us had touched the controls.

'It takes about a week's work to set up,' I told him. 'I've put it all down on paper, as you asked. It takes about 20,000 bucks' worth of parts.'

'I want you to order three more sets,' Ric said. 'Have them brought here.'

'There's still the problem of getting it to land. I can have it land itself anywhere with a precision approach, hooking it up to the radar altimeter, but I don't think that's the idea.'

'We'll tackle that later,' Ric said. He was relaxed for once, his voice almost dreamy. 'Order the parts. Do it today.'

'Okay.'

I brought the MU-2 on a curving approach on to final. The thought flicked through my mind that for some reason Ric wasn't interested in the automatic MU-2 being able to land itself. I put down the gear and allowed the thought to vanish. There could be no point at all in loading up a bunch of executive twins and having them blast off into the sky like a lot of flying-bombs, unable to land themselves. The idea was foolish.

We came over the numbers and the tyres kissed the tarmac. The air was like silk.

NEW YORK

The lights of the cars rippled like white fire coming up the blacktop, and the tyres of the Ninety-Eight hissed through the water filming across the road. The wipers clacked rhythmically and the beads of rain on the edges of the windshield slowly became garish as the dark changed to neon. Spencer pulled off on to the lot to park among the trucks and pick-ups and other second- and third-hand vehicles, and the big Oldsmobile halted like a regular.

'There used to be a joint like this on the road out of town where I was raised,' Spencer said. 'Served cold longnecks, chicken fried steak, sawmill gravy and biscuits. I shouldn't think we'll get that here. The Yankees can't cook. People who wanted to leave used to go out to the bar and hitch a ride out with one of the truckers. That's what I did when I went off to college.'

Yossif Petrovsky grunted. 'How'd they get back? Same way?'

'Nobody came back. You wanted to leave, not come back. Sorry we keep meeting in these places. Hassan's friends can still stop this thing cold by simply getting rid of me.'

'You could always go back to teaching modern political history, Victor.'

Spencer smiled. 'Hardly.'

With the wipers off, the lurid lighting flickered and blurred through the sliding rain on the windshield.

'You must be KGB, Victor.'

'How's that now?'

'Whoever KGB is in this country. Who is it? Who do

184

you work for? Too much power . . . people vanish, people get tortured, people get killed, and no one hears a thing . . . all because of Dr Victor Spencer. The Mayor thought that he was using you, he didn't know it was the other way about.'

'He was encouraged to think that way . . . I'm sorry that you got hurt, Yossif. I never thought that they would go to work on you so fast.'

'Why?'

'It's customary to soften the person up psychologically first.'

'It worked just fine on me, Victor. I'd have sold them my granny the moment they put that thing on my balls, let alone when they turned on the current.'

'Sorry. We had to wait until they had got you out of the vehicle.'

'KGB, as I said.'

'Let's go and have a beer, and something to eat.'

'Being with you has caused me to become connected to the output of the local electricity supply company and to wear skin from my thigh over my balls. I'm not sure I want to go anywhere with you.'

'Maybe I can give you what you want.'

'What can I want? I'm here, in the home of the brave and land of the free. I'm here already.'

Spencer grinned amiably in the garish, filtered light.

'Come on, let's get a beer.'

They went through the rain into the bar. Around the walls were wooden booths and on the floor round tables and chairs. There was a bar and a stage for performers. On it an ageing Elvis Presley look-alike was finishing a weary medley of the singer's hit songs. They took a booth and ordered a pitcher of Blue Ribbon, with home-made hamburgers and french fries.

'Well, all right,' said the singer, sweating under the light. 'You got some requests now?'

Two tough-looking bottle-blonde women were sitting at a table drinking margharitas, and one called out, 'Yeah. Get off the damn stage.'

The beer came, together with frosted glasses, brought by a waitress not unlike the women. The Presley impersonator shuffled off and was replaced by a vigorous young man who launched into a Huey Lewis number which seemed to please the audience better.

'What were you doing in 1969, Yossif?'

'Going to school. Carrying messages for my parents. They taught Hebrew and Jewish history, you know. It wasn't safe to talk on the telephone, but a young boy would not be suspected.'

'That's right. I was at the war. Not the big one that everyone knew about in Vietnam, but a little one that almost no one knew about up in the Shan Hills and the Meo highlands. It was called the Golden Triangle and it was filled with the remnants of the Kuomintang: assorted gangsters of many races, various warlords, generals and opium barons – often one and the same man – Pathet Lao, Meo and North Vietnamese armies, and more opium than anywhere else in the world.'

The hamburgers and french fries came. The fries were hand-made and large, and Spencer shook salt over them and put hot chili sauce in his bun. Two men in cowboy boots and jeans went over to the table where the two tough girls were, they got up and the four began dancing as the band launched into a twenty-year-old T. Rex number.

'Also, in this war that is now a small footnote in the history books, I met a man who read history. We got on very well, as you can imagine. I arranged to get him all the books he wanted, and he was very grateful. We got on so well that when I left we made a very unusual agreement; we decided to stay in touch.'

'What's so strange about that?' Yossif said through a mouthful of bun, lettuce and mayonnaise.

'His name was Yuly Borodin, and he was my opposite number. He was a Captain in the KGB. So you see why he was grateful to get the history books.'

Petrovsky nodded. 'Sure. He wouldn't have got them along Nevsky Prospekt, that's certain.'

'Access to any hard historical information is difficult inside, isn't it? Wasn't that what your father found? Didn't he want to write a history of the Russian Jewish people? Simon Dubnov's been dead since 1941, it's time for a new work. Your father's history had to be oral – which he passed on to you.'

'Telegram Sam' crashed to a close, the band went off to get a drink from the bar and there was silence for a few seconds before someone put the Pet Shop Boys on the jukebox. Spencer ordered another pitcher of Blue Ribbon.

'Yuly was from Azerbaijan. His family have been in politics there for years. Have you ever been there?'

'It's one of the republics in the south, isn't it? Borders with Iran. I don't know it.'

'It used to be a part of the Tsarist empire. After 1917 the Azerbaijanis declared themselves an independent nation, but had their ideas changed by Trotsky's Red Army. There's still a lot of nationalist feeling there. They have a sizeable Shi'ite Muslim population who don't relate to the Greater Russians particularly well. Yuly is Russian, but they make up only a small part of the population. Anyhow, we were sitting on top of this mountain near Burma waiting for the Long Pot opium harvest, and for Vang Pao to get his troops organized, and Yuly said he thought that history was repeating itself. He said that the situation between the USA and the Soviet Union had many similarities to the revolutionary and Napoleonic wars between Britain and her allies, and the France of Napoleon. In effect, the wars saw the culmination of the long struggle between Britain and France for mastery of the world. The two sides were different – the whale and the elephant – and the struggle took place over a vast arena. The French had tremendous military strength – it took a combination of the British, Austria, Prussia and Russia to defeat them – but it was the British who won. They won because of the strength of their economy, their sophisticated financial system, their overseas markets and their navy, which was by far the best in the world. They also won because of the growth of nationalist sentiment in the lands which the French occupied. As the saying went, a European was someone whose country had been occupied by foreign – French – troops. The times were against the construction of a pan-European power such as Napoleon had in mind.

'At the time, when Yuly put this forward, I thought he was right. The USA had all the advantages the British had, and the Soviet Union the disadvantage of its system of government – also the fact that it was not the monolithic, united entity its leaders would have you believe, but instead the world's last great empire; and history has been unkind to great empires, not least the history of the twentieth century. I saw no reason why we could not put the screws to the Soviet Union and, once she was defeated, go on into the kind of glorious century the British enjoyed up to 1914.'

Spencer poured more beer into their tall glasses. The Pet Shop Boys sang about rent.

'I won't say it's turned out entirely like that. We've got our problems with Japan, and there's China on the horizon, but by and large it looks good. Except that the Soviets are trying to get their act together. And they might succeed. They still have all the resources, human and otherwise. I don't think it's in our interests for the Soviet Union and their clever new Peter the Great to do it. I'd like them to stay ossified and antique, like a latter-day Habsburg Empire, with the subject races slowly pulling the whole affair apart at the seams.'

Spencer paused to drink some beer.

'Have you ever read *The Sword in the Stone*, Yossif?'

'I don't think so.'

'Lovely book, a fairy tale about the early life of King Arthur, who as a young boy – known as the Wart – is educated by the wise wizard, Merlyn. While out in the woods with his friend Kay he is captured by an evil witch, Madame Mim, who plans to eat the two boys. In the nick of time, Merlyn arrives and he and Madame Mim engage in a duel to the death. Rather like the game with your fingers where you play scissors, paper, stone, the idea was for one of them to turn themselves into some kind of animal, vegetable or mineral which would destroy whatever animal, vegetable or mineral was selected by their opponent. Merlyn and Madame Mim each turned themselves into a variety of ferocious beasts – dragons, wildcats, dogs, snakes, falcons – and Merlyn appears to be losing when his elephant is trumped by a giant aullay – an enormous mythological beast. He vanishes and appears to have conceded defeat that way when the aullay gets hiccoughs, turns red, swells, begins whooping, comes out in spots, staggers and dies. Merlyn has turned himself into the microbes of hiccoughs, scarlet fever, mumps, whooping-cough, measles and heat-stroke, from the effects of which the witch Madame Mim expires.'

'Are you Merlyn, Victor?'

'I hope so.'

'And you plan to give the Soviet Union a fatal disease?'

'Yes.'

'When?'

'Very soon. President Thomas only has three years to go. We won't get another like him.'

'I said you were KGB. What do I get if I am your wizard's assistant?'

'I thought you could answer that.'

'I get to go home?'

'Yes. In the end. You're not a refusnik, you're in exile. You want to go home.'

'What do I have to do?'

'Yuly Borodin is now a colonel in the KGB. I want you to join him.'

The band were tipping back their drinks and trooping on to the stage.

'What happens if we lose, Victor?'

Spencer motioned to the waitress for the bill.

'You and I are all right. We already speak Russian.'

'Sure. We'll understand the fire orders when they put us up against the wall. Why would they win?'

189

'Maybe they thought of it first,' said Spencer. 'Maybe we're the ones who'll get the disease.'

The singer sent a blast of noise from his guitar through his loudspeakers. The two tough girls had joined the men in cowboy boots at their table.

'Well, *all right*,' bawled the singer. 'Now for all you rednecks out there, a song that puts the cunt back into country music. Onetwothree – '

The tough girls yelled with enthusiasm and the waitress brought more margaritas.

SANTA MARTA

We flew back to Nicaragua, landing at the dirt strip on the Mosquito Coast. Ric's three Hispanics were there waiting. We loaded up a number of heavy plastic-sealed packages, and also some very weighty 5-gallon cans of the type the farmers brought along at spray time, with the poison in. I made these very secure, because for sure we didn't need a 5-gallon can coming through the side of the MU-2 when we hit turbulence. Then we took off again bound for our destination – a small, disused strip up in the mountains, near Spartanburg, North Carolina.

Not long after take-off I began to feel nauseous. It just wouldn't go away, so I let Hank fly. He was fine. We landed in North Carolina at two in the morning. Two men in a pick-up and a tanker were waiting for us, we offloaded the dope and the drums while we were refuelled and were ready to turn around in minutes. Nobody said much. We barrelled out of the strip in a hurry and returned on our path. My nausea had got worse, not better, so I told Hank, gave command to him, went into the back and lay down, where I passed out.

I woke up briefly and it was dark, dark. Lying there I couldn't see anything – no light from the windows, or from the cockpit. I didn't have the strength to get up. I lay there, and very soon went back under.

When I woke up again, bright sunlight was streaming in through the windows. I got up with a mouth like owl shit and went through to the cockpit. We were over the ocean, an hour out from Colombia. I had slept through everything. It was most odd. I felt pretty tired and stayed in bed most of the day once we landed. I figured it had probably been something I ate before the flight, or maybe the water, and I made a mental note to be more careful and to boil everything.

Otherwise the trip had run perfectly. Ric let us know that later on he would want us to make three more trips, to Louisiana, New Mexico and California.

In a hospital in a small town in Georgia a woman died. In Atlanta a nineteen-year-old black girl went missing. Billy Lee and I flew home, one of us to bury the woman he'd married and the other to find his daughter.

WAYCROSS, GEORGIA

Billy Lee went to Atlanta and I went to church. It was a quiet morning funeral which Claire would have hated – but then, it wasn't as though she had many friends in the town. When we'd planted her and the black men in dungarees were shovelling the dirt in the hole, I went back to the Forestry strip in the pick-up and made my way, carrying tools, through the heavy undergrowth until I came to the wreck of the Thrush by the power line. You could see where the fire had razed the area, but already small creeping plants and little shrubs and the beginnings of saplings were at work; in a couple of years you'd never be able to find the wreck. It was in truly terrible shape – there was nothing on it at all that was salvageable – and it took a long time, and a lot of heaving, cutting and use of the cold chisel before I got the prop and governor off. When I did, I found what I had been looking for. I had been very slow, but finally I had got to put two and two together to make a number other than three or five.

That evening, I went to visit John G. Darlby III.

He wasn't in. He was down at the bank working out new ways to fuck people, so I picked the lock on the door and let myself in. It was a real handsome house, had antique furniture and silver and maids, I guess, and shit like that. You could put a beautiful person in there; she wouldn't mind at all.

He came back in the end. I was still sitting in the dark in a handsome old armed wooden chair, real solid walnut, and he put on the lights and headed for his liquor cabinet – done worked out a new way to cheat niggers and white trash out of their money. He'd poured himself a drink, and had himself a shot of Mr Daniels No. 7 in his hand before he turned and saw me.

'Evening, John G.'

'What're you doing here, Marvin?' he asked slowly.

'We didn't see you at the funeral, John. We was wondering where you was.'

'Your trashy wife died,' he sneered.

'That's right. My trashy wife died.'

He put down his cut-glass tumbler on a little round table which probably cost more'n a Thrush's main gear and walked to the door.

'I'll oblige you to leave. Before I call the law.'

He opened the door and I sat where I was and Billy Lee came in and shut the door behind him.

'D'you know Billy Lee, John G.? Billy Lee's my partner in the business. He's also an ex-football player and an ex-Marine sergeant, which just naturally makes him one mean and ornery niggah. He also hates rich fat corrupt folks like you, so that if'n we decide to tear your nuts off I'm gone let him be the one to do it. Bring the president of the bank over here, Billy Lee.'

'This way, mothahfockah.'

I got out of the good strong wood chair and we put John G. Darlby III in it, and tied his arms and legs and body to it so's he wouldn't move around too much when we did it to him – and by the time we were through getting him restrained his attitude had changed somewhat.

'R.D.,' he pleaded. 'Sir. If this is about your wife, I'm sorry, but surely, she ain't worth it? You know, like I know, she was worthless, she was a tramp, you – '

Billy Lee gagged the man and I bent down to talk with him.

'John G.' I said softly. 'You've been a bad man. Everyone in town knows you're a grasping son of a bitch who'd sell his own granny for another niggah shack to rent out, but ain't many know that you'd kill. Yes, that's right. Now, let me explain. Billy Lee here was in the Marine Corps. I was in the Air Force. And after that I

194

went to work for Air America, which was the CIA's own air force. I could already do all kinds of clever things with airplanes, and to make me even more smart they taught me some things to do *to* airplanes. How to sabotage them so's no one would know. Everything from the simple rubber band around a grenade with the pin pulled out in your fuel tank to some real sophisticated devices.

'Now, you may recall that earlier this year I had an accident after take-off in my Thrush. There's an element of risk in my business, so after it was over and I survived I put it down to the Lord calling out my number in that day's lottery. For a while.

'Then I got to thinking about it. I'm a bit slow, but I get there in the end. The governor quit *and* the pin sheared in the dump handle. That's not happenstance. I went back this afternoon and got a good look at the wreck, and you won't believe what I found. Well, you will of course, you will, John G., because you arranged to have it put there. One of those sophisticated devices I was talking about? Yes, sir.

'Now, I started putting things together and there was more. I was set up putting out 2,4,5-T, got a heavy fine. That was you. My wife was taken very ill. Cancer. I paid the bills, as I guess you knew I would, but the young doctor told me something interesting. He said that Claire had swallowed something carcinogenic. You know what that means? Something real toxic, gave her cancer. That was you too, John G.'

I sat back on my haunches and looked at him, white and sweating, and his eyes bugging out of his head. I continued.

'And for what? Just to get my land, so that the shopping mall would be all yours. Ain't that something?'

I reached round the back of my waistband and pulled out the Colt. Darlby began making mewing sounds through the gag.

'Now. Ain't any good me trying to prove any of this. We're holding the trial right now. This Colt auto here comes from Air America too. It's a good weapon. It's

195

untraceable. I'm going to blow your head off with it and ain't no one going to know who did it.'

I checked the action on the Colt and Darlby was threshing about in the chair. There was suddenly a terrible smell as he shit himself, and the piss ran through his pants over the chair. I cocked the pistol and squeezed the grips to take off the safety and held it up to his temple, and a huge black hand came around mine and pushed the gun up.

'Ain't no need, R.D.,' Billy Lee said. 'He didn't do it. He ain't a man. You got to be a man to do those things. A bad one, shore, but a man. He ain't. Look at him, sitting there in his own shit, terrified out of his mind. He ain't got the balls for that. All he good for is sucking on the blood of the poor folk.'

I slowly got up from my crouch and put the safety back on.

'Yeah. Yeah, you're right, Billy Lee. I didn't see that.'

'He ain't good for anything now, R.D. He afraid for the rest of his life. He knows his money don't buy protection now.'

We went out, leaving Darlby for the maid to find in the morning. I had the pick-up parked down the way, we got in and rumbled off along the road.

'Did you find Maybelline?' I asked.

'Yeah, I found her,' he said flatly. 'I checked around, places where she was known, but I didn't find her, R.D. In the end I went to the po-lice. Talk to a Sergeant there, man called O'Steen. We didn't like each other. I say I'm looking for my daughter, Maybelline Williams, and he calls the morgue. I say hold on, mothahfockah, what you looking among the dead folk for? He says you a country boy, I kin see that. Well, when we in the big city and someone missing, we call the morgue.'

There was silence for a few minutes, just the sound of Rosanne Cash on the radio. Then he spoke again.

'Mothahfockah was right, R.D. Ah went down the morgue and she lying there in a box in the wall. She dead. Found in a motel. She inhaled her own sick. My little girl.

She was on heroin, R.D. My little girl was a junkie, working as a whore to keep her habit.'

A car came by the other way and lit us up in the can with its lights. I looked across and the tears were streaming down the big black face.

NEW JERSEY

The sun was in Yossif Petrovsky's eyes. It shone straight and low down the street, between the buildings, to strike him in the face. Someone should have considered that, he thought – and the parade could have taken place later, or down a different road. But no chance of that, since this was the Presidential Avenue. He should have put on his dark glasses before he got out of the car, but no chance of that either, because they were in his jacket pocket and he was wearing a light raincoat. If he undid it people were sure to see the Ingram MAC 10 sub-machine gun gripped in his right fist. And there were many people to see. They lined the boulevard, waving their flags, their cheering breaking over him like a torrent falling down a mountain. The man was behind him and his eyes searched constantly along the people pressed against the barrier as he walked towards the monument.

Yossif Petrovsky paid much attention to what he was doing, because the man was behind him and it was his job, if necessary, to die instead of the man, to take the man's place on the cold slab in the morgue by accepting the bullet meant for him, by falling on the grenade meant to shatter the man's body, and Yossif Petrovsky liked living too much. What he wanted to do was make the *assassin* take that cold place reserved in the morgue. He gripped the Ingram through the pocketless pocket of the raincoat, the safety off but his forefinger straight on the outside of the receiver as he had been trained to do.

The avenue bifurcated around the statue of the Liberator, and his work-load doubled as he had to check both the people on his left and those who ringed the

198

monument. Straight ahead, twenty yards away, a young woman held a baby in a shawl in her left arm and waved a flag vigorously with her right. A schoolboy applauded patriotically. To his left, coming up, a big, powerful black man stood waiting; his face was a mask of stone.

The woman smiled excitedly, ignoring the baby which screamed and struggled in her arms. The schoolboy stood stiff as the man approached. The big black reached one gigantic paw inside his combat jacket and Yossif's weapon began to track. The hand emerged with a flag, looking like a toy in the great fist, and the granite face cracked with pleasure.

'Long live the Revolution!' he bellowed, and Yossif heard him over the roar of the crowd.

The woman's right hand moved down to her baby, but she wasn't looking at it. Its face was purple as it screamed. As the man approached, her hand came smoothly out of the shawl. The schoolboy pulled his satchel around, slipping the strap over his head.

The baby dropped downwards as the woman brought the gun out from the shawl, her face contorted with hatred. Bringing the Ingram gun up to position, Yossif shot her three times, in the chest, throat, and head, and she vanished backwards into the crowd. The schoolboy screamed, the satchel strap taut in his hand, tracking across. Yossif shot him, shattering his arm, shoulder and head. The satchel fell to the ground and there was suddenly a silent, sweeping explosion that brushed away the figures by the monument.

Yossif stood in the street and the noise died away. The people froze, and vanished. The lights of the simulator came on, and in the silence he could hear only the harsh rasp of his breath. A door opened and his instructor came out of the control booth; his name was Pasquale, he looked as though he had been fashioned from a great block of oak and then brought to life. He came up to Yossif and put one hand on his shoulder.

'Well done!' He looked into his eyes, deep black ones questioning the bright blue. 'It's scary as hell, isn't it? I

199

still can do a walk-through and believe I'm really there.'

Yossif was aware of the sweat beading his lip and the heat rising around his neck. He nodded, not trusting himself to speak.

'CGHS,' Pasquale said proudly. 'Computer Generated Holographic Simulation. Eight million bucks to make that real. That's why we train everyone's bodyguards. So tell me, what gave them away?'

'The woman. The baby was very upset, but she was not paying any attention to it. No mother would let her baby scream so without trying to comfort it. Therefore the baby was not hers, therefore she was not what she seemed. The schoolboy . . . he did not look right. The clothes were correct, the blazer, the cap, the satchel. It was him. He was young, but savage. He was unused to the clothes. A violent young panther, not a scholar.'

'Good. Good. Okay, get out of your rig and we'll go to class for this afternoon's session. We'll get away from the classic business of protecting a public figure performing ceremonial duties and get into something a little different. We can run it a few times, because this will be more your kind of thing.'

After lunch, Yossif Petrovsky stood on the beach in a sea mist. Just off shore, he felt that there was a boat waiting. He stood with two men, both Arabs, in Western dress. Their Renault van was parked on the edge of the sand. The wood walls of a beach restaurant stood bleakly, awaiting summer and the tourists. A Peugeot saloon appeared through the pines, travelling along by the field of twisted, lifeless vines which waited for the heat.

The Arab at his side, a young man, hissed an oath.

'They are here. Arm your weapon. Kill them quickly.'

'We have to wait,' Yossif said. 'We cannot be sure it is them.' He spoke in Arabic. The Peugeot came bumping up the road and Yossif moved away from the van towards the shelter of a brick booth that sold cold drinks from May to September. Fifty yards away, a dark tube poked from the rear window. Both fired at the same instant, and missile and bullets passed each way.

WAYCROSS, GEORGIA

In the little wooden chapel down the dirt road the organ was blowing soft and sad. It was a beautiful clear morning, the buds were showing on the trees and the blossom was white and pink. I'd seen the blue wooden building one Sunday morning many years before, mid-season and the armyworm in town. I'd come over and suddenly realized where I was, and looked down at the sea of black faces that had come out to watch – everyone in their Sunday best – and when I'd got through I landed the Stearman in the pasture and walked over to apologize for interrupting their service. They all said to give it no mind, they'd enjoyed the show and thereafter some Sundays I'd go along to their chapel and be with them. I'd be the only white face there, but no one took offence.

Old Reverend MacArthur held the service, and we sang and the organ played, and then old MacArthur stopped to say a few words for Maybelline. He'd aged, his hair was snow-white and his face was lined, but in his white robes he was still a fine figure of a man and his eyes still sparkled for the love of the Lord.

'We are here to pay our respects to Maybelline Williams,' he said softly. 'Maybelline has left us. We miss her. I miss her. She was of this parish. She was a good scholar, clever and hard-working, and when she left to go to Atlanta we all wished her well. She called me once or twice from that city; I thought her mind was troubled and sought to counsel her. It may be that I was derelict in my duty, for Maybelline is dead, the victim of an evil drug.

'But we should not grieve for Maybelline, although we miss her, for now she is happy, she sits with Jesus and

Jesus has taken away her torment. He has soothed the pain in her breast. Now Maybelline is with the Son of God, and will rejoice throughout Eternity. The Bible tells us that the Lord takes the sweetest flowers, and that may be why He took Maybelline so young.'

He paused and looked down on the congregation, letting his fierce eyes roam over us.

'I am looking here at you,' he continued, his voice calm and measured in the little wooden building. 'I see her brothers and sisters, her mother and father. I see friends from her schooldays. I see Mr Marvin, her father's partner, and our friend. I see others who have come to pay their last respects.'

He paused and his voice became low and hard.

'But there is someone missing.'

He looked around us. 'Someone is missing, who should be here. Someone should be here to see the grief and devastation his acts have caused. Someone should be here to see what has happened to the fine young woman whose life he destroyed.

'The man who sold for money the drug that destroyed Maybelline Williams should be here today.'

He drew himself up and gripped the pulpit with his old hands.

'He should be here to know that the everlasting fires of Hell are awaiting him. For him, and his ilk, who poison the towns and cities of our country, who destroy the lives of our young people for silver – for them, the mercy of the Lord is not infinite. I say again, this man should be here.'

We rose and sang the last hymn before we took Maybelline outside and put her in her last resting place.

I'm here.

The flowers flew through the air and scattered on the coffin.

Lord, won't you have mercy on me, I'm here.

The gravediggers' shovels bit into the earth and filled in the grave.

I'm here.

QOM, IRAN

Musavi Yasdi lived in a single, small square room known as a *hojrah*. It was the traditional place of residence for such as he – the *talabehs*, the seekers who might one day become *mujtahid*, capable of guiding others. On his journey, a *talabeh* might one day become a *mullah* or *akhund*, or even achieve the higher ranks of Hojat al-Islam, or Ayatollah. To this end, reviving a way of life that had been dying out before the Grand Ayatollah returned, they attended a *madrasseh*, a kind of free theological seminary. Musavi Yasdi attended the politically important *madrasseh* of Hojat al-Islam Tasdeeq, but not because he sought to become *mujtahid*, or to attain clerical rank, but because he was a spy.

Hojat Tasdeeq sought to follow in the footsteps of the Grand Ayatollah and so, like he had so many years before, set up as a religious leader in the Holy city of Qom, a hundred miles south of the politically more important capital of Tehran. Since the overthrow of the *Shahanshah*, the King of Kings, religious power equated with political muscle and in Qom Hojat Tasdeeq was both *marja-e-taqleed* – the source of imitation, the master of his *madrasseh* to which he attracted important disciples, thus increasing his own power – and was also head of the Islamic Council of the Revolution. Iran was a post-revolutionary country involved in a seemingly endless war. Administratively confused, rival organizations fought each other for power as viciously as the enemy, and one of the most feared and functionally ill-defined was Tasdeeq's Council.

Musavi Yasdi was a spy, an agent in place left behind by a retreating force, beaten by their opponents. There had been many who had opposed the Grand Ayatollah before he could consolidate power; among them had been the left-wing organizations, the Mojahedin and their uneasy allies the Tudeh, or masses, known for their pro-Soviet sympathies. Both had been defeated. The leader of the Mojahedin, Mas'ud Rajavi, set up a government-in-exile with the former prime minister Abol Hassan Bani-Sadr in Paris in 1981. Many of his followers, including lieutenants like Abdul Karim, were judicially murdered by judges such as Khalkhali afterwards. Musavi Yasdi escaped to fight another day. He was able to join the *madrasseh* of Hojat Tasdeeq, and from time to time to send out messages.

In his *hojrah* Yasdi knelt on his prayer mat. It was before dawn and any who heard his murmuring voice would assume he was attending to his devotions. This was far from the truth. Yasdi believed more in Marx than in Allah, and was speaking into a small black Sony micro-cassette recorder.

'It is said that the Grand Ayatollah's health continues to fail,' he said softly to the little machine. 'It is thought that he may not last the year. This is why Hojat Tasdeeq has revived the ancient practice of the pilgrimage to the shrine of Ma'assoumah, the Chaste One, on *Nowruz*, the first day of the New Year. The celebration of *Nowruz* by the people is a very old festival, and one suppressed when the Grand Ayatollah first came to power. Its revival and association with the pilgrimage to the shrine here in Qom, formerly undertaken by the Khan or Shah in order to bind the loyalty of the people to him, is undoubtedly in order to perform the same function for Hojat Tasdeeq, who feels that the presence of the Grand Ayatollah with him in his town of Qom during this ceremony will aid him considerably in the power struggle that will inevitably take place once the Grand Ayatollah dies.'

Yasdi paused and moistened his lips with some water from his earthen water-jar. It was still dark outside. He raised the little recorder again.

'Tasdeeq's principal opponent in this struggle will be

Shaikh Jazayeri. Jazayeri operates from Tehran where he is Speaker of the *Majlis*, the parliament. Jazayeri has secured a strong power base by becoming the patron of the Pasdaran, the Islamic Revolutionary Guards Corps, which has taken much of the brunt of the fighting in the war. IRGC soldiers are noted for their fanaticism and willingness to court martyrdom for their cause, and have thus become favoured by the Grand Ayatollah himself. Under Jazayeri's patronage they are on their way to supplanting the regular armed forces, and Jazayeri has ensured that they get priority on whatever equipment is available. He cultivates close links with them, often flying down to the front to visit Pasadaran units.

'Tasdeeq is a radical cleric in the mould of the Grand Ayatollah. When he refers to the submission – Islam – of Arab countries to the teachings of the Qur'an, he means just that. Tasdeeq would go further. He advocates a return to mediaeval concepts of conversion by the sword for the infidels of the West, who he sees as polluting the mind, spirit and body of the true believers. Western civilization is seen by him as a barrier to achieving a oneness with Allah. Although the USA is to him the Great Satan, and chief among the *muharib an al-Allah* – those who wage war upon Allah – we especially should note that our own ally the USSR is at risk from his desire to export the Islamic revolution. Should Tasdeeq emerge as the new leader of Iran he would undoubtedly link up with the resistance movement in Afghanistan, which itself seeks the establishment of an Islamic state. Were the USSR ever to withdraw from Afghanistan, it is a certainty that Afghanistan would ally with a Tasdeeq-led Iran, and that together they would attempt to destabilize the Central Asian republics like Azerbaijan and Kirghiz – and probably also the Soviet satellite of Bulgaria, which has a large Moslem population. Moslems will constitute more than 25 per cent of the population of the Soviet Union by the end of the century, so the ideas of men like Hojat Tasdeeq can be seen as a threat to both the USA and USSR.

'The rhetoric of the Shaikh Jazayeri is hardly less extreme than that of Tasdeeq. With the depth of fervour whipped up by the involvement of the USA – the Great Satan – in the Gulf War, he cannot be seen to be any the less hard line than the radical clerics. However, this may not be so. Jazayeri came to prominence and erected the first framework that his power now rests upon through being there when the students occupied the US Embassy on Taleqani Avenue in 1979. With the "Muslim Students Following the Imam's Line", he gained access to the classified files of the Embassy and the CIA station there. Do we not remember how he used carefully selected information to ruin those who sought a share of power? Did his advancement not commence then? Many suspect that he has knowledge still hidden, which he uses to persuade people to this very day – in the American phrase, he "knows where the bodies are buried". But few remember that he was among the very first into the Embassy. Was there not a file on one Moussa Jazayeri, which he quickly took and burned? And what did that file say? Few remember, and those who do dare not say that Moussa Jazayeri was a student in the USA once, before the King of Kings fell. If Jazayeri and not Tasdeeq comes to power, there may be a lessening of rhetoric about the Great Satan and a pro-Western realignment. There are many still in exile who would be glad to come home under such circumstances, bringing money and skills with them.'

Yasdi paused, his ears pricked for any indication that he was being overheard, but the warren-like building was quiet. He bent his lips to the machine one last time.

'It is obvious that neither Tasdeeq nor Jazayeri is suitable as a leader in our eyes. While Tasdeeq is rabidly anti-American, his plans will inevitably bring us into conflict with our ally, the USSR. For all his hard rhetoric, Jazayeri is at best indifferent to the USSR and is probably pro-American. Indeed, there is the whisper – which will get you buried up to your chest and stoned – that Jazayeri might be a tool of the Americans.

'The day is not far away. The Grand Ayatollah is ailing. The *Nowruz* pilgrimage to the shrine of Fatima the Chaste One may well be the last time he is seen in public. Tasdeeq and Jazayeri have formidable allies. Our technique must be that of judo, of *coup d'état*, to turn their strengths against them. Above all we must be ready, for the day is not far off.'

Yasdi stopped the machine and put the tiny silver and red cassette into a small paper envelope which he slipped into his pocket. The faint light of dawn was filtering through the small window. He put a knitted cloak around his shoulders against the cold and crept out down the bare passage, then out into the narrow alley. He hurried along the winding way until it spilled him out into the vast arena of the courtyard of Fatimah's shrine. At this early hour it was still empty, and he went across to the great Mosque that flanked the shrine, its two enormous golden domes beginning to lighten in the dawn. Inside the Mosque he paused at the entrance to the huge hall, dominated by its windows and great chandelier, to make obeisance, then turned off to the corridor that led to the *takieh* where those who wished to remember the Imam Hussein might perform their worship. It was a far smaller affair, simple, with wooden benches at the back and along the walls; it was empty at this hour. Yasdi slipped into a row at the very back. Here women might sit if it was their time of the month and they were unable to worship. He peeled the covering off the strip of two-sided tape that was stuck to the envelope and pressed it to the underside of the bench. This done, he went forward and performed his correct rituals to begin the day's worship. As a spy, he had to live his part.

Later in the day the buses would arrive, bringing the blind, the lame, the hunchbacked, the sick and mentally infirm, all of whom would have travelled to the grim city in the hope of being cured by Fatima, the chaste sister of Imam Reza. Amongst their number would be a young woman who would make her way to this one bench and collect the message. Among those who had opposed the

Shah were women who had benefited from the Westernization he had introduced; they had not thought that the revolution they had assisted in would bring with it the darkness of mediaeval culture; now that it had, there were still some working for the revolution of their choice. However Muslim scholars might present it, under Islam women were inferior to men, and this could stick mightily in the craw of those who knew they were not.

The sun was up when Yasdi emerged. People had come to the huge courtyard, where in a city devoid of all entertainments public life was lived out. Almost immediately, as he came down the steps, professional beggars accosted him. Qom had beggars as a slum has cockroaches, there were almost as many beggars as begged upon. Yasdi avoided them skilfully, his eyes held firmly a short distance ahead of his feet, as any practised cleric would. He made his way back through the rabbit-warren of winding alleys where the *seeghahs* or temporary wives plied their trade, along with the fortune-tellers and turbaned miracle workers, undertakers and gravediggers. Qom was a city that prepared people for death; the faithful came from all over Iran to be interred there.

Yasdi emerged into the square containing Khaneh-e-Hojat, the *madrasseh* of Hojat Tasdeeq, a large, bleak mud-brick building of the old style. He entered and made his way to the big *mehman-khaneh,* the main room where Tasdeeq's pupils gathered. That day Tasdeeq, donning the role of the Master, was due to give the outside lesson, the *dars-e-kharej,* that represented the highest degree of Shi'ite education. Like all Shi'ite thought, the lesson would not in any way encourage the *talabehs* to think for themselves in an enquiring manner, but would emphasize the importance of preservation of a fixed and unalterable view of existence.

As always, Yasdi mentally braced himself to enter. A dedicated Marxist, he lived his life according to very different laws from those of the men he was about to join. The effort to be one of them was great.

To his surprise, the room was full. Hojat Tasdeeq was

sitting cross-legged on a straw mat on the floor. As Yasdi entered, he slowly raised his eyes from their contemplation of the ground in front of his feet.

'Yasdi,' he whispered. '*Al-fikri.*'

The word literally meant 'the thinker', but Shi'ism opposed thought and *fikr* was a deadly sin, a sign of mental derangement that led inevitably over the precipice.

Tasdeeq stared burningly at him from a face of parchment, and all around the mad, rabid faces looked at the traitor.

'We have been waiting for you,' said Tasdeeq, and from all sides hands like claws reached out for him.

PARIS

Yossif Petrovsky left his hotel in Montmartre and descended in every sense as he walked towards the Arab quarter in Barbes. He left the beauty of Sacré Coeur and the solidity of old grey houses and little neighbourhood shops and passed through the bustle of restaurants, the garishness of neon-lit boutiques – selling flimsy clothing to whores and transvestite whores, selling transient relief and disease – into the drabness of Barbes. Here the Arab immigrant labour huddled, and recreated a shanty existence to be found in Algiers and Tunis. Here the clothes, luggage, utensils and people for sale were all second-hand and used, here the meanest hole in the wall could be graced by the title of shop or café. Smells of smoke, old cooking and washing drifted through Yossif Petrovsky's nose as he walked purposefully along – out of place, too fit, too European, too positive. Yet the people accepted his presence, because shark moved in these waters too; here were men who dealt in terror, men from Beirut and Tripoli, men who dealt in gold, guns and flesh, men who were spies and agents, men from the Sureté, from Mossad, from the CIA and the KGB.

The restaurant he entered was smoky from the grill where an Arab in a greasy shirt tended to the brochettes and couscous. He sat down at a little table with an oil-skin cover and was brought a coffee, thick and sweet. Arab expatriates infested the room, crouched around small coffee cups and glasses of rough red wine; tangled fantasies of revenge, retribution and victory crazed men's minds, and were fuelled by those whose business it was to keep such hatreds alive.

Petrovsky spotted those he sought easily. They sat in a corner like a small group of predatory birds, young, keen of eye and hand, suspicious. It was their youth that struck him; they must have been mere children when they escaped from Tehran. Now the daughter and two sons of Abdul Karim waited for revenge too. Their hatred had been carefully tended by experts, now it was time for it to be used. What was Yuly Borodin? Morteza Cheragh, Petrovsky reminded himself. Cheragh, the name meant light. It was an inappropriate name for the undercover KGB Colonel, he thought. Perhaps that was why he had chosen it; he was not without a sense of humour.

It was time to activate the brothers and sister Karim. As he rose from his cheap wooden chair Petrovsky wondered what others were in the smoky room. The Grand Ayatollah had his men in Paris too, they had killed Abdul Karim there – Abdul Karim, one-time Mojahedin leader, one-time member of the long-gone government-in-exile.

He walked over to the table and the young predatory eyes watched him in anticipation.

Hussein Sultani crossed the Seine just south of the Tour Eiffel, having left his comfortable apartment and comfortable mistress in the Boulevard Garibaldi some minutes earlier, and a short time later was among the morning traffic on the *Péripherique* heading for St Denis, his Volkswagen Golf GTI cabriolet humming sweetly in fifth gear. Warm in his stomach were the *croissants, confiture* and *café au lait* that had made his breakfast. Hussein Sultani would have choked to death on goat's cheese, unleavened bread and a handful of dried dates. He prided himself on his civilization. Warm in his loins was the comfortable memory of the satisfaction that had preceded his pleasant and civilized *petit-déjeuner*. Normally, at about the same time that he changed up into fifth and blasted past some *paysan* in a 2-CV, he would reflect on the incredible good fortune which had brought

211

him here, to the most civilized city on earth. Hussein was an engineer, one sent abroad from his native Iran to learn his craft – first in the USA, where he took a degree at George Washington University, and later, practical experience in London and Paris. He had returned to Tehran about the same time as most Westernized Iranians were leaving with bagfuls of banknotes in both hands. He was still there when the dying King of Kings departed. A rational man, he found the idea that his country – the fifteenth largest in the world in size, ranking thirteenth in GNP, with the sixth largest army and the mightiest arsenal of weapons in entire Asia – could be taken over by a crazed and infirm *rowzeh-khan*, an old rabble-rousing preacher who had been in exile for over fifteen years; this, he found ridiculous. It was a view that he shared with the President of the United States, both men having their minds changed for them shortly afterwards; President Carter by the occupation of his embassy and the seizure of hostages, and Hussein Sultani by the gun-butt of a revolutionary guard breaking his nose shortly before he took up occupation of a very horrible cell in Evin Prison.

Clean-shaven, *fokoli* in his Western clothes, he had little doubt that as a thoroughly civilized *mufsed felardh*, a corrupter of the earth, sooner or later his time would have come, once the fanatics on the *komitehs* had worked their way down from the higher levels of Shaytan's servants, the generals and former ministers, through those who had ever committed 'grave offences' against any mullah . . . sooner or later they would arrive, in some casual gaol-clearing, at one highly-trained most experienced civilized engineer, and one cheap bullet or length of twisted cord would put an end to fifty thousand dollars' worth of education in a prison courtyard.

What saved Hussein Sultani was the war. In the war with Iraq, the ayatollahs and mullahs found themselves with a gigantic stock of weaponry, but few who knew how to use it. They armed child-soldiers, but had no trained officers to lead them. Thus was Hassan Sadeq, former Guards officer in the Immortals, released from jail with his fellow Captain, Ali Bahonar. However large a stock of weaponry one begins with, a war chews through it at fantastic speed. It was not long before tanks could not move, jet fighters could not fly, guns could not fire and the oil terminals to pay for it all were ablaze. Furthermore, the fanaticism of his country's new leaders had alienated the great nations who might re-equip their fighting forces. It was for this that Hussein Sultani was released from prison, cured of his various ailments, fed and clothed once more in *fokoli* dress, given funds and sent to Paris.

Hussein Sultani was an expert in reverse-technology. If he was provided with a particular machine, he could dissemble it to its component parts and then dissemble the component parts into *their* component parts, which could then be analysed. This done, he could design and have made a perfect copy of whatever part was required. A Soviet-built T-62 tank went through track treads and road-wheels, air and oil filters, clutches and gearboxes, and all of these had to be supplied in quantity. When hit, armour plate was needed. The tanks were becoming short in supply, and they were always worth repairing. Reverse-technology was at its simplest with something relatively crude like a tank, and at its most difficult with more sophisticated weaponry like fighter aircraft and missiles. Nevertheless, beyond the level of a bayonet almost all modern weapons required access to the industrial infrastructure of a modern state of the first rank, and this Iran had never become – not even under the Shahanshah – and whatever achievements he might have made towards this goal had long been destroyed and submerged beneath an ideology that reached back for the seventh century AD.

Only a Western country would do, and political considerations ruled out almost all the NATO nations, especially the USA and Great Britain, and it was to France – traditionally amoral as to the destination of armaments, not indifferent to being friendly with any of the Middle Eastern countries in search of a profit to be made, even the Ayatollah's Iran – that Hussein turned, setting up his base among the industries around St Denis. It was a Saturday morning and normally Hussein would have been lying abed before planning the pleasures of his Parisian weekend, but he was on his way to work. Normally, as he hit fifth and pressed the accelerator to the metal to enjoy the pleasure of driving one of the best products of German automotive technology, he would revel in the joy of living, of having been rescued from certain death, of being able, very soon, to make that rescue, that fine way of life, permanent into old age.

But it was Saturday and he was on his way to work, trundling dismally along in the middle lane as fatter, more arrogant men swaggered past, for Hussein was worried. To be more accurate, and he prided himself on his accuracy, he was afraid. He had a visitor.

Shaikh Mohammad-Najafi had asked him to give some time to see this man, this one Morteza Cheragh. The surname meant Light, but its owner brought no brightness to Hussein. On the Islamic Council of the Revolutionary only Hojat Tasdeeq stood higher than Shaikh Mohammad-Najafi. This Morteza Cheragh was a Lebanese businessman, 'someone who has helped us'. What did he want with Hussein? The hedonistic little engineer was mortally afraid of all the fanatics the Islamic Council was so representative of.

The firm Hussein owned rented accommodation in a modern industrial estate. He had a large warehouse and a small engineering shop with offices above, where Hussein worked with his IBM computer. Being Saturday, his employees were all at home, where he wished he was. He parked his Golf outside and went into the metal-sheet and concrete building; there he prepared the Moulinex filter-coffee machine and, taking a cup, went over to the computer terminal. One enjoyable part of reverse-technology was being able to improve upon the original design. The engine of the Soviet-built T-62 tank had an oil filter which managed to combine all the disadvantages

214

of bureaucracy by being expensive, constructed from a committee of twenty-three different parts and inefficient. Hussein was finalizing his own design which was effective, made from three components and cheap. Furthermore, its efficiency would pass benefits down the line in terms of savings on engine oil, components and Time Between Overhaul that translated into T-62 tanks penetrating Iraqi soil and firing shells at Iraqi troops. Hussein became absorbed with this and had begun to feel the familiar sense of enjoyment that he got from his work when he heard the door open. When he turned, a tall, beautifully-besuited man was standing in the doorway.

'Morteza Cheragh,' the man said. 'I hope I am not disturbing you. I believe that you are expecting me.'

At the very moment of seeing Cheragh, Hussein felt that there was something wrong. As he played the host, sat Cheragh down and brought coffee, he told himself that he was wrong, it was simply that he was naturally apprehensive. Cheragh was a mixture of bloods; there was Persian there, but not also Arab as one might see in Iran, but what looked like Slav. Still, there were many strange mixtures of races in the Middle East, and especially from the melting-pot of the Lebanon. His expensive suiting was what a successful entrepreneur would clothe himself in, and the cold sneer of command that Hussein detected beneath the pleasant smile would be necessary in a man who could request an introduction from such as Shaikh Mohammad-Najafi. But O, that he had wanted to see someone else!

Cheragh accepted a mug of black coffee and placed it on the table beside his chair.

'Everything is so clean and tidy,' he said pleasantly. 'I had a vision of foundries and casting-shops, lathes and arc-welding machines.'

'We act as head office here,' Hussein explained. 'Downstairs we dissemble and examine, we analyse and quantify. Here I design and prepare specifications and drawings. We have a warehouse. All work is sub-contracted. We are ideally situated here, for we have

215

access to many industrial firms from foundries to very high-tech electronics.'

'All designed by computer,' Cheragh murmured. 'So efficient.'

Hussein had thought that there would have been a certain amount – fifteen, twenty minutes, perhaps even half an hour – of formal conversational waltzing in true Arab spirit before the subject of the call was broached, and he was taken aback when Cheragh came brutally to the point.

'My good friend Shaikh Mohammad does not know the purpose of my visit to you,' Cheragh said. 'I merely asked for an introduction to someone with the qualities I need.'

'Ah,' said Hussein. 'What might they be?'

'I want an AT-6 tube-launched missile, NATO-designation *Spiral*. Do you know the one I mean? It is a Soviet weapon, suitable for use from a tracked vehicle or helicopter. It is current-generation, comparable with the American *Hellfire*.'

Hussein forced himself to smile benignly, even slightly incredulously, as real terror flared up inside his belly.

'Of course,' he said, as though it was all a good joke. 'Would you like a *Hind* helicopter or a BMP to go with it?'

'No,' said Cheragh, unsmiling, 'but I will need the KDT laser-designation equipment to go with it.'

Hussein spread his hands in bewilderment and allowed the smile to vanish from his face, a man on whom a joke is being played out far too long.

'Mr Cheragh, you have come to the wrong man. I am not an arms dealer, I am a citizen of the Islamic revolution, working solely for my country and Allah. I provide parts for our T-62 tanks. Reverse-technology can make road-wheels or oil filters. It cannot construct something as sophisticated as a laser-designated air-to-ground missile like *Spiral*.'

'That was so five years ago . . . Three years ago . . . perhaps even last year. But not now. You can do it. Those who own you believe that you can do it. They have sent you two missiles and associated laser-designation equipment. They arrived yesterday and sit in your warehouse as we speak. I have come to take one from you.'

Hussein forced himself to his feet and contorted his face in simulated fury.

'My task is to work for the revolution of Islam! I work to propagate the teaching of Allah. Be careful with me! I am prepared to die for Allah, but also I am prepared to kill for him too.'

Cheragh stared cynically at Hussein and mockingly clapped his hands together a few times.

'Very good, Mr Sultani. In the Iran of today it is as well to proclaim your loyalty to Allah and his revolution as often as possible. Those in charge are ever anxious to seek out the spies and disloyal ones in their midst. Shaikh Mohammad himself told me the very last time I saw him that they had uncovered a spy among them, one of their very own members of the Islamic Council.' He reached inside the breast pocket of his impeccably-cut suit and withdrew some photographs, which he tossed in front of Hussein on his desk. 'Here, see.'

The photographs had spread themselves in front of his eyes. He blanched in terror and pushed them aside.

'He confessed to being an American spy for the CIA, apparently,' said Cheragh. 'Though I expect by then he would have confessed to anything, wouldn't you say? Do you think you would confess, Mr Sultani?'

Hussein fought to control the heavings of a stomach that enjoyed good food and closed his eyes to the horrors on the desk.

Cheragh extracted a plastic envelope from his pocket and took a leather folder from it, tossing it on to the photographs in front of Hussein.

'Shaikh Mohammad gave me the photographs in this.'

Hussein picked up the wallet, which was crudely constructed of some sort of light brown pigskin. It felt greasy to his fingers, and as he lifted it up he noticed a vile, sweetish smell rising from it.

'It's his skin,' remarked Cheragh.

Hussein's breakfast rose violently from his stomach and he ran for the little bathroom leading off his office. *Croissants, confiture, café au lait*, prepared with love and so enjoyably eaten, spewed up into the basin. He stood – his legs trembling and his breath sobbing with terror – for some minutes before he calmed and washed himself. Outside, he could hear Cheragh talking to someone: as he listened, he realized that they were talking Russian. He came out and sat down carefully, like an elderly man. Cheragh had been joined by a tall, slim man in his twenties, cold-faced, with chill blue eyes, very bright – a Jewish man, perhaps, a Russian. He stood by the door with his coat casually open, and underneath it in his hand was a small sub-machine gun.

'You work for very frightening and terrible people, Mr Sultani,' Cheragh said, almost sympathetically. 'I too would wish to escape far from their clutches if I were in your position. Though, given the fact that their country is at war with Iraq, I might have picked a better method of raising my capital than trading with that enemy.'

Courage returned to the little engineer. 'Why not?' he demanded, looking up at his tormentor. 'I owe these fanatics – these crazy men who want to take us all back to a dark age – I owe them nothing. Let them kill each other. What better way to make enough money to escape? Iraq has T-62 tanks too. *They* need spare parts. They do not know it, but they buy them from me.'

Cheragh smiled, and Hussein thought that he saw genuine admiration in his eyes.

'Why not indeed? A masterly solution. Mr Sultani, your secret is safe with me. You may continue to trade with both sides just as long as your nerve holds out, or until you reach whatever sum of money it is that you have decided upon.'

'Three million dollars,' said Hussein, 'from the Iraqis. You see, I must work for loyalty alone for the men in Qom and Tehran.'

'All I require from you is the missile and its guidance system. We have our van outside.'

'Bring it round to the warehouse. I will open the door.'

'You will still have one left. If you work hard, you will soon be producing replicas. The Iraqis will pay well for them.'

Hussein thought of the home he owned in Sydney, so very far away from all the terror, in a country where a man with mechanical ability might put his three million dollars to good use. Not long now.

'Yes,' he said. 'About fifty should do it.'

SANTA MARTA

I got in, strapped it on and wriggled about in the dawn's early light getting myself comfortable while they waited impatiently for me to get on with it; the armyworm had got into the marijuana and brought all his cousins with him, been in there two days, pigging out on the leaf, and the stinkbug was busy doing nasty things to the coca bushes – and everyone wanted it *stopped*, Ryan was positively hopping up and down on the tips of his red and white Pro model sneakers, but the cord on my Cal Mil helmet was hanging up somewhere, and I took the time to get it free, no hindrance. I learned that from old Joe Powers one time, after the Mexicans stole his Stearman he hired out to a big outfit in Arkansas. I was there myself that year – we were working the rice with B model Ag Cats – and old Joe was down there in his field one bright spring morning. He got down by the light line on the downwind edge of the field, got the spray rolling nicely under the wires, and the cord on his helmet was bothering him; he had it caught up somewhere on his harness, and he was fiddling with it to get it loose – and the next thing he knows he has done gone snagged his top wing on the wire, and it has a hold of it and won't let to. And old Joe, he flies all the way up the wire to the pole, which he smites at over one hundred miles an hour, and he has full power on and even as he's shitting himself as pieces of pole and insulator and chunks of Cat fly all about him, he's still flying – done got it made, he reckons – but the wire has looped itself sneakily around his wing and a short distance farther on it causes him to make the shortest snap roll seen in Arkansas that year, puts him flat on his back in the road on the other side of the rice paddy.

He told me all about it as he was lying there in the little room they had put him in; it was all very clear in his mind, I had a can beer under my coat and I'd slip him a sip when no one was looking. 'It was the top wing done saved me, R.D.,' he said. 'Man, they build them things strong. I ain't gone fly anything but a Cat from now on.' And old Joe, he a man of his word, he never did. He died three days later with 75 per cent burns.

So I got myself comfortable, and Billy Lee had the bird filled; we were using Pounce for the bugs, get them to quit eating and lie on their backs with their little feet in the air. I was real proud of that. I'd managed to hold on to my breakfast that morning. I gave it the fuel and waddled out and began work.

About midday the wind was blowing strong, the turbulence in the field was vicious, made your arm ache from the control pressures, and when I got down from my load Billy Lee didn't have another waiting for me.

'What's the matter with you? Give me the chemical, dammit.'

'Wind's up.'

'Piss on it.'

'Must be twenty knot out theah.'

'Give me the damn chemical.'

'It yo ass.'

He shrugged, but yanked the Briggs and Skatton to life.

'We are two thousand acres behind here,' I reminded him. 'Damn worms is mowing the field while you watch.'

'When in doubt, put it out,' he said.

It took us two days, and I was as tired as I could remember. I flew fourteen hours each day, shutting down once for a sandwich and a piss which took all of five minutes. When I had done, I went back to the hotel and showered and went to bed.

It was time to put out MH-30 on the tobacco on the coast, for sucker control, and with the really valuable crops out of the way I went down the next day to take care of six hundred acres. I got it done and flew back up to the valley in the afternoon. Ryan was there and he looked like the doctor'd just told him he was pregnant.

'R.D., I want you to come see. Something terrible has happened.'

His face was completely ashen and he was trembling.

'What is it?'

'Just come and see.'

We got in his Jeep and drove off up the valley. His face was working, he looked ten years older. We stopped by one of the poppy fields I had first sprayed and we got out, but you could see it without even going into the field. It didn't shine and wave in the wind. The poppies were tightly coiled like watch-springs. Dessicated. Brown. And very, very dead.

'Ho Lee Shit,' I said slowly.

'I was on my training run when I saw it. It's not disease.'

'Shit, no. That's chemical burn. Something's burned the heck out of it.'

I went over by the edge of the field and pulled up a few dried plants from the rich earth.

'Paraquat'll do that. That or 2,4,5-D.'

We drove back and opened up the big chemical store, and among the orderly piles were the big square boxes of Ortho Paraquat. I opened one and pulled out one of the four dark plastic gallon jugs.

'We were using Pounce,' I said. 'Pounce is totally safe, won't harm the crop at all.'

'How could it happen . . . ' he wailed, completely distraught. A multi, multi-million dollar crop was dying out there.

On impulse I opened the jug, gingerly unscrewing the wide cap, because the only problem with paraquat is it'll do the job on you. I sniffed, cautiously. There was no smell. I poured some of the contents over my hand and they were free and clear. Ryan stared in horror.

'Water,' I said.

222

I went to one of the Pounce cans left over from the spraying and again, I was very cautious. One sniff was enough.

'This is Paraquat,' I said. 'Do you see what has happened? Someone has switched contents on us.'

Ryan's face was aghast. 'But *who*?' he cried beseechingly.

'I could make an educated guess. Has to be government organization. President Thomas is getting pretty hawky about all this. Hasn't the Drug Enforcement Administration gone into Bolivia and places in Chinooks? Burnt the shit out of all the drug fields and all? You want my opinion, that's what happened.'

'Oh, Jesus . . . ' Tears were streaming down Ryan's face. 'All my life I've wanted to be rich and now this . . . oh, shit I had it made . . . '

He fell to the ground, sobbing and beating on the dirt with his hand. He didn't seem to need me, and I hate to see a grown man make an ass of himself, so I went off home. Sure wasn't much urgency in looking after a few thousand acres of dead vegetables.

The heavy white shutters had been closed all day and the room was cool. I lay in the half-light on the rough cotton sheets and debated whether to have a second beer, which I knew would put me away. The two previous days had left me about to give out.

'Yeah, I guess President Thomas'll be real proud of his boys, pulling off this one.'

'Real secret agent stuff,' Ellen said solemnly.

'Well, they probably train these guys up real good. I knew a special forces man in 'nam one time who could make a bomb out of anything you got in your kitchen. Man, you should have seen Ryan. He was sobbing and chewing the dirt. I don't think that boy's bread is done.'

'Ryan's infected with the American dream, he wants to be a millionaire. He's dangerous though, R.D.,' she warned. 'Don't let him think you're laughing at him. Ric didn't employ him just because he knows how to harrow a field. Ryan's a killer too.'

'I won't . . . ' I ached, I ached all over.

'You're tired,' she said. The thin white cotton shirt rode up over her smooth buttocks. 'You've been working hard. What will you do now?'

'I'll stay to work the tobacco on the coast. It won't require much more, maybe a month. The lower leaves are starting to yellow. They went in and topped it out last week. Then I'll go home.'

She chuckled, I saw her nice white teeth gleam in the half-light, felt her round breasts push against my side.

'Yes, it'll be safe for you to go home then,' she murmured mysteriously. I could smell her scent as she rubbed herself against me and I was hard and all thoughts of beer a million miles away. 'Do you like me or something, honey?' I said.

She laughed and came up sliding on top of me, and my hands felt her slippery with the sweat of desire.

'Like you? Darling, I love you.' Her voice hissed in the quiet, dim room as I slid inside her. She bent and her mouth was very close to my ear. She shivered with an excitement I did not know, her skin burning hot with fever. Her eyes were glossy and dark, all pupil.

'Mother knows,' she whispered, and the words had a terrible fever. A fever of joy. Her nails were sharp and she bit my ear. 'Mother *knows*.'

THE VAR

In the grey light Yossif could now see, but he kept the lights of the van on for safety. After leaving the *autoroute* and climbing along the winding road over the hills – travelling in the opposite direction to Napoleon, beginning his last 100 days, on his way to defeat and exile – a sea fog had awaited them as they descended the other side, and Yossif proceeded cautiously. His cargo was such that no sane man would have risked an accident. In the seats beside him the brothers of Gohar Karim, Morteza and Ahmad dozed. On the floor of the cab lay the remains of a very late supper, the packets which had contained couscous and unleavened bread, a thermos of coffee.

Driving down from Paris through the night, the darkness had been filled with excited talk, the re-living of past exploits, the memories of those dead, the dwelling for a while on the wickedness and evil of their enemy, the jubilant gesturing towards the rear cargo area of the van, the extravagant praise of their ally and friend forever, KGB Captain Yossif Petrovsky. And again and again the wonderful, glorious end to the story, with evil defeated and right triumphant. It had filled Yossif with a sense of dread and foreboding.

Two or three times a minute, Yossif triggered the wipers to clear the fog that settled on the windscreen. At dawn in February, the coast road was deserted. A faded sign advertising a beach club loomed up out of the mist and Yossif turned off down the rutted and muddy track. The change in motion awoke his two companions.

'We're here,' said Yossif. The two Iranians rubbed

their faces and stretched and prepared themselves to do some work. The heater pushed out warm air over them. By the door, Morteza wound down the window to let a little cold rush on to his face. The pine trees passed on either side, dark and dripping with moisture. They turned the corner and the beach was ahead, shaped and washed by the winter sea, littered with jetsam. The wood walls of a beach restaurant stood bleakly awaiting summer and the tourists. A small pier, at which rich men's boats would tie up or fishermen cast off stretched into the fog. The sea was flat. Yossif parked at the foot of the pier, close by a brick booth that sold cold drinks in the hot weather. They got out to relieve themselves, and the clammy chill wrapped itself about them. The metal of Yossif's weapon suddenly felt warm under his coat.

Something white flickered through the trees. Ahmad, the younger brother hissed through his teeth and grasped Yossif's arm, an automatic pistol appearing suddenly in his hand.

A Peugeot saloon appeared through the trees, travelling along by the field of twisted, lifeless vines, waiting for the summer heat. Ahmad swore.

'It is the Ayatollah's men. Arm your weapon. Kill them quickly.'

'We have to wait,' said Yossif. 'We cannot be sure it is them.'

His mouth was dry and his heart thumped in his chest. The Peugeot came bumping up the road and Yossif moved away from the van towards the shelter of the brick booth. Ahmad and Morteza were behind him. Fifty yards away a dark tube poked itself from the window of the car and Yossif brought his Ingram gun smoothly up to the aim, as he had been taught. As he squeezed the trigger, he could not believe that he was doing it.

There was a flash of light from the car and the front of the van blew up. The Peugeot veered sharply, pieces flying off it, and crashed into the wood wall of the restaurant. Yossif stood staring at it by the booth, but no one moved. Someone was screaming. He forced himself to take his finger off the trigger.

Half-way between the van and the booth, Ahmad lay on the sand. Part of his head was missing. His brother writhed like a beached fish, his arms clasped around his stomach. There was a lot of blood everywhere, the van was burning, and above Morteza's screams Yossif could hear someone shouting. Footsteps pounded down the wood planking of the pier and he turned to see Hassan Sadeq.

The former Guards officer jumped down on to the sand and heaved Morteza over his shoulder.

'Quickly,' he gasped. 'The van will explode.'

They left Ahmad and ran along the pier into the fog. Emerging at the end was a white Chriscraft, its engines burbling under the water, as it rested against the old tyres lining the pier. Hassan ran up the small gangplank. Morteza was over his shoulder, blood gushing rhythmically from his mouth and down Hassan's back. On board, Yossif pulled in the plank as Hassan unhitched the ropes, and suddenly the fog vanished as the cargo in the van exploded. The blast sent the powerboat heeling and Yossif ducked his head as fragments of metal and wood began raining into the water. As the fog swirled back into the pocket of heat, Yossif saw someone running in the pines. Then the fog swept back in, black and stinking of explosive, and Hassan pushed the throttles forward.

With the use of Loran and the bridge radar Hassan navigated the big powerboat rapidly and accurately through the fog. Yossif tended to the wounded Mojahedin, who had been shot in the stomach. There was little he could do, except wad the entry wound in an attempt to stem the bleeding. He went to inject him with morphia, but Morteza stayed his hand.

'Wait,' he urged, gasping. 'I would see my sister.'

Half an hour after the short battle Hassan conned the craft into a small artificial harbour. Pines lined the little bay and there was a house on the hill. By the quay stood a

227

white Renault Traffic, Gohar Karim standing by it.

She seized the lines and tied up, and then came running on board.

'Aiii . . . *Haider*, brave one, what has happened?' She knelt by her brother.

'The Ayatollah's men . . . they followed us . . . Ahmad is dead . . . Yossif the Russian killed them with his gun . . .'

Hassan touched Yossif on the arm.

'Quickly. We do not need to linger here.'

The two men went to the Renault van on the quay where, opening the doors, they saw the long wooden case inside. It was mounted on wheels in the manner of an ambulance trolley and so, despite its weight, they were able to manoeuvre it out on to the quay. Using an electric derrick on the Chriscraft, Hassan lifted it on board and they wheeled it inside. Then there were the various boxes that accompanied it.

This is insane, thought Yossif. I am in a foreign country, in the company of a man who has tortured me and two terrorists, one of whom is dying. I have just killed people in a gun battle and I am helping my companions load an ultra-modern Soviet laser-seeking high-explosive missile on to the boat that will take it on the next leg of its journey. Will people believe me when I say that this poor Russian Jew, this little historian did this?

When all was loaded, they turned to Gohar and her brother.

'Enough . . . this poor *mustadh'af* must do *derang* . . .' whispered Morteza. 'I am a *rassoul*, I will take on the message.'

The fighter had gone a bad blue colour, and he gasped with pain.

'The morphia now,' Gohar ordered, without looking up. She held his hand as Yossif slid the needle into his arm and depressed the plunger.

Morteza smiled up at his sister.

'The fear of death is a disease whose only cure is faith, is that not so?' he asked.

228

'It is so.' She smoothed his head with her hand. 'Rest, *haider*, rest. I will take care of all.'

A few minutes later Morteza stopped breathing. His sister reached out and closed his eyes.

'Only I am left,' she said. 'Of the house of Karim, there is but myself.'

She stood up. 'Let us go,' she ordered. 'It is time for *ma'ad*, it is time for the Day of Reckoning.'

On the quay, Yossif watched the Chriscraft edge out of the little harbour. The water foamed at its stern and it quickly vanished in the fog, leaving just the boom of its engines fading away. Yossif got into the cab of the van, reversing along the quay, then turned it round to climb up the track on the steep hillside. When he emerged on the coast road he headed east, taking the route to Nice. A few kilometres down the road he saw a figure standing by a grey Mobylette moped in a parking area overlooking the sea. He drew up alongside and the man got in; it was Spencer.

'Has it gone to plan?' he asked.

Yossif shifted into gear, and they went back on to the road. 'Yes,' said Yossif. 'It has gone as you wanted.'

The road doubled around the steep red rock walls of the coast, and Yossif kept his eyes fixed on where he was going.

'That is, I assume they have gone as you planned,' he said. His mouth was a straight line. 'You did mean to kill Ahmad and Morteza?'

Spencer was silent, sitting across the seat, looking at Yossif.

'I knew, when I saw them in the rotten little bar, the girl and her two brothers. They were young, they knew nothing. They had been involved in a moment of history, now they were refugees in a new land. They should have been left that way, left to forget the past and forge new lives, get married, bring up children. That is what happens to refugees – that is the good, the sane thing to do. But someone had taken them and kept their hatred alive, made them believe they still had a cause, that it still

229

burned back in their homeland. Someone would not let them go, someone kept them like little animals caught in a trap, fed and watered until the time came for them to be let loose – for one brief moment in the air before being gunned down by their captor, the one they had thought their friend. I knew. Listening to them in the van last night, they were full of myths and legends. They knew not the truth. Why did you kill them, Victor?'

'The girl, Gohar Karim, she has to be dependent upon Hassan. She does not need to have other support.'

'And the men in the Peugeot? The ones I killed? The ones Morteza and Ahmad called the Ayatollah's men?'

'They were.'

'And who told them where to go?'

'Yuly Borodin.'

'I was set up for this, Victor. In the simulator, with that man Pasquale, the bodyguard. You knew where it would be. I shot them without thinking because you trained me to.'

Yossif's eyes suddenly filled with tears and he pulled the van off on to the side of the road, unable to see.

'I thought we were the good people, Victor. We can't be good when we do horrible things like this.'

'But the problem with good men is that they will not take the measures necessary. That's not an original thought: Sir Robert Walpole pointed it out a very long time ago, and he knew what he was talking about; he made life so safe for the Whigs that they stayed in power for a hundred years, and the Whigs saw to it that Britain became the greatest power on earth once the French were defeated. We have to defeat the Soviet Union, and to do that you have to take the necessary measures.'

Yossif wiped the tears from his eyes.

'And more people will have to die first?'

'Yes.'

'So what is the truth, Victor? What is really happening?'

'The truth? The truth isn't important. What is important is what people *believe* to be truth – whether it is or not. The Karim brothers and their sister trusted Yuly Borodin of the KGB because they believed that the Soviet Union were their allies. In *fact*, the Soviet Union sold the Mojahedin to the Grand Ayatollah for goodwill in 1982. It proved to be a good bargain. But poor Gohar and her brothers *still* think that the Soviets are their friends. King Charles the First of England was not really a Catholic, and Archbishop Laud's Arminianism was not really "the little thief put in at the window to open the door of the Church"; but sufficient of his nobility and gentry believed that he was, and that it was. Nearly a decade of civil war didn't change their minds, and in the end they made him shorter by a head because of it. His son James the Second *was* a Catholic, but he was not really planning to reconvert England to his religion by the sword and invite in the Inquisition; but enough of his nobility believed that he did and *they* invited in his son-in-law, William of Orange, with a large army, and when his allies and commanders had deserted him the Virgin Mary was left to do all.'

The sun was beginning to burn off the sea fog. Yossif switched out the lights of the van.

'Always religion,' he said.

'Of course,' agreed Spencer. 'Religion is immune to reason. A religious man *knows* what the truth is, and no one may persuade him differently.'

SANTA MARTA

Ric's equipment came – the servos and relays and electrical motors, the solid state circuitry, radio beacons and computers that could make three more MU-2s start themselves up, taxi out, take off and fly a pre-programmed path. We still couldn't land them. I went down to the airport in the truck and picked it all up, then headed for the valley, deciding to store it in the hangar until Ric decided what to do with it. When I came up the road I saw the MU-2 in the air, flying a pattern. Someone was doing touch and gos in it. There was a fierce crosswind blowing, and as I came up I could see the wings of the aircraft rocking in the turbulence on final. I turned in by the hangar and Hank was standing there.

'If you're over there and I'm over here,' I said, getting out, 'then who is in the aircraft up there?'

'That's Ric,' said Hank. 'He got in, only just heard about the crop being destroyed. Came out here, said he wanted to practise some.'

'What's he need to practise for? He's got pilots. That airplane is not for beginners.'

'It's his,' Hank said shortly.

The MU-2 arrived on short final and Ric got fooled by the sink rate as he came close to the numbers. There was a howl from the turbines as he came in with the power and went around.

'That boy is set to make a hole in something,' I said.

Ric got it wrong again the next time around, but he was keen to put it on the dirt by then and kept on coming. He was short, and the nose came up.

'Go around,' I said.

The port wing dipped and you saw the tremor of stall buffet.

'Go around,' I repeated.

Ric put the nose down as he'd been taught and the bird sank like a stone as he still wanted to be on the ground. He got his wish. The MU-2 thumped into the runway like an F-4 making a carrier landing, and the starboard main tyre blew with a bang we heard a quarter of a mile away. He was probably unlucky that the nosegear collected one of the runway lights. When we arrived in the truck the MU-2 was sitting with its nose on the dirt, and Ric had shut down the engines.

'Hullo, R.D.,' he said. He seemed unmoved. 'Can you move it?'

'We'll shift it,' I told him. He looked in the back of the truck.

'Are those the parts? I'll take them. I'll store them at my quarters in town.'

I looked at the MU-2, working out how to tow it in. Ric slid behind the wheel of the truck.

'Pity about the crop,' he said. 'It could almost have put us out of business.'

'Yeah.'

'I'll just have to make other arrangements.'

233

PARIS

Spencer got into Orly off the Eastern 747 about the time Parisians were getting ready to go to work, and his cab joined the flowing traffic on the Left Bank as they were doing so. Housewives had begun their shopping on the lively markets along the rue de Buci when he got out and strolled a short distance to his hotel. Having eschewed the breakfast on the aircraft, after checking in he went down to the basement where he enjoyed fresh French coffee, croissants and rolls. The hotel had begun life as a small abbey in the sixteenth century, and Spencer was eating in what had once been the chapel. The conversion had been managed with beautiful taste, and he smiled to himself, thinking how Yossif Petrovsky would have complained at being left out of the first hotel with any class.

When he was through, he went up to his room, where he took a shower and changed. The room looked out over an attractive courtyard where one of the staff was tending the tubs and hanging baskets of spring flowers, and he was standing at the window when the knock on the door came. He opened it and Yuly Borodin came in.

'I came as soon as I got the message from O'Neill,' said Spencer. 'Is it about Nowruz?'

'No,' said Borodin. He sat down in a good copy of a Louis XIII armchair. 'Not directly. All is on target for Nowruz. The New Year is not far away. This concerns your Ade Jumbe, the 747 that crashed into Harlem and Hojat Tasdeeq's soldiers of God. I can tell you who Yusuf Ghesuda who kidnapped Ade Jumbe, was – and what he was doing.'

Spencer sat on the edge of the twentieth-century bed, with its hard square pillows.

'Okay,' he said.

'To understand the story fully you have to go back to the return of the Grand Ayatollah Khomeini to Iran in 1979. The Soviet Union had built up support among the people, using especially the pro-Soviet Tudeh party, and for some while it was considered that it was wisest to lie quiet and wait for Khomeini's Islamic revolution to consume its children, with Tudeh and their allies waiting to inherit the homeland. By 1981 it was clear that with the assistance of the war against Iraq Khomeini had secured control over the country, and that the policy of lying in wait was fruitless, as was confrontation. The decision was made to ride the tiger, and to buy goodwill and trust from the Ayatollah's regime. Accordingly – I was there at the time and a party to this – we sacrificed a very large number of those we had in place, including the entire top Tudeh leadership, all of whom were executed, along with some 10,000 supporters of the Mojahedin who with Bani-Sadr had attempted insurrection in '81. The tactic worked very successfully and much goodwill was obtained. In the meantime, we concentrated on building up a new network of supporters, using junior elements of Tudeh, so that today we are in a far stronger position than we were in 1982. It was when this goodwill had been bought that it was decided to use Iran as a stalking-horse for a very ambitious operation directed against the United States.

'For the past decade, the Soviet leadership has noted that America seems to be in decline. American leadership of the West has faltered ever since the Vietnam war. The American system of government is visibly running out of steam. Political confusion at home is reflected by incompetence and an inability to define policy and objectives abroad. Once the strongest in the world, the American economy has been overtaken, and the government has allowed the greatest creditor nation to become the greatest debtor. The stock market has crashed. More than anything else, there is a lack of any national will and

235

purpose. At best, it seems that America has entered a period of introspection.'

Spencer grunted. 'The USA is in decline, Yuly. What do you think we are doing here with 'Ashura? It's the gambler's last throw of the dice. If we win we get enough money to sit it out on the porch while the younger nations get at it with tooth and claw.'

Borodin nodded in agreement. 'Forget about *glasnost*, CFR, the reunification of Germany and all the rest of it. Simply remember that the KGB can only exist while there are "enemies". It is pathological about enemies, and must search, discover and eliminate them. Without this impelling drive it will cease to breathe, to be. The USA has been, is and will remain the principal target of such external activities. The congruence of the rise of militant Islam, the worrying weaknesses appearing in Soviet foreign policy and the possession of a piece of peculiar technology gave the impetus to the plan. It has long been felt that the USA is vulnerable in three areas. Firstly, to the effects of narcotic drugs on the younger people. Two, to the effects of racial hatred, as so many different races make up her population. Three, to the effects of a sustained and successful terrorist campaign. It is felt that efforts made to promote these three factors would pay enormous dividends in terms of damaging the leadership and national will of the USA. Accordingly, given the current conditions in America, it was decided to go ahead and do just that.'

'You'd need enormous teams. It would be the equivalent of a declaration of war.'

Borodin nodded in his new antique chair.

'Certainly. Which is why the operation was set up to emanate from Iran. Then, if discovered, the Iranians could take the punishment that would be handed out. But not teams. Individuals. The soldiers of God.'

'Of which Ade Jumbe was one.'

'Yes.'

'He was turned into an *entehari*. In a matter of a few weeks. How was it done?'

'The actual process took but one night. A few days for preparation. Ade Jumbe was brought up as a Muslim, as a young boy, though his faith lapsed and he forgot Allah. One night, in the holy city of Qom, Hojat Tasdeeq returned him to the power of his Lord. He was assisted by the man known as Yusuf Ghesuda. Ghesuda was a Spetznatz soldier, a man from Khirgiz who could pass for Arab. He was equipped with certain drugs, drugs developed in the Soviet psychiatric hospital at Dzherzhin, the hospital that has specialized in the destruction of a man's will since the early days of Stalin. With these drugs there is no need for the old methods, the days of forced kneeling, the deprivation of sleep, the entombment in the box filled with tens of thousands of bedbugs, the incarceration in the concrete coffin with ice water trickling over the victim – all these methods of destroying a man's mind, of sending him insane, became obsolete. The drugs leave no marks, save on the mind. The mind they break. The course nearly always destroys the will to resist. Some victims commit suicide afterwards, so terrible is their pain.'

Borodin leaned forward and held up one finger. 'The drugs work with all but the very strongest of minds. For a very few, very strong, very ruthless, very committed people, the drugs simply serve to enhance the strength of will already present. Then the person becomes exceptionally dangerous. The only course then is to shoot them.

'Yusuf Ghesuda and Hojat Tasdeeq selected a very few such people. Each was fully adult, each knew America well. Each had already shown great ability, and great ruthlessness. They were very, very strong in the mind. All had once as children been brought up in the faith of Islam. This faith they had forgotten, and allowed to lapse. One by one, these people were brought to the little *hojrah* the little devotees' cell that Hojat Tasdeeq prepared for them in Qom.

'The leader of the Assassins, Sheikh-al-Jabal, prepared his devotees, those who would die to accomplish their mission, by granting them great pleasures in their

237

fortresses, as a foretaste of the Paradise which they would enter when they had died completing the task set for them. Hojat Tasdeeq used a different method. Under him the soldier-to-be was returned to Allah. In the name of Allah, they felt His displeasure. They burned in Hell for a full hundred years. Then their Lord in His mercy rescued them, to do His will. The release from Hell was entry to Paradise. Once sent on their way, programmed, nothing should be able to stop them. They would be intent on entering Paradise once their mission was completed. So they became God's soldiers, and would carry out His will. They feared failure above all else; they feared eternal torment.'

There was quiet in the room. The scent of the flowers in the courtyard drifted up through the window. Below, the gardener's shoes scraped on the flags as he watered the pots.

'Ade Jumbe was not the first,' Borodin said. 'They began with a woman.'

'Did your Spetznatz man Ghesuda know who she was?'

'Yes. He was the one who freed her from prison. She was Saada Mohammed.'

Spencer stared at Borodin for some time.

'So that's what happened to the bitch.'

Saada Mohammed was post-Baader-Meinhof, the spoiled daughter of a Beirut businessman, a prescient man who foresaw the future and moved his family to America. Saada was an Arab until she was ten, and an American until she was twenty. Good-looking, fit and intelligent, with a Master's degree in computer engineering, she acquired direction to her life when she met Elizabeth Meyer on a research trip to Heidelberg University. Elizabeth was a member of the Siegfried Haag terrorist group – she had been there when they sliced Hans-Martin Schleyer's throat from ear to ear for being an industrial-ist – and she was ever on the lookout for suitable talent.

In Saada Mohammed she found it, and although she was responsible for her training and indoctrination the pupil outshone the teacher.

Saada Mohammed shed her old life like a used set of clothes. Her uncle was a man who had an engineering firm in partnership with her father; it sold electronic equipment to Panavia for NATO's Tornado fighter-bomber. She made an appointment to call for tea one afternoon and killed him and his family with three bursts of fire from an Uzi sub-machine gun, and incinerated the bodies in the pyre of their home.

GSG-9 caught up with Elizabeth Meyer, who died in a gun-battle in a safe house near the French border. Saada Mohammed simply went on to greater and greater exploits. She founded her own terrorist organization, funding it through a series of bloody and successful bank robberies, and began a two-year campaign against NATO targets. Highly intelligent, and by this time seasoned in her art, she split the group into two; one to carry out terror, a second, political wing to co-ordinate activities with the fringe radicals, the useful tools, during the 'militant pacifist' campaign against President Reagan for deploying US nuclear weapons in NATO bases.

During this campaign she established links with other terrorist groups in Europe, including the Inge Viett group of the Red Army Faction, the 2nd June Movement, the French Action Directe and Red Zora. She was a guiding force behind the formation of the Red Cells, training groups of men and women with far left, anti-imperialist, anti-Zionist leanings, from whom the pick of the new terrorists was selected. She showed considerable political ability by having her political wing build links with the Greens, the ecological party. In her depth of understanding of the methods required to de-stabilize a Western society she was unmatched, and far superior to her predecessors like Ulrike Meinhof and Andreas Baader.

Saada Mohammed possessed a genius for her profession. That was the simple opinion of the federal attorney-general's office in Karlsruhe, who prosecuted her at the

239

great trial. It was also the opinion of the judge, who sentenced her to detention without limit in Stammheim prison.

A riot broke out in F-Block, in Stammheim, at twenty minutes past three in the afternoon. Saada Mohammed, pacing round and round in the little exercise yard, heard it. It was quickly brought under control by the guards, but in the short time it lasted two men were injured. One was a guard, and he had been stabbed. They called for an air ambulance.

Two armed guards were with Mohammed and the prison itself was overlooked by six towers. The guards in them were armed. The yard where she walked was small, and walled.

They heard the noise of the helicopter coming. The clatter of the blades took on the characteristic thump as it slowed to a high hover. The guards in the yard saw it arrive, hovering some fifty feet up and two hundred feet away. One guard wondered why it did not go to the helipad. Then he wondered why it was different. The usual air ambulance was a Messerschmitt-Bolkow-Blohm B0105, and this was a Bell UH-1. Still it was painted white, with large red crosses. The noise it made may have silenced alarm bells in his mind as well as made him deaf to the noise of the two Aérospatiale Gazelle helicopters coming up from the south. Looking up, he did catch sight of a very small helicopter circling round the prison at about 2,000 feet, and heard its faint buzzing as of an exasperated wasp.

Then the Gazelles were upon them. They were fitted with 7.62 Chain Guns, and in a single pass they took out the guard towers with a mixture of incendiary and armour-piercing rounds. As he saw the Gazelles pass under him, the pilot of the Hughes 300 hovering above dropped the collective and began to auto-rotate downwards. In the big Bell, hovering by the exercise yard, the large side door rolled back. A sniper positioned inside shot both guards dead with two perfectly aimed shots. Saada Mohammed ran to the side of the yard, as she had been instructed to do.

She was just in time. There was a sudden burst of noise as the pilot of the Hughes brought the power back on, a hundred feet up. The tiny helicopter was dropping like a stone, its blades windmilling. The pilot flew it backwards as he descended, to acquire the very small target he had – the walled exercise yard – then forward, and as he entered the yard vertically, arrested his descent with collective. It was a superlative piece of flying; the yard measured fifty feet by fifty, and the helicopter was just over thirty feet long.

The doors were off and the cockpit open. As the helicopter landed, Saada Mohammed ran the short distance under the blades and scrambled into the right-hand seat. The second set of controls had been removed, and as she made contact with the seat the pilot raised the collective. He had the rpm at 3,300 in the red arc and the helicopter came out of the yard like a pogo stick. As the rpm decayed, he put the nose down and they skimmed away over the German countryside. They landed in a field four miles away, where the crews of the Bell and the Hughes transferred to the Gazelles. The two Gazelles were over 60 mph faster.

The German police found the Gazelles early the next day, at rest. They were parked together on a remote landing strip south of Reutlingen. The grass of the runway was charred from the exhaust gas of a jet engine, but like the guns and engines of the helicopters it was cold.

QOM

In his grim dwelling Hojat Tasdeeq had prepared a *hojrah* for Saada Mohammed. In years gone by those who sought to learn the truth had dwelt as hermits in very simple stone caves, and the word was kept, as was the function and style, when the seeker – the one who would become *mujtahid* – lived in a building. The floor was swept stone and there was no furniture other than a coarse tribal rug, a prayer mat, a plain table on which stood an earthen water jar and a bowl, and an unlit candle. Saada Mohammed knelt in *chador*, the prayer mat spread before her. Dim light filtered in through a high window.

She was sedated – fully conscious but lacking individual will. The drug Yusuf Ghesuda had used to induce this state had been developed for the treatment of schizophrenia. By the woman's side knelt her *modarre*, Hojat Tasdeeq, her instructor. In a shadowy corner stood the Soviet special troops officer, Ghesuda.

'There is no God but God,' Tasdeeq intoned.

Her body jerked, as though touched by electric current.

'There is no God but God,' she repeated, 'and Mohammed is His prophet.'

Breath hissed through Tasdeeq's large teeth, set in a face like a starving mule, and joy awoke in his heart. He was certain that the woman had not repeated those words since she had been a little girl.

'It is dawn,' he said. 'Mecca is ahead of you.'

Saada Mohammed washed, performing the long-forgotten rituals correctly. Her feet were bare, her head

242

covered as she prostrated herself on the prayer mat and praised the Lord for the first of the five times in the day.

'In the name of God, the merciful, the compassionate. Praise be to God, the Lord of the worlds, the merciful, the compassionate, the ruler of the Judgement Day! Thee we serve . . . '

When her prayers were finished Tasdeeq allowed her to pour a glass of lukewarm water from the jar. It was the water of Qom. That bleak place was built on the site of what had once been a huge salt lake. Passing through layer upon layer of salt, the water that emerged was bitterly revolting in taste and had the peculiar quality of promoting in the thirsty who drank it an even greater desire for water. With this horrible drink Saada Mohammed was allowed a few raisins and a bite of unleavened bread and goat's cheese. After the meagre meal Tasdeeq bid her sleep for an hour, the *ghaylulah* recommended by the Prophet himself.

Living in the ghastly city in the summer was akin to camping out close to a blast furnace. For the next two days in the stifling little room, afflicted by the swarms of biting flies, the heat and the raging thirst promoted by the water of the city, Hojat Tasdeeq, assisted by Ghesuda, returned Saada Mohammed to the correct, the one true faith.

During the second day Tasdeeq began reminding her that she had forgotten her faith which she had had as a child. He linked her loss of faith with her failure to destroy the machinations of *Taghut, Shaytan Bozorg*, the United States. Her will had been removed from her by drugs, and she became very agitated and filled with guilt.

Outside it was dusk. Darkness seemed to pour through the little window into the stone *hojrah*. It was time for Saada Mohammed to enter Hell.

This was the crucial part of the programming. The drugs used would break the minds of all but the supremely strong, and were administered in combination. The first made the body exceptionally sensitive to all stimulation. The second was toxic, it caused immense pain and a rise in body temperature. The rise was such that the victim became delirious, racked with thirst and subject to terrible and terrifying hallucinations. The sophistication of the treatment lay in the third element. It was derived from a synthetic hallucinogen, and when under its effect time for the victim slowed thousand-fold. Tasdeeq's treatment would last but the night. For Saada Mohammed, it would be one hundred years spent broiling in the very furnaces of Hell.

'It is the Judgement Day,' said Tasdeeq. His voice echoed in the bare room. 'The angels Gabriel, Michael, Azrael and Uriel have summoned all before the Lord their God. You have failed your Lord.'

Saada Mohammed moaned in protest. 'No . . . I tried, I did well . . .'

'You forgot your Lord. Had you believed in Me, you would have succeeded . . . you failed . . . America is still strong, she is still *Shaytan Bozorg*.'

'Another chance . . . please, another chance,' the terror leader begged.

In the dark room Tasdeeq pulled back the sleeve of her gown and slid the sharp needle of a syringe into the soft flesh. He pressed the plunger, and she groaned in pain as the chemicals entered her body.

'You have failed Me. You failed in your task. I cast you into everlasting torment.'

Tasdeeq rose. The chemicals were beginning to work, and she shuddered at the impact of the noise as she moved. Ghesuda was by the table; he struck the match that lit the candle and she shrieked in agony.

For most of the night the task of the two men was to monitor their victim, to ensure that she did not choke, that her body temperature did not rise so high that she burned up and her life force become consumed in the blaze. In the small hours, Tasdeeq began the programming, implanting the commands within her brain for her to act upon.

'Americans must fear . . . aircraft will crash into cities, water will poison from taps . . . '

They kept going through the night with coffee, endless black cups. Ghesuda occasionally smoked a cigarette.

'Americans must fear . . . white must fear black, black hate Hispanic . . . each must blame the other . . . there must be plague . . . '

The noise was terrible.

'Americans must fear . . . they must fear to go out at night, they must fear to act . . . '

There was another room in the building where there was a cool bath, crystal-cool water to lie in, to bring down the raging heat of her body, to take away the temperature that turned agony into the hallucinations of Satan, to bring her back to the real world. Programmed to act, no matter what. In a refrigerator there was fresh bottled water, chilled, to soften the parched mouth. Ice-water, more delicious than nectar. There was a soft bed to lie in, in cool conditioned air. She would be in Paradise.

The light of dawn was filtering through the little high window as Saada Mohammed lay on the stone flags, barely recognizable as human. A murderer of many, she had paid for her sins. She was stained and stinking, her body contorted by cramps of agony, her skin drawn tight from the dehydration of torment. Yet her chest still rose and fell in shallow breath. She was alive.

Tasdeeq cradled her in his arms. Ghesuda brought a glass of cold, fresh water and Tasdeeq raised it to her lips.

'Drink, my servant . . . ' The parched, cracked and bloody lips rustled as they tried to take from the glass. 'Do not waste it . . . to waste a drop is to pluck a feather from the wing of an angel . . . '

The precious fluid trickled into her mouth, running over and round the swollen, purple tongue.

'Mercy has been given to you . . . you have your mission to perform . . . you must not fail . . . '

The eyes of Saada Mohammed opened. Her lips moved, reopening the fissures created by the night, and blood trickled down.

'There is no God but God,' she whispered, 'and Mohammed is His prophet.'

Down in the courtyard, small tables had been set on the old flagstones where the monks used to gather, and now guests were drifting by for an aperitif before heading into Paris for shopping and sightseeing. In the room above, Spencer got up from sitting on the bed and looked down.

'The Lord must wonder what we're doing down here,' he said. 'We're all assembling our soldiers, and each in His name. How many of these creatures are there? How many did Tasdeeq programme?'

'There were four,' said Borodin. 'Saada Mohammed was the first, and then the African, Ade Jumbe.'

'Who were the other two?'

'Ghesuda never knew. After the first two, Tasdeeq sent Ghesuda away for a while, with soft words, for a rest. But Ghesuda was suspicious and watched Tasdeeq secretly. Tasdeeq had two more men brought to him, and these he programmed himself. Ghesuda was powerless to interfere and, reporting back, was withdrawn. There was only enough of the special drugs for four. Ghesuda was withdrawn because someone finally started thinking clearly and realized that if the programming worked, if it was effective, it was a weapon that could quite as easily rebound upon the user. It is known that Tasdeeq hates the Soviet Union – not as much as the USA, but he does. "People in glass houses" . . . so Ghesuda was withdrawn, and all information relating to the programming and the drugs used destroyed. There will be only four soldiers of God.'

'Ade Jumbe is dead. He died to prove that it worked, and as the beginning of Saada Mohammed's campaign of terror. I wish I knew why it started and ended there. It should have been the first lash of the whirlwind. Maybe we got lucky. Maybe the bitch fell under a truck. With her, and two more, that gives enough for one for terror, one for drugs and one for racial hatred. What are the other two? I wish we could capture Tasdeeq and have him tell us what he knows.'

'We can't risk it,' Borodin said firmly. 'It would endanger 'Ashura.'

'I know. We're going to have to cross our fingers. There is nothing going on to indicate any increase in the areas we've been talking about. No great rise in drug use, no terror, no racial hatred. Maybe this programming doesn't work that well after all.'

'Maybe,' said Borodin. He got up from his chair. 'I must leave, Victor. I have to be in Tehran by tonight. It's nearly the third of June.'

'Right. Don't leave it too late to go, Yuly. You're going to be the most hated man in Iran.'

'I'll go in time,' Borodin said reassuringly.

'Is everything in place?'

'Everything.'

'Leave everything behind when you go.'

Borodin looked at Spencer in friendly exasperation.

'Victor, I think we have only been over all this one hundred times already!'

'I'm sorry, Yuly,' said Spencer placatingly.

'All generals worry on the eve of the battle. Once the battle starts it will be out of your hands.'

'Yes. How odd that we should both think of soldiers of God. We must trust that ours are better than theirs.'

Borodin smiled. 'Isn't God on the side of the big battalions? We have many more than four.'

Spencer remained in Paris until the following morning. He spent the day walking in the city, ate supper in a popular restaurant on the Ile St-Louis, and after breakfast the next day took a taxi back to Orly. In the terminal he paused to buy a paper after checking in and the headlines blazed: EPIDEMIC OF DEATH. THOUSANDS DEAD.

'Oh, Jesus,' he whispered. 'The bitch has woken up.'

He went to a payphone and dialled Yossif Petrovsky in

247

New York. It was a little while before dawn and Yossif was deeply asleep after an exciting evening spent having his handwriting analysed.

'Hullo?'

'Yossif, this is Victor. I'm in Paris, at Orly. I'm catching the Eastern flight back. This business in North Carolina. Tell the Mayor the person they are looking for is Saada Mohammed. She was a terror leader in Europe towards the end of the seventies, with a group called *Fatih*. It was bound up with Red Zora, Action Directe and the rest. The Germans captured her and sentenced her to life, with a minimum of forty years in Stammheim. The trial judge said he considered her the single most dangerous person, woman or man, to ever come before him, hence the very long sentence. She was sprung from Stammheim two years ago in a very well organized and daring operation using helicopters, but has never been heard of since. Get the Mayor to put her picture on television. Someone must know her. There is also a man called Davidson. He worked as a scientist at Fort Detrick, making nerve gas. He's missing. Put his picture on television and ask anyone who knows where he is, or has seen him, to call.'

Yossif pushed back the bedclothes and sat on the edge of the bed. A vodka headache was tightening around his forehead.

'Okay, Victor. I'll pick you up at the airport.'

He was there waiting when Spencer came through the customs at JFK. His car was in the short-term park, and as they walked across the bridge he said, 'We've found Saada Mohammed.'

Spencer stared at him in real surprise, amid the turbine noise all around them.

'Already?' he asked. 'That's very good indeed.'

Petrovsky shook his head as the great aircraft took off and landed, one after the other.

'No,' he said. 'It isn't.'

*   *   *

248

The building was dingy and run down. A smell of ancient cooking, excrement and madness hung in the air like a miasma. The balding man who stood in front of Spencer and Petrovsky in the bulb-lit corridor was responsible for the building, and failure dwelt in his eyes. Now, however, they were illuminated also by a curious mixture of apprehension and excitement at being close to notoriety. He was a doctor, but one who had ultimately settled for the small security of working for the state, passing paper through his hands and looking after people like Saada Mohammed.

Saada Mohammed had not washed in some while. A thin, disagreeable odour arose from her body, and her once-lustrous black hair lay lank and greasy around her face.

'I'm sorry you see her like this, gentlemen,' the little doctor said apologetically. 'This is kind of the place of last resort for people like her. She's paid for by the state, you see; there's no one to pay for her.'

The little room was painted a dull cream, with bars on the outside of the dirty windows. Saada Mohammed was on a flimsy mattress, with a grey blanket rumpled at the end of the bed. She lay in a foetal position and did not move.

'She was found in a hotel almost two years ago,' he said. 'She's been here ever since.'

'Like this?' asked Spencer.

'Like this. She's very heavily sedated, gentlemen.'

'Why? What's the matter with her?'

'She's suffering from some very deep-seated religious mania. When she is not sedated she is as she was when she was found in the hotel – she shrieks as though in terrible torment, and begs God for forgiveness.'

'Any chance of her recovering?'

'No. You wouldn't want to hear her, gentlemen. I've been in this business many years now, and even I can't stand it for long. The agony is very real, even if it is just in her mind. She is in terror of burning in Hell, and if we take away the sedation in her mind she feels as though she really is burning there. It simply isn't kind, or even medically sound. You wouldn't treat a dog that way, let alone a fellow human being, even if she is this terrorist.'

'She is,' said Spencer.

'Well,' said the doctor, 'if she's done bad things in the past, then the Lord has surely sent them back to live with her now.'

They drove away, and even the Brooklyn air seemed clean.

'She was in there when the 747 crashed,' said Petrovsky.

'Yes. Ade Jumbe did that on his own, because he was programmed to do so. Afterwards Ali and Hassan killed Adam Ross, because he wasn't needed any more. Hojat Tasdeeq knew that one of his soldiers was inoperative, that the campaign of terror which Saada Mohammed was programmed for would never take place.'

'If Saada Mohammed is inoperative, what about all the dead in North Carolina?'

'There are two more soldiers,' said Spencer. 'One of them must not be.'

SANTA MARTA

They had it on television. You could see a town, an ordinary American town, not very big, nestling across the floor of a small valley in the mountains. There were army trucks parked in the street and soldiers were moving on foot, unarmed, although they appeared in full combat outfits. The cameraman cranked up the zoom; he must have been a very long way off, because the picture was shaky, and you could see that they were wearing their NBC – Nuclear Biological and Chemical protection. An agitated voice was speaking in Spanish. The soldiers moved slowly along the street – it was most strange, nothing else moved. A dog was sleeping on the pavement. A soldier prodded it with one foot but it did not move.

'What are they saying?' I said. Ellen was listening to the Spanish commentator.

'He says . . . there is no damage . . . the bird is still alive . . . what bird? Oh, I see, look, the soldier has a bird in a cage.'

On the screen, one of the soldiers was carrying what looked like a parrot, in a cage.

'All along the valley there are dead birds on the ground . . . they lie under the trees where they were sleeping in the night. Animals are dead in the fields . . . they are going up the valley to see how far . . . it is twenty miles they are finding dead animals and people.'

The shot switched; soldiers were carrying a shrouded stretcher out of a house and putting it into a field ambulance. Then another, and then three more, small, small mounds under grey blankets.

'No one knows what has caused this . . . can it be

251

radiation? Some sort of poisoning? They are picking up reports from the radios of the officers that say everyone seems to have died in their sleep. They are unmarked . . . there are no injured . . . only the dead . . . '

'Where is it?' I asked urgently.

'They haven't said.'

We had to wait fifteen or more minutes before they told us. Fifteen minutes of dread before I knew who was responsible for the death toll of birds, animals, men, women, their children.

'Here . . . North Carolina . . . a small valley up in the mountains, north-west of Spartanburg . . . '

The picture changed and a still photograph of a man appeared, a thin, bespectacled man.

'The American authorities want this man . . . Dr Curtis Davidson . . . he may be with two children . . . a boy of eight and a girl of five . . . there is a number to call . . . '

My fingers took a pen and noted it down, as I counted to ten, like you do when things are really bad, in the worst weather, short of fuel, before you talk to the man, get you down.

They would be bringing the bodies out soon, laying them in rows. I was there when they shot the Galaxy down with the refugees on board, I knew how it was done.

This would be tidier, of course. There would be no mud or wreckage, no blood or mutilation, no hasty improvisation of covers, no damp field to have to use to lay out the dead. This was America; there would be all the facilities they needed and no need to search in the ditches and among the debris of the accident for the dead. All they needed to do was break into the houses the fathers and mothers had made secure the night before, to keep their families safe. They would find everyone neat and tidy in their beds: men who had gone to sleep with a problem to be solved on their minds, one that a good night's rest might provide an answer to; women worrying about their children; young men and women with plans, exams to take, leaving home, getting married; young children with no anxieties beyond hoping for good weather to go fishing, to play with their friends. The friendly cat, curled up in the most comfortable place, the loyal dog, nose on paws outside.

It wouldn't really have been similar to the Galaxy at all. And there were so very many more people. It wasn't me, the man who pulled the trigger as the great Galaxy lumbered into view.

'I reckon that's nerve gas,' I said. 'Hank and I flew the 5-gallon cans it came in into Spartanburg. We took them from Ric's strip on the Mosquito Coast. After take-off I was nauseous, I couldn't fly. After we'd off-loaded and were flying back I felt even worse. I had to go lie in the back. Now, Hank wasn't affected by it. But before I ever came here, I had an accident last season; I crashed on take-off and got covered in the spray – it was bad stuff, methyl parathion. Parathion's related to nerve gas, and I'm hypersensitive to it. I went to see a doctor, and he ran some tests on my blood and says I'm sensitized. I reckon that whatever we took into that valley in the drums is a nerve gas in liquid form. They'd better just take me out and hang me. I took Davidson and his children to Nicaragua for Ric. That's where he is.'

I picked up the phone and dialled. I heard the numbers clicking as the relays sent the call to the USA. It rang, and someone picked up at the other end.

'This is Yossif Petrovsky.'

QOM

On the morning of March 22, Hojat Tasdeeq
awoke before dawn. It was the Spring Equinox, the first
day of the New Year, and this year the day coincided
with mourning for the sixth Shi'ia Imam, Ja'far Sadeq. It
was Nowruz, the New Day. When Tasdeeq had finished
the rituals of his morning prayers, he found a messenger
waiting for him. It was this person who told him of the
search for and the finding of Saada Mohammed in New
York. Tasdeeq pondered a moment, then ordered the
man to wait outside for a few minutes. From a drawer in
the simple chest in his room he took a small Sony Micro-
cassette recorder, similar to the one used by the unfortunate Musavi Yasdi. Using this infernal machine, a
frightful anachronism in the mediaeval setting of the
room, he recorded a short message on to the tape. Re-
winding it, he then took a plain brown envelope, wrote a
name and address on to it and put the cassette inside.
Summoning the messenger he gave it to the man, together
with instructions. The messenger left then, to travel the
hundred miles north to Tehran where he would catch a
flight to Paris. Once in Paris, he would apply postage and
send the little package on its way. It was a message, an
order two sentences long, sent to the Fourth Soldier.

Hojat Tasdeeq then broke his fast with some lukewarm
water sweetened with raisins, and a bite of bread and
goat's cheese. Dealing with the messenger and passing his
instructions on had robbed him of the time for the short
ghaylulah sleep before the sun had fully risen. The sun
was up, and next door he could hear his seekers and
mullahs gathering in the *madrasseh*. He checked his
dress, which was austere. The flowing black robe of the

Shi'ite clergy, topped with the black turban of the *sayyed*, and simple *na'alayn* slippers on his feet. As a *sayyed*, or gentleman, one who could claim direct descent from the Prophet Mohammed, Tasdeeq could also have worn a green belt. Many clergymen dyed their beards with henna, but he did not. In his personal life Tasdeeq followed the teaching of Shaikh Abu-Sa'id. 'Your vanity is a barking dog,' taught the Shaikh. 'Silence it.' For himself, Tasdeeq wanted nothing. For the Lord, he would do anything.

Outside there was the noise of people moving in the streets, preparing for the great day. The air was crisp and Tasdeeq put an *abas*, a knitted camel-wool shawl, around his shoulders. He went out to lead his followers from the *madrasseh* to where the great procession was to assemble, before setting out on its solemn way to the great shrine of Ma'assoumah and the majestic Mosque next to it.

The golden domes of the shrine to Fatima – the Chaste One, sister of Imam Reza – and the Mosque dominated the city of Qom. They were visible from afar. From her little apartment in the block a mile away Gohar Karim, only daughter and last surviving offspring of Abdul Karim, one-time revolutionary leader of the Iranian Mojahedin, could see them clearly. Through her Zeiss tripod-mounted 4×10 binoculars she could pick out the individual figures in the procession which was preparing to depart on its way to them.

The apartment was a small one, suitable for a young widow of the war, which was how she portrayed herself, in a drab tower block, one of several erected under the rule of the Shah in the 1950s. Her neighbours hardly knew she was there – a quiet person whose family, they thought, had been entirely wiped out in the fighting for Khorramshahr, she emerged only infrequently and dressed fully in *chador* and veil. Now, standing in her little living room, she was dressed in combat fatigues for ease of movement and psychological boost. Next to her binoculars, mounted on a far heavier tripod, in olive drab was a boxy piece of military equipment, in size and shape not unlike a very early camera. In detail, however, it was clearly a most modern piece of machinery. Powered by a NiCad battery that sat on the floor inside the tripod legs, two 'spectacles' peered out from the front of the box, looking at the Mosque. One was an optical transmitter and one a receiver. The box was a KTD or *kvantovy dal'nomer* laser rangefinder and designator. When used to assess range – the 1.452 km from the living room to the great window of the Mosque – when commanded it produced a pulsed 900-volt discharge from its capacitors, a 'clot' or *sgustok* of light energy that was transmitted to its objective. As the ignition circuit was activated a signal was also passed to a counter, which began turning. Once a small amount of reflected radiation was received back through the receiving assembly, the counter halted. Since a chip in the KTD knew the speed of light, it was a simple task for it to multiply time and speed to obtain the distance. The KTD was in service with Soviet artillery target acquisition units, and the particular version then resting in Gohar Karim's apartment in Qom was in service with Mi-24 *Hind* ground attack helicopters, which required a designator facility to illuminate targets for their *Spiral* air-to-ground or ground-to-ground missiles. In the *Hind* the designator was powered by electricity produced by the three generators turned by the Isotov turbines, which gave unlimited use of the designator. For portable ground use the NiCad battery gave sufficient power for target illumination of up to two minutes. It was more than enough.

In the distance a slowly moving wave appeared to be passing through the crowd lining the route, running parallel with the head of the procession. Looking through the binoculars Gohar could see men and women prostrating themselves. At the very tip of the procession was a most aged figure, white-bearded, black-robed and turbaned, walking slowly, seeming to look only at the ground before him. It was the Grand Ayatollah, who for many of the religion he led had become *nabi*, the Emissary of Allah, one almost on a par with the

Prophets, one who had the right to wield political and military power on behalf of the Almighty.

Tracking along the way to the shrine and Mosque, Gohar could see the television crews recording the event. The Grand Ayatollah had not been seen in public for many months, it had even been rumoured that he was dead, and such was his age and ill-health that this would surely be one of the last times his people would see him. Behind the great old man came serried ranks of men with beards and turbans of black and white; some way back, as befitted their place in Islam, came the veiled women in their *chadors*. At the front Gohar could see Hojat Tasdeeq flanked by his *talabehs* and mullahs, and Shaikh Jazayeri with a scattering of IRGC officers in attendance, whose olive drab contrasted with the black robes of the clergy.

A double knock came at the door, she ran to open it and Hassan Sadeq quickly slipped inside. He was dressed very like Tasdeeq, as a mullah.

'I am worried,' she said. 'I thought that you would be late.'

'I had to be sure I came here unseen. Security is heavy.'

At one side of the little room was a Soviet ZK/441 radio communications set. As was standard, it had the capacity to frequency-hop and was hooked up to use the apartment block television aerial as its own. Hassan sat down at the keyboard and began to tap out commands. In a cave five miles outside the city relays clicked shut, gyros began to spool up and the AT-6 *Spiral* missile came alive on its launcher.

'*Spiral* is active,' he said.

The procession had reached the great Mosque, and the principal members were beginning to file inside. The rank-and-file would hear the service outside, through loudspeakers. As they entered the magnificent building, with its great windows and fabulous glass chandelier suspended from the golden dome, Shaikh Jazayeri edged to one side. Very pale and sweating, he pressed a white cotton handkerchief to his mouth.

257

'One moment,' he murmured to his aide. 'I shall return in a moment, I am temporarily unwell.'

He refused offers of help, ordering his people to remain in the Mosque and to wait for him. He slipped quietly along a corridor into the *takieh*, where the Imam Hussein was remembered, and which had a small lavatory. He went in and shut the door. The pill he had taken before joining the procession was making his stomach churn, and he bent suddenly and vomited. With the emetic gone, he felt better. He settled down to wait.

From the fifteenth floor of the apartment block, Gohar could see the crowd swelling around the front of the Mosque as the doors were shut. The white walls and golden dome shone in the sunlight. Through the clear spring air the trained voice of the *muezzin* in the tall minaret came clear and beautiful, like a bird, calling the faithful to prayer.

In the lavatory, Shaikh Jazayeri took a small but sharp knife from his pocket and, gritting his teeth, used it to gash himself nastily across his scalp. The blood spouted from the vascular skin, staining his white robe.

In the mosque, the doors were shut and the service ready to begin. The Grand Ayatollah knelt facing Mecca, and behind him the ranks of his subjects did the same. Above and behind him glittered the great glass chandelier.

In the apartment, looking through the open window to the little concrete and rusting rail balcony, Gohar and Hassan were ready. Looking through the sighting tube, Gohar lined up the cross-hairs of the *zritel'naya* at the back of the KTD on the great window of the Mosque. She selected the designator mode, and checked the charge built up in the capacitors of the pulse modulator block.

'Ready?'

'Ready,' said Hassan.

Gohar squeezed the button marked *pusk* and the laser came on.

'Target illuminated,' she said.

In the Mosque the centre of the great chandelier was suddenly charged with light and the cut glass fragmented the light into every colour of the rainbow, casting it throughout the huge hall. Exclamations of wonder burst out from the congregation and the more simple-minded began crying out, calling God's name and linking it with that of the Grand Ayatollah, who steadfastly ignored all, thinking only of his worship.

In the lavatory of the *takieh* Shaikh Jazayeri heard the noise and crouched down by the wall. Blood spattered on to the floor from the cut on his head.

Hassan typed out the command signal and pressed the key to transmit. A relay closed inside the *Spiral* missile five miles away, the solid-fuel motor ignited and with a shattering roar the missile came out of its launch-tube, brushing through the light screen at the front of the cave and accelerating out and up into the clear air. In its nose, a laser-seeking unit began looking for illumination to guide the missile.

There were few who would know what the light in the chandelier was, and most were mixed with Persian mud and sand, but one was in the Mosque – a Revolutionary Guards Corps officer familiar with modern technology. Displaying remarkable speed of mind and foot, he turned and ran for the door.

Shaikh Jazayeri closed his eyes and put his arms around his head.

The *Spiral* aquired its target at an altitude of 1200 feet AGL, two and a half miles out. It locked on, and even had the illumination ceased it would thereafter travel to the target, which in design terms would be a heavily-armoured Main Battle Tank.

Gohar Karim keened with excitement and anticipation.

Hassan Sadeq pulled off his turban and slipped the black robe over his head.

Hojat Tasdeeq saw the grand Ayatollah bow his head in prayer, saw his lips frame the words, and did likewise as the glittering green, gold and red light shone about them.

259

Gohar caught the briefest glimpse of the missile as it streaked in, descending from altitude at just below the speed of sound, diving like an arrow for the huge window and the chandelier behind it. It exploded with enormous force just after passing through the centre of the chandelier, some twenty feet above the bowed heads of the praying clergy, and the great hall was filled with white-hot metal rain. Watching from the apartment, Gohar saw the windows blow out and the ancient structure of the minaret topple in slow motion, flinging the *muezzin* from it. His black robes flapped like the wings of a shot crow as he tumbled over and over through the air. His death scream reached her with the noise of the explosion, after he had hit the ground. The Mosque began to burn.

She lifted her hands in triumph.

'Father! My brothers! You are avenged!' she cried in delight.

Much of the ceiling of the *takieh* fell in, covering Shaikh Jazayeri with ancient plaster. Dust and smoke filled the corridor connecting the *takieh* to the Mosque, and he ran up it. The screaming of the wounded was in his ears. The walls of the Mosque were covered with blood, and shreds of bone and meat. He went to a side entrance and pushed the door open, emerging into the fresh air with a billowing cloud of smoke and dust. Behind him, the flames began to crackle as the old building provided fuel for the fire. Men and women outside were screaming and crying. There would be no need for *mointat al-boka'as*, the tears assistants today. He saw one of the television crews filming, and an IRGC officer standing nearby. As he went over, wiping the blood from his face, the camera tracked him.

'The Grand Ayatollah is dead,' he said clearly. 'I am taking command.'

Gohar Karim's upraised arms slowly came down and she turned, still beaming, to Hassan. The smile left her face. He was standing by the door, which was now half open, and was wearing his Revolutionary Guards Corps uniform which had been hidden under his robe, now stuffed into a haversack with the turban.

'What?' she asked, in puzzlement. 'Why is this?'

Hassan Sadeq raised his Tokarev automatic sidearm and shot her through the heart.

In the IRGC command post Shaikh Jazayeri issued orders. Reports were just starting to come in of the Masses – the Tudeh – taking over the streets of Tehran. Yuly Borodin's *coup d'état* had begun.

Frightened faces peered around shabby doors at Hassan in the corridor.

'You have kept a traitor in your midst!' he screamed at them. He reached out and jerked a man out into the corridor, where he fell terrified on his knees and begged for mercy. Hassan heaved him upright and stood him beside the open door.

'Stand here and allow no one inside until I return,' he ordered.

Hassan went out, heading for the Mosque. A few streets away he found what he was looking for, an enterprising young reporter with a cameraman, seeking some exclusive coverage. He stopped them and took them back to the shabby apartment block where the body of Gohar Karim, only daughter of Abdul Karim, one-time Mojahedin leader, lay dead among her Soviet-supplied hardware. She lay in a pool of blood but her face was untouched, looking out at the sky, and people said how like she was to Abdul el-Ahmar, Abdul the Red. The young reporter and his cameraman filmed the room, the dead woman and her KTD laser designator, pointed at the now blazing Mosque. They travelled to Tehran, where they filmed the pro-Soviet Tudeh fighting for control of the capital with the IRGC. They got the film out that evening, and their pictures went around the world.

SANTA MARTA

Ellen Tyler stood with Ryan near the big yellow Thrush that sat at the side of the stained mixing rig, and the great 5,000-gallon water bowser and pile of 5-gallon cans, marked with skull and crossbones: Danger, Can Kill You. They were in the shade of the hangar there. A breeze blew off the sea, bringing a welcome hint of freshness, and all around the tobacco rippled. Ellen Tyler had her hands tied behind her back.

Out to sea, they heard the faint screech of turbines, and low on the horizon a small dot began to turn into an aircraft; it skimmed over the beach and touched down at the end of the strip, rolling to a halt by them. An MU-2, dark blue with a thin silver line, it was identical to the damaged one up in the valley. It was its twin brother and had once sat on a line in Florida, waiting for collection. The propellers whirled to a halt and Ric and three soldiers got out. The three men pushed the MU-2 out of sight in the hangar, and Ric came over to the couple waiting.

'Good,' he said.

'Marvin'll be here soon,' said Ryan. 'I told him you'd be coming to the strip. This little lady here has some airline tickets. I think they thought they'd take you along as a bonus.'

'Tyre, and the nigger?'

'Fishing, apparently.'

'Together?'

'No, they don't get on. One in the hills, one on the coast. I'll take care of them.'

'Okay. You get on and do that. We'll look after things here.'

262

'Right.' Ryan went over to the two vehicles waiting by the hangar and got in the car, leaving the Jeep behind.

Ric stood by Ellen. The three soldiers stood a few yards away at the side of the hangar, their automatic weapons slung. Ric had a short Uzi over his shoulder.

'I've had to change plans,' he said pleasantly. 'First the crop being destroyed, then the cans leaking. That was deliberate, you know. Davidson was hoping to kill me. I've explained the error of his ways to him. He's making some more, and his children are sleeping next to the new batch. Brimstone's corrosive, you see. You have to seal the can, which Davidson didn't do. He's sealing this batch.'

'I wish you wouldn't tell me this, Ric,' Ellen said.

'It's good to be able to talk for once. I've had to do it all myself . . . I haven't been able to tell anyone. These are only goons,' he gestured towards the soldiers. 'They don't speak English. They're bought for money, some killing and cheap sex. You can buy anyone, can't you?'

'Why are you doing this, Ric?' Ellen asked, but he only smiled. From the hills came a faint buzzing. Ric issued some sharp orders in Spanish and the soldiers deployed.

'Time to tidy up the ends,' he said. 'You all know a little too much.'

Ellen and Ric stood in the shelter of the hangar and watched the little blue Piper descending towards them – a pretty, frail butterfly. You could tell that Marvin was ex-military; he flew a standard curving approach on to final without separating it up into sections, keeping the threshold in view at all times. He came over the palms and slipped it gracefully on to the turf where the little bird touched on all three.

Then one of the soldiers stood up in the grass and opened fire. He was the stupid one, the one they shouldn't have brought, the one who liked to shoot the women after he had raped them.

Marvin came back in with the power and the tail rose. One main tyre burst; they were all standing up in the grass firing. Ellen Tyler suddenly ran behind Ric and threw herself into the back of the nearest; he went down and the little plane swerved, but Marvin held it up with aileron, keeping the ruined tyre clear, and the little machine was airborne, nose down, going for speed. Then it was hit, smoke pouring back from the engine, the note changing, losing power; it cleared the scrub at the end by a few feet as he milked it for all he had left to him, and entered a shallow turn to the right, losing altitude. There was a heavy explosion of spray as it hit the water a few hundred feet out. Just before it crashed they could see flames gushing from the top of the wing. The broken machine sank rapidly, leaving a pool of burning gasoline rising and falling on the water. No one got out.

Ellen stumbled to her feet, being kicked by one of the men on the way. Ric looked at her curiously.

'You were always brave,' he said. He seemed to shake off his past memories and beckoned to his gunmen.

'Bring him here.'

The two soldiers grabbed their companion, the man who had opened fire early, and dragged him over to Ric.

'That was stupid,' he said unemotionally. He kicked him viciously in the groin and the man fell to his knees, vomiting. Ric shot him in the head with his Uzi.

'Go check down there,' he ordered. 'Kill the pilot if he swims ashore.'

Chico, the one of two left, went jog-trotting down the strip; Luis, his companion, dragged the corpse off to one side. When Chico came back he shook his head.

'Nobody, boss.'

'Bring the woman here.'

They brought Ellen Tyler over to Ric, standing by the Jeep. He checked the Uzi as they dragged her up.

'Ric,' she said desperately. 'Please don't kill me. Don't. I've always been loyal to you, haven't I? Don't kill me . . . '

'Boss,' Luis said urgently. 'If you want the woman dead, let us do it. We would be happy to perform the service. If we could have a little fun first . . . ?'

'Are you tired of fucking chickens?' Ric said coldly. 'I have never seen people like to fuck chickens like you.'

264

The Nicaraguan grinned, showing stained teeth.

'The result will be the same,' he leered ingratiatingly, looking across at his comrade to see if he enjoyed the joke. 'You fock a chicken, it die.'

The laughter was cut short by the expression on Ric's face. He found living in the world burdensome, always in his mind was the knowledge of Hell and its agony was wearing him down.

Ellen saw his face and suddenly began struggling violently.

'No . . . ' she screamed. 'No . . . '

'Throw her down,' Ric said irritably. He was unable to shoot her without including his men. They threw her to the ground and she turned to look at him as he drew aim. She looked deep in his eyes as he prepared to kill her, and recovered her courage.

'Fry in Hell,' she whispered.

Ric howled, like an animal on fire. The gun jerked in his hand as the clip fired, spraying bullets across the strip.

'Burn, burn for ever,' the woman said intensely and he ran, throwing away the gun. He jumped into the Jeep as the men stared at him in amazement.

'Kill her,' he yelled, and then he was gone, overcome with terror, hurtling up the road.

They waited until he was out of sight, then tethered Ellen Tyler joyfully to the aircraft while they discussed who would have her first. They were not animals, they could take their turns.

The air in the tyre was giving out. When he wrote the manual we had them practise on the wreck in the pool; we got them so they could get unstrapped, get out and start on the first reservoir of air; when you ran out on one you could go switch to the other, but one main was shot out and the smallest damn thing we ever used was a Bird Dog – man could probably stay down a week on something the size a Caribou. I took the last lungful of oily air it was going to give me and released the match I held between my teeth, holding the valve open. It floated up to the waves and I followed it, leaving the Cub to begin its career as a cave for fish.

I came to the surface and kept low in the swell; I couldn't see anyone on the shore. Keeping to the cover of some rocks, I swam in. Events had clearly got ahead of me, what had whistled through the sides of the Super Cub hadn't been bees and I still had a vision of Ric standing by the hangar, and Ellen with her hands tied behind her back.

I had lost both my shoes and was bleeding from some superficial cuts, which spread the blood all over because I was wet, but I hadn't been hit by a bullet. Through the palms I could see the yellow of the Thrush and I set out towards it, walking through the scrub and long grass, keeping very low and moving slowly, like stalking deer with a bow. It took me a little over five minutes to get into range. I was very angry.

There were two of them, leftovers from the set of extras of a spaghetti Western, and I recognized them: Ric's Nicaraguan goons. They had Ellen tied to the boom of the Thrush and were arguing over something. One appeared to have won, and began amusing himself by cutting her clothes away with a knife. The other stood, looking both surly and anticipatory. Their weapons were lying on the ground. They were poor soldiers. But I had lost my Colt in the wreck.

The cans of chemical were piled high, and I crawled up behind them so that they hid me from view. As I squinted through a gap, they both had their backs to me. The man with the knife cut away Ellen's bra and squeezed her breasts. She spat full in his face. I stood up with one full heavy can and threw it at the man watching; it caught him like a bowling ball collecting skittles. The other turned with his knife in one hand, but Ellen put out her foot, tripping him, and it went flying. I got him as he came up and we went rolling across the grass, kicking and biting and tearing; he was partially trained, but younger and stronger than I was. We wound up under the water tank and he was winning; I was on my back with him on top of me, his fingers clawing for my arteries, and it began to go black, and I did what I'd been trained to do twenty years before: I reached up and removed his eyes.

I came out from under the bowser, leaving him screaming and flopping, and Ellen yelled 'R.D.' very loud; she was at the end of her rope and the man was crawling away from her to the guns. I went across, picking up a half can of methyl, and swung it round like a club, and he died with his hand on the butt of his rifle.

I took the knife I'd dropped and went over to the blinded man, who was thrashing about by the tanker, I put the point just below and behind his ear and pushed, and he was still. I went and cut Ellen free, then I noticed that I had methyl all over my arms and chest. I opened the valve of the tanker and while I was doing it the nausea hit me and I buckled. I was washing it off when little twinkles started appearing around my eyes, and then suddenly I couldn't see.

'Where are you, sugar?' I said.

'I'm here.'

'I can't see.'

'We must get away from here. Ric may come back.'

'I got to get to the valley, honey. I got the antidote for this shit there.'

'We'll drive in the van.'

I shook my head in the dark. 'Cain't,' I said, choking. I bent and was suddenly sick. 'I'll be dead soon if I don't get the antidote. I'll die, sugah. We'll have to fly.'

'You can't fly if you're blind.'

'*You'll* fly.'

'I can't fly that enormous thing, R.D.,' she whispered.

'You want to stay here and have Ric come back?'

She led me to the big bird and I crawled in with difficulty. My muscles were beginning to twitch and I had a hard job making my body do what I wanted.

'Fire it up, sugah. Master on. Mixture rich. Pump the throttle a couple times 'n crack it. Cleah. Turn that key.'

The big radial turned lazily and caught.

'Taxi it up the end, honey. Get the feel of it, it's just like a big Cub, there ain't nothing to it. You put the stick forward to release the locking tail. There you go, that's good.'

I felt the airplane begin to move and we rolled over the bumpy strip with Ellen gingerly operating the controls. Suddenly racked by cramp, I bent over and vomited some mucus over my knees.

'We're lined up, R.D.,' Ellen said. She was making a great effort to keep her voice calm.

'Good gal. We'll shut the doors.' I got mine shut and latched, with a lot of effort. 'Put the trim on the black mark.'

'It's on. Wish me luck, R.D.'

'You know it. The bird likes a lot of right rudder to keep it straight.'

'Whatever it takes,' she said, and I knew she'd got something from the lessons.

She came in with the power and the engine bellowed. The airplane seemed to accelerate sluggishly, but I couldn't properly tell, being blind, and it was my duty to let the pilot in command handle it.

'It doesn't want to *fly*,' she shouted desperately, and I felt her come back on the stick in an effort to get it to come off. We were in ground effect and I felt the tailwheel strike back on the ground; then we were flying, but I felt the shudder of pre-stall buffet shaking the airframe.

'Put the fucking nose down!' I yelled. The buffet stopped and suddenly there was a godawful bang and the airplane groaned – and I knew what it was. I'd committed a cardinal sin, I hadn't gone through the checks and the airplane was still fully loaded with 300 gallons of water we'd put in to flush the system. The impact had thrown me forward in the cockpit as I wasn't strapped in; I reached over beside Ellen and shoved the dump handle and it felt like the bird went straight up.

'Put the nose down,' I said, beside her ear. 'Get the speed on 85 and climb it out.'

I waited a little more and there was just the bellow of the 600 horses in front of us, and we were still flying.

'What did we hit?'

'A palm tree.'

'Controls feel all right?'

'Yes.'

'Bring the power back to 22 inches. All right. Put the rpms on 20. Use the little lever closest to you by the throttle.'

I heard the noises come back into the right gauge and knew she'd done it correctly.

'That's good. Take me home, sugar.'

We flew for a quarter of an hour and the spasms and shaking in my body grew worse. I had vomited everything I could, but my stomach didn't believe it.

'Ellen, if I ain't talking when we get there, the stuff's in a little black box in the top drawer of the desk. Shoot me full of it.'

Dimly I heard her coming back on the power.

'We're coming in, R.D.'

'Same as the Cub?'

'Put it on 85. Give yourself 20 degrees of flap. When you got it made, cut the power and let it on down.'

She made the sweetest landing . . . kissed it on. Then there was a vibration from the gear, then it broke and there was the screech of metal on the concrete which swung us around in a ground loop fast as a snap roll. My head smacked into a piece of the roll cage and I departed the scene.

There was a little yellow liquid left in the syringe, I lay on the little ragged cot where Ellen had managed to drag me from the wreck, and it was the first thing that told me I was still alive. She had my head in the crook of her arm and fed me little sips of water from a glass. My mouth was as dry as defoliated cotton and my head felt like an old pigskin left out in the sun.

'What's in that stuff?' I croaked.

269

Ellen looked across. 'It says 2-PAM and Atropine Sulfate.'

'When I have a son he will be called Atropine Sulfate Marvin.'

'Sorry about the aeroplane, R.D.'

'The hell with it! That was my damn fault for not remembering we still had a load on board. You did a hell of a job to get it off the ground at all.'

She smiled with pleasure. 'We did hit a palm tree,' she pointed out.

'The fault of Captain Numbnuts here. Damn, I'm glad my old instructor ain't here to see me screw up like that. I can hear him now: "Marvin, grab aholt of your left ear with your right hand. Now, your right ear with your left hand. On the count of three, HEAVE, and pull your *head* out your *ass*." Old Bo Galloway – as pretty a pilot as you ever saw, afore he started adding vodka to his cornflakes 'stead of milk.'

'R.D.,' she said softly, 'we have to do something. Can you get up? I'm going to need your help.'

She pushed me up into a sitting position and I got my feet on the floor.

'What do you want me to do, honey?'

'We have to kill Ric. Do you remember me once saying Ric was different? That something had happened to him? I know what it is, I know what's different, and the only way to stop him now is to kill him.'

I couldn't fault her. 'Okay,' I said.

'If we drive back to the strip he'll come for his aircraft. We can shoot him with one of the rifles.'

'Okay.'

She helped me up and I got my arm around her shoulders. We got out the door and I only saw Ryan at the last moment before he hit me.

There comes a point where, when they hit you again, you don't feel the pain, you just hear the noise. After a while the noise stopped and all I heard in the room was the breathing of Ryan's goon. He had two, like the ones I had killed earlier in the day.

'Who got to you, Marvin? Who got you to do it?'

Ryan's voice rasped in my ear.

I explored a hole where one of my teeth had been and spat blood on the stone floor. Billy Lee would have been proud of me; it looked like I'd been to spit school.

'Nobody,' I whispered, and the noise started once more.

When it stopped, he asked again, 'Who do you work for? What have you told them about our work?'

'Self-employed . . . ' I said. 'I did it all myself.' Now that the noise had stopped, it was starting to hurt again and breathing was difficult.

'I burned your drug crop. I thought it all up myself, and went out and did it.'

'We made you rich, didn't you think you owed us something?'

'Bat-shit. Don't owe you a thing.'

A boot went into my ribs, and it hurt now, but Ryan held up a hand.

'Nothing?'

'Nothing at all. I'm kind of slow, but I get there in the end. This has been a bad year for me, see? I got a contract to put out 2,4,5-T on timber. Someone tipped off the feds and I got a hell of a fine. You did. *You* organized it, you got me fined. A little later my prop governor failed on take-off and I crashed. When I stripped it, much later, I found it had been sabotaged. *You* did it. 'Course, things weren't good anyway; I'd done sold my house to pay my wife's medical bills. She had cancer, you know. The doctor told me it was something in her food which had done it. I thought he was a health-food nut, and took no notice, but it was you.'

'We needed you desperate. We had to have the very best. You're the best, so we made you desperate.'

'You're stupid, Ryan. I'm the best, but Ric didn't need the best just to put out spray. Did you think Ric was just a drug baron? Did you think you were all in it just for the money?'

271

Ryan stared at me lying on the floor.

'The money, and the power . . . '

'There's people dead, thousands of them, in North Carolina, because people like you and me only thought of the money . . . '

Ryan shook his head in fury. His world had all gone to pieces and he couldn't work out why. And he knew nothing about the dead in North Carolina, and he didn't care.

'It's time for you to pay.' He looked up at the goons. 'Bring the bitch as well.'

They hustled me to my feet, and Ellen was there. We went up the steps, I staggered and she put her arm around to hold me up. It was dark, we were outside. Weak from the methyl and the beating, I sank to my knees on the grass, and Ellen knelt beside me.

'I'm sorry,' I said. It was my fault.

'I should have killed Ric when he changed. I always knew I should do it, but I was afraid.'

I found her hand on the grass, it couldn't be too bad when you had your best friend there; it was like the last time. I heard someone work the slide on a gun and I could smell the hydraulic fluid and the blood so sharp – there was the scent of crushed grass and flowers and gun oil, but no strip to get it down on, no tricky skill to save me this time.

I heard Ryan shriek with revenge, howling mad with hatred, then there was a sudden ripping burst of automatic fire, a blazing of light, the smell of blood like copper in the air.

I was lying on the ground and Ellen had thrown herself across me. I could feel the thumping of her heart, hear the rasping of air in her lungs.

Then she was gone and a man was looking down on me. In the light from the house I could see him; he was young, with bright blue eyes. He had a short automatic weapon in his hand.

'I'm Yossif Petrovsky,' he said.

NEW YORK

'Have you seen the news?' asked Spencer.

'Show me,' said O'Neill.

Spencer took the cassette he had recorded earlier and put it in the machine. The familiar features of the CBS newscaster appeared.

'KGB Colonel Yuly Borodin was killed today by an Iranian suicide bomber. Borodin, who had sought asylum in Paris following the failure of the Soviet-backed Tudeh *coup* in Iran, was believed to have been the mastermind of the operation. The new government of Shaikh Jazayeri has produced documents captured in the Soviet embassy – destroyed by Iranian Revolutionary Guards during the fighting – which seem to back their claim. The suicide bomber, Captain Hassan Sadeq, was hailed today in Tehran as a hero of the Islamic Revolution.

'The assassination was captured on video by a *paparazzi* cameraman who had succeeded in following Borodin to a supposedly safe house. The Soviet Colonel was leaving with French security men when Sadeq attacked.'

On the screen there was a Paris street. Borodin and three Frenchmen were coming quickly down a path. A man on a Mobylette came down the road and suddenly mounted the pavement. Within feet of the group of men there was a blinding flash and the picture vanished as the cameraman was blown off his motorcycle. When the vision came back the camera was on its side, showing the road and the lower parts of a parked car. Blood had spattered the lens and slowly trickled across.

'In the holy city of Qom today, Shaikh Jazayeri pledged the Shi'ite people everywhere to *jihad*, or holy war, against those responsible for the assassination of the Grand Ayatollah.'

Spencer pressed his remote control and the picture vanished. The two men looked at each other without speaking for some moments.

'Okay,' said Spencer. 'The third Soldier of God is one Ricardo Abdul Coluccio. Born of a Sicilian father and Beirut Arab mother. His father was a successful Mafia figure involved in Euro-Middle-Eastern crime, who was killed in a feud by rival gangsters when Coluccio was four. The boy was brought up by his mother, which explains the Islamic element vital to Tasdeeq's programming. Coluccio was educated in the USA as a young man, and was a highly successful and ruthless CIA agent in the Golden Triangle when we were involved there. He returned to the USA following the end of the war in Laos, and qualified as a lawyer. On his way home he is believed to have passed through Sicily and assassinated the two men responsible for the death of his father; they were discovered crucified, inverted, in an olive grove.

'Coluccio had acquired a truly expert grounding in the drug trade through his work in Laos, and even while studying at UCLA was building a career as a drug baron. He was unlucky enough to be caught in Thailand a few years later, although fortunate not to be executed, and emerged from jail there some eight years ago. He set about rebuilding his career with remarkable energy, dedication, skill, charm and the utmost ruthlessness. We must suppose that these qualities brought him to the attention of whatever computer programme the Soviets used in compiling a short list of suitable candidates for their truly terrible conditioning process. Coluccio's name was on the list that Tasdeeq had, and he arranged for him to be kidnapped and taken to Qom, like Ade Jumbe and Saada Mohammed, although this time without the knowledge of Ghesuda, the Spetznaz officer who was meant to be in charge.

'The Soviets clearly meant Coluccio to be the drugs arm of these dedicated super-soldiers, just as Mohammed was meant to be the mainspring of a giant terror campaign. It is clear that Tasdeeq, realizing the potential of the weapon in his hand, programmed Coluccio to commit maximum destruction upon *Shaytan Bozorg*. Coluccio used his drugs expertise to acquire a large operation in Colombia with which to finance access to fast turbine aircraft, refuelling bases in the USA and an organization there, plus the considerable sums needed to set up a base in Nicaragua. Coluccio was responsible for the kidnapping of Dr Davidson and his children. The cache that leaked in Spartanburg was the first of four sites across the southern USA, from which automatically programmed MU-2 aircraft were meant to fly, heading north, spraying Brimstone nerve gas from 12,000 feet. The death toll would have been measured in tens or hundreds of millions.

'Coluccio is in Nicaragua. I want you to arrange observation by KH-11 reconnaissance satellite to find him. The manufacture of Brimstone gas is a lengthy, if relatively simple – in scientific terms – process. It also leaves an effluent which can be measured by the equipment the National Reconnaissance Office has. There is also Davidson and his two children. They're all white, which should help. I want a Special Forces team to be standing by in Honduras, together with one of their MH-47E Chinooks. They will need fighter support – maybe have a carrier off-shore. Once we have Coluccio found, I want the team to go in and get him. Can do?'

O'Neill slowly got to his feet.

'Victor, I want to tell you that the President is very, very pleased with what you have done. He cannot tell you so personally, as you realize. As we have seen . . . ' he gestured towards the VCR and television, ' . . . events have gone exactly as you planned. It is for this reason that we cannot risk the main thrust of the programme by official sanction – Special Forces teams and fighters striking into Nicaragua. I can get you the information from the NRO. I can get a KH-11 moved. We'll find Coluccio, but you'll have to get him yourself.'

SANTA MARTA

I spent a couple of days in hospital. They changed my
blood both times, and stitched me together, but I can't
stand those places – and Ellen came and got me, put me
in a wheelchair and took me back to her little house. She
made up a little bed on her verandah, and I spent the day
there and slept inside at night, and by the end of the week
I was in fair shape – could get up and walk some, eat a
proper meal.

She came in at the weekend, in the mid-morning, and
said there was a man who wanted to see me.

'What's his name?'

'Spencer.'

'Yeah,' I said. 'I've been expecting him.'

He came on to the verandah and pulled up a chair. He
hadn't changed much, still wore those tweedy clothes,
looked like a college professor in Oxford or some place,
still pronounced his words precisely. He came from
Bumfuck, Arkansas, but you'd never have guessed. He
left young and never came back.

'R.D.,' he said. 'It's been a long time.'

'You're wearing well,' I told him.

'You've taken a bit of a beating.'

'Yeah, man,' I said. 'We had us an old-fashioned
square dance and I was the floor.'

'We should find Ric soon. He's in Nicaragua.'

'That's good.'

'When we know where he is, we'll need to take him
out.'

'Send in the B-1s,' I said. 'Bomb everything flat
around him. Stand on a soap-box, see the whole town.'

'I'd like to, but my employers object. Congress wouldn't like it.'

'Send in the Marines.'

He sat in the old wicker chair, one polished brogue crossed over the other, looking very like he had when I was lying in the army hospital with five bullets in my leg and a wrecked Caribou out on the hill – sitting in the little canvas chair there, wondering how long it would be until I'd be any use to him. It had turned out to be longer than he had expected. About twenty years.

'No,' he said, 'I'm going to send you.'

LOS ANGELES

The woman lay in bed with the morning sun lighting up the carpet, planning her day. More specifically, she was debating whether to begin an affair. She was having lunch with a most attractive man who had already indicated that he found her very desirable. It would be reassuring for the ego, and probably good for the body. She needed it, her husband had not touched her for two years.

She heard the clack and thud of the mail arriving and shortly afterwards the padding footsteps of her husband going down the hall from his own bedroom. They halted as he picked up the communications from the rug, then went off. She resumed her contemplation of the possible delights in store, and wriggled sensuously in the bed. Her pleasant ruminations were broken by a terrible, bubbling scream.

She threw back the bedclothes and ran out of the bedroom and down the corridor. It was her husband's habit to sort through the mail in his study; when she pushed open the door she found him at his desk. Some letters were there, in front of him, together with an opened brown envelope and a small Sony microcassette player which appeared to be on, but silent. Her husband was rigid in his chair, although he was controlling his breathing. All his skin was drenched in sweat; his face, dead-white, glistened.

'What in God's name – '

'Nothing,' he said flatly.

'You *screamed*.'

'It is nothing,' he said again. She saw that his tongue was running with blood where he had bitten himself.

'Go away,' he told her. It had been this way for two years. Someone she had never met was inhabiting the body of her husband.

'I shall be away for a few days,' he said. She went out, shutting the door behind her. There was no point, she knew, in continuing to beat her head against it. As she went back to her bedroom she decided, very firmly, that she would begin the affair that very day. She was badly in need of solace. Her husband's career had never been more successful; he dedicated himself to it night and day. He was well-read, informed, persuasive; he knew where the bodies were buried. His aides and his party management were very pleased with him. He was a political coming man. Only his wife knew that he was completely and totally insane.

In his study, the Fourth Soldier rewound the tape. It only had a short distance to travel. He pressed the play button and listened again to the words of instruction.

'This is the command of the Lord your God. You will kill Victor Spencer.'

279

NEW YORK

When Judge Connel came home his house was empty of occupants, except for a man he had never met who was sitting patiently in a chair waiting for him. He got up as the Judge came into the room.

'Good evening, Judge,' he said politely. 'I hope you don't mind me waiting in here for you. Your wife let me in.'

Nonplussed, Connel stood in the doorway to his library, where he worked. To come across a man one had never met in one's own house normally presumed that one had surprised a burglar, but this man was tall, handsome, well-dressed and seemingly at his ease. He was also familiar in some way.

'Do you recognize me?' the man asked.

Connel made the identification then.

'Why yes, of course . . . ' He looked around. 'Are you on your own?'

'Yes.'

Despite his identification of his guest, Connel's initial sense of unease grew. Where were the man's aides? Why hadn't he made an appointment?

'Ah . . . is this an impromptu visit?' he hazarded.

'No,' the man said calmly. 'Planned.'

'I didn't know anything about it.'

'No.'

'So what do you want?' said Connel, his unease making him irritable.

'I want you to do me a favour.'

'Now hold on . . . '

The house was quiet. His children were usually there to meet him; his wife would have a cocktail waiting.

'You say my wife let you in? Where is she?'

The telephone rang as he spoke and the man smiled. He had a glacial calm.

'I think you'll find that is her now,' he said. 'Answer it.'

Connel was white and sweating as he put the phone back in its cradle, and his hand shook. He looked in disbelief at his unwanted visitor.

'You must be completely mad,' he said certainly. 'What in God's name are you doing?'

'I want you to do me a favour,' said the Fourth Soldier, dismissing Connel's protests. 'After which your wife and children will be released to you unharmed. I want you to make an appointment to see the Mayor. I want you to call Carmine now.'

MADISON, NEW JERSEY

The airfield was an old wartime training base. When the military had left, private enterprise had crept in from outside, until now there was a thriving small fixed-base operator who provided flight instruction, fuel, maintenance and home-made hamburgers to those passing through; a number of light aircraft owned by locals; and a few large hangars where some corporations had decided to take advantage of the lower rates out of the city and base their flight operations.

The operator of the FBO was taking a short break from supervising a one-hundred-hour inspection to take a cup of coffee when the Unicom came to life. The airfield was uncontrolled, and incoming or outgoing aircraft announced their intentions and asked for advice on a frequency of 122.8.

'Madison, this is Grumman Eight Eight Echo. Like traffic and active, please.'

Eight Eight Echo was a corporate Gulfstream III that travelled the world with its executives, working from its base on the airfield.

The FBO operator got up from the table to go to the set.

'That ain't Harry, is it?' he commented to his wife, sorting through the sectional charts for those out of date.

'This is Madison,' he said, picking up the microphone. 'Active is Two Four, traffic one Cessna 150 taxiing out for take-off.'

'Eight Eight Echo, thank you.'

'Harry with you today?' he enquired.

'Harry's on vacation. I'm standing in for him.'

The operator clicked his button twice, to indicate that he had heard. Shortly afterwards they heard the GIII announce its presence on downwind and saw the handsome white jet sweeping past at eight hundred feet, gear and flaps down. The corporate hangar was on the far side of the field; after the jet landed it turned off and taxied over. The pilot cut the engines as the aircraft was on the ramp, and allowed it to roll directly into the open hangar.

'Hot dog,' commented the operator to his wife. 'I'd laugh if his damn brakes failed and he came out the other side.'

The electric doors rolled shut and the T-tailed jet vanished from sight.

'Well, all right,' he said. 'This ain't going to get the baby fed. Back to work.'

Spencer was inside the hangar as the aircraft rolled in, and it was his hand that operated the switch which closed the doors. A black Cadillac with tinted glass stood waiting by the car exit. The door of the GIII sprouted a handle, which turned, then the whole door hinged outwards and down, its interior curve growing steps. The pilot who had operated it stood back and two men came down. They were Yuly Borodin and Hassan Sadeq. Both looked tired, but extremely relieved.

'Welcome to America,' Spencer said formally. 'I am here to convey greetings and thanks from the President and people.'

Borodin stepped on to the concrete and embraced Spencer.

'But do the people *know*, Victor?' he asked, and laughed.

'They know you're both dead,' Spencer answered. 'Didn't they see it on television?'

He turned to Hassan. 'Your wife and daughters are waiting for you. Shaikh Jazayeri got them out and we flew them in yesterday.'

Hassan's eyes filled with tears. 'Will they know me? I have so much blood on my hands. So much killing . . . '

283

'The killing is over for all of us. We shall kill no one, and no one will seek to kill us. The war is over. We won.'

They went over to the long black Cadillac and the taciturn pilot slipped into the driver's seat. Borodin and Hassan got into the back, which smelled of leather.

'Are you coming, Victor?' Borodin asked.

'I'll join you at the safe house in a few hours. I have to go and see the Mayor. For the last time.'

The fixed-base operator looked up from the Bonanza in time to see the Cadillac slipping along the road through the trees. A short while afterwards he saw the big old Ninety-Eight following it. He drove a modern, small Toyota and suddenly felt a pang of nostalgia for the days of the old gas-guzzlers.

In Manhattan Spencer found a meter and walked a few blocks to City Hall. It was a glorious spring day. He felt almost light-headed with success, and the relief that it was nearly over. No more living in hotels, no more fear of the man coming for you in the dark. The war was over. He went up the steps of the building two at a time.

Carmine Santucci's secretary collected him and took him up to the penthouse, where the Mayor had his offices. There was a superb view over the city. The Mayor was waiting for him and came forward, beaming, to shake his hand.

'Victor! We meet again,' he said effusively. He was beautifully dressed in a grey silk suit, and had a white carnation in his buttonhole. 'Do you know, this is the first time we've met since the first time? I've been kept up to date by young Yossif.'

'I'm sorry that Saada Mohammed wasn't the one,' Spencer said. 'But maybe you got some prestige from finding her.'

'Oh, oh sure,' said Santucci. He seemed surprisingly unconcerned.

'So what can I do for you, Mr Mayor?' Spencer asked. 'You sounded rather insistent that we should meet.'

'That's right, Victor.' Santucci seemed uncharacter-

284

istically embarrassed for a moment. 'I got to be honest with you, it's not so much me as Judge Connel.'

'Judge Connel? He wants to see me?'

'That's what he said. Ah, I expect you know, Victor, I've been having a few problems . . . Judge Connel is the man heading the inquiry. I've not been optimistic, you know . . . and then yesterday he calls, says maybe we can work things out . . . '

'Connel's known as an honest man. Incorruptible.'

'Yeah, well, everyone has a price. Anyhow, he says to meet today. But he says you have to be here.'

Breath hissed through Spencer's teeth. 'I've walked into it . . . ' he whispered.

Santucci looked enquiringly at him.

'Someone is going to kill me, Santucci,' Spencer said clearly. 'I've been slack, it'll happen here . . . '

Santucci looked alarmed. He was familiar with assassination.

The intercom bleeped.

'Yeah?'

'A messenger from Judge Connel.'

'Send him in,' said Santucci. He looked at Spencer. 'Let's see what's going on.'

Spencer slid backwards into a corner of the room, and his hand slid inside his jacket.

The door opened and a black man in a chauffeur's uniform appeared.

'Good morning, Mr Mayor,' he said. 'Good morning, Dr Spencer.'

He had a black leather briefcase in his hand.

NEW YORK

The senior nurse came bouncing angrily across the floor to Yossif Petrovsky.

'I don't know who you are, but now you're here you make it fast,' she said furiously. 'I've been forbidden to continue his treatment until you've seen him. It's unheard of. If he dies, it'll be your damn fault.'

'How is he?'

'He's probably going to die. He'll certainly die if I don't get to work on him. He's staying conscious on will-power, so listen to what he wants to tell you and get out.'

Petrovsky went over and stood by the bandaged figure which lay on the bed. It seemed held together with sticky, transparent fabric and black stitching that zig-zagged about, and tubes and wires connected it to bags and machinery. A nurse sat close by, checking monitors.

'Victor. It's Yossif.'

The thing hissed faintly and Yossif leaned down to hear.

'Santucci?'

'Dead,' said Yossif. 'The media are saying it was Mafia.'

Spencer made a noise that could have been amusement.

'The briefcase had a microphone in it,' he whispered. 'Once the chauffeur had said my name, he triggered it by radio signal.'

'Who did?'

'Not the Mafia. The Fourth Soldier. Ric is the third. There is one more, the fourth.'

Fluid bubbled in his throat and the nurse pushed Yossif aside, wielding a suction tube.

'That's enough!' she said angrily. 'Leave now.'

The thing on the bed made a sound like a snake hissing and she stood back, shooting Yossif a glance of pure hatred.

'Judge Connel.'

'Dead. With his family. All shot in the back of the head. The media are linking it to Santucci and the Mafia.'

There was silence for a while as Spencer worked at getting breath into his body. Then he spoke again.

'Listen then. Look on the cabinet there. Take the envelope to R.D. It contains the satellite photographs he needs. He's picking up from the road. I couldn't get any F-16s, but he'll have some electronic assistance.'

The breath wheezed in his throat as Yossif took the thick envelope.

'Okay, Victor. I'll leave now.'

'Tell him his Uncle needs his help. Say the last time pays for all.'

There was silence again, and the nurse motioned imperatively at Yossif with her head. He turned to leave, but on the way to the door heard Spencer hiss again. He retraced his tracks as the nurse slid a needle into an undamaged part of the arm.

'What is it, Victor?'

The nurse withdrew the needle and wiped the site.

'Watch the news.'

SANTA MARTA

Managua was an unhealthy place. It hadn't been healthy for Americans even when Somoza was running the show. I'd flown in there more times than I could remember, back then, and it was full of flying things that bit you, and swimming things in the water that went and lived in you if you didn't boil them dead first, and navigational aids that went off when you most needed them – and which could kill you.

It hadn't got better. To get there from Colombia you flew over the Caribbean for 600 miles, at which point you crossed the Mosquito coast. If you were wise you did it at 50 feet, because they had radar. You flew up the San Juan river to lake Nicaragua. This you crossed, avoiding the small islands and volcanos that rose from its surface. You hoped you didn't go into the water of the lake, which was infested by a unique breed of freshwater shark. Once you crossed the lake, you were in Managua. It wasn't wise to land at the airport, because they took you away and put you in jail for twenty years as an Imperialist Capitalist saboteur. It wasn't really wise to land there at all, what with it being full of Russians and East Germans, not to mention loads of excitable folk armed to the teeth with armoured personnel carriers, automatic weapons, rocket-launchers, mortars and artillery supplied by the Russians.

We were going to land on the road.

Spencer had pictures of it, taken from the KH-11 satellite. He had a computer read-out that measured the shadows and the position of the sun and told us how high the power lines and wires were. At night, we wouldn't be able to see them. At night, we would be lucky if we could see the *road*.

Hank didn't want to go. Spencer persuaded him – he said there was a twenty-year jail sentence waiting for him – one was guaranteed, in America, the other was possible, in Nicaragua.

Yossif Petrovsky brought the information. I was at Ellen's house. The MU-2 waiting up in the valley, with its nose-gear mended, and the automatic equipment I'd installed for Ric removed. I'd spent some time in the day getting the aircraft ready, and I was through by early afternoon. We were due to launch at midnight E.S.T.

I left the MU-2 and went back to the villa on my own. I found Ellen there and we fixed a couple of sandwiches in the kitchen and then went on up to our room. I took a shower and when I came out and dried myself I looked at the great blotches of bruise and realized that I was starting to heal, turning yellow.

'I look like a goddamn Chinaman,' I said.

'So thoughtful of you,' said Ellen. 'My favourite colour. Why don't you lie down, let me give you a rub? I saw you taking the stairs one at a time. You need to be fitter than that if you're going to fly.'

'That's sitting-down work. Sedentary, anyone knows that.'

But I lay down and she rubbed gently, relaxing all the bunched-up places, and although it still hurt in the boot-marks it was very soothing.

'You're full of dents,' she said. 'They half killed you.'

She worked steadily, freeing all the stuck-down places, and I dozed off with gentle little fingers working on all my tied-up muscles. When I awoke the sun was low in the sky. I got up and dressed in my O.D. nomex flight suit and boots and went down. Ellen was sitting on the verandah with Yossif Petrovsky, and had her little portable television there on a table.

'Yossif wants to see the news,' she told me.

'It's always the same,' I said, but it wasn't. The shot

289

opened with a parade of troops rolling past in lorries and tanks.

'Soviets,' I said.

'Red Square,' said Petrovsky.

He was there, up on some great slab, in front of a line of other powerful folk, the one Russian everyone recognized. Stocky, balding, the man. The camera jerked in zoom and two lorries slowed, their canvas sides rising. Combat troops were inside, they had their Kalashnikovs on full auto. The grunts used to call it rock and roll. They had him by surprise. The lorries accelerated away out of the square. As they went they fired a salvo of RPGs back into the carnage and blood and fragments ran over the stone. They cut to a different camera and there he was, lying in front of his dead colleagues, so much blood all over him that the birthmark on his head had vanished in the gore.

'Who the hell were they?' I said.

'Disaffected elements from Azerbaijan, apparently. Muslim soldiers,' Ellen said, having listened to the commentary.

There was someone else on the screen, a tall figure in a black turban and black robes, with a face like a buzzard. He howled at the crowd seething beneath and they howled back.

'And who the hell is *he*?'

'That's the new Ayatollah, Hamidullah.'

'You know what he's saying?'

'He's declaring Holy War, *jihad*. On the Russians. In the name of Allah, the merciful, the compassionate. He has declared it *fard ala'l-kifaya*, and the sixth *rukn*, the fundamental duty of all Muslims. Those who die killing Russians will enter Paradise,' said Petrovsky.

Ellen looked sharply at him. 'How do you know that?'

'Spencer said that he would.'

The picture changed again, to an old, slab-faced man staring grimly at the camera as words came from his mouth like chunks of cast iron.

'Kulikov. Former head of the KGB,' said Ellen, translating from the commentary. 'He's the boss now. He says all the reforms introduced are null and void. He's banned any political activity outside the Communist Party. The Soviet-Union is to return to the principles of Lenin.'

'Back to the Stone Age?' I said.

Petrovsky got up, and switched off the television.

'You'll have to read my book about it,' he said.

'What book?'

'The book I shall write telling the story of how America won the war.'

'What war?'

'The Cold War.'

'Ain't it over?'

'The President didn't think so. He thought the Soviet Union had the power to shake off the shackles that had been put on it by communism. He thought that such a freed Russian Empire would be both powerful and as nationalist and expansionist as it always has been since Ivan the Terrible. So he gave his country's best soldier the job of seeing that it didn't happen. That soldier chose the only weapon that would do it, which was resurgent Islam. Over a quarter of the population of the Russian Empire is Muslim.'

'Why're you going to write this book?'

'Because I'm a historian. You see, when the Russian Empire begins to go – and it will go fast once it happens – there will be people who will say, "The Americans did it." And my book will come out, and they will say, "Look, here it is, it was a great covert operation." But my book will be flawed, and I'll have written it with KGB backing, and it'll all come out, then the other people will say, "See, it was Soviet disinformation all along, even you liberals should have known that." And the whole notion will have been taken out and aired and totally discredited, except among people who believe in conspiracy theories, and it'll remain buried for about fifty years, and *then*, some enterprising young historian of the dusty carcass of the USSR is going to say, "Hold on, this guy was telling the truth all along." I might even be around to see it. An old, old man. At home.'

'You're going back?'

'Yes. I'll be able to go back on the strength of the book. Do you find it odd that I should want to go home?'

'Everyone wants to go home,' said Ellen.

'Ellen's going home,' I told him. 'Spencer fixed it. There'll be no charges.'

'*You* fixed it,' said Ellen. 'You said you wouldn't go unless I could go home.'

'Well,' I said. 'No one can go home until I do my bit. We'd better get on out.'

Ellen picked up the Ingram gun Petrovsky had given her. None of us felt very safe in Colombia any more.

'I meant to tell you,' said Petrovsky. 'Spencer said that Ric's plan would be flawed in some way.'

'Why?'

'Because of his conversion to Islam. Muslims believe that only Allah can create something perfect. An Islamic artist might make a beautiful wall-frieze, so lovely that it would take your breath away, but somewhere in it there will be a tile just totally wrong and out of place.'

'Ric did pretty good. If he'd got lucky, we'd all be dead.'

'Good luck,' said Petrovsky.

It was dark by the time we got to the valley. In the half-light from the building the MU-2 looked shiny and cold. The door was open and Hank was walking to it; he had a bag in one hand and a Jep approach plate binder in the other.

'You ready to go, R.D.?'

'We aren't leaving until midnight,' I said.

'I thought we'd leave early. Go direct Miami. Spencer got blown up by a bomb, right?'

'He did.'

'Probably won't live. So, listen, we don't have to do it,' Hank said gleefully. 'Let's get in and go home.'

I reached out and slipped the Ingram gun off Ellen's

292

shoulder, and sat on the step with it across my knees.

'What about Ric, the poison gas, all that, Hank?'

'What do you think Spencer sent his team in for? That's what they're doing, right now. We fly to Miami, get on to the right people, tell them what's going on, and if Spencer's team didn't do the job then they send another. But sure as hell, there ain't no point in us getting our asses shot off when we don't have to.'

'Yeah, but those guys are waiting for us to take Ric out. Ric ain't safe left on his own, you know that.'

'Like I say, R.D., let the professionals do it.'

'We are the professionals,' I said tiredly. 'Ain't nothing's changed. Nothing at all. Why do you think Spencer set it up that way? We still got to go to Managua as planned, all the way.'

'You crazy,' he said angrily. '*We don't have to*. Not now.'

'Nothing's changed,' I repeated. 'Billy Lee's over there. Spencer sent him with the Cubans. And the only way he's gone get out, is if we go fetch him.'

I sat with the gun across my knees and listened to the mosquitoes whizzing in the night air.

'You are crazy,' Hank said quietly, certainly. 'You are going to risk your life and a million-dollar airplane for a *nigger*? I swear, R.D., there are about forty-eight million niggers in the USA, I *know*, because about five hundred thousand of them live three blocks from where I do. I see them every week when they drive past to get their welfare cheques. Let's forget about this stupidity and get in drive this bird to Flo'da, and when we get there you need a new nigger for your business then *fine*, we go down the stoah and *buy* you one.'

He was angry. 'Look, you ain't thinking of the whole picture,' he continued. 'So Billy Lee's a pretty good, stand-up coon. Okay, I'm sorry. What we looking at here is one and one half million dollars' worth airplane, *with no fucking owners*. We can take it, it be *ours*. Don't you see? Do you *know* how long it takes to earn one and one half million dollars, tax free? Shit we be back in *business*.'

'Yeah,' I said, 'it's all very attractive. Be nice to get rich before we die.'

'You got it. You *got* it.'

'But we all got to die. I die, and the Lord's gone say to me, "R.D., did you haul dope that killed people and destroyed their lives?" and I'm going to have to say, "Yes, I did." And if He says, "Did you do it for money?" I'm going to have to say "Yes, I did." And if I go ahead with what you have planned He'll say, "Did you leave your friend, who saved your life, who trusted you, did you leave him to get killed over there waiting for you to come and get him while you cruised home fat and happy in your one-million-dollar airplane?" and I will have to say, "Yes, I did," and He will send me along to the hot place, and be right to do it.'

I shifted the gun over so that it covered him.

'I've done a lot of bad things this past few months. I'm trying to change that.'

'Shit, R.D.,' he shouted furiously. 'If I want to listen to a fucking sermon I'll go to church.'

'It might do you good,' I agreed. 'And you will find one at the other end of the DC-8 that leaves for Miami.'

We'd removed the chocks and gust locks, we'd drained the kerosene for water, the fuel that Ellen had a hard time smelling. Now it had got cool, and we sat in the cockpit in the soft green light and went through the check list. We checked the annunciator panel and the override, fuel quantity and balance, emergency attitude gyro, alt. auto power, compass switches slave, cabin air, oxygen and bus ties. Hank was two hours gone, headed for a DC-8. I told the Omega/VLF where it was, and where I wanted it to go. Then there was nothing to do but wait for the clock to tick round to the right place.

'Billy Lee went into the Marines when he came out of school, went fought in the same place I did, and when he

294

came out he tried out for the Falcons, got a number two slot, sixteen grand a year. He was doing well, in his second season with them, when he crippled his knee, and he'd been on his way to a starting position.

'It all went to rat shit for him then. He was kind of over-extended, had to give back his Z model Toyota, move out of his nice apartment; day it happened, his pretty young wife filed for divorce – she wasn't about to stay with a damaged ex-athlete with no future.

'He showed a lot of sense. He didn't stay in the city, drift into crime, be an enforcer, he was a country boy and he went back to his roots. He didn't go on welfare, neither. He knew me and he came up one morning, start of the spray season, said how 'bout a job, and he worked so hard that after three years I cut him in.'

It was quiet in the cockpit. I watched the hand tick round the dial.

'Anyway, he's my partner,' I said. 'I let him go get shot and killed over there, he liable to sue.'

'What you're doing is right,' she said. 'You don't have to make explanations.'

It was getting close to time.

'Do you want me to come with you?' she asked.

'No, sugah. Even if you had a ticket, this isn't a Cub. This is a big girl, and she is three parts mean. If you tried to fly her she would get away from you.'

'I could help, perhaps?'

'No. Thanks for offering.'

She turned and I saw her smile in the dim light. 'I'd have been terrified if you'd said Yes.'

'It took guts to offer. You're a brave girl,' I told her sincerely.

She shook her head. 'No, I'm not. I should have killed Ric myself when he changed. I knew he was going to do something terrible, but I was too frightened of him. I knew I should do it. If I had, none of this would have happened.'

Lights were coming up the runway.

'R.D.?'

295

'Yeah.'

'You never told me what it stood for.'

'Been so long, I've about forgotten myself.'

The vehicle turned in to the ramp and put out its lights.

The airplane rocked slightly as someone got aboard and squeezed into the cockpit.

'You sitting in my chair, lady,' he said.

'What's the matter, couldn't you get on?'

'Airlines don't take my class of passenger, you know that. Now shift out of there and let me in.'

She got out and Hank fitted himself through the narrow gap between the seats and slid into place.

'You need another pilot along, right?' he said.

'Sure would help. Be back-up, if I get hit.'

'Then I'll do it. For a price.'

'So name it.'

'We get back, the MU-2 is mine. Alone.'

'If that's what you want, then you got it.'

'Okay. You got a pilot. It's time. Tell her bah.'

'Be back around dawn,' I said, 'if it goes to plan.'

'We'll be at the airport,' said Ellen.

She went out and we shut the door and got out the check-list and the strobes lit up the area twice a second. I hit the button and the AiResearch turbine began to spin, a rising whine. I kept my eye on the interstate temperature gauge, there was a muffled bang as I lit the fire, and the torque meter ITT gauge, tach and fuel-flow indicators began shifting around their dials as the turbine spooled up and the noise increased. We did it again and when they were both ready I came off the brakes and taxied out, checking compass systems, vertical gyros, turn/bank, flaps, trim, ammeter.

At the numbers we lined it up and checked the engine instruments, hydraulics, cabin pressure, voltmeters and ammeters, controls, pitot heat, put the radar on standby and set the V-bars 10 degrees up. I told the Omega/VLF that we were ready to go and gave Hank the V speeds, which he said he knew, damn me. There wasn't anything left to do after that, no clearance to get, so I gave it the

fuel and we hauled down the runway, left rudder to keep
it straight; damn props went round the wrong way, when
the speed came up I hauled back on the wheel. With its
negative angle of attack at rest you had to overcome it
and then almost immediately relax pressure as the
drooping wings grabbed lift; you tended to over-rotate if
you weren't expecting it. Hank pulled up the gear and we
climbed out at 200 knots. I allied the autopilot to the
Omega/VLF and we punched into the 3,000-foot cloud
base shortly after. Then we sat on our hands waiting for
the time to tick away, and watched the gauges.

MANAGUA

Billy Lee was field-stripping his M1 Carbine when the Cuban came over and sat with him.

'I can give you an M16 instead of that, if you prefer,' he suggested.

'Ain't fond of it, Enrico,' Billy Lee said. His huge fingers handled the parts of the gun like pieces of Lego. 'That sorry fockah Lyndon Johnson done give it to us in d'Nam. Damn thing fire good on a range, but when we used it theah it jam good. Cain't take a little dirt. I done seen good boys stacked like wood, waitin' on the Huey to bring the body-bags.'

'Yeah. They got that sorted out now. It's a good weapon, especially with the grenade launcher.'

'Ain't strong enough, neither. Damn thing made of plastic. When the officah say go, you want to get out yo fightin' hole, 'n' when you get to the enemy if you done run out of ammo you want to be able beat him to death wif the butt, no have the gun break ovah his head. M1's good and strong.'

'You were in the Marines.'

'Yeah man. Done two tours.' He twisted the bolt, lifted it and took it out of the receiver. Then he looked at the Cuban. 'You got something you want to tell me, Enrico?'

'Yeah. Someone got Spencer with a bomb. He's still alive, but he may or may not make it.'

Billy Lee paused. The air was scented with solvent and oil.

'You think it may affect this heah?'

The Cuban shrugged. 'It might. This was Spencer's

thing, you know. You think your airplane will still come?'

'Sure. R.D.'ll be here. What you planning to do, Enrico?'

'I'll be honest with you, Billy Lee. I'm gonna do what I was going to do anyhow. Spencer gave me plenty of stuff for all this, but it was going to cost. Lose a few men. It's got to be worth while. We captured this Ricardo Coluccio and the scientist, there was always going to be a lot of trouble for us. So make it worth while. We're going to knock off the bullion store. The Russians got silver and gold coin, piles of hundred-dollar bills. We're going to take it.'

'Uhuh. Say, Enrico, what you doin' here? You sound like you 'Muhricain.'

'I am. Got a nice house in Pompano Beach. I'm a mercenary, Billy Lee. The CIA hires me to fight for Uncle Sam down here. These Contras ain't up to too much, and they need some guys like me to provide know-how. Being Cuban, the CIA can always disown me if I get caught. Now, this operation was funnier than most at best, and it's even funnier now, and I reckon this is my chance to get what I need to retire.'

'Enrico, you can do whatevah you want, long as you git Coluccio for me, slap the incendiaries round the nerve gas, get Davidson and his kids across the border and have me and Coluccio standing by the road when the aircraft come by, collect us.'

'That gas is mean stuff.'

'It burn. That the way to get rid of it.'

'You sure the airplane'll come? There's one hell of a storm brewing out there.'

'It'll come. Ain't no little storm stop R.D.'

'Okay.' The Cuban mercenary got to his feet. 'We'll be moving out in twenty minutes.'

'Okay.'

'What if it don't come, Billy Lee?'

Billy Lee used a cartridge as a screwdriver to secure the sling swivel, slipped it into the 15-round magazine and jacked it into the chamber when the magazine went home.

'Then we just S.O.L.,' he said.

'S.O.L.?'

'Sierrah Oscah Limah. Shit Outa Luck.'

In the distance, thunder rumbled in the dark, and rain spattered on the window-pane.

The MU-2 was cruising at 310 knots at flight level 220, the night was black and we were passing in and out of cloud; every time we knifed in we felt the rocking turbulence, like the swell of the ocean telling you the storm was coming. If you flicked on a strobe there it was, white all around, and wet on the windshield, and it was coming. The storm was there.

We had the weather radar set on a hundred miles, but as we drew closer we brought it to fifty, and it looked bad. I was dreading turning it to twenty-five; by the looks of it the screen would be just filled with red.

'Jesus God,' said Hank. 'Will you look at the size of it?'

The cumulo-nimbus clouds spread across the sky in front of us, extending far off the edges of the scope, Charlie Bravo, CB, Mr Charles and all his relatives forming one terrible squall line that had set the severe cell alert flashing on our weather radar, and we'd turned it off – we *knew* there were things out there that could turn us into chaff-sized pieces, we didn't need a stupid machine to remind us of it.

The red areas were awful close together. Going through a line you tried to pick a hole, you picked the biggest piece of green you could find, but I was looking at what it was painting, and the artist had left his kelly behind. Thirty miles ahead the terrifying energy machines were on the fire, boiling up from the sea and reaching high into the cold, cold night air at sixty thousand feet, and you want to fly that high, you work for your uncle and wear a special suit.

300

Mr Charles had more energy than a hydrogen bomb. He just took longer to spend it. It didn't mean he couldn't do to you just what the bomb could, if that's what he felt like; he just took a little longer, so you could appreciate what was happening to you.

I squinted away at the scope and finally came up with a decision.

'That looks like the best bet,' I said. Hank grunted something unintelligible because it was the sort of bet that sent any sane pilot into a one-eighty the other way, and I set about slowing it down to manoeuvring speed. We wound down our seats as low as they would go and turned up the instrument lighting to the highest notch. Once we got in the vertical winds inside the cells would be in excess of a hundred knots; we'd be seeing 5,000 feet a minute either way, and it was way too much for the autopilot to cope with. I uncoupled and took it by hand.

Ag pilots hate thunderstorms. All pilots hate thunderstorms, but ag pilots have honed their dependence of hand and eye to such a degree that it becomes ingrained, and when you got it, it don't matter how good you get at instrument work – at the back of your mind you're still uneasy because the vision of where you are, in what attitude, what condition is only a picture in your head, assembled from the information given to you by your instruments, and the longing to *see* becomes very real.

In the clear air in front of the line we could see, all right. Three miles out the vast roiling columns glowed with an evil light flickering high above us, reducing us and our high-technology aircraft to the status of an impertinent gnat. We entered the crevass suggested by the weather radar and the air was still, as smooth as silk. A moment later we were in cloud, and the first edge of the rain hissed over the cockpit like stepping on a nest of cottonmouths, and then it went to work. We weren't an airplane, we were a submarine doing 180 knots through the ocean. We hit the updraught with an impact like a midair collision – it jarred the teeth and sent the breath grunting from your body – and the VSI wound round the dial and told us we were going up at four thousand feet a minute. I dropped the gear and reduced power to flight idle, and Mr Charles continued to spit us upward towards the stratosphere.

Then we hit the other side and the impact threw us up in our straps and the cockpit was filled with flying objects; pencils, dust, charts, approach plates. I hauled in the gear and came back in with the power, putting the chip into the V-bars at ten degrees up, which should have given me two thousand feet higher every minute, and the VSI informed me that I was heading for the Caribbean below at three thousand feet a minute and that there was nothing that I, R.D. Marvin, could do about it.

The rain came over us like a fire hose, the thunder was right by us. It wasn't the jolly, exciting kind that rolled over you as you stood sheltering under your porch and said Lawdamussy, what a storm, it came on you like field guns firing in your ears; they got our range and the lightning bolt slammed into the wing and while I was blind and deaf the gushing water put the fire out in the left engine.

I realized it as my vision came back, and saw the MU-2 trying to roll on to its back. I slammed in rudder and reduced power on the one that was working, and with the nose down, reluctantly, annoyed at having its fun spoiled, the bitch came back, and I got it cocked into the good engine as best I could in the turbulence, and Hank got on with trying to start the dead engine.

The giant storm kicked us in the balls a couple more times, then tiring of its sport, contemptuously spat us out the other side. We were at eight thousand feet, running over a dim overcast below us. Hank coaxed the recalcitrant turbine back to life and we turned the lights back down, and jacked up the seats, and said well goddamnit, and fuck, a couple times each.

We had a problem. We hissed through the still night, very quiet, just the steady breath of the 300-knot air rubbing against the airframe, and a small red light had

302

come on on the Omega/VLF. It was telling us that it didn't like thunderstorms.

We sympathized.

It was telling us that it now *did not know exactly where it was*, that it was in DR mode, dead reckoning, and that was just flat plain not good enough.

It was time to get down. As we descended I took a five-degree cut on the heading, to the south. Hank was busy with the charts.

'See heah,' he said, holding up a sectional. 'They got themselves a tower, the north edge of the estuary.'

'That'll do,' I said, and he got the coordinates out and fed them to the Omega/VLF. We descended through the overcast into light rain over a heavy sea. I had the helmet and goggles powered by that time, and through the light intensifier I could see the white caps to the rolling waves as though it was day.

We had the weather radar tilted down and set on five miles, and it picked up the coast just like it was on the map. My cut on the heading had brought us there south of the San Juan river, and we turned north, about a quarter of a mile off shore and a hundred feet up. The river estuary came up on schedule and I could see the tower on the north side, it was about three hundred feet high, with guy-wires extending from it, I could see them like cord. It was just like spraying next to the widow-makers, I came by about thirty feet away and Hank informed the Omega/VLF where we were. It thanked us by switching out its little red light. I cranked it round 275 degrees and we shot up river.

The radar altimeter stuck on fifty feet and I was looking out the front. There was no colour through the goggles; the muddy river below was a murky grey, wide and sluggish with the mangroves lining its edge, their long sinuous toes for ever testing the water. The mach. meter read 250 knots, and we had the straps done up tight. The squall line was coming down from the north-east, and we were running through the turbulence like a fast patrol boat planing on a heavy sea.

303

Twenty minutes after entering the river we were able to cease our twisting and turning along the river and flatten out over the surface of Lake Nicaragua. Once again, the weather radar gave warning of ships, islands and volcanos in our way, and I was able to use the Litton goggles to pick them up and weave our way over the lake. We were beginning to run in and out of rain as the squall line approached. The constant buffeting made us breathe in short gasps, and it was a relief as the shoreline came up to begin slowing the bird down. The outline of Managua came up on the radar, and I gave it over to the Omega/VLF to shoot the initial approach for us. The city was lit up by flashes of light where we were going. They weren't celebrating the date of the revolution. They were fighting.

We were low as could be, to avoid being picked up by the radar. The Omega was bringing us in, that creepy feeling as you sat on your hands and the airplane banked and turned on its own, as we came over the very roof-tops, I sure hoped they hadn't put up a new hoarding of noble peasants hanging Uncle Sam since Spencer's IBM had read the pictures from the KH-11 for us. We came by the two big towers and it cranked it round on to final approach, low over the houses, close enough to break glass. I had the goggles back on and I was scanning for the runway, for our street, and then I had it – and I took it on a final that had us looking up at the office buildings, gear out, flaps down, set up to go under the power lines, smoke gushing from a blazing building, someone firing in the rain; and suddenly there was a truck coming out of a turning and I was back on the power, skimming up like a flat stone off water, just high enough to clear the truck and it swerved across the road, crashing into the building, and some soldiers fell out into machine-gun fire, falling like scythed hay.

When I got back off the power and put it down the road was clear, and we were by a long wire fence, smacking it down on the yellow line and pouring in the reverse thrust, blasting garbage high into the air. Hank was out of his seat as I chopped the left engine, fast taxi back, and my mind was holding a picture for me, only I was concentrating so hard I didn't take it in, rain spattering and swirling in the street, lining it up, the shriek of the turbine battering back from the buildings.

They were running, a small group of men, one big one forcing another along in front of him: Billy Lee and Ric.

Then the explosions came, the first blew in the windows in the office buildings. The next threw a car high in the air in a sheet of flame that half blinded me through the goggles. The third sent them across the street like skittles.

The fourth was close enough to damage the airplane. Small hammer blows erupted down the glossy skin, little knives carved into its body, my hands were on the levers – let's *go*, go *now*. Hank fell in the aisle behind the cockpit. Outside one big figure was up, half-dragging another, supporting a third; it was Billy Lee, through the goggles I could see the blood spilling from the rubberized suit, slick and wet; the MU-2 quivered with power as I unconsciously came forward on the right engine, they were tumbling through the door, there was another explosion that sent debris high into the air and I spooled up the left engine as the door shut, lit the fire and came forward on the levers. We were going, the turbines howled in the enclosed street, there was a truck turning in ahead; I reached down and turned off the torque limiter and the power went to 100 per cent, kicking us in the back, and the picture in my mind came clear, I looked to the left and the other side of the fence was a building, low and flat, and beside it was the second MU-2.

I saw Vmc on the dial and came back on the wheel, allowing it to over-rotate as I hauled in the gear, and we left under a power-line. As I did so, the building exploded. It erupted in a long, red and yellow tongue of flame that reached out for us. Hauling in the gear, I cranked it round as much as I dared; for a second we flew straight through the flame, and suddenly the air tore at my throat.

Gas.

I was like a diabetic now, never separated from my syringe, I clamped the oxygen mask over my face in the depressurization drill. The gas had hurt – I had the syringe out, and slammed the preloaded needle into my thigh.

We were clear of the buildings, I put the nose down and we started accelerating back up to 300 knots. The weather radar was out. Screen blank. I snuck a glance down as I reached to put the torque limiter back on and the Omega/VLF was dead. Autopilot gone. And then the goddamned light-intensifier goggles started to quit.

I turned up the wick but the light continued to dim. Without the goggles, without the Omega or radar we couldn't stay low over the lake, pick up the river and still avoid the squall line. At 50 feet and 300 knots we would fly slap into the nearest piece of granite cumulus. I cranked it round to the south-west, heading for the Pacific coast, and edged it up a little.

The light through the goggles got worse and worse. I cursed, and took the helmet off.

It was dark in the cockpit.

I guessed that the hits had taken out the cockpit lighting, so I pulled out my little Sanyo rechargeable flashlight, the one I could hold between my teeth as I flew.

It didn't work.

I had back-up in the flightbag, always did, so I hauled out the big 5-D cell flashlight, and of course it worked perfectly, just like the little Sanyo – it was just that I couldn't see it.

At 200 feet and 300 knots, I was going blind.

I was going to hit something very soon if I stuck with it, and so I made the decision and went for the clouds, trusting that Spencer had pulled the strings he said he had.

The instruments were very dim. I concentrated on the attitude indicator/flight director, using altimeter and airspeed and VSI as back-up, and heading indicator/HSI to tell me what compass heading we were on. With the radar out I needed to go around the east edge of the squall line, and I headed 130, passing through 4,000, hauling 220 knots, 1,800 feet a minute. At least, that's what I thought we were doing.

The turn co-ordinator was working.

The flight director, HSI, No. 2 VOR, ADF all waited for me to use them to bring us home.

And not one of them any use at all, if I couldn't see.

We were in the clouds and someone knocked into me as they pushed their way into the right-hand seat.

'Hank,' I said. 'You got it. Take the airplane.'

Someone put the barrel of a gun next to my head.

'Hank's dead,' they said quietly. 'Bring it down, R.D., we're going back to Managua.'

'Hullo, Ric,' I said, after a while.

'Take it on back,' he repeated, and jammed the gun further into my ear.

'Can't do that, I'm afraid,' I told him.

'You're going to have to. You'll do as I say.'

'No. Firstly, they'll shoot us down. We just done flew over the Air Force base. If their radar's any good at all they'll have people running for their Mig 23s right now. We go back, we're a sitting duck. Out *here*, we got some help you can't see. Go back, *nada*. And even if they missed, they'd stick me up against a wall, and from that range they won't.'

'Any other reasons?'

The instruments were very dim indeed. Little twinkles were beginning to appear around the edges.

'Yes,' I said. 'I'm going blind.'

A hard hand twisted my head around, the fingers sticky with blood.

'You've got no pupils,' he said savagely. 'Can't you see *anything*, damn you?'

'No. Ric, this airplane will not fly itself. You'll have to help me.'

I pointed to the flight director.

'I want the chip on the horizon. The orange chip is the airplane.'

I pointed to the turn co-ordinator. I knew where they all were, I was so familiar with the panel, I always figured I could find them blindfold.

'I want the little airplane to have its wings level.'

'It is left wing low.'

I made the correction.

'Level.'

'Keep talking to me. If we have to turn, no more than the little airplane's wings on the dot, either side.'

'Okay.'

'Heading. I want to fly 190 degrees. One niner zero.'

'You're on two hundred and ten.'

I coaxed it back to the left.

'Airplane's over the dot.'

I took some out.

'One-ninety.'

'Okay. Altitude, about ten thou. That's less important. Keep talking to me. Now let's find out what we got.'

I drew out Managua VOR from my memory and had Ric put 115.9 in the No. 1 Nav radio. I pointed to the HSI.

'Any flags? Has the bar done shifted?'

'No.'

We did it again with the No. 2 radio.

'The needle's jumped. It's all the way over to the right.'

I turned up the volume and there it was, the morse coming through clear.

'Okay. Twist the knob here and put one-ninety in the top.'

He did it. 'Needle's half-way over to the left.'

'Okay. Let's go one-eight-five for a while. We got ourselves a radio. Now at least we can go some place and land.'

'Where are we going to land, R.D.?' he asked softly. 'We haven't decided where we're going to go.'

'We're in it together, Ric. I can't fly it without you,

and you can't do it without me. We got to make a deal, decide where to go.'

'All right.'

I heard him breathing heavily beside me, shifting in his seat.

'You hurt?'

'I've got some splinters in my leg. I'm binding it up. What about you? You going to live till we get down?'

'I got the shakes in my leg, and I can't see, and it feels like I drank a quart of mountain dew last night, but the injection's holding. What about everyone else?'

'Hank's dead. The nigger's hurt bad.'

Nausea was building in my stomach and suddenly all the muscles contracted, I arched forward and vomited over my knees.

'Going *right*,' Ric called intensely. 'Right and down.'

I couldn't get straight, the muscles were locked solid in spasm. I got it up and back as best I could, we were pulling gees; I pushed back down and we went negative. Vomit splashed up from my face and then the spasm diminished, and within thirty seconds I got it back under control with a running commentary from Ric.

'Did you nearly lose it?'

'Yes.'

'Why can't I fly it?' he asked softly.

'Don't even think about it,' I said coldly.

'I've flown on my own. I flew the other to Santa Marta and back.'

'In daylight, with the autopilot on. In clear weather. This bitch is mean, she is for professional folk at the best of times. Without the autopilot, at night. If I die here in the seat I want you to go back there, sit in the back with the others and wait for the loud noise, because you will be as much use back there as up here all on your own.'

'So where are we going to go? You're not going back to Managua and I'm not going back to Barranquilla to be shot.'

'How about Panama? I done flown the Canal Arrival

into Colon more times than I can remember. You'll be safe there and so will I.'

'All right,' he agreed calmly. 'We'll do it. How do we find the damn place?'

'Fly the STAR, the arrival route. Stick 113.7 in that thing. Turn the knob till the needle centers. What does it say at the top?'

'One nought five.'

''Kay. Let's fly it. That's the beginning of the Canal Arrival.'

We turned to one-nought five, where the arrival route waited for us out in the black night.

Thirty-five thousand feet over the Pacific, two aircraft held station together. They were off the USS Coral Sea; one was an F14 Tomcat, the other an EA-6B electronics aircraft. The big fighter had a crew of two, the Prowler four. Both crews watched the progress of the MU-2 as it headed off the wrong way, overflew and departed in a drunken fashion to the south, wandering about as much as thirty degrees from its heading either way. The second crew member of the F-14 – the Guy in the Back Seat, known as the Gibs – monitored the turboprop's progress as it weaved about.

'I don't know what those guys are up to,' he said.

The Commander in the front grunted. The huge fighter cruised at 300 knots with its wings outspread.

The radar picked up three blips leaving.

'Three bad guys, off the ground, heading for the target.'

Missiles hung under the Tomcat's wings and were snugged up against its broad belly. The fighter could engage up to six enemy aircraft at any one time, its on-board computer automatically selecting the most appropriate missile, the most dangerous of the enemy. It was a formidable opponent, even more so if it was accompanied by an EA-6B. The Commander keyed his mike and spoke to the EA-6B operator.

'Blind them,' he said.

In the electronics aircraft the computer had identified the frequencies of the Russian-built fighters, and its ECM system was armed. They turned it loose and below the radar screens of the three interceptors went white, as though struck by a blizzard. Their radios were filled with a terrible howl, forcing their pilots to first try to change frequencies and finally to switch off. Without radar or ground vectoring the fighters were helpless, reduced to impotence in their task of finding the target in the vastness of the night sky.

On the radar screens in the aircraft above them the crews saw the MiGs waver, fall off course and finally turn hesitantly back towards land.

The Commander grinned.

'Deaf, dumb and blind,' he called triumphantly. 'You can't fly when you're blind.'

The tremor in my leg was getting worse. My foot was beating a tattoo against the rudder pedal and there was nothing I could do to stop it. The cockpit stank of sweat and blood and vomit, and I could feel Ric's hands on the controls as he called out the interpretation of the flight instruments and felt me make the corrections.

'Take your damn hands off the controls,' I said angrily, but he didn't reply, he just said left wing low, nose a little high, and felt me correct, right wing low, heading one-one-five, and felt me correct. I knew what he was doing, what his plans were.

My stomach was giving me cramps, spasms that buckled me over. There was nothing left to vomit, but it tried.

'You don't look too good, my friend,' Ric said, and his voice was confident.

'If you do what you are thinking of doing,' I whispered hoarsely, 'then you will die. You cannot fly this airplane.'

'I don't think it's so difficult. I see a blind man flying it, and I have eyes. Eyes that work.'

311

'You will die.'

'I don't think so. I don't need you any more, R.D.'

I couldn't see it, but I sensed it. I had my arm up and partly blocked the blow the first time he hit me, but I couldn't see him, and the second time he got himself set and wound up properly, and that time the first thing the gun hit was the side of my head – and it was dark, all the way from the outside in.

In the rear seat of the F-14 the Gibs watched his radar screen and observed the erratic progress of the turbo-prop far below. They had given up trying to contact the crew. In his own mind he had decided that whoever was at the controls was either badly injured, or was a passenger with limited flight experience. He had no way of knowing that he was right on both counts.

Ric flew with his right hand on the wheel, keeping his left free, as he had originally been taught. He was what they termed a very quick 'study', he had an ability to learn new crafts, his co-ordination was excellent and he was a natural athlete. He followed the routine the pilot had instructed him in, the 'scan' of the instruments, not concentrating on any one but moving his eyes from one to the next, one, two, three, four, five, one, two, three . . .

On the radar screen, the course of the MU-2 seemed to have straightened out. It was holding a fair heading.

Flight director, HSI, altimeter, VSI, turn co-ordinator, flight director, HSI . . .

Ric concentrated on flying straight and level for nearly two minutes. The next step was to turn the aircraft around, to make a one-eighty-degree turn. He was acutely aware of the necessity of making small move-ments under these instrument conditions, everything had to be gradual and smooth. He began a turn to the left, using the little airplane of the turn co-ordinator to judge his angle of bank.

On the screen, the Gibs saw the MU-2 turning back

towards Managua. In disbelief he informed his pilot. In their turn, the F-14 and the EA-6B also came around.

The turn was successful. Having been there and felt what happened when the American had had the terrible spasm and the turboprop had got away from them, Ric treated the machine with great respect, handling the controls very gently.

The next step was to find Managua. He knew that the VOR worked by twisting the knob until the needle centred. If the flag said From, and you wanted to fly away from the station, you flew whatever course was at the top of the compass ring. If you wanted to go to the station, you twisted it until it said To, and was centred, and flew that. If the needle began drifting off to the left, then why, you flew a bit to the left too, until it came back.

Ric had graduated top of his class when they were training them at the Agency.

But first, you had to know what frequency to put in the radio.

There was a chart lying on the floor, in the blood that flowed sluggishly there. He bent down to pick it up, lowering his head, and wiped the blood off on the American's britches so he could see.

When he looked back at the instruments, they said that the machine was in a dive to the right and gaining speed.

It took him nearly forty-five seconds to re-establish level flight. When he had done so, there was but one thing wrong. He was convinced that the aircraft was in a climbing left turn. Sweat ran freely from his body into his clothing, and even the pain from his wounds was forgotten. A wholly alien, new emotion stirred in Ric's mind, like nothing he had ever felt before.

It was panic.

He brought the nose down and the wing down, fighting to control what was infiltrating his arms, his hands, his mind. It was better. Level flight.

Now he had a new problem, and the monster in his brain fed on it voraciously. Although he felt he was level, all the instruments said that the aircraft was rolling to the right and gaining speed. The airspeed indicator wound rapidly towards the red line and the hiss of the air turned into a roar. The tentacled thing in his brain took charge and heaved back on the controls.

On the radar screen, the Gibs considered that the MU-2 looked like a bug crawling up a corkscrew.

The instruments said that the aircraft was rolling to the right and going down. Ric tramped on the rudder to bring the nose round and heaved on the yoke. The MU-2 obliged by snap-rolling to the left at 260 knots. In the cabin the blood rose up off the floor, coating the inside of the aircraft; the bodies flew, smacking into the ceiling and sides of the cabin; the sleek turboprop tucked in its chin and began to spin.

On the radar screen, the Gibs saw the blip become nearly stationary, and after a little while it vanished. They waited a short time then they called up the Coral Sea and set course for the carrier.

Ric had lasted nearly five minutes in control of a sophisticated machine in pure instrument conditions, without experience. It was an amazing feat of skill, even if not nearly good enough.

It was the noise that dragged me conscious, that and the vibration of an aircraft trying to break up. If it had not been for that, I believe that I would have stayed under longer and died, but there was the terrible booming roar of an airspeed way over never-exceed, and the shake and shudder of control flutter that jarred your teeth. I was a pilot, it was the only thing I was really good at, and the airplane reached down deep into the blackness to tell me it was dying.

I was still in my seat, held there by the harness. I reached forward and pulled the power levers back to flight idle, then found the gear-handle and pulled it Down. As the undercarriage extended the vibration and noise was appalling, the aircraft screamed and through my seat I felt pieces tear away in the giant wind. I was hurled forward in my straps by the deceleration; it put me up by the panel and I reached forward and cruelly put the flaps down. In the banging and shuddering, things I could not see flew around the cockpit, striking me from time to time in the process.

Someone was screaming.

I thought perhaps it was me, but it wasn't. It was Ric.

From the gees, we had to be spinning. I threw a fist out to where I figured Ric was; my knuckles crunched into bone and the noise stopped.

'Which *way*? Which way are we spinning?'

'I don't *know*,' he screamed, and there was something in his voice that I had never heard before. It was fear.

'Left or right?' I stabbed at the Flight Director.

'It's on its side.'

We had to be getting very close to something hard, and in desperation I touched the turn co-ordinator.

'Which way is the little airplane? Which wing is low?'

'The left. God, the left . . . '

I pushed the wheel forward and trod on right rudder, the gees began diminishing and then sharply increased as I came back on the wheel, and the roar of the air began to diminish.

'Talk to me.' I punched him again. 'Talk to me, damn you, tell me what the instruments say.'

I put the flaps back and the gear in, and the aircraft screeched with the effort; there was a lot of bent machinery out there. I came in with the power and we began a gradual climb.

'Altitude,' I said.

'Four hundred feet.'

'Give me one-one-five.'

'Turn left,' he said, and his voice shook.

'You cannot fly this thing, bastard,' I said.

'No, I can't,' he agreed, and his voice was sincere. 'I will help you all I can.'

I waited until we were calm again and working as a team before I spoke to him.

'You're not ready to die yet, are you, Ric?'

He didn't answer.

'You have a mission to accomplish, don't you? I mean, you still have, haven't you?'

He still said nothing, and I sighed.

'Ric, it don't make no difference to me if I live or die, I'm damned anyway after all I done. Now either you answer, or I'm gone sit on my hands and wait for the loud noise. And then we'll both be dead. You want that?'

'No.'

'So what do you have to do?'

'Americans must die. Americans must die in their millions, on the streets, in the fields, in the cities, on the land.'

He said it as a chant, and I realized the words were graven upon his brain.

'Who says so?'

'It is the Commander of the Lord,' he said.

'Spencer said your plan would have to have a flaw in it – that only Allah could make something perfect.'

'It is so.'

'What was the flaw?'

'You were. I had to have you, because you were the best. I had to take the chance you wouldn't realize what was happening in time.'

I was losing control of my muscles. My left leg beat against the rudder pedal and tremors were invading my shoulder and right arm. Muscles twitched in my face and saliva poured in my mouth, spilling over my chin. But we were at the Intersection, inbound to the VOR.

'Come back on the power,' I said. 'Give us sixty per cent on the meter.'

I no longer had faith in my right arm to do what I told it. We began a descent to 2,500 feet.

'When we cross over the VOR, the needle will swing and the flag will change from To to From. When it does

316

it, put one-fifty-six in the top and turn us until the needle gets back into the centre. Understand?'

'Yes.'

We waited and the air was smooth; there was just the shaking of my body, like an old man in his wheel-chair.

'How long?'

'Not long. We'll hit the ground one way or another, I promise.'

'The needle's twitching . . . it's swinging . . . the flag's changed.'

'Give me two-zero-zero. Start the time.'

We swung roughly outbound.

'Are we still in the clouds?'

'Yes. But they're lighter than before.'

'Dawn's coming.'

The minute was up.

'Left to one-fifty-five.'

I swung it round, roughly procedure turn outbound.

'Put zero-two-zero at the top. That's inbound course to the station.'

We made the procedure turn, brought the power back and put the gear and flaps down, and sank down to one thousand five hundred feet.

'Got anything?'

'Still clouds.'

'When we pass over the station then zero-four-two, that's the 42-degree radial outbound, takes us to the field. Put it in when we pass overhead.'

'Do I start a time again?'

The tremor and pain were worse. I was flying it on the electric trim mostly, as my left hand was still working, and there was no turbulence to upset me, but I knew that the involved movements of a missed approach and go-around were beyond my fading capacity to control the aircraft. It was only because the air was smooth in the pre-dawn that we remained upright at all.

'No,' I said. 'This one's shit or bust.'

We came over the VOR and swung on to our new

317

course that would bring us to the airfield – either one way or, if we were lucky, the other.

'There's just one runway. It'll be lit. There'll be flashing lights at the end of it. You got to say left or right. You got to say when we got it made.'

I was back on the power, letting the bird come down. Busting minimums, for sure. The last flight, anyway. There was a bad flutter from some part of the airframe, a banging of metal. Even if we got it down all of a piece, they were going to park this one, put Hank's jewel on one side, rip out the few good bits left as salvage.

'*Lights*. Lights. To the left,' he shouted, and his voice was tight with relief.

I brought it around.

'The lights got to look like you can put them between your feet,' I reminded him. 'Not the middle of the airplane. *Your* feet.'

'Right a little. About two miles.'

I told him to push in power, to maintain altitude.

'How high?'

'Three hundred feet.'

'Hold it until the lights begin to go under the nose. We got lots of runway.'

'Coming up . . . ' he said. 'We're here. We're here!'

'Put the power on thirty. Let the nose come down.'

'Left a little. Left.'

'How high?'

'Fifty, forty, thirty . . . '

It looks like you're higher than you really are, at night. At twenty I said shut it, and pulled back on the trim with my loyal left thumb that still did what I asked of it while the rest of my body was departing from me.

We hit the ground, and came home. We smacked it into the concrete with enough force to burst the tyres; it started to ground loop, the bare gear screeching, some banging and splintering as we took out the runway lights and came to a halt fifty yards off in the scrub.

My last act as the pilot of faithful Forty-Seven-Juliet, poor damaged bitch, was to cut the fuel and switches with my good left hand. The turbines began spooling down with a long-drawn-out moan of relief. By my side, Ric unclipped his belt and scrambled out of his seat.

'Well done,' he whispered. 'I think you're dying, R.D. There's no antidote here.'

Then he was gone, and I heard him unlatching the cabin door. He was wrong. Ellen would have a syringe with her.

Cool air flooded in and there was the noise of the rescue vehicles coming. I coughed and fluid spilled up over my filthy shirt.

Ric was waiting outside. A vehicle stopped.

'Hello, Ric,' Ellen said.

I heard him scream with sudden fury.

'*Where is this?*'

'This is Barranquilla, Colombia. Welcome back.'

'We flew the Arrival. R.D. said it would bring us to Panama.'

All arrivals bring you to an airport. The Canal Arrival will take you to Panama. The one we had flown took us into Barranquilla.

'R.D.,' Ellen called. 'Are you alive?'

The fluid was filling my lungs, filling up, drowning me. I tried to call, and it spilled over my chest.

'R.D.?'

I coughed and struggled, then there was clear air in my lungs and I managed to speak.

'*Kill it.*'

There was the sudden ripping explosion of the Ingram gun and then the screaming. Ric's life-blood gushed out on to the concrete of the runway and he screamed. He screamed as though dragged through the very gates of Hell, as though consumed by fire and brimstone.

319

Acknowledgements

With Thanks. To Nick, Barbara
and Andrew, Imogen and Debra.
As always, to Anne, and to Kim
Nobles, the best ag pilot in Georgia.